THE
ENCHANTER
HEIR

THE
ENCHANTER
HEIR

CINDA WILLIAMS CHIMA

HYPERION
LOS ANGELES NEW YORK

First Hyperion paperback edition, 2014
10 9 8 7 6 5 4 3 2
FAC-025438-18138
Printed in the United States of America
ISBN 978-1-4231-9253-4
Library of Congress Control Number for the Hardcover Edition: 2013013816

Visit www.hyperionteens.com

SUSTAINABLE FORESTRY INITIATIVE
Certified Chain of Custody
Promoting Sustainable Forestry
www.sfiprogram.org
SFI-01054
The SFI label applies to the text stock

For Eric: After all these pages turned and scenes shared between us, you are writing your own stories.

꩜ PROLOGUE ꩜
THORN HILL, BRAZIL

Jonah awoke to suffocating heat and the sound of screaming.

He jerked upright, his sheets drenched with sweat, his head pounding. The screams came from outside, through windows that had been left open to capture the night breeze. A wan, gray light oozed between the shutters.

Inside the dormitory, the other Sevens were moaning and the sound foamed up from the beds all around Jonah. He squinted through the darkness, but his vision flickered and swam like one of the paintings in Mama's books.

"What's going on?" he whispered, his voice hoarse and strange. As he swung his legs over the side of the bed, the smell of sickness smacked him in the face.

He sat still until the churning in his middle settled a little. He would not throw up. He was nearly seven years old— old enough not to make work for other people. That's what Mama said, anyway. *People will always be willing to do things for you because you're an enchanter, because of your gifts of empathy, charisma, and persuasion. But that's wrong, Jonah. You need to learn to do things for yourself.*

His chest burned, smoldering like someone had lit a fire inside him. He pressed his hands against his T-shirt, as if he could put it out. Somebody in one of the other beds was calling, "Daddy?" over and over.

Where was Jem, the dorm-master? He would know what to do.

Jonah slid off his bed, his bare feet hitting the floor with a thunk. For a moment, he stood, head swimming, as the flame in his chest burned hotter. Then, staggering, holding on to bed frames for support, he worked his way toward the door.

Just as he reached it, he nearly stumbled over a body sprawled across the threshold.

It was Jem, eyes rolled back in his head, his blackened tongue sticking out, his hands fisted. Like he was still fighting.

"Jem," Jonah whispered, kneeling beside him. Jonah could no longer sense the mingled love and exasperation that was Jem.

Jem was dead, but some of the Sevens were still alive. A healer. Jonah needed to find a healer. And Mama and Dad and Kenzie and Marcy.

Jonah pushed the door open, carefully stepped over Jem's body—and walked into a nightmare. People in nightclothes filled the *okara*, blundering around the square, running into things as if they were either blind or out of their heads. Bodies lay everywhere, like broken dolls flung aside. Some, he recognized. There was Foster, who worked in the metal shop and gave Jonah interesting bits of metal to play with. And Lilith, who helped make the medicines the healers used. She lay, facedown, just outside the lab building, her pale hair spread around her head like a halo.

Somebody ran into him, nearly knocking him over. It was Patrice, who built the sets for the theater, still in her night-gown. She was the first grown-up he'd seen who wasn't dead.

"Patrice!" Jonah cried, snatching at her sleeve. "Have you seen Mama and Dad?"

Patrice swayed, holding on to Jonah to keep from falling over. Foam bubbled on her lips, dripped down her chin. She stared at him, wide-eyed, like she didn't recognize him, then floundered backward and wobbled on, heading for the lake.

People were running in all directions, some toward the lake, maybe hoping to cool themselves in its waters. Others toward the healing halls. Some ran, screaming, flailing their arms, like they were being chased by monsters. Jonah saw one man barrel into another. They both fell to the ground, punching and kicking each other.

Terrified, Jonah ran for the cluster of family homes, called *oka*, that housed those that worked in the performing arts. Until a month ago, Jonah had lived there with his parents, his younger brother, and baby sister. Then, since it was getting crowded and he was nearly seven, he'd moved into the Sevens dorm. All the seven-year-olds stayed there, regardless of what guild they came from.

Some of the *oka* were dark, ominously quiet. Others were ablaze with lights. Dogs barked at Jonah from open doorways as he followed the familiar path to his own family's dwelling. He had to stop once and throw up into the bushes.

The house was dark, but through the front windows, Jonah saw an odd flickering light. Like flame, but more blu-ish than orange and red.

He burst into the house, calling, "Mama? Dad?"

No answer.

He slid back the screen that divided his parents' room from the main room.

They were still in bed. He could see their familiar shapes in their double hammock, but no reassuring rush of love came his way. Jonah inched closer. Mama lay on her back, a rag on her forehead, face milk white, her lips blue. There was a cup on the window ledge next to her. His father lay facedown beside her. They were dead.

Jonah had been punched in the stomach once—so hard that he couldn't seem to drag breath back into his body. It felt a lot like that.

Shaking his head no, he backed out of the room, hands raised in front of him. Once in the main room, he smelled smoke. Something was definitely burning, and the smell seemed to be coming from the space that Kenzie and Marcy now shared. Jonah eased open the screen to his old room.

Marcy was standing in her crib, giggling and pointing, the light from the flames painting her face an odd color of blue. Kenzie's side of the room was ablaze, and now and then a flame arced out from the inferno as if someone were shooting off rockets. At the center of the fire, Jonah's five-year-old brother, Kenzie, burned brightest of all, like a human sacrifice to the old gods one of the healers, Jeanette, sometimes talked about. Burning and burning, yet not burning *up*.

Dizzy, sick, and confused, Jonah wanted to lie down on the floor, close his eyes, and go back to sleep. He wanted Mama to wake him from this nightmare and stroke his hair and tell him it was all a dream. He wanted a grown-up to figure out what to do.

But there was only Jonah, and he was almost seven years old, and if he didn't do something, nobody would. Blotting the tears from his eyes, he snatched up a blanket draped over the side of the crib and wrapped Marcy up in it. Dropping the side of the crib, he lifted her out.

Marcy pointed over Jonah's shoulder and cried, "Kee!" which was her word for Kenzie.

"Come on, Marcy," Jonah said. "Let's get out of here before this place burns up."

She struggled in his arms as he crossed the threshold. "Kee!" she cried. "Kee!"

She continued to kick and squirm, and Jonah's strength was dwindling fast.

"Marcy," he pleaded as they left the shelter of the trees. "Hold still. I can't carry you if you're wiggling."

"Kee!" she said again.

"I know," he said. "I didn't forget him. I just can't carry both of you at once."

Two of the Twelves were plodding toward him, girls who'd helped out in the healing halls. They looked half dead themselves, moving like they were sleepwalking through a nightmare. One girl's skin was covered in blisters. Jonah tried not to stare.

"We're meeting in the *okara*," one of them said dully. "Go there."

"Take my sister," Jonah said. "I'm going back after my brother."

"Jonah!" Marcy cried, clutching on to his nightshirt.

"It's all right," Jonah said. "I'll be back." He bent his head and kissed her on the cheek.

Marcy's blue eyes opened wide, then closed. A smile

curved her lips. Her color faded like a winter-blasted rose as she died.

Jonah didn't know how long he drifted between waking and sleeping. He was strapped down, so he couldn't move, and there were tubes and needles poking him everywhere, and thick mittens covering his hands so he couldn't rip them out. Hardly anyone came in, and when they did, they left in a hurry. He slept most of the time, anyway.

Then one day he woke up, drowning in his own vomit. When the healers finally came in, they seemed angry, like it was his fault. After that, they unstrapped him so he could use the basin by his bedside. They unhooked all the tubes, but they left the mittens and a big clanking chain attached to his ankle. It was long enough for him to get to the bathroom and walk around the room, but that was it.

He knew a few things. For instance, he knew where he was—in one of the classrooms at school. But why was he here, all by himself, instead of in the healing hall?

They must have been giving him something that made him sleep most of the time, because now he was more awake. Now that he was awake, he saw who came in. There were two in particular—strangers who must have been healers, but they were unlike any healers Jonah had ever known. Not at all like Jeanette, who'd cared for him since he was a baby.

These healers never touched him unless they had to, and then only with gloved hands. Whenever they came close, their fear slopped over him like a cold fog. Often, they stood by the door and talked in low voices. He guessed they were talking about him.

Jonah called them Thing One and Thing Two.

Jonah wasn't used to being feared. He was used to affection. He wished Jeanette had stayed—she always knew how to make him feel better when he was sick. She'd left Thorn Hill before any of this happened. But, if she'd stayed, then she'd probably be dead, like all the other grown-ups.

They brought him food to eat, leaving it on the bedside table, even though half the time he was too sick to eat. Every time one of them came in, Jonah asked a question, collecting information like puzzle pieces. The wells had gone bad, they said. Mama and Dad and Kenzie and Marcy were all dead. No, he didn't have anything catching. No, he couldn't take the mittens off.

His seventh birthday came and went without anyone noticing. Meaning two months had passed since everyone died. Jonah rested, and ate, and kept the mittens on, and wondered why he was still alive. The more he rested, the stronger he got and the more he saw and heard, whether he wanted to or not. His ears seemed to hear better than they ever had before. And if he looked out the window, through the bars, he could see all the way across the lake, to where white tents had sprouted, like mushrooms after a rain.

Most importantly, now he could hear those muttered conversations between Thing One and Thing Two. Thing One did most of the talking. Thing Two didn't say much.

"He's not paying us enough to do this work," said Thing One. "Nobody told us they'd need twenty-four-hour nursing care."

"Mm-hmm," Thing Two said.

"They brought this on themselves, you know." Thing One scratched his neck. "Did they think the Wizard Guild was going to stand by and let them build an arsenal?"

"But that's not the kids' fault. Besides, Mandrake claims they weren't making weapons."

"And you believe that?" Thing One snorted. "Guess the Wizard Houses didn't. Now their parents are all dead, and nobody knows what kind of monsters they'll grow up to be. They're in agony, most of them, and they'll probably die anyway. More die every day. It seems to me that the kindest thing to do would be to put them out of their misery."

"What are you suggesting?" Thing Two said sharply. "I need this job. I don't plan on leaving until the mine's played out. A few more months in Brazil, and I'll never have to work again. I consider it combat pay."

"I'm just saying that it'd be easier if there weren't so many."

"Mutant kids or diamonds?"

Their laughter faded as they walked on down the hallway.

Fear prickled the back of Jonah's neck. Were he and the others going to die? Jonah touched his chest, which still burned sometimes, enough to wake him from sleep. Sometimes he still had to use the basin they left beside the bed. Sometimes he sweated blood.

But at least now he was strong. Strong enough to explore.

As he slid to the floor, he caught a glimpse of himself in the mirror over the sink. He didn't look like a monster. He looked the same as always—shaggy black hair, blue eyes, the tattoo of a flower on his arm, like everyone else's. Maybe thinner and sadder than before.

Jonah gripped the cuff around his ankle, trying to slide his foot through. It wouldn't fit. All he did was scrape off some skin. Frustrated, he yanked at the ankle band, and it came apart in his hands. Startled, he let the pieces fall onto the coverlet and looked around, but of course nobody was watching.

If he'd known it would be so easy, he'd have done it before now.

He snuck to the door, only to find that it was locked. Frustrated, he wrenched at the handle, and managed to pull the door right off its hinges. He tumbled backward on his rear, the door on top.

He scrambled to his feet in a panic. I didn't mean to, he thought. I didn't mean to break the door.

They shouldn't have locked me in.

At the end of the hallway, in what had been the gym, he found dozens of children lying in row after row of beds. Some he recognized, and some he couldn't. Some were covered in wounds and blisters, others in scales and feathers. Some were beautiful, frail, pulsing with light, like the fairy children in Jeanette's stories. Some didn't look like children at all. All were hooked up to machines and bags of fluids that dripped into them. It was a horrible place. A horrible room.

"Jonah?"

Jonah flinched, startled. The voice came from a nearby bed. It was Alison Shaw, another Seven. She looked thinner than he remembered, and pale, with dark circles under her eyes.

"Alison!" he said, thrilled to finally find someone he knew. "Are you—?"

"Shhh!" Alison put her finger to her lips. "Don't let them hear." She held up her hands, and Jonah saw that she had mittens on, too. And chains that bound her to the bed frame. "How did you get out? They said you were locked up."

"I broke the door," Jonah said, to keep it simple. "Why do they have you chained up?"

"Never mind. Can you get me loose?"

Jonah took hold of the chain and broke it.

"How did you do that?" Alison asked, squinting at him, looking impressed. "Show me."

Jonah shrugged. "These chains aren't very good, I guess. Where is everyone else? What about Rudy? And Miranda?"

"I don't know. They never let me out of this room. Have you seen Kenzie?"

"He's dead," Jonah said around the lump in his throat. "Didn't you know?"

"No, he isn't," Alison said. "They have him locked up, too."

Jonah's heart stuttered. Then started up again, beating hard and fast. "Where? Where is he?"

Alison slid off her bed and onto the floor. "I think it's this way."

They crept out of the Horrible Room and down the hallway. They turned a corner and practically collided with Thing One and Thing Two. Two of the nursing assistants were with them. Jonah might have run back the way he came, but now they stood between him and Kenzie.

"Jonah!" Thing One said, taking a quick step back. It was the first time he'd called Jonah by name. "How'd you get out of your room?"

"Where's Kenzie?" Jonah demanded, fisting his hands.

"We were just coming to get you," Thing One said, glancing at Thing Two. "Would you like to see him?"

Alison and Jonah looked at each other. "Why'd you tell me he was dead?" Jonah said.

"We didn't want to get your hopes up," Thing Two said, his eyes flicking down to Jonah's mittened hands. "He's been very ill, and so have you. We thought it was better to wait." He gestured down the corridor. "It's this way."

Thing One blocked Alison's way as she tried to follow. "Not you. You need to go back to bed."

"I want to go with Jonah."

Thing Two nodded to the nursing assistants. Each took one of Alison's arms and dragged her, still protesting, in the other direction.

"Why can't Alison come, too?" Jonah asked.

"Your brother's too sick. One visitor at a time. You'll see."

Fear quivered through Jonah. He'd just gotten Kenzie back, and now he might lose him again.

They made several twists and turns, and Jonah realized they were on their way to the dining hall. Why the dining hall?

They passed through it and crossed the yard toward the kitchen, which was in a separate building. Jonah heard helicopters, at a distance, but coming fast. That was odd. Helicopters often came and went, bringing medicine and supplies, but never at this time of day.

Thing One and Thing Two didn't seem to hear them. Jonah scanned the slice of murky sky overhead, but the Things hurried him along, into the kitchen building, and back to the storerooms and freezers.

"Kenzie's *here*?"

"It's the safest place," Thing Two said, unlocking the door to a huge, stainless-steel freezer.

"He's in the *freezer*?" Jonah's voice came out in a terrified squeak.

"It's not turned *on*," Thing Two said, impatiently, pushing open the door.

He switched on the light, but it wasn't necessary, because Kenzie himself lit up the entire room. He sat on the floor in the corner, knees drawn up to his chin, his arms wrapped around his knees. Flames flickered across his skin—the same blue-white flames Jonah remembered from the night his parents and Marcy had died.

"He's still on fire!" Jonah cried. "Why don't you put it out!"

"We can't," Thing One said. "He makes the flame himself. He's been burning since the night of the massacre."

Kenzie didn't have any clothes on. Maybe that was why Alison hadn't been allowed to come.

Jonah crept closer. Though Kenzie was burning, he shivered and shook constantly, his teeth chattering, his eyes rolling back in his head. Now and then his head banged against the wall.

"You should give him a helmet," Jonah said, because he couldn't think of anything else to say.

"We'd *like* to help him," Thing Two said, shrugging his shoulders. "I mean, we've been leaving him food and water. But, unfortunately, we can't get near him."

"Kenzie," Jonah said. "It's me, Jonah."

The sound of Jonah's voice seemed to catch Kenzie's attention. The shaking eased, and his little brother leaned forward, hands on his knees, eyes wide with fright. "Jonah? Help me! Please help me! I'm so c-cold. And hungry."

Jonah was desperate to help. "Can't you at least get him a blanket?" he said.

"They just burn up," Thing One said. The two Things

looked at each other, then Thing One continued. "You *can* help him, though."

"Me?" Jonah blinked up at the tall man beside him. "How?"

"You can put the fire out, Jonah," Thing Two said softly. "There are so many children here you can help. Will you?"

"I guess so," Jonah said warily, looking up into Thing Two's face. "I do want to help."

Thing Two brought out a shiny pair of scissors. Thing One held Jonah's wrists while Thing Two carefully cut Jonah's mittens off. Then stepped back quickly.

Jonah flexed his fingers, glad to have the mittens off, but puzzled at the same time.

The freezer door was slightly ajar. Outside, Jonah could hear people talking and footsteps coming closer. Thing One and Thing Two didn't seem to hear, maybe because Jonah's hearing was better than theirs.

"I'll wait outside," Thing Two said, turning away.

"You'll stay right here," Thing One growled under his breath. "You agreed to this, now man up." He turned to Jonah. "Now, Jonah. Just take Kenzie's hand. It will put the fire out."

"Why would that put the fire out?" When they didn't answer right away, Jonah said, "Won't I get burned?"

"We think the fire will go right out. Give it a try," Thing One coaxed.

Why were they coaxing him? He wasn't a healer. Jonah looked up at Thing One and saw the lies behind his eyes.

"No," he said, turning his back on Kenzie and facing the two Things.

"Look at him," Thing Two said. "You think he's happy the way he is?"

He took a step toward Jonah, and Jonah raised both hands in defense. To his surprise, Thing Two flinched back, his face going fish-belly pale.

Thing Two was afraid of Jonah. Why? They wanted him to touch Kenzie. Why?

"We can't help Kenzie," Thing One said to Jonah, his voice roughening from silk to burlap. "We need to focus on the ones that might actually survive."

"No," Jonah said.

"Would you want to live like that? This is the kindest thing you can do for him now."

"No," Jonah said.

"I told you this wouldn't work!" Thing Two said.

"He'll come around," Thing One said. "He's a smart boy. He'll figure it out."

"That's the problem. He *has* figured it out," Thing Two spat. "Why don't you—"

The door to the freezer banged open. In the doorway stood one of Jonah's music teachers, a man named Gabriel, who only stayed at Thorn Hill part of the year. Who'd been away the night everybody died.

"Who do you think you are?" Thing One spluttered, blocking Gabriel's path. "This is private property, and if you think you—"

"I'm Gabriel Mandrake, I own this property, and I pay your salary, I believe."

"Mandrake!" Thing One seemed to shrink, right before Jonah's eyes. "You should have told us you were coming. We could have prepared—"

"That was the idea," Gabriel said. "A surprise visit. It looks to me like you've been spending more time working the mines than doing the work I'm paying you for."

Thing One licked his lips. "Well, you know, we thought it was important to keep it going, to raise funds for the kids— for their future and all."

Gabriel pushed past the Things and on into the freezer, followed by Alison and—

"Jeanette!" Jonah cried.

But Jeanette didn't answer. Her eyes were fixed on Kenzie, her face displaying disbelief and then growing horror.

When Gabriel saw Kenzie—when he saw him naked on the floor in the freezer—he flinched, his face first going pale as milk, then dark with fury. "Good God," he said, turning on the Things. "What were you thinking? They're children."

"That's easy for you to say," Thing One said. "They're dangerous. If you'd seen what we've seen, you—"

"I've seen enough," Gabriel said, his voice low and hoarse. He looked different than Jonah remembered, thin and scruffy and sad.

Jeanette crossed to Kenzie and knelt beside him, talking to him soothingly. She wasn't afraid. As Jonah watched, she reached into her carry bag and pulled out a brown bottle.

Jonah squatted next to Jeanette, as close as he dared come. "What's that?" he said as she poured some of the sludgy brown contents into a spoon.

"It's a medicine that might relieve his symptoms some by dampening down the magic." That was one thing Jonah always liked about Jeanette: she always told the truth.

Jeanette tried to guide the spoon to Kenzie's mouth, but he flailed around so much she couldn't hit her target.

"Kenzie," Jonah said. "What's that song you like? That John Lennon song?"

Kenzie blinked up at him. "'Imagine,'" he whispered through cracked lips.

Jonah began to sing, softly. Kenzie's body relaxed and his movements slowed enough that Jeanette was able to slide the spoon between his lips.

The Things were still arguing with Gabriel. "I have the baseline numbers," Gabriel said, his voice low and tight. "Two thousand adults and three thousand children dead. There were a thousand children who survived. Where are they? How many have died since you took over?"

Thing One and Thing Two looked at each other. "Maybe a couple hundred?" Thing One ventured.

"No," Gabriel said. His entire body slumped, and he covered his face with his hands. Tears leaked between his fingers. "I never thought—I never even guessed it would be this bad."

"Yeah, well, now you know," Thing One said. Like usual, Thing Two wasn't saying much. He slid to the floor in the corner, and pillowed his head on his arms.

Kenzie's fire had finally gone out, and he sagged back against Jeanette's shoulder, exhausted. Jonah would have thought he'd be covered in blisters, but he wasn't. Maybe the flames he made himself didn't burn him.

"Alison," Jeanette said, rocking Kenzie back and forth, rubbing his back, her voice calm as ever. As if she took care of flaming boys every day. "Can you bring Kenzie some water and some of those animal crackers he likes? And a box of chicken broth."

Jonah could tell Alison wanted to stay and listen, but she left anyway.

"Jonah," Jeanette said, giving him a tired smile. "I'm so glad to see you up and walking around. Do you think you can find your brother a blanket?"

As Jonah ducked through the door, Thing One said, "So, I guess now you can see what we're dealing with here. It hasn't been easy, believe me."

"Is that why you've been chaining children to their beds?" Jeanette's voice stung like a whip.

There was a new nervousness in Thing One's voice as he replied. "You have to understand, there's been too much to do, too little manpower, not enough—"

"Yes, it's no wonder you're shorthanded, when I found ten people working in the mines," Gabriel put in. "Ten people I'm paying to take care of children."

Jonah found a blanket back in the Horrible Room, where newly arrived healers were busy unchaining children and examining them, questioning them in gentle voices. Some of the healers were weeping.

When Jonah returned with Kenzie's blanket, Thing One was scowling, his voice rising in protest. "Listen, some of these kids haven't stopped heaving since we came here. Others are so deformed they make *us* want to throw up. And that's just the tip of the iceberg. You fire us, we leave Brazil for good. Then good luck finding other healers to come out here to this godforsaken place and take care of *that*." He pointed at Kenzie as Jonah wrapped the blanket around his brother's shoulders. "Do you even understand what you're dealing with? See his big brother here? Cute kid. Only thing is, his touch is lethal. His lips, his hands . . . and we don't know what else. He killed his own sister."

Thing One kept talking, but Jonah wasn't listening.

Marcy? He'd killed Marcy? He extended his hands, studying them. Turned them over and looked at the backs. They didn't look any different than they always had.

"Don't worry, Jonah," Jeanette said, softly, brushing his hair out of his eyes. Leaning down to kiss his forehead. "Whatever happened, it wasn't your fault."

Tears came to Jonah's eyes. Nobody had kissed him—hardly anyone had touched him for two months. Jeanette wasn't afraid of him. And, yet . . .

Jonah shook his head and backed away from her. "No," he said. "I'll hurt you, too."

"The point is," Thing One said, "most sorcerers wouldn't set foot in here after what happened. They don't want to risk the Wizard Guild coming after them."

"Maybe some people are braver than you," Gabriel said. "Now get out, before I have you arrested."

❦ CHAPTER ONE ❧
MEAN OLD WORLD

By the time she woke up in the booth at Mickey's, Emma Claire Greenwood hadn't been home in three days. She knew it was wrong, that Sonny Lee would be worried, even though she'd called him every day. They'd agreed on that the last time they'd had a sit-down about her wild ways.

But it was sweet summertime in Memphis, and the call of the streets was like a siren song—impossible to resist. School was out, and there was no place she had to be.

Sleep all day, then stay out all night, walking pavement still breathing heat at midnight. Passing open doorways, letting the delicious music sluice over her from all the little clubs. Music that picked your heart apart and put it back together again. She was just sixteen, but she had a ticket into every club in Memphis. She'd sit in with bands all over town, big names and unknowns. Mickey put it this way: "That girl Emma? She's an old soul. That girl can play the blues."

It sure didn't hurt that she was Sonny Lee Greenwood's

granddaughter. Sometimes she'd cross paths with him in some smoky dive. She'd hear him before she ever saw him— he played slide guitar like nobody else. Sometimes they'd coax her onto the stage and she'd play alongside him, the air thick with cigarettes and beer and sweat—the smell of the blues.

Sonny Lee warned her about the streets. He told her there was danger out there. But she'd always fit in better there than anywhere else. Better than she'd ever fit at school. Besides, she was street-smart enough to say no to the pretty boys who'd try to sweet-talk her into making that first big mistake. To the older men who wanted to buy her a drink. It was the music that seduced her—nothing else. She looked out for herself because nobody else did.

She'd slept all night on the vinyl seat, her long legs and arms hanging over the edges, stirring only when the staff started trickling in. The clatter and bang of Robert as he racked dishes finally woke her up for good.

Yawning, she checked her phone. Two in the afternoon.

She had one text from the guy who'd ordered a guitar months ago, wondering where it was. Three calls from Sonny Lee. He'd be in the shop by now. Where she should be.

Sonny Lee should fire her and get some good help is what he should do.

Her mouth tasted like sawdust, which she totally deserved. Stretching the kinks out of her back, she hobbled over to the bar, where Robert comped her a Coke. She carried it to the ladies' room and sipped at it while she cleaned up as best she could—raking her fingers through her tangle of hair and gathering it into a rubber band. She dabbed at a spot of mustard on her T-shirt with a wet paper towel. Where'd that come from? Was it new? Or had it been there when she put it on? At home, laundry was hit-or-miss.

Good intentions rattled around her brain like dice against an alley wall. *I'll stay home tonight. I'll get caught up on my custom work and anything Sonny Lee asks me to do. I'll cook Sonny Lee a nice supper.*

Cooking was hit-or-miss, too.

She shoved open the door, letting it bang shut behind her, squinting in the sunlight. It must have rained overnight, because the wet cement was steaming. The air hung honey-thick, pressing all the scents of the city close to the pavement.

Emma turned off Beale Street and followed the cut-throughs and alleyways to the shop. She stopped at Sweetie's along the way and bought two of the sticky buns Sonny Lee liked, though they cost her last few dollars. A peace offering.

The neon sign in front of the shop flickered. S. L. GREENWOOD, LUTHIER. CUSTOM GUITARS AND REPAIRS. And underneath, their new sign, put up a month ago as a symbol of their new partnership. STUDIO GREENWOOD. To her surprise, the sign in the front window had been flipped from "open" to "closed." Way too early.

Maybe business had been slow, and he'd closed up early so he could get some work done. Which he probably needed to do since Emma had let him down. Again.

Or had he not opened up at all? Sonny Lee wasn't as young as he used to be. He sometimes had trouble making it down the stairs after a late Friday night. But music was blasting from the speakers inside the shop, turned up louder than Sonny Lee allowed, during business hours anyway.

The front door was locked, so Emma let herself in with

her key. "Sonny Lee?" she called, but there was no way he'd hear her with the music blaring. She circled behind the counter and hit the off button, and an eerie silence descended. "Sonny Lee?" she repeated. "It's Emma. I'm home." No answer.

The air in the store had a charred quality, as if Sonny Lee had been using his wood burner recently. The coffee in the pot had boiled away to a thick syrup and the carafe had cracked. Her heart flip-flopped.

She pushed through the swinging door that divided the store from the workshop. It was dead quiet. Spooky quiet. Tools lay scattered on the workbench and sawdust littered the floor. The drawer in his workbench hung open. Her grandfather hadn't cleaned up the night before. He always cleaned up. His apartment was a disaster, but you could eat off the floor of the shop.

"Sonny Lee!" she shouted, circling around behind the workbench.

And that's where she found him, crumpled on the floor, his head haloed by a pool of blood.

Emma screamed, an anguished animal sound, and fell to her knees beside him. She pressed her fingers under his gray-bristled chin, felt for a pulse, and found one—thready and weak.

"Hang on, Sonny Lee. Hang on," Emma whispered, reaching for her phone and punching in 911. The dispatcher had barely answered, when Emma burst out, "I'm at Greenwood's on Hoopeston. My grandfather—Sonny Lee Greenwood—he's been hurt."

"Hurt how?" When Emma fumbled for an answer, the dispatcher said impatiently, "Is he shot or stabbed or what?"

"I don't know. I think he fell, and hit his head. His head's bleeding, anyway."

"Is it bleeding a lot?"

"Looks like it was, but it's scabbed up now."

"How long ago did this happen?" To Emma's guilty ears, the dispatcher's voice sounded accusing.

"I—I don't know. I haven't been home."

"Is he breathing? Does he have a pulse?"

"Yes, ma'am."

"Does he have a history of heart disease? High blood pressure?"

"Who knows? He's seventy-three, but he never goes to the doctor's. Look, can't you ask these questions later? My grandfather, he needs—"

"EMS is on the way, honey," the dispatcher said. "What's your name?"

"Emma Greenwood."

"And you're Mr. Greenwood's granddaughter?"

"Yes."

Emma heard the clatter of a keyboard as the dispatcher took down the information.

"Anything else, Emma? Can you see any other injuries? Broken bones?"

Emma shook her head, which of course the dispatcher couldn't see through the phone. "No."

"Any history of stroke?"

"Not that I know of," Emma said.

"They'll be there any minute. Listen for the sirens. Are you on the first floor?"

"Yes. Door's unlocked. Come in through the shop. Studio Greenwood. I won't hang up." Emma set the phone down on the floor next to her and leaned over Sonny Lee.

To her surprise, her grandfather opened his eyes. He tried to speak, but the words came out garbled.

"Sonny Lee! Hang on," Emma said. "The paramedics are coming and you're gonna be fine; all you have to do is lay there and wait."

In answer, Sonny Lee flopped his right hand, banging it on the floor. He clutched an envelope in his gnarly fingers.

"What's that?"

He flopped his hand again in answer. Carefully, she extricated the envelope from his grip. On the outside, *Memphis Slim* was scrawled in pencil.

Memphis Slim. Sonny Lee's name for her.

Emma sat on the floor next to him. "Just hang on a little longer," she said, pressing her hand against his cheek, blinking back tears. He breathed out, a long sigh of letting go. His head drooped back and his eyes glazed over, like a skin of ice on a blackwater puddle. He was dead.

Emma tilted her head back, closing her eyes against the fly-specked ceiling. Tears ran down her face as that place in her heart that never quite healed broke open once again. Emma could hear the faint sound of sirens through the open windows, too late. They couldn't bring Sonny Lee back to life. What would happen to her now? Would she end up in foster care? That old fear kindled and burned.

No. She had places she could go, people she could crash with for a night or two.

A night or two. What about the rest of her life? And what about the shop, with all its woodworking tools? And Sonny Lee's collection of vintage instruments, many of them one of a kind. What would happen to them?

She needed time to think. To plan, and she wouldn't have it if she stuck around. She needed to get out of there.

She could at least take the guitars that she'd built herself. She could claim that much. Maybe she could get the rest later somehow. When she had a place to stay.

In a daze of grief, Emma climbed the stairs to her bedroom. She yanked a backpack off a hook on the wall and stuffed four T-shirts, a pair of jeans, a flannel shirt, and socks and underwear inside. That was most of her clothes, when you counted the ones on her back. She pushed up the loose ceiling tile over the mattress she used for a bed and pulled down her money stash—the proceeds from the sale of two guitars. She slid the money into the backpack pocket, and Sonny Lee's letter into the front pocket of her jeans. That was about it: her whole life inside one backpack.

Sirens clamoring right outside pulled Emma out of her thoughts, and emergency lights bloodied the windows. There was no time to pack anything else. The two Studio Greenwood guitars she'd finished leaned against the wall, still in their cases, where she'd left them the last time she came back from Mickey's.

She pulled one of Sonny Lee's fedoras down low over her eyes, slung the backpack over her shoulder, scooped up the guitars, and descended the outside stairs to the alley as the paramedics came in the front.

Moments later, she was walking down Beale Street, a guitar in either hand. Emma looked just like a hundred other guitarists in Memphis, heading for a gig. Except for the tears streaming down her face.

❧ CHAPTER TWO ❧
TOO LITTLE, TOO LATE

By the time Jonah broke into the dungeon, Jeanette was dead. She hung from the wall, her long plait of gray hair matted with blood, her face swollen, her body bruised and broken. Tools of torture had been flung carelessly aside—useless now.

Jonah knew she was dead because he couldn't feel her pain. The pain he was feeling was all his own. "Jeanette," he whispered, his voice breaking, along with his heart.

He snapped the manacles around her wrists in two with his fingers, letting the chains clatter back against the wall. Gently, he lowered her to the stone floor, giving her damaged body the care it deserved, that it should have had. She'd saved his life many times over, but he'd failed her now.

Until five years ago, Jeanette had worked in the infirmary at the Anchorage, where Jonah had spent much of his early life after leaving Thorn Hill. She would hold his head over the basin until the black sick was out of him, then clean his face and mop his sweaty forehead and change the mitts on his hands. After his doses, she would cradle him and sing songs to him until he slept. She'd loved him when nobody else could. Most important of all, she'd saved his brother's life. She'd left the Anchorage when he was twelve, but not a week went by without a phone call or text or e-mail from Jeanette.

Even at the worst times in his life, he'd never stopped believing in Jeanette Brodie. And she'd never stopped believing in him.

Stripping off his leather glove, he cradled her cheek with his bare hand, knowing he no longer posed any danger to her. "Be at peace," he whispered, closing her eyes with his fingertips. He texted Gabriel and Kenzie, one word only: *Dead.* He resisted the urge to send a second text to Gabriel alone. *Told you so.*

Jeanette might be at peace, but a fine, fresh anger flamed inside of Jonah. Why would anyone—even wizards—target Jeanette? She was one of the gentlest people he'd ever known. She'd only left Gabriel's service because she could no longer steel herself against the dying of children.

The world was full of monsters, and Jonah meant to find out which one was to blame for this.

He mounted the stone steps two at a time, at savant speed, quiet as the vapor of death. As soon as he reached the first floor, he heard voices. When he breathed in the stench of conjured magic, he knew: wizards.

Jonah ghosted down the hallway. The voices spilled from a large, arched entryway into an adjacent room. His unusually good hearing was, ironically, a gift from wizards.

He edged his head around the door frame so that he could see.

Three people stood around the fireplace, though the hearth was cold on this summer day. One was a young man with sun-streaked brown hair, his lean body rigid with impatience. He looked to be in his early twenties—but it was always hard to tell with wizards. The fifty-ish woman with raven-black hair would be Jessamine Longbranch, the owner of the house Jonah had broken into minutes before. The other man was older, gaunt, with a badly scarred face. That was likely Geoffrey Wylie, a known associate of Longbranch's.

"Well? What did you find out?" The younger man was an American, his voice as penetrating as a sliver of ice.

"Not as much as I'd hoped for," Longbranch said, scowling.

"So you've given *up*?" The scarred man snorted.

"I didn't have much of a choice, Wylie," Longbranch said. "She's dead."

After a strained pause, the American spoke again. "If there was any chance at all she knew anything—which, for the record, I doubt—then *why the hell* did you kill her?"

"I didn't mean to, clearly," Longbranch said, her voice low and tight with anger. "Sometimes they just die."

Everyone needs a hobby. Jonah's was tracking wizards. Something that his mentor, Gabriel Mandrake, discouraged. In Gabriel's view, Jonah's mission was elsewhere—hunting shades. The undead victims of the Thorn Hill Massacre.

"Well," the American said, glancing at his watch. "That's that. This has been a colossal waste of time. I've got to get back to New York."

"Hang on, DeVries." Longbranch leaned back against the sideboard, swirling her drink. "The Thorn Hill angle *is* worth pursuing, and you know it. The best sorcerers of the age flocked there, because they knew that they could source any botanicals they needed without the risk of anyone coming after them in Brazil. Their expertise could be the key to freeing ourselves from the underguild tyrants in Trinity."

"No doubt," DeVries said. "After all, the Thorn Hill conspiracy was a smashing success—or would have been, if they hadn't managed to poison themselves."

"Fine," Longbranch flared. "Moss and her cohorts can go right on killing wizards until we are extinct."

"What's the count now?" Wylie asked.

DeVries shifted his gaze to Wylie. "Fifty-seven dead," he said. "And I understand that some from the underguilds have been killed as well."

"Red herrings, no doubt," Wylie said. "To obscure the real culprits."

"Maybe," DeVries said, as if he didn't care one way or the other.

"Are there truly no clues at all?" Wylie asked.

"Some of the bodies don't have a mark on them. Others have been found—to be blunt—dismembered. The commonalities are that their Weirstones are destroyed, their magic drained, and all of the bodies have dead flowers scattered over them."

"Roses?" Longbranch guessed.

DeVries shook his head. "Nightshade."

Nightshade? Jonah's hand crept inside his neckline, to his Nightshade pendant, brushed over the engraved design. Really? Was it possible that someone from Nightshade was moonlighting? Somebody besides him?

"Any updates on the Interguild Council investigation?" Wylie asked.

"Don't look for any help from *them*," DeVries said bitterly. "Some on Council are probably responsible for the killings; the rest merely celebrate them. Madison Moss has to be involved. Wizards just aren't that easy to kill."

"That's exactly why we need to take matters into our own hands," Longbranch said. "The survivors of Thorn Hill represent the greatest reservoir of knowledge about materials magic and Weirstones that exists."

"Existed," DeVries said.

"Don't you see?" Longbranch continued undeterred. "What if we could modify Weirstones so that they no longer require the connection to the Dragonheart in order to function? Failing that, if we could determine exactly what agent got into the water supply at Thorn Hill—"

"Why? Are you planning some kind of mass murder, now that we're finally at peace?" DeVries said, his voice dripping with sarcasm. "Look, investigating Thorn Hill *seemed* like a good idea," he said, as if Longbranch had crocheted an especially clever potholder at the old folks' home. "But we've no way to pursue it if there aren't any records, and if everybody who knew anything is dead."

"The healer survived. There must be others," Longbranch said. "More who left before the disaster." She paused. "Perhaps some of them are working for you."

"Working for me?" DeVries said, his eyes narrowing. "Do go on."

Wylie and Longbranch exchanged glances, as if negotiating the next move.

"We're well aware of your expertise in poisons and toxins," Wylie said, trying for charm, and failing. "You were brought up in the business, after all. And isn't it true that your father was murdered by some in the underguilds who blamed him for this so-called Thorn Hill Massacre?"

"I have no idea who murdered my father," DeVries said, clearly not seeking a heart-to-heart with Wylie. "He was a successful businessman, and successful businessmen attract enemies. Those were violent times, if you recall. As for poison, that's a sorcerer's weapon. Wizards have other options."

"I've heard rumors that the Black Rose is back," Wylie persisted, "that it's resurfaced in response to the recent killings. We thought, perhaps, that you—er, the Black Rose—might have recruited some Thorn Hill survivors to—"

"Shut up, Wylie," Longbranch said, glaring at him. "We don't want to imply that young DeVries here is in any way involved with assassinations and the like."

"Another day, another conspiracy theory," DeVries said, rolling his eyes. "People who consort with assassins have a rather short shelf life, don't you think?"

⚘ After another exchange of glances with Wylie, Longbranch decided to change the subject.

"What about the Anchorage?" she said. "Every one of the inmates there is a Thorn Hill survivor. One of them might know something. They may even have records and archives from the camp."

Jonah stiffened. He didn't like that these wizards had the Anchorage in their sights.

"I can't imagine that *they* would be of any help," DeVries said, his voice laced with contempt.

"Why haven't you mentioned this place before?" Wylie asked, seemingly annoyed to be on the outside. "I never heard of it."

"I only just thought of it," Longbranch said. "The Anchorage is an institution that houses the children of the rebels at Thorn Hill, the few hundred who didn't die with their parents. The ones that survived the mass poisoning ended up as magical cripples. Some are barely functional, requiring round-the-clock care. Others are kept confined, because they pose a danger to themselves and to everyone else. A few run loose on the streets."

"Fascinating. But who would want to *do* that—take care of underguild freaks, I mean?" Wylie mused. "Moreover, who would want to pay for it?"

"You've heard of Gabriel Mandrake—the American music promoter?" When Wylie nodded, Longbranch continued. "He's a sorcerer who's adopted the labrats, as they're commonly called, as his pet charity. If you ask me, it would have been cleaner to have dealt with them at the time. It's easier to dispose of mutants and monsters when they're small."

Bitterness boiled up in Jonah. *This proves, once again, that wizards are the monsters we should be targeting, Gabriel. Not our own kind.*

"You have a point, Jessamine," DeVries said, paging through messages on his phone. "The magically damaged are really quite . . . useless." He looked up at Longbranch, a smile curving his lips. "They shoot horses, don't they?"

Longbranch's face paled and her lips tightened. Jonah felt the sharp push of her rage meeting the chill of DeVries's indifference.

Wylie broke the charged silence. "Why don't we go after Mandrake? He might know something. Or be able to finger someone who does."

DeVries shook his head. "Gabriel Mandrake is an extremely visible figure who lives a stone's throw from the headquarters of the Interguild Council. He also has the best security system money can buy. I don't need that kind of attention."

"Fine. Maybe the Anchorage is out, but there must be leads we could explore," Longbranch said. "We can't give up now."

"Who says *we're* giving up?" DeVries smiled, more a showing of teeth than anything else. "Don't contact me again unless you have a solid lead. It's too risky. And, next time, turn your prisoner over and let us handle the interrogation. No doubt we'll get better results."

Jonah ducked away from the doorway to allow DeVries to stride past him. He left through the front door, closing it behind him with a soft click.

Jonah returned to his vantage point just in time to see Longbranch snatch up a vase and smash it against the door-frame, sending shards of glass flying past Jonah's ear. "What an insufferable, smug bastard," she snarled. "We don't need him."

"Yes we do," Wylie said. "If we want to regain any real power, that is." He motioned toward the sideboard. "I'll have a drink, if you're offering."

"Pour it yourself!" Longbranch stalked to the large windows that overlooked the gardens and pulled them open. The scent of roses wafted in. "For all we know, DeVries is behind the killing. Everyone knows the Black Rose will murder anyone for a price. Maybe the council gave him a contract."

Jonah rubbed his aching head. He'd had enough. He had no interest in hanging out, listening to bickering wizards. He knew who to blame for Jeanette's death, and that was what counted.

He yanked off his gloves with his teeth and tucked them into the waistband of his jeans, then rounded the corner and walked toward the two wizards.

Longbranch was the first to spot him. Her eyes widened at first, then narrowed speculatively. "How did *you* get in here?" she demanded.

Wylie spied Jonah in that same moment, his face contorted in surprise. "What the—?"

"How did you get over the security fence?" Longbranch interrupted.

"Well," Jonah said, shrugging, "it wasn't much of a fence."

Longbranch rolled her eyes, as if Jonah's presence were more an annoyance than a threat. "Why am I paying for twenty-four-hour security? I'm going to fire them all."

"No need," Jonah said, raking his hand through his hair. "They're dead."

"Ah." Longbranch nodded. "Well, then. That's the price of failure, I suppose. How many of you are there?"

"Just me," Jonah said. "That's usually enough."

"Why, you arrogant son of a—" Wylie began.

"Shut up, Wylie," Longbranch said. Her eyes traveled over Jonah approvingly, lingering on the sword hilt poking up over his shoulder. "Has anyone ever told you that you are a *breathtaking* young man?"

A thousand times, Jonah thought. A lot of good it does me.

"Are you a warrior, then?" Longbranch continued. "Or a wizard?"

Jonah shook his head. "Neither." Wizards were unable to identify Weirstones—one of the few advantages the underguilds had.

"Hmm . . . definitely not a seer. They are so tiresome. A sorcerer—no—an enchanter, perhaps?" Lust glittered in the wizard's eyes. "An enchanter with a sword? Like—like a gladiator. How intriguing. And versatile. Would you like a job?"

"I have a job," Jonah said. "I'm here about Ms. Brodie."

Longbranch smiled. "Wylie, our luck may be turning. Just when we think we're at a dead end, fate hands us this second chance." She took a step toward Jonah. "Who was she to you?"

It was a verbal ambush. "She—she—" Jonah's words stuck in his throat. He took a ragged breath, then regained control of himself. *Get a grip, Kinlock. You ought to be used to losing the people you love by now.*

"I'm not here to answer your questions," Jonah said, back to icy calm.

Wylie thrust his hand under his sweater and produced a massive pistol, which he pointed at Jonah. "Think again," he said, waving the thing like a movie badster.

Compensating for something? Jonah thought wearily.

Longbranch tilted her head back, studying Jonah like she was hungry and he was dinner. "Brodie wasn't much help, even after hours of torture. In retrospect, I'm thinking that maybe she didn't actually know anything. You, on the other hand . . . you're *much* more promising." Her cheeks were flushed, her breath coming faster. Like most wizards, she took pleasure in inflicting pain.

Jonah, on the other hand . . . not so much. He pushed back his sleeves. He had to try to come away with something, anyway. Something that would convince Gabriel to act.

Easy questions first. "You're Jessamine Longbranch, right?" he said. "And you're Geoffrey Wylie?"

"Shut up," Wylie said, motioning with the gun. "Put the sword on the floor and step back from it."

"No," Jonah said.

"No?" Wylie looked down at the gun in his hands, as if to make sure it was still there. Then back up at Jonah. "What do you mean, no?"

"I mean I'm keeping the sword. It was a gift," Jonah said.

Fragarach was one of the Seven Great Blades made at Dragon's Ghyll. Gabriel had given it to Jonah when he signed on with Nightshade. It was ensorcelled bright metal, good for killing both gifted and Anaweir, for cutting up cadavers to free the shades inside. Ideal for multitaskers like Jonah.

"Now," Jonah said. "What did you want from Jeanette?"

"Drop the sword or I'll shoot!" Wylie roared, his face going purple.

Jonah sighed. Fine. He needed to make an example of one of them. "So shoot me," he said, feinting a move.

Wylie fired, but Jonah was already across the room. He disarmed the wizard before he could get off a second shot. It was as if Wylie were moving in slow motion, his eyes widening, his mouth opening, and words rolling out slowly, along with drops of spittle.

Jonah closed his bare hands around Wylie's neck. A light touch, a gentle kind of violence, but enough. Wylie's eyes went wide with wonder, and then his face took on a familiar, blissful expression.

He crumpled, and Jonah let him go, his still-open eyes glazed over before he hit the floor.

This was how Jonah's interrogations tended to go, since he couldn't deal with the blowback associated with inflicting pain. Still, killing wizards was so much more satisfying than killing shades. Especially these particular wizards.

Jonah stepped over Wylie, advancing on Longbranch.

Her eyes had gone round with horror, her complexion dead-fish pale. Her mouth opened and closed, but it took some time for words to emerge. "Who *are* you?" she croaked. "And *what* are you? An enchanter with a sword *and* a deadly sting?"

"Me? I guess you could say I'm kind of a monster hunter."

"M–monster hunter? I don't understand."

"You know how in the movies the monster turns on the evil scientist who created him?" He shrugged. "That's me. I'm a monster who hunts monsters."

"Look," she said. "I have lots of money. You want this house? You can have it. There are five cars in the garage. Choose any or all of them." When that didn't draw a positive reaction, she added, "I—I have a boat."

"I'm not a thief," Jonah said. "I'm more of an assassin, really."

"*You're* the one who's been killing wizards!" Longbranch took a step back.

"No," Jonah said, with a sigh. "Actually, I'm not."

"Of course not," Longbranch hastened to say, "but if you are, you should know that I don't have a functional Weirstone." She paused. "So, technically, I'm not a wizard."

"Not a problem. If you're not a wizard, you're definitely wizard-ish."

Longbranch licked her lips and said, "You mentioned— weren't there some questions you want to ask me? Before—before you—"

"Why did you kidnap Ms. Brodie? What did you think she could tell you?"

"We were hoping to get files and records from Thorn Hill. Information about the weapons they were working on."

"Weapons? You mean like perfumes and skin creams and medicines?"

"Oh, come on," Longbranch snapped. "Don't be naive."

She really believes that Thorn Hill was the center of some kind of antiwizard conspiracy, Jonah thought. "What do *you* need weapons for?"

"To protect ourselves."

Why are there ever wars? Jonah thought. Everyone only needs weapons to protect themselves. Jonah noticed that the ex-wizard had moved three or four feet to the left over the course of the conversation.

"Do you have anybody else on your list? People to torture, I mean?"

Longbranch shook her head.

"That DeVries that was here—tell me about him."

Longbranch seemed more than happy to give up her co-conspirator. "That's Rowan DeVries, an American, of course. Very wealthy. He's a new member of the Interguild Council, but he's also the principal in a syndicate of assassins for hire."

"The Black Rose?"

Longbranch looked thunderstruck. "You've heard of it?"

"The Black Rose has been around for a long time," Jonah said. "Do *you* think Madison Moss is behind these killings?" When she hesitated, he took a step closer. "Tell me."

"She could be. She's certainly capable of it. Only . . ." She paused. "Why would she? She's got all the power. Moss disabled my Weirstone, but I'm still alive—if you can call it that. If it's her, then why are these wizards dead? If it's her, why doesn't she just do everyone at once and get it over with?"

"It's not just wizards," Jonah reminded her. "Other mainli—guildlings are dying as well."

Longbranch snorted. "What happens to the other guilds is no concern of mine."

She was still moving, and now Jonah could see that she was headed toward a desk at the side of the room.

Jonah watched her inch along with part of his brain while the rest wrestled with Longbranch's revelations. "And it's happening all over?"

"Everywhere," Longbranch said. "Starting about two years ago." She'd reached her goal. Now she stood, her hips braced back against the desk, leaning on the heels of her hands. "May I ask you a question?"

"You can ask. I may not answer."

"Who sent you? If you're not working for Madison Moss, then who *are* you working for? McCauley?"

"McCauley?" Jonah shook his head. "No."

"Hastings? Hastings, then?"

"No. Not Hastings."

"I have it!" Longbranch said. "You're working for DeVries. You were sent to find out how much we know. And then to kill us."

"I told you. I came for Ms. Brodie. But you tortured her, and then you murdered her." He paused, long enough for his words to register, then said, "I want to know why. Specifically. Who's working with you, and what are you planning to do?"

Just then Jonah's secure cell phone went off. Incoming text from Charlie Dugard, head of Nightshade's European operation.

He scanned the screen. *Slayer down. Regent's Canal, near Camden Lock. All hands.*

That would go out to any slayer within range.

Taking advantage of Jonah's momentary distraction, Longbranch scooped a dagger off her desk, turned, and lunged at him, attempting to bury the blade beneath his breastbone. Jonah intercepted her hands, gripping both wrists, and slammed her up against the wall.

Longbranch looked down at the dagger between them, just pricking his sweatshirt, at his hands gripping her bare wrists. Then looked up into his eyes.

"Oh," she said, her lips curving into a dreamy smile. "My dear. You are *such* a pretty one."

Jessamine Longbranch died happy. Now Jonah Kinlock had someplace he had to be.

∞ CHAPTER THREE ∞
SLAYER

Jonah took the Northern Line to the Camden Town stop. It was likely the quickest way to get there, but still—it seemed to take forever.

Slayer down. Was it someone he knew? He'd heard that Charlie's group had been investigating shade activity along the Regent's Canal. An eighteen-year-old warrior savant, Charlie was tall, buff, and totally bald, with the gift of picking up any language within a few minutes of hearing it. That made him a good choice to head Nightshade's European operations.

Exiting the station, Jonah veered right, up the Camden High Street toward the lock, following the signal from Charlie's cell phone. Crossing the canal, he descended the steps to the towpath, turning toward Regent's Park. The breeze blowing down the canal brought with it the stink of mischief, the mingled scent of free magic and rotting flesh that signaled that hosted shades were nearby. "Where are you, Charlie?" Jonah said into the phone. "I'm close. Talk to me."

"On a boat," Charlie gasped. "The one being foundered by shades. Can't miss it."

Rounding a curve in the canal, Jonah saw, up ahead, one of the narrow cruise boats that plied the canal. It sat low in the water, drifting nearly crosswise in the channel, as if it had lost its rudder.

On all sides of the boat, the water teemed with hosted shades, swarming up the sides, boosting themselves up and over the rail. Organized, coordinated, planned. This wasn't a mob—it was an army.

Shades were lone wolves, notorious for squabbling with one another, competing for fresh meat, and backstabbing, so to speak. This was something new.

Unhosted shades were nearly invisible to the naked eye, seen as a flicker of movement or a thickening of the air, like one of those transparent jellyfish in the ocean that you never notice . . . until you get stung. Shadeslayers wore Nightshade amulets to make unhosted shades easier to see.

Though they weren't substantial enough to physically attack anyone, unhosted shades might startle someone into falling, or jumping out into traffic. Every shade's goal was to acquire a host—to possess a fresh cadaver to walk around in. To experience the world in. To kill the next host in, since fresh cadavers never stayed fresh very long. So even hosted shades were always hunting new hosts.

Up ahead, a bridge arched over the canal. Jonah put on speed, threading his way between late-night joggers and bicyclists. He sprinted up the stairs to street level and crossed to the center of the bridge. Ripping off his gloves, he drew Fragarach. As the stricken boat passed beneath him, he leaped onto its roof, flopping down on his stomach so he wouldn't be raked off by the low bridge.

When they were clear of the bridge, Jonah vaulted down to the deck. Some of the shades had been scraped off by the narrow channel, but others were still attempting to clamber aboard. He ran the perimeter of the boat, swinging Fragarach, scything through corpsy arms, allowing the bodies to drop into the river. There was no time to finish the free shades now. He had to get below.

He threw himself down the stairs. The main cabin looked like a fancy party turned into a drunken brawl. Tables were overturned and broken glass and bodies lay scattered over the floor. Charlie and Thérèse had herded the dozen or so survivors into a corner, forming a bristling wall of blades between the shades and the civilians. Most of the dead were wizards. The survivors were Anaweir.

Jonah launched his attack from the rear, cutting four cadavers in half before they knew he was there. Free shades escaped their hosts, fleeing in all directions as their hosted comrades turned on Jonah.

We can't finish them when they come in numbers, he thought. Clever. Who thought of that?

After that, it was a matter of slash and dismember. The shades wielded a mixture of weapons—everything from swords to iron bars. Some may have been crude, but they were still deadly if they connected. Jonah was everywhere, cutting down bodies until there wasn't enough left to come back at him.

Suddenly, as if they'd heard a signal, the shades abandoned the attack and swarmed back up the stairs. Jonah walked among the bodies, looking for survivors, while the other two slayers kept the civilians penned up and out of the way.

One of the downed wizards, a young woman in a sequined cocktail dress, was moving, struggling to sit up. Jonah crossed to her and knelt beside her. "Are you all right?" he asked.

She looked up, and that's when he smelled the free magic and noticed that the back of her head was entirely gone. Right before she tried to take his head off with a knife. He gripped both her hands to keep her from having another go. There ensued a deadly wrestling match. Hosted shades were uncannily strong, and not even Jonah Kinlock could kill a cadaver. He couldn't get at the shade as long as it was hosted.

Happily, Thérèse rode in on her white horse and sliced the shade in two, the tip of her blade slicing through Jonah's sweatshirt. The free shade emerged from the corpse, trying to escape, but Jonah pinned it to the floor. It shrank, dwindling under his bare hands until it disappeared.

"Thanks, Thérèse," Jonah said, looking up at her.

"I didn't know you were in London, Jonah," Thérèse said shyly, wiping blood from her face.

That brought it all crashing in on him again—Jeanette and the rest.

You need to grow a thicker skin, Jonah. That's what Gabriel always said.

Jonah shoved to his feet. "Charlie said somebody was down?"

Thérèse pointed to a crumpled body against the wall. "Summer."

Jonah hurried over, but he could see already that he was too late. "She's gone," he said. "She must have split in the confusion."

"Damn it!" Charlie kicked the wall in frustration. They

both knew that, by now, the undead Summer had joined the army of free shades, relentlessly searching for a new body.

"What about them?" Thérèse asked, pointing her sword at the huddled survivors, who shifted nervously under their scrutiny.

Gabriel's rule was—slayers don't leave witnesses. Secrecy was their best protection. But it was one thing to slay one shade in a back alley and keep it quiet. It was another to fight off an army in broad daylight.

"Leave them alone," Jonah said. "It makes no sense to stop a bloodbath and then riff the survivors. None of them are gifted. Let them try to explain to the authorities that they were attacked by zombies."

❧ CHAPTER FOUR ☙
LIES AND SECRETS

Mickey didn't ask any questions when Emma showed up at the club teary-eyed and told him she needed a place to stay. He agreed to let her bus tables and wash dishes in trade for a meal and a bed to sleep in. He knew that squabbles between Emma and Sonny Lee never lasted very long.

She'd decided to keep the news of Sonny Lee's death to herself for as long as possible. There was too much chance she'd get tangled in the county welfare web. But word would get out quick. She needed to move fast and have a plan before it did.

Late that night, after the final table of poker players had left, Emma locked the door to the spare room over Mickey's bar. She slumped down onto the bed and pulled the envelope out of her jeans pocket.

She traced the words on the outside. *Memphis Slim.* That had become her grandfather's nickname for Emma during those wary, standoffish days when she'd first come to stay with him. When he didn't really want to admit he was a grandfather at all.

You're all eyes and hair, he'd say. *You have to stand twice to cast a shadow.*

A lump formed in her throat, and she blinked back tears. She tore open the envelope and unfolded the notebook paper inside. A wad of crumpled bills dropped onto the bed. She spread the creased paper over her knees.

Dear Memphis,

If you're reading this, then likely I'm dead. I want you to have my guitars, my tools, and all my wood and supplies. I filed papers down at my lawyer's office saying that. Anything you want to sell off, go ahead. It won't hurt my feelings, since I'm dead. I just wish I had more cash money to leave you.

I'll be straight with you: I wasn't happy when you first came to me. Now I don't know what I would've done without you. You're the best (only) apprentice I ever had. I should have kept a better eye on you, should have made sure you spent more time in school, but you turned out pretty good anyway. So far.

If I was murdered, or might of been, you're in danger, too, because of some of the bad things that went down when you were a child. None of it was your fault, but if I was murdered, you need to get out of Memphis.

So call this number and ask for Tyler Boykin. He'll look out for you—he's got to, now.

Love, Your Grandfather, Sonny Lee Greenwood

A phone number was scribbled underneath. It had been erased and rewritten, crossed off and changed, so often the paper was worn thin.

She flattened out the money and put it in a little stack. Two fifties, four twenties, two tens. Two hundred dollars. With what she'd saved from the sale of the guitars, that made . . . $3,200. Walking-around money for a while.

Tyler Boykin. Who was he, and why would he look out for Emma? And why would she want him to? She'd rather stay in Memphis. She had a little money, and a roof over her head, and all the music she needed within a city block. If she stayed, she could pretend like Sonny Lee was still around. He'd might be just around the corner, or down the block, his whiskey voice and slide guitar leaking out of some after-hours club.

It wouldn't seem so much like she'd lost everything.

The question was—would Mickey let her stay? Could she stay out of the way of the police and the county?

As if called by her troubled mind, Emma heard footsteps on the stairs. She hurriedly stuffed the money under the mattress.

Someone pounded on the door. "Emma!" It was Mickey.

"Come on in," she said, sitting cross-legged on the edge of the bed.

Mickey pushed open the door and closed it carefully behind him. When he turned back toward Emma, his face was taut with worry. "Emma," he said. "The police was just here, looking for you."

Emma's heart sank. "Looking for me?"

Mickey nodded. He crossed the room and gripped Emma's hands. "They said Sonny Lee's dead. Did you know that, honey?"

Emma looked up into Mickey's kind face, and her control crumbled. "I—I f-found him in the shop, on the floor. I guess he fell, and hit his head." Then she let go and cried, big heaving sobs that shook her whole body.

LIES AND SECRETS

"Oh, honey, I'm so sorry," Mickey said, enfolding her in his meaty arms. "What a world this is. Why didn't you tell me?"

"I just—I was afraid I'd have to talk to the cops, and be sent to foster care," she said. "I just—I felt like if I didn't talk about it, it wouldn't really be true."

"They said you called it in, but you left before they got there."

Emma nodded against Mickey's broad chest. "Sonny Lee—he was still alive when I got there. But . . . then he died."

"That's all right," Mickey said, stroking her hair. "That's all right, honey. At least you got to see him before he went. The thing is—you can't hide in Memphis. It ain't that big a town. Everybody knows Sonny Lee, and most everybody knows you. You should go to the police. Otherwise, they'll keep looking until they find you."

Emma stiffened and pulled away, panic rising within her. "Me? They think *I* had something to do with Sonny Lee's death?" She searched Mickey's face.

"No, of course not," Mickey said. "It's just . . . you have been a handful. Plus they have to try to keep you safe. It's the law."

"No," Emma said. "I'm only sixteen, and I have nobody. You know they'll put me in foster care until I'm eighteen, even if they don't put me in jail." She hesitated. "You know, Mickey, I was hoping . . ." She stopped talking when she saw the *no* in Mickey's eyes.

"You got to go to the police," Mickey said. "If you stay here, they'll find you—they already been here once. It would be better to turn yourself in and answer a few questions, show them you had nothing to do with it. And they'll make sure you get taken care of, till you finish school."

Emma would have kept arguing, but she could tell it wouldn't do any good. Mickey was right: they would find her, sooner or later, if she stayed in Memphis. If they found her staying with him on the down-low, he might lose his liquor license.

"You know, Mickey, I just remembered. There *is* someone I can call," Emma said. "Let me sleep on it and maybe we can figure something out in the morning."

"All right, Memphis." Mickey hesitated. She knew he didn't quite believe her, but also didn't want to deal with not believing her. "Good night, then. You need anything?"

Emma shook her head. "I'm fine," she lied.

After Mickey clomped back downstairs, Emma stuffed the money back into the envelope. Before she could chicken out, she pulled out the note Sonny Lee had left for her and punched the telephone number into her cell phone.

It rang—several times—and just when Emma thought the call would go to voice mail, a man answered in a gruff voice. "Boykin."

Her heart did a flip-flop. "Are you Tyler Boykin?"

"Now, what'd I just say?" After a pause, he added suspiciously, "Who is this?"

"My name's Emma Greenwood," Emma said. "My grandfather, Sonny Lee Greenwood, said I should call you."

Tyler Boykin was quiet so long Emma thought maybe he'd hung up.

"You still there?" she said, her fingers sweaty on the phone.

"Emma Claire Greenwood," he said finally. "I knew this day would come. What happened?" It was like he knew it was something bad.

"Well . . ." Emma cleared her throat. "Well, Sonny Lee is . . . he's dead. He fell. In his shop."

Tyler Boykin swore softly. Then went quiet. Finally, he said, "Did he fall or did somebody knock him down?"

Hmm, Emma thought. It seems like both Sonny Lee and this Tyler Boykin suspect foul play. "He was down when I found him," Emma said, "so I don't know. I didn't have anything to do with it."

"I didn't say you did." Seconds passed, and Emma could hear him breathing in the phone. "Where are you now?"

"I'm in Memphis. At a club."

"That figures. What club are you at?"

"Mickey's," Emma said. "Do you know it?"

"Yeah." More silence, as if Tyler Boykin were thinking hard. "Look, sit tight, and I'll come get you. Take me about twelve hours if I drive straight through."

"Twelve hours! Where are you?"

"Up north in Ohio. Near Cleveland," Boykin said. "You ever been there?"

"No, never," Emma said. One thing she knew: she wasn't going to be getting into a car with someone she didn't know, even if he came recommended by Sonny Lee. "Give me the address. I'll drive there myself."

"You can drive?" Boykin sounded stunned. "How old are you now?"

"I'm going to be seventeen," Emma said. "Next March."

"Time flies," Boykin muttered. "You got a car?"

"Well. Sonny Lee has—had an old Element he'd drive to

gigs," she said. "It's not much to look at, but it runs good." That was stretching it, but she'd need a car to get around. Emma didn't worry that the police would be looking for it because Sonny Lee had never transferred the title from the man he'd bought it from. It was kind of an informal deal. "Now, what was that address?"

"I'd rather come get you," Boykin said.

"And I'd rather drive."

He sighed. "All right, but you can't tell anybody where you're going. I don't want anybody following you up here."

"Why would anybody follow me up there?" Emma said, about to lose patience.

"Just promise, okay?"

"All right," Emma said. "I won't tell anyone. I don't want anybody coming after me either."

He gave her the address and she scribbled it on the back of Sonny Lee's note.

But she wasn't going to drive all the way to Cleveland without getting some answers. "Look, I know Sonny Lee said I should call you, but . . ." There just wasn't any other way to put it. "How do you know him? Who are you and what's your connection to me?"

Boykin laughed a low, bitter laugh. "Me? I'm Sonny Lee's son. I'm your daddy."

❦ CHAPTER FIVE ❧
DEBRIEFING

"**M**r. Kinlock!"

Jonah lifted his head from his desk and peered, bleary-eyed, at Constantine. If it was Constantine teaching, it must be calculus. At the Anchorage, the teachers moved from classroom to classroom while students stayed put, to allow some of the more physically challenged students to be mainstreamed.

But staying put made it that much more difficult to stay awake. And even harder to keep track of what class was in session.

"Sorry," Jonah mumbled. "I was just resting my eyes."

All around him, muffled laughter.

"Well, rest your eyes on your own time. I'm not up here to compete with your dreams, delicious as they may be. I'm up here to teach you a little something about differential equations."

Constantine was a recent hire, and a bit less mission-driven than most of Gabriel's handpicked faculty. And, of course, he knew nothing about Nightshade. What he thought he knew about Jonah's delicious secret life was totally wrong.

I will never use calculus, Jonah thought. I won't live long enough to use differential equations. I have other problems I need to solve. But part of the bargain at the Anchorage was that students cooperate with their Individual Education Plans, or IEPs. It went along with the shared fiction that any of them would live long enough to need a career.

Jonah was an erratic student, mostly A's with the occasional F. He didn't obsess much about the failing grades. What was Gabriel going to do, flunk him out? When he missed things in class, it was because (a) he hadn't had enough sleep because of his work with Nightshade, or (b) he was distracted by the background drama. Right now calculus was the least of his worries.

Even on the best of days, Jonah felt like he was under siege in class. On this particular morning, it didn't help that he was jet-lagged and emotionally bruised from the events in London. Any gathering of teens was bound to be a cesspool of emotions, and the classroom was no exception. Jealousy, embarrassment, grief, unrequited love—it was all there on any given day.

He was most aware of lust. Lust hung in the air like September pollen. Sometimes it was a kind of broadband hormonal yearning that splashed everyone in the room. Other times it had a specific target. Rudy Severino, for instance, was gazing longingly at Jonah's best friend, Natalie Diaz, looking for a reaction to the sizzling texts he was sending. She'd read them, smirk, and text back. They were at that stage in their relationship where their desire for each other made everyone else feel like an extra. Even in the middle of a classroom.

Jonah was glad that Natalie was going out with someone, but he couldn't help wondering how it would all turn out. Nat and Rudy were in a band together, and failed romance was a major cause of band breakups. Jonah wouldn't want to be on Natalie's bad side. She was tough. She used to run with the Outlaws in Lorain—before her extended family sent her to the Anchorage.

Nat worked in the clinic and dispensary that served students at the Anchorage. A healer savant, she could spot disorders through the skin. Often, she was the only one who could determine whether a therapy was working or not. Jonah had always thought of healers as gentle, tender souls, his model being Jeanette. Not Natalie. She was a warrior who played to win.

Calculus finally ended and Jonah stuffed his tablet into his backpack. His debriefing with Gabriel was next on the agenda. He could have slept in and gone straight to the meeting with Gabriel, for all the math he'd absorbed.

Natalie and Rudy were waiting for Jonah outside the classroom. Well, actually, they were totally entangled, as if being apart for an hour of class was more than they could bear.

"Get a room," Jonah suggested.

They jumped apart, Natalie apologizing profusely. As always, she was hyperaware of Jonah's celibate status. The two of them kept a measured foot apart all the way over to Gabriel's office. Which was almost as annoying as the embrace.

"Who else is in town—do you know?" Rudy asked.

"Charlie and Thérèse came back for the debriefing. I don't know who else. I just got back last night." His eyes felt like they had sand in them.

"Rudy and I have some new songs we'd like to run by you," Natalie said. "Could we go back to your place after the meeting?"

"I'm going to go see Kenzie," Jonah said. "I need to talk to him about Jeanette."

Natalie squeezed his shoulder as they turned down the alley next to the Keep.

The Keep Nightclub was housed in a rehabbed warehouse perched on a bluff overlooking the river. Gabriel Mandrake's offices were above the club, on the uppermost floor, where walls of windows offered a stunning view. In one direction lay downtown, a forest of glittering buildings; in the other, the river and the lake beyond. Several stories below lay the gritty industrial landscape of the Cleveland Flats.

They entered the main building through the alley door, touching their palms to the sensor by the entrance. Gabriel was a geek for gadgets and high tech. He'd been a materials man from way back, a kind of Renaissance minister of rock and roll. Part musician, part tech guru, part artist, part cutthroat promoter, part healer/pharmacist/drug dealer. A self-created sorcerer turned savant.

Gabriel had found a kindred spirit in Rudy Severino, who'd helped design and build the security system. Jonah was never sure how much of Rudy's talent was extreme nerdistry and how much was magic, but when Rudy built systems, they worked like a charm.

The three of them climbed the narrow staircase to the second floor, then waited while the iris biometrics scanner did its thing. The locking mechanism shifted, and they were in.

The outer office was where Gabriel met music-industry

big shots, prospective clients, venue owners, talent, and the like. The walls were lined with photographs—Gabriel at the Rock and Roll Hall of Fame induction ceremonies; Gabriel with an array of up-and-coming musicians; with the governor, the mayor. Gabriel introducing eight-year-old Jonah to the president.

At least Gabriel had put away the big-eyed Jonah posters when Jonah threatened to go on strike. Even though they'd been fund-raising gold.

It was the first of many small battles between Jonah and Gabriel. Jonah's failed rescue of Jeanette had begun as an unauthorized investigation of the healer's disappearance. His brother, Kenzie, had helped him track her down via the Web, which might mean the Kinlock brothers were in trouble again.

It would be worth it if it forced Gabriel's hand. He can't ignore this, Jonah thought. He can't.

Patrick looked up from the reception desk. He served the dual role of personal assistant and bodyguard. "Jonah!" he said. "Glad you're back! You three can go on in. The others are already here." He buzzed them in.

Gabriel's private office enshrined the sorcerer's wide-ranging interests. A large showcase to the left of the door displayed an array of antique bottles—some extremely elaborate, in glass, metal, and enamel, with jeweled stoppers. Others were time-blackened, their tops layered in yellowing wax.

One wall showcased images of tattoos, in color and black-and-white. They represented just a fraction of Gabriel's designs, many of which were inked into his skin. Skin art was the sorcerer's tool Gabriel worked with most often, art that protected and healed. Many of the students at the Keep were covered with Gabriel's work. It was the therapy that kept them alive and functioning a little while longer. Another gallery displayed line drawings of botanicals, reflecting his intense interest in drugs and medicinals.

The other slayers were sprawled around the conference area. It was glass on three sides, overlooking the Flats and the lake beyond. Leather couches and ottomans surrounded a low granite table with a platter of sandwiches and snacks.

Alison Shaw was there, of course. Charlie Dugard and Thérèse Fortenay from Europe, and Mike Joplin from South America. Like Jonah, they were still nominally in high school. Even Mose Butterfield was there. He'd been too ill to deploy for the past year, but the others pretended he'd be going back out again. Gabriel must have told them about Jeanette, because they all wore glum, dispirited expressions.

This was as large a quorum as they ever had. Most of Gabriel's shadeslayers were in the field at any given time, hunting shades—their former classmates, families, neighbors, and friends—the undead victims of Thorn Hill. Making the world safer for everyone but themselves.

Unfolding to his feet, Gabriel crossed to where Jonah stood, just inside the door. Embracing him, he said, "Glad you're safe. I just wish you'd brought better news." Gabriel looked into Jonah's face for another long moment before he let him go.

Well, Jonah thought, at least we're not going to argue about my going after Jeanette.

Gabriel's eyes were riveting, his pupils unusually large, all but obscuring their irises, so that his eyes seemed to swallow you. Whether it was his natural physiology or a consequence of the drugs he took, the sight of them could be unnerving. Gabriel was a man of many demons, with a dump load of pain to forget.

Gabriel returned to his seat, and Jonah threaded his way around furniture, murmuring greetings to the others.

"Jonah!" Mose said, with an eager smile. "Glad you made it back safe."

"It's great to see you here," Jonah said, squeezing Mose's shoulder. Odd. The more Mose's body declined, the more brightly his spirit shone through.

"Charlie was just filling us in on what happened in London," Gabriel said as Jonah slumped into his usual chair. "Go on, Charlie."

"Feel free to chime in, Jonah," Charlie said. "Like I said, we'd been monitoring the towpath for weeks. Three of us followed two shades onto a canal boat. It was a private event, with several mainliners on board."

"Then all hell broke loose," Thérèse said. "The boat was attacked by an army of shades. We think they were targeting the mainliners."

"What makes you think that?" Gabriel said.

"That's what we've been hearing," Charlie said. "Mainliners are being killed, all over Europe. As you can imagine, the guilds are in an uproar."

"Any change in the old modus operandi?" Mose asked. When met with a blank look from Charlie, he added, in a loud stage whisper, "How are they riffed?"

"All different ways," Charlie said. "Tossed off buildings, hacked to pieces, throats cut—nothing too high-tech. Some don't have a mark on them. They're just dead."

"It's the perfect crime, Watson," Mose said. "So many suspects. Everyone hates wizards."

"It's not just wizards," Thérèse said. "And, anyway, the Anaweir authorities don't know that." Anaweir meaning the nongifted. The civilians.

"Let's get back to Regent's Canal," Gabriel said.

"Summer went down fighting," Charlie said. "We might've, too, but Jonah showed up and waded in. The shades split soon after that. To sum up, six civilians dead, including two mainliners."

"Mainliners aren't civilians," Alison murmured.

"Dozens of shades freed, two shivved," Charlie said, "counting Jonah's. And one slayer down."

Freed. That was Gabriel's term for removing a shade's borrowed body so you could get at it and kill it. That's putting a positive spin on it, Jonah thought.

Alison looked up at the ceiling. "Only two shivved?" She slid a smirk at Charlie.

"I'll match my long-term stats against yours anytime," Charlie said, unruffled. "Then again, why would I want to do that?"

Jonah spoke up for the first time. "The shades were organized, working together. When they come in swarms like that, it's really hard to do anything but chop them down."

"Is that it, then, Charlie?" Gabriel said, as if eager to move on.

"Yeah," Charlie said, "Except we're running low on shivs." He slid one of the enchanted daggers across the table to Gabriel. "We like this design the best."

"We're running short, too," Alison said to Charlie. "Better make 'em count, Dugard."

"Alison." Gabriel raised his hand to quell her. "We're making them as fast as we can," he said.

Shivs were slender silver blades encrusted with runes—the weapons slayers used to dispatch free shades. All shadeslayers, except for Jonah. The runes were layered on, so they took months to make in the Anchorage metal shop.

Gabriel rubbed at his stubble of beard and turned to Jonah. "Now," he said. "Tell us about Jeanette."

Jonah kept the report short and matter-of-fact.

"But, I still don't get it," Rudy said, when Jonah had finished. "Why would they kidnap Jeanette? She's retired. She lives—lived—on that farm in Massachusetts."

"They were interrogating her about weapon development at Thorn Hill," Jonah said.

"Thorn Hill!" Gabriel's head snapped up. "What about Thorn Hill?"

"You know the wizard line—that Thorn Hill was a terrorist camp, and the massacre was some kind of an accident," Jonah said. "Now they're looking for some of that terrorist expertise. To fight back against Madison Moss, they claim."

"Who's Madison Moss?" Thérèse asked.

Jonah stared down at his hands, biting his lip to keep from speaking his mind. We should know this stuff, he thought. We're Gabriel's key operatives. We have to navigate this world whether we like it or not.

"She's the young lady who holds the Dragonheart," Gabriel said. "The source of power for Weir magic. It gives her the ability to cut off the spigot of power. It's completely changed the relationships among the mainline guilds."

"In other words, it's reduced the power of wizards,"

Jonah said. "And they don't like that. Amazing she's survived this long."

"The good news is, I don't think Ms. Moss wants to control anybody," Gabriel said. "She is, shall we say, a reluctant despot. On the other hand, Rowan DeVries is on the Interguild Council."

"So the person who murdered Jeanette is on the council?" Mike snorted. "These are the good guys?"

Try to find a good wizard, Jonah thought. Betcha can't.

Jonah finished relaying what he'd seen and heard in the mansion on the Thames. "Even in private, Longbranch, DeVries, and the others kept to the script, claiming that the massacre was something we did to ourselves."

"I'm sure some wizards actually believe that," Gabriel murmured.

"But if the Black Rose engineered it, and Rowan's father, Andrew DeVries, was in charge—" Jonah began.

"Rowan DeVries was just a little older than you were when Thorn Hill happened," Gabriel said. "Frankly, it's unlikely that the wizards who kidnapped Jeanette were involved in the Thorn Hill disaster."

Here we go again, Jonah thought. Gabriel will diffuse blame and keep us from going after the real villains.

"They mentioned the Anchorage," Jonah said. "But they didn't seem to think we were much of a threat, and didn't want to tangle with you."

"Good," Gabriel muttered. "At least they're not blaming us."

"Well, not yet," Jonah said. "But that could change. Now they're finding clues with the mainliner dead: nightshade flowers, scattered over the bodies."

"Nightshade!" Gabriel levered out of his chair and stalked to the window as six slayers reflexively grabbed for their amulets. "My God."

"So someone *is* trying to blame it on us," Mike said. "Who would do that?"

"I don't know," Gabriel said, staring out through the glass. "Did the wizards connect that to us? Or mention any other clues around the bodies?"

"No," Jonah said. Nightshade was hiding in plain sight, just an hour away from mainliner headquarters at Trinity. Most mainliners had heard of the Anchorage, of course, but they *didn't* know anything about the existence of Nightshade and its targets.

I wish we didn't know, Jonah thought, fingering his *sefa*. I wish we could just throw away these amulets and pretend that shades don't exist.

"How did they find Jeanette?" Gabriel asked, in a low, tight voice. "Do you know?"

All of a sudden Gabriel cares, Jonah thought. When it seems like the Anchorage might be a target. "If they talked about it, it was before I arrived. But it couldn't have been too hard. It's not like she was hiding."

"Did you leave any witnesses? Anyone who could identify you?"

"No. Longbranch and Wylie are dead. DeVries left before I came out of cover." Jonah paused, then plunged on. "I should have riffed him, too."

Gabriel spun away from the window, visibly agitated. "That's the last thing we need right now," he snapped.

"What are you afraid of, Gabriel?" Jonah demanded. "First, wizards tried to murder us. Now they pretend that it

was our fault. The other mainliners treat us like—like—*we* should be going after *them*."

Natalie rested her hand on Jonah's shoulder. "I know you're upset at what happened to Jeanette," she murmured. "We all are."

"I'm more than *upset*," Jonah hissed. "*Upset* is what happens when you lose your cell phone. You're *upset* when you break a string on your favorite guitar."

Gabriel stood over Jonah, glowering down at him. "You agreed to the mission when you came here, remember?"

"That was ten years ago!" Jonah retorted. "I was seven years old. Maybe we should think about changing the mission."

"You always have the option to leave," Gabriel said.

"I never said I wanted to leave." Jonah tried to get his anger under control. "Anyway, I wouldn't want to leave Kenzie behind."

"Then you need to follow the rules that protect us all," Gabriel said flatly, returning to his seat. Pulling a bottle out of his desk drawer, he popped two pills into his mouth and swallowed them dry.

"Gabriel," Mike began hesitatingly, "why Jeanette? If they want to find out how the poisoning was done, shouldn't they be talking to wizards?"

"Wizards aren't that good with material magic," Gabriel said. He flipped the shiv, catching it by the hilt again.

"But . . ." Alison looked lost. "You always said—"

"Though wizards would have planned the operation, it would have been sorcerers who developed and compounded the poison," Gabriel said.

They all stared at him.

"Why haven't you told us that before?" Jonah said finally.

"I thought it was obvious." Gabriel shrugged. "That's the role of sorcerers—compounding medicinals and the like."

"Why would sorcerers collaborate with wizards?" Alison said, grimacing like she had a bad taste in her mouth.

"They may have been forced to do it. Perhaps they didn't know what the intended use was." Gabriel ran the edge of the dagger along his thumb, and blood welled up. He watched it drip onto the desk, as dispassionate as if it were someone else's. Given the drug regimen he was on, he probably didn't even feel the wound.

"Shouldn't we find the survivors ourselves, then?" Jonah said. "Before they do? Or confront the Black Rose, head-on?"

"We can't afford to draw attention to ourselves. Not right now."

"If not now, when?" Jonah exploded, his frustration and exhaustion getting the better of him again. "What the *hell* kind of evidence do you need? Wizards kidnapped Jeanette, they tortured her, and then they murdered her. Now they're trying to track down survivors from the Thorn Hill Massacre so they can figure out how to do it again!"

"Was the word 'massacre' mentioned?" Gabriel said quietly. "I think you're jumping to conclusions."

"What do you need, a signed *confession*?"

"Jonah," Gabriel said. "If mainliners are dying, if the clues left with the bodies point directly at us, that means that someone knows enough about us to frame us. How long do you think it will take others to make that connection? Or for the framer to lead them to it?"

"They're not blaming it on us! They seem to be blaming it on this Madison Moss."

"They're not blaming it on us *yet*," Gabriel said. "If we confront them, they will. You don't remember what it was like, but I do. When I established the Anchorage, mainliners viewed the survivors of Thorn Hill like . . . like mad dogs. Like dangerous mutants who should be slaughtered before they hurt someone."

Gabriel's words eerily echoed what Longbranch had said about the "labrats," as she called them. *It would have been cleaner to have dealt with them at the time.*

"So we don't go after the Black Rose directly," Jonah persisted. "If there are sorcerers out there who created those poisons, we find them. They could help us figure out how to treat the effects. Maybe they'd be eager to help."

"That's a waste of time," Gabriel said. "Do you really think that the Black Rose would leave their collaborators alive to tell tales?"

"Looks like Longbranch, DeVries, and the others don't think it's a waste of time," Jonah persisted. "Maybe they know something we don't."

Gabriel just kept shaking his head.

Jonah jackknifed to his feet. "They murdered Jeanette. Now we're just going to *sit* here and do nothing until they come after us?"

"Jonah," Gabriel commanded, "Sit down. You're out of control."

Jonah didn't sit.

"Anyway, we're not doing nothing," Gabriel said, an edge in his voice. "We're going to upgrade our security and extend our eyes and ears."

"So we're going to hide in our bunkers like we're *guilty*?" Jonah demanded.

Gabriel surged to his feet, "I know you're tired, and we're all grieving for Jeanette, but I expect you to stay on task and on mission and to recognize *no* when you hear it.

"Now," Gabriel said, turning away. "I mean to do everything in my power to avoid another Thorn Hill. We have no reason to think they'll come here, if we don't draw their attention. If what you said is true, and they don't view us as much of a threat."

Why not? Jonah thought. Why aren't we more of a threat?

"If they're planning a massacre, you can bet we're not the targets, or at least we shouldn't be," Jonah said. "After all—if they wait a while, we'll die off on our own."

He strode to the door and yanked it open, then turned to fire a parting shot. "You know what I think? I think you're scared they'll come after you. I think you've lost your nerve."

And he slammed out of the office.

❦ CHAPTER SIX ❧
KENZIE

Safe Harbor—the skilled care unit at the Anchorage—was homey in a warehouse kind of way, with exposed bricks and beams and battered wooden floors polished to a warm shine. Next to each of the "residences" was a brass nameplate. Permanent. Those who lived at Safe Harbor rarely ever moved to a different building.

"Safe Harbor," Kenzie liked to say. "Where nobody gets out alive."

Jonah came in through the back door—the one with the disabled alarm. He climbed the stairs to the second floor, only to find Kenzie's room empty. Jonah swore softly. He'd hoped to find his brother at home. The tablet display outside his door said, *I'm in the gym. Rescue me.*

So it was back down the stairs, toward the skylighted gymnasium. Residents at Safe Harbor generally used the specialized gym located in their own building, since it was too hard to transport them to the main gym.

Jonah heard raised voices, clear down the hall.

"Kenzie, could you *just* give it a try." The therapist sounded pissed. "We need to loosen up those tight muscles."

"Let's not and say we did," Kenzie said. "I'll never tell."

"You know as well as I do that we need to stretch out those legs. Now. Let me know if you feel any pain, all right?"

When Jonah walked into the gym, he found Kenzie strapped into a chairlike device designed to stretch out his arms and legs. The therapist stood beside Kenzie, coaching him as she manipulated the levers. "Extend, then release. Extend, release. Keep breathing."

"That's one I'm good at," Kenzie gasped. "Breathing." His red-brown hair was plastered down with sweat, so they must have been working out for a while.

The therapist knelt beside the machine, adjusting the weight setting.

Kenzie spotted Jonah. "Jonah! Thank God you're here! They've got me on the rack again!"

"It looks good on you, Kenzie," Jonah said, brushing the damp hair off his brother's forehead. "Let's tighten up those screws a little, shall we? That will no doubt loosen your tongue." Kenzie rolled his eyes. It was an old joke between them.

"We'll be another fifteen minutes," the therapist said briskly, without looking up. "Shall I call you in when we're finished?"

Jonah knew most of the therapists, but he didn't know this one. She seemed unimpressed with Kinlock humor.

"I'll take over," Jonah said. "I'm an old hand at torture, and Kenzie's my favorite victim."

Now she did look up. "Oh!" she said, and stood so quickly

she nearly bumped her head on the equipment.

"I'm Jonah Kinlock. Kenzie's brother."

"I—I'm Miranda," the therapist said, her cheeks pinking up. "They told me about you. I'm . . . um . . . filling in for Julie. And . . . ah . . . I'm sorry if I—"

"I've been away," Jonah said, to put her out of her misery. "Has the treatment plan changed?" He touched the screen next to the machine and Kenzie's chart came up. He scanned the progress notes. "Same PT and OT. What's this mean, 'minimal stimulation therapy'?"

Miranda shifted from one foot to the other. "It's something they're discussing . . . a new treatment to dampen drug-resistant seizures and hyperkinesis."

"Hmm. How does that sound, Kenzie?"

"Horrifying."

"My thoughts exactly. Do you have plans for him after this session?" Jonah asked. "Or can we go to the spa?"

"The spa?" Miranda said uncertainly. "Well. He has group at seven."

"He'll be back in plenty of time," Jonah said.

"This is the life," Kenzie said, biting into a Cadbury's Screme Egg, then squinting at it. "What's this green stuff in here anyway?"

"Guts," Jonah said. "They already had their Halloween candy on display at Cadbury World. I guess it's the next big chocolate holiday."

"Crunchy Spider?" Kenzie said, offering a pouch of candy. "Or would you prefer a Dead Head?"

"I'll stick with the truffles," Jonah said, popping one into his mouth. "I'm too squeamish for the rest."

"Squeamish? You, who fight the zombielike walking dead on a daily basis?"

"That's exactly why I'm squeamish," Jonah replied. "I don't like to bring my work home."

The spa was a little-used oasis on the roof of Safe Harbor, including an all-weather pool, sauna, massage therapy area (by appointment), and the hot tub the Kinlock brothers were presently sharing—Jonah in his boxers and leather gloves, Kenzie wearing nothing but the waterproof earbuds Jonah had brought back from the UK. They'd spent the last hour eating chocolate and reminiscing about Jeanette.

While Kenzie ate, Jonah studied him, looking for signs of deterioration or improvement. His brother was thin—all bones and brilliant eyes and a mop of red-brown hair. He burned so much energy that his caloric intake could never seem to keep up.

Kenzie looked up and caught him staring. "This is the best invention *ever*," he said, tapping his earbud. "Who is this?"

"Manygoats," Jonah said. "Navajo punk band. Hot in the UK right now."

"You know, leather and boxers is a good look for you," Kenzie said. "Classic, yet just a big dodgy—"

Jonah splashed him.

"Hey!" Kenzie said, snatching his chocolate out of danger. "Respect the candy." He stretched out his legs, allowing the churning water to support them. His body seemed relaxed, free of the electric, hyperkinetic movements that had plagued him all day long. It had taken the full hour to get to this point. "Let's build a fort up here and stay forever. Remember when we used to build forts?"

"We never built forts," Jonah said, leaning his head back and looking up at the stars. Steam rose up all around them, eddying in the wind off the lake.

"We built forts," Kenzie insisted. "In the jungles of Brazil. You saved me from a tiger."

"There are no tigers in Brazil, bro."

"A jaguar, then."

Jonah rolled his eyes.

"Anaconda?"

"You just keep thinking, Kenzie," Jonah said. "I haven't saved anybody from anything so far."

"We did our best," Kenzie said, "if you're talking about Jeanette."

"You did *your* best," Jonah said. "But apparently *my* best is not good enough," Jonah said. "And it's not just Jeanette. It's a whole lot of things."

"You're protecting the public," Kenzie suggested.

"Am I? It feels more like murder to me. Anyway, what do I care about the general public? They have no idea they're being protected." Sitting up a little, he sipped from his steaming mug of drinkable chocolate. "More?" He waggled the thermos.

"I'm good," Kenzie said.

For a while, they said nothing, each lost in his own thoughts.

"I'm going to write a symphony for Jeanette," Kenzie said finally.

"Good idea." Jonah nodded. "Will you be wanting lyrics?"

"Maybe. But it seems like we should do something more than write a song."

Jonah blotted condensation from his face with his fore-arm. "I riffed Longbranch and Wylie. They're the ones who kidnapped her."

"That's not enough," Kenzie said.

"What—you want me to kill more people? Got anybody in mind?"

Kenzie rolled his eyes. "I do, but that's me. Her death has to *mean* something. It has to make a difference. I keep think-ing . . . what would Jeanette want? And I think what she would want is for us to fix this." He waved his hand, spraying droplets over the roof.

"Fix what?"

"You know, save the children of Thorn Hill. This can-not stand. We need a plan." He looked up at Jonah, his eyes bright with tears.

"I know," Jonah said, squeezing Kenzie's shoulder. "We need a plan."

"To Jeanette," Kenzie said, raising his mug in a toast.

"To Jeanette," Jonah echoed, clanking mugs with his brother. "She would love the fact that you're toasting her with Cadbury's."

❧ CHAPTER SEVEN ❧
MOTHERLESS CHILD

Emma was glad she'd decided to drive herself to Ohio. Twelve hours is a long way to drive, but it's also a long time to ride in a car with the father that you just found out about a few hours ago. Though maybe it would've been a good time to ask questions, since he'd be trapped in there with her.

She was bone-weary and itchy-eyed by the time she reached Cleveland. It didn't help that she couldn't sleep.

Cleveland Heights was a mingle of twisty streets lined with older homes on tiny lots, commercial streets with stores, bars, and restaurants, and broad boulevards bordered by mansions in brick and stone. She parked in a garage on Coventry Road and called Tyler from a nearby coffee shop.

She half expected he wouldn't answer, that he'd have disappeared on her again, but he answered on the first ring. "Boykin."

"I'm here," she said simply. "In Grinder's Coffee on Coventry Road. Can you meet me?"

"Be a few minutes," he said, and clicked off.

She knew him as soon as he walked in. He reminded her of Sonny Lee—though Tyler was taller, and lighter-skinned, with that smudgy glow that some people have, like there's a light on inside.

He came straight at her and stood awkwardly next to the table. "Emma? I'm Tyler. I'm going to get some coffee. You want anything?"

Yeah, Emma thought. I want to know where the hell you've been all this time. But she shook her head.

Tyler returned to the table with a large coffee, a big slab of cake, and two forks.

"I just had a feeling you wanted some cake," he said, settling into the chair across from her and handing her one of the forks.

If you knew anything about me, Emma thought, you'd know I don't like carrot cake.

She studied him across the table. He was handsome, with Cherokee cheekbones, as Sonny Lee called them. Yet he seemed timeworn, too, like he'd lived a hundred years in forty. Emma brushed her fingers over her own face, wondering if one day she'd look the same.

"I've seen you before," she said. "Haven't I?"

He nodded. "When you were real little, of course," he said. "And I brought you back from Brazil."

"You were a lot younger," Emma said. "I remember dragging this old suitcase around. You carried me on your shoulders sometimes."

"I think you've changed more than me," he said. "Guess you think people just stay the same when you're not looking at them."

"How'd you recognize me?" she asked.

"You favor your mama," Tyler said. "And Sonny Lee sent pictures, now and then. Though not lately."

"He said you were dead."

Tyler chewed his lower lip, as if embarrassed not to be. "Not yet."

"He knew *exactly* where you were all this time?" Emma's voice trembled. "And he never told me?" Hurt and betrayal washed over her once again.

"That was the deal between him and me," Tyler said. "He insisted that there be no contact."

"Why? Are you some kind of a—a—pedophile, or—"

"No," Tyler said. "Nothing like that. I made some bad choices, is all. He was pissed, when I handed you off to him."

Emma recalled Sonny Lee's letter. *I'll be straight with you: I wasn't happy when you first came to me.* "I know it was—must've been burdensome, having me to look after," she said, her voice trembling in spite of herself. "But it—it seemed like we got along good. Later on, I mean."

Tyler rubbed his forehead with his thumb and forefinger. "When I said he was pissed, I meant he was pissed at me, not you. None of it was your fault." He hesitated, then hurried on. "If you knew the whole story, you'd—"

"Why don't you tell me that story?" Emma said, sitting back in her chair and looking her father in the eye. "I got no plans."

Tyler gazed at her, a muscle working in his jaw. Thinking thinking thinking. "So the old man never told you nothing, did he?"

"I didn't even know you existed," Emma said.

Tyler snorted. "There was no one could carry a grudge

like my old man. He was the most stubborn—"

"I know enough about Sonny Lee," Emma said. "I want to hear about you." She paused and, when he said nothing, asked, "If you're Sonny Lee's son, then what's with the name Boykin?"

"That's a stage name. I'm a musician."

Of course you are, Emma thought. "What's wrong with Greenwood?"

"I don't use that name anymore."

"How did you meet my mother?"

Tyler did that flicker-eyed thing that people do when they're choosing between a truth, a half-truth, or a lie. "We met at a club in New York. I was in a band, and we had a regular gig there at that time."

"What do you play?" Emma couldn't help asking.

"Guitar," Tyler said. "Bass guitar, mostly, these days. I do some teaching, too. Anyway, your mama started coming to see us, and one thing led to another, and we got married."

"What was she like?"

"Your mother?" Tyler shook his head. "She was a beautiful woman. Me, I was head over heels in love with her. After I met Gwen, there was nobody else. We had some good times, that's for sure." He paused. "I'll tell you one thing—she was crazy about you."

That thought warmed her a little. "Do you have any pictures?"

Tyler dug out his wallet, flipping it open to a photo taken in one of those coin-operated photo booths. Gwen stood in front, holding Emma, who was the best dressed of the three of them. Tyler stood behind with his arms draped around both of them, as if to pin them to the earth. Her mother's head was cocked so she could look down into Emma's face. Her hair was as pale as sapwood ash, her eyes a clear gray.

The photo was crinkled and worn, like it had been pulled out and looked at thousands of times.

Emma looked up from the photo and found Tyler gazing at her. "Like I said, you remind me of her. Oh, I know your coloring's different," he rushed to add. "But you have that same . . . wildness about you." He grimaced. "I don't mean to be creepy, I just don't know what else to call it."

"So I should blame her for the way I am?" Emma twisted a lock of her hair, the piece that was always falling in her face.

"I don't know that I'd use the word 'blame,'" Tyler said. "It's one of the things I liked about her."

"What happened? Between you and my mother? How did she end up at Thorn Hill, and you back here?"

He paused, did the flicker-eye. "After you were born, she complained about her job, more and more, and wanted to leave it, but she was afraid to. Afraid of what Mr. DeVries might do."

"Mr. DeVries?"

"Her boss."

"Because she quit her *job*? Was she cooking meth or what?"

He shook his head. "Mr. DeVries was somebody you'd never want to meet. A wizard."

"A *what*?"

"A wizard. *You* know." He took a big bite of cake.

"I have no idea what you're talking about."

Tyler nearly choked on his mouthful. He dabbed at his mouth with his napkin. "Sonny Lee never told you about the magical guilds either?"

"Maybe that was *your* job," Emma retorted, unwilling to hear Sonny Lee criticized.

"Maybe it was," Tyler said, with a sigh. "I just figured you'd know, since you're gifted."

"One thing I am *not* is gifted," Emma said bluntly, recalling the endless round of conferences at school. "Not a single person in all my life has called me that."

"But . . . you have an aura."

"A what?"

"You can see my aura, right?"

"That glow?"

He nodded.

"Lots of people glow. I asked Sonny Lee about it, once, and he acted like I was crazy, so I shut up about it."

"Because he is . . . was . . . Anaweir. Meaning he wasn't gifted, so he can't see it." Tyler paused. "You don't have any . . . special abilities? Unusual talents?"

Getting into trouble? Emma thought, but it probably wasn't the thing to say to your father that you'd just met. "I play a little guitar," she said. "And I helped Sonny Lee in the shop. I'm not much of a student, but I'm real good with my hands." I might as well lower expectations from the start, she thought.

Tyler scowled at her, brow furrowed. "If blood is true, you should be a sorcerer, like your mother and me. I just can't get a read on your stone. It's like it's muddied up."

"My stone?"

"Your Weirstone." Tyler brought his fist to his chest. "It's right here."

Huh, Emma thought. Good thing I never got in a car with this one.

"You think I'm nuts," Tyler said, with a twisted smile. "Don't you?"

"Oh, no," Emma blurted, thinking, Don't make him

mad. "I'm just confused. Like—aren't wizards and sorcerers the same thing?"

Tyler shook his head. "Wizards can do fancier spells, what we call conjured magic. With charms. Sorcerers make magical things—herbs, medications, potions, magical tools, and like that. Seers predict the future, warriors are good fighters, and enchanters—stay away from them. They can talk you into anything. So . . . there are five Weirguilds in all." He counted on his fingers. "Wizards, sorcerers, seers, warriors, and enchanters."

Right, Emma thought. Uh-huh. She slid a look at the door. Should she make a break for it?

What's your hurry? You got no other place to go. Might as well sit here in the warm and keep him talking.

"So," she said, settling back into her chair. "How do you know what guild you're in? Or can you try out for different ones?"

"You don't choose. It's based on what kind of Weirstone you're born with, inherited from your parents." Again, Tyler pressed his fingers against his chest. "In my case, from my mother, your grandmother. In your case, from me and your mother." He studied her face, then looked down at his hands. "I know it's hard to take in, all at once."

Emma hadn't expected much of Tyler Boykin—a man who knew just where to find her for sixteen years but never made contact. Who let his father raise her, after a fashion. She'd expected a deadbeat, a drinker, an addict maybe. Not someone who was a good mile past eccentric. *Guess that's why Sonny Lee had to keep me.*

"How come I haven't heard of any of this?" she said. "I'd think the newspapers would be full of stories about magical people. You know, like they do with aliens."

"Most Anaweir don't know about us," Tyler said. "It's just easier that way. And people like us—in the underguilds— we tend to lay low. We don't want to come to the notice of wizards."

"But you're saying my mother was working for one," Emma said.

Tyler nodded, staring down into his coffee. "She was. A lot of sorcerers worked for wizards, and not always by choice." He seemed edgy, like he was teetering on the edge of a truth and might topple into it by accident.

So Emma gave him a push. "What kind of work did she do for him?"

"You don't need to know that," Tyler growled. He looked up at Emma, and it was like storm shutters had slid down over his face. "Some things are better left alone."

Emma shoved back her chair and stood. "I guess some things are." She stuck out her hand. "Good to meet you, Tyler. I mean, who knew I had a father and all? Thanks for coming out."

He stood, too, in a hurry, practically knocking his chair over. "What? Wait a minute. You're leaving?"

"There's no point in this. I ask you a question, and you either make stuff up or refuse to answer."

"I'm not—but . . . where will you go?"

"I don't think that's any concern of yours," Emma said. "I'm used to taking care of my own self. I'll be fine." *Ha! Speaking of making stuff up, that was pretty close to a lie, right there.*

"Emma, I'm sorry," Tyler said, wiping his hands on his jeans. "What I said about the guilds—it's true, and I can prove it, if you'll give me the chance. As for the rest, it's just—there's some secrets you're better off not knowing."

"*I'm* better off, or *you're* better off?"

Tyler hunched his shoulders and drew his head in like a turtle's. "A little of both, maybe." He smiled, crookedly, and Emma could see how he'd charmed her mother. "All right, you win. Sit down, and I'll tell you the dirt."

Emma sat, and Tyler sat. By now, she was half afraid to hear it, half sorry she'd asked, but her ironwood spine wouldn't allow her to admit it.

Tyler took a deep breath. "See, the main thing your mother did for Andrew DeVries was make poisons."

It took Emma a moment to get her voice going. *"Poisons?"*

Tyler nodded. "DeVries only employed the very best, and your mama was the very best."

"But . . . what would he need with poisons?"

"He was the head of a syndicate of assassins. At the time, wizards were killing each other, right and left, even though it was against their own rules. DeVries was the one who saw the potential of poison. It's almost impossible to defend against. Little pinprick on the street, and you die of a heart attack. You could put a drop on somebody's pillow and be a continent away when he died. If you want your enemy to die scream-ing, that can happen. Or maybe he just goes crazy. Some of Gwen's brews took a month to kill you, and others—"

Emma raised both hands. "I get the picture," she said, her voice trembling.

"Now, then," Tyler said, with a bitter smile. "Are you glad you asked?"

"I like to know the truth," Emma said. "That's all. I just wish the truth was different." She rubbed her eyes with the heels of her hands, as if to wipe away the image of her mother she'd built for herself.

"If it makes you feel any better, she hated the work. We needed the money, though, so I tried to get her to stick it out. That made her mad. One day, she came home with this idea of moving to Brazil. People from the underguilds had started a commune there—a place called Thorn Hill. They figured there was safety in numbers and distance.

"I said no. My work was here, and you were just two years old. I worried about what would happen if you got sick or hurt in a remote place like that. Plus, like I said—you don't just resign when you work for Mr. DeVries. But Gwen kept bringing it up and bringing it up. And then, one day, she disappeared, and took you with her."

He grimaced. "I guessed where you were, but to tell the truth, I didn't come looking for a long while, because I was pissed, you know?"

"We called it the farm," Emma said. Memories surfaced, of steamy air and a sea of purple flowers. Of horses and pigs and parrots. Scratching in the dirt with a hoe. Running barefoot through tall grass. Singing together in a large auditorium. Her mother guiding her hand with a paintbrush. Reading to her in a chair big enough for two. Emma could picture flowers on the table, framed prints on the wall, window boxes spilling flowers. Mama always wore a sun hat when she worked outside, because her skin was so fair. While her mother worked, Emma ran wild with a pack of children from dawn till dusk and never put her sunscreen on.

She looked up and caught Tyler staring at her, a wistful expression on his face. As if he knew what he'd missed out on.

"What finally happened?" Emma asked.

Tyler kept staring down at the table. He sure wasn't one

to look a person in the eye. "I finally went to Brazil, hoping to talk your mama into coming back. Gwen refused to come back with me, but let you come back to the States with me until Christmas. Not long after that, she, and nearly everyone else at Thorn Hill, died." It was like he'd fast-forwarded through a scene.

"What do you mean?"

Tyler's eyes flicked up to her face, then back to the table. "The wells at the commune went bad. It may have been toxic leakage from the mines, pesticides—something like that, though there were lots of conspiracy theories. Thousands of people died—all of the adults, in fact, and a lot of the kids. That put an end to the commune. Now I was on my own to raise you, but it was the same old, same old. I was always on the road. Couldn't make a living otherwise. As a musician, anyway. So I asked Sonny Lee to help."

"Seems like Sonny Lee did more than help," Emma observed.

"When I called him, he was pissed at me for getting myself into this kind of a jam. So he said he'd keep you, but only if I stayed out of the picture. He was worried that being connected to me would be dangerous for you."

Emma recalled Sonny Lee's words: *You need to get out of Memphis, because they'll come after you, too.*

"Why would it be dangerous?"

"Like I said. You don't just resign when you work for Andrew DeVries. He didn't like loose ends."

"But—if Mama was already dead . . . ?" Emma cocked her head.

"Just trust me on that, okay?"

"Why should I trust you on anything?" Emma snapped.

"And don't try playing the daddy card, because you lost that hand a long time ago."

Tyler whistled. "You don't hold back, do you?"

"I just don't like being lied to," Emma said. "I never have."

"Nobody does," Tyler said, looking down at his hands. "But you'd better get used to it."

Emma stretched, trying to ease the clenched muscle over her shoulder blade. "How did you end up here?"

"I came here five years ago, figuring I was getting too old for the road. I bought a house, found some regular gigs here in town, where the cost of living is low." He rose and carried their empty plate and cups to the trash, then returned to the table.

"Why here? Why not Memphis?"

"Too many people know me in Memphis," Tyler said. "This is a great music town, too, and nobody would look for me here." He snorted. "Who knew this was going to turn into the center of the Weir universe."

"What?"

"Never mind." He paused. "I thought of trying to get in touch with you after I settled here. But a deal's a deal, and it seemed like you were doing fine in Memphis. You're almost grown, and I didn't want to mess that up."

"It got messed up anyway," Emma said. They both sat and stared down at the table. When Emma couldn't stand the awkward silence any longer, she said, "So? Now what?"

Tyler twisted his napkin between his fingers. "First a question, Emma . . . did you tell anyone you were coming here?"

"No," Emma said. "You told me not to."

He nodded, looking relieved. "Good. That's good." He paused again. "Look, you're welcome to stay with me. We can get you enrolled in school and all, see how it goes." When she made a face, he said, "Aw, come on, it won't be that bad."

Emma thought about it. It wasn't like she had a lot of choices. It could be risky, moving in with a stranger, but she'd chance it if it kept her off the streets and out of foster care. No law said she had to stay if he turned out to be crazy dangerous.

"You'd have your own room," Tyler persisted. "We can fix it up, any way you like."

He really wants this, Emma thought, scarcely able to believe it. After all this time.

"The thing is—I'm used to doing pretty much what I want," she said. "Coming and going as I please. Sonny Lee didn't nanny me much. I don't want to move in and have you all of a sudden setting up rules and curfews."

"If you live at my house, you'll go to school," Tyler said. "These days, you can't make a living without schooling. No drinking, no drugs, no friends in the house when I'm not there. No staying out all night when I don't know where you are. Most everything else, we can talk about."

"Sounds like a lot of rules," Emma observed.

"Well. You don't have to sign anything," Tyler said. "If you don't like it, you can leave."

"Is there a place for a woodshop?"

"A woodshop?" Tyler raised his eyebrows.

This is my father, and he knows nothing about me, Emma thought.

"I rescued some things from Sonny Lee's shop on my way out of town. Things he left to me. They're big tools—that take a lot of space. If you got a place to put them, it's a deal."

The sun was just breaking over the horizon when Jonah arrived at the fitness center. It was new—a state-of-the-art facility with glass walls overlooking the lake, funded by the Anchorage Foundation. The adaptive equipment and tailored exercise programs received considerable media attention. Medical personnel came from all over the world to learn from the Anchorage experience.

Hidden under the skin of the Anchorage was another school—an academy to train Nightshade assassins in the specialized skills needed for their work as shadeslayers.

It wasn't all assassination, of course. Operations also needed healers, weapons designers and fabricators, intelligence and tech experts. Savants interested in joining Nightshade trained under Gabriel's lieutenants—shadeslayers expert at evaluating gifts and determining their usefulness to the cause.

Slayers were at a natural disadvantage when it came to fighting shades. Shades never hesitated to risk their borrowed bodies in a fight, since they felt no pain and could simply move into another body if the old one suffered heavy damage. Shadeslayers didn't have that option. So considerable time was spent on weapons training and weaponless fighting techniques. All slayers were expected to schedule time in the gym . . . even those who, like Jonah, got plenty of practice in the field.

Jonah's physical gifts and fighting experience made it difficult to match him with an appropriate sparring partner. Alison came closest, and he sparred with her at least once a week. Charlie, when he was in town. Since those two weren't always available, Gabriel had hit on the strategy of matching Jonah against entire packs of slayers-in-training.

Jonah's sparring sessions were closed to the public.

On his way to the gym, Jonah stopped in the armory and selected an array of shivs and cutting blades.

As he left the armory, he looked up at the board. Today it was a group of nine who had been training together. They must be getting close to deployment. Gabriel wouldn't have assigned them to Jonah otherwise. Whatever Jonah thought of Gabriel's priorities in this fight, it was important to prepare slayers with the skills they needed to survive.

In the gym, nine preps stood in a jittery half circle, masked up and ready for bloodshed, their numbers displayed on the outside of their scoring vests. Jonah recognized one or two of them from their voices, their builds, and the way they moved. He didn't know most of them, though. He didn't mingle much with the preps. He didn't mingle much with anyone.

When Jonah appeared in his street clothes, a surprised murmur ran through them. One of them—Number Six—said, "You're fighting like *that*?"

Jonah shook his head. "You can ditch the fighting gear," he said. "We're not sparring today."

"We're not?" Number One ripped off her mask, revealing a scowl. "Why not?"

"This is the first of three sessions," Jonah said. "Today, we're going to review weapons and theory."

This was met with the usual chorus of groans. Newbies were always eager to fight Jonah. Until they actually did.

"All right," Jonah said. "Let's review what you've covered in class. What equipment do you need for a riff—minimum?"

Number Three raised her hand. "Doesn't it depend on what kind of shades you're hunting?"

"Explain what you mean," Jonah countered.

"Well . . . you need shivs for free shades, and cutting blades for hosted ones."

"And a mask to cut the stench," Number Six said, holding his nose.

Jonah ignored this. "Number Three—if you free a hosted shade, what do you have?"

"Oh," she said, getting the point. "You have a free shade."

"Right," Jonah said. "You have a free shade, and so then you need a shiv to finish the job. If you free a shade, it simply goes looking for another host. So don't leave home without both shivs and cutting blades. What else do you need?"

They all looked at each other, seeming at a loss.

Jonah fished his Nightshade pendant out of his neckline. "*Sefas*. What do they do?"

"They allow us to see unhosted shades," Five said.

"I know you don't have these yet, but you will when you deploy. Now." Jonah spread an array of shivs on a table. "What can you tell me about these?"

"If you stick a free shade with one, it dies," Number Six said. He'd been fidgeting and rolling his eyes throughout Jonah's presentation.

"Elaborate," Jonah said. "How are they made?"

"Do we really need to know all this? I mean, come on. We're fighters, not metalsmiths."

"Number Six, you're excused."

Six blinked at him. "Wha—?"

"You're not ready for deployment."

"But I'm the best fighter in this group," he protested. "I win every match I—"

"Don't worry. Get your head straight, and you can join the next training session. If you can't, we'll find another role for you to play."

"That's bullshit," Six said. "I've been training for this for months. We're not allowed to make a joke? We're not allowed to ask a question? You act like we're some kind of—of holy warriors."

"The people we're hunting were your friends and classmates, Six," Jonah said. "Here or back at Thorn Hill. The difference between you and them is that their bodies were too damaged to survive. Maybe they took in more of the poison than you did, or maybe their bodies were smaller, or maybe they were more susceptible for some reason. Maybe they were killed during a mission. Can you imagine what it's like to spend day after day hunting for a body? To have people recoil when you come near them? To know that your body is decaying around you and your survival depends on killing someone else before it falls apart?"

"But . . . I don't get it," Number Six persisted. "You've riffed more shades than anybody else! Anyway, everybody knows shades don't feel pain." Heads nodded all around.

"Hosted shades don't," Jonah said. "But a free shade screams when you kill it with a shiv. You can't hear it, but I can. They're as eager to go on living as you or me." His voice softened. "My point is, we're not bloodthirsty butchers. If you begin to love this job, it's time to leave. Our mission is to protect the public and put shades to rest in the kindest way possible." Even as he said this, he felt like the world's biggest hypocrite.

Six broadened his stance, like he was putting down roots. "Is it true what they say about you? Is it true you secrete toxins through your skin, like one of those poison frogs?"

"You're dismissed," Jonah said. "We have work to do."

No doubt believing he'd found a chink in Jonah's armor, Six warmed to his subject. "So is every part equally deadly? Is kissing enough, or do you have to, you know, get to second base? Is that why you're so sentimental about shades?"

For a long moment, Jonah just looked at him. Looked at him until Six dropped his eyes.

"I don't know," Jonah said, emotionless. "Why don't we find out?" Gripping the hem of his tee shirt, Jonah pulled it over his head and tossed it aside, drawing a collective gasp from the class. Now bare-chested, he extended his gloved hands toward Six. "Come here."

Six's eyes widened, and he backed away. "N-no," he said.

"I promise I won't kiss you, all right?" Jonah said.

Six fled the gym. Jonah turned back to the others. "Soldiers need to know how to take care of their weapons. They are the tools of the trade. What's the difference between sharpening a shiv and sharpening a cutting blade?"

"You use different stones to sharpen them," Number Four

said. "If you use the wrong whetstone on a shiv, it destroys the runes, rendering it ineffective."

"Which would be a nasty surprise, if you're counting on it, out in the field," Jonah said. "Let's talk methods. You encounter a hosted shade—a shade inhabiting a body. What's your weapon?"

"Cutting blade," Five said promptly.

"What's your method?"

"Dismemberment."

"Why?"

"A hosted shade can't be killed as long as it inhabits a body. Our goal is to render the body uninhabitable. That frees the shade."

"Ah," Jonah said, looking at Three. "Now you have a free shade. What's your weapon?"

"Shiv."

"Method?"

"Impalement."

By the end of the session, Jonah felt a little better about their prospects. "Next week, we fight," he promised. "Gear up."

❧ CHAPTER NINE ❧
GOOD MORNING, LITTLE SCHOOLGIRL

The conference room at the high school was stuffy and hot, and Emma couldn't help feeling like she and Tyler were besieged. Outnumbered, anyway. Three teachers, a counselor, and somebody called an "intervention specialist." All members of Emma's "team," as Ms. Abraham, the counselor, kept pointing out.

Then why did she feel like they were playing on the other side?

Emma stole a glance at Tyler. He'd put on a collared shirt for the occasion—the first time she'd seen him in anything other than a T-shirt in the three months she'd been there. He kept pulling it away from his neck as if it was too tight. His face gleamed with sweat. Not glad to be there, but at least he'd shown up, she thought, with a rush of gratitude.

"Our goal, Emma, is to all work together for a positive educational outcome," Ms. Abraham said. She frowned at her laptop screen as if she didn't like what she was seeing.

"Although you were admitted as a junior, you have less than half of the class credits you'll need for graduation. Which means you have some catching up to do."

"She's taking a full load, right?" Tyler said, wiping his hands on his jeans. "What more can she do?"

"First and foremost, she needs to pass the courses she's taking," Ms. Marmont, her algebra teacher said. "We're midway through the semester, and her current grade in Algebra One is . . . let's see . . . sixty-eight percent. She has to pass both Algebra One and Algebra Two to meet the core standards."

"I don't get it," Tyler said. "Emma's good at math. She does all kinds of measures and calculations in the shop."

"The shop?" Ms. Beaumont, the intervention specialist, raised an eyebrow.

"Her woodshop," Tyler said.

Emma's team looked at one another. They had nothing to say.

"I'm good at word problems," Emma said. "Problems where you know where you are and where you want to go and there's a reason to get there."

"Many colleges are looking for calculus these days," Ms. Abraham murmured, typing a few notes into her computer.

"What if I don't want to go to college?" Emma said.

It was like she'd sprayed a flock of hens with a hose. Everybody started squawking at her at once, a mingle of *What are you thinking?* And *Let's not be hasty* and *Don't sell yourself short.*

Ms. Abraham raised her hand to quiet them. "What would you like to do, Emma, after high school?"

"I want to be a luthier," Emma said. Met with a circle of blank looks, she added, "I want to build guitars."

"That's great, Emma," Ms. Beaumont said, "but how do you want to make a *living*? What are your plans for a *career*?"

"What I said. I want to build guitars," she repeated stubbornly. Even though she knew that wasn't on the official list. She had a plan, after all.

They all looked at one another. They wanted to roll their eyes. She knew they did.

"In a classroom, I can't help but feel boxed in—sitting in the same spot, every day, while people talk at you. I need to move around. I need to make something *real*—that I can hold in my hands. Something out of wood."

"Perhaps there is something in career and technical ed," Mr. Boyd, her English teacher suggested.

"What about automotive technology?" Ms. Beaumont suggested, scanning a list. "Or audio engineering?"

"That doesn't sound like what I want," Emma said. "I was in an apprenticeship program in Memphis. I'd like something like that." *Apprenticeship program* sounded more official than *I helped my grandfather in his shop.*

"I don't think we should rule out the idea of college just yet," Ms. Abraham said, pushing back from her desk. "You're just two months into your junior year. We've arranged for tutoring in language arts and math. You'll need those skills, whatever you do, and a high school diploma gives you lots more options. I'm going to refer you to Ms. Britton to test for special needs. I don't find any evidence that you've been evaluated for that."

Thumbing through a file, she pulled out a sheet and handed it to Tyler. "Mr. Boykin, I'd appreciate it if you would fill out this questionnaire and return it to me in the next few days."

Emma read the title upside down. *Does My Child Have ADD/ADHD?*

Ms. Abraham followed Emma's gaze and put her hand on her shoulder. "Don't worry, Emma. Everybody has a different learning style. We need to figure out what works for you. Meanwhile, I'll find out if any of the CTPDs in the area offer a woodworking track."

"CTPDs?" Tyler asked.

"Career and technical education," Ms. Abraham said. "We used to call them vocational schools. When we have all that, we'll meet again at the end of the semester." She paused. "You also need to come to class, Emma. None of this matters if you're not in your seat. If your attendance is good, there are waivers we can apply for when it comes to testing and the core curriculum. But your attendance in Memphis was—what's the word I'm looking for—awful. All right?"

"Yes, ma'am," Emma said.

They drove back to Tyler's in silence, worry on both sides. She still thought of it as Tyler's, even though he'd done his best to make her feel at home.

Her father lived in one of those neighborhoods that teeter on the knife's edge between chic and shabby. From the outside, his house had crossed to shabby a long time ago, but inside it was all beautiful oak woodwork and rooms big enough to throw parties in. And, surrounding the house, the remains of an overgrown garden.

It was a lot of house for a single man who never had any visitors. Not one, since she'd been there. Emma was used to all the comings and goings at Sonny Lee's shop. Tyler's

place seemed designed more to keep people out than welcome them in.

It was fitted out like a fortress, with iron bars behind the
leaded windows and dead bolts on all the doors. It was good
Emma had a knack for tools and devices; otherwise she'd
never have mastered the alarm system.

"You must have a lot of crime here," Emma had said,
when he gave her the tour.

"Better safe than sorry," Tyler said. He led her around the
house to show her all his hiding places—the gun safe behind
the bookcase in the office, and the regular safe hidden at the
back of the closet in his bedroom.

He had her unlock and lock it several times. The combination was her birth date.

"What do you keep in here?" she asked as he locked it
back up again.

"I have some things put away for you, Emma," he said,
"that I want you to have after I'm gone." It was like he was
just sitting in the eye of the hurricane, waiting for the wind
to start howling again.

He took her to the shooting range and taught her how to
fire his gun, with both hands on the grip, feet spread apart to
provide a good base against the kick. It was something that
near strangers could do together.

Emma had to admit: Tyler had done his best to give her
a sanctuary; a place of her own. Maybe it was because he was
so solitary himself. He'd moved several years' worth of clutter
out of the basement and covered the walls with soundproofing, creating a space where she could amp up the sound—like
a bare-bones sound studio.

Her shop was divided into two rooms—the "clean room,"

where she glued things up and applied the finishes. Where she kept Sonny Lee's vintage guitar collection. Where she could plug in and play and sing as loudly as she wanted.

Through a closed door was the "dirty room," housing the lathe, band saw, jointer, sander, and drill press, where she did the major cutting and shaping, making the sawdust fly. It was lined with racks of seasoned wood—wood that had come from Sonny Lee's Memphis shop, along with the blanks and plates they'd made together.

A luthier has to know what he needs ten years in advance, Sonny Lee always said. Because it takes that long for the wood to settle and decide what it wants to be.

Maybe me and Tyler are the same way, Emma thought, with a spark of hope. Maybe we just haven't settled yet.

She'd hoped Tyler would be willing to share stories of her childhood. He didn't seem eager to go back there, though. In that way, he was nearly as closemouthed as Sonny Lee.

He did give her a five-by-seven photograph of Gwen, one of those black-and-white studio portraits that look like nobody in real life. Emma set the photograph on her bedside table.

How my parents ever got together, I'll never know, Emma thought. Some stories just don't have happy endings.

Emma still found it hard to think of Tyler as Daddy or Papa or any of those family kind of names. He was not a family kind of man. And yet, she kept stubbing her toe on ways they were alike. They even dressed a lot alike—in jeans, flannel shirts, and random T-shirts that came their way like T-shirts always do, promoting this show or that club or an up-and-coming band. They had that in common, along with the music. Aside from his aura, she'd seen no sign that her father was magical. If he had it, he did... wouldn't answer questions about it either.

Tyler pulled around behind the house and ... garage. They scuffed through gold, brown, and ... to the back door. Leaves spiraled down from the ... head like flakes of gold.

"I kind of like Ms. Abraham," Emma said as Tyl... gated the door-opening routine. "I'm not too fond ... Monts."

"The Monts?"

"Beaumont and Marmont," Emma said.

Tyler laughed, his shoulders shaking, and dabbed tears from his eyes. His laugh reminded her of Sonny Lee's . . . a mix of whiskey and honey that went right to your heart.

"Are you all right with the plan, Emma?" he asked.

"I don't have much choice, if I have to stay in school." She eyed him sideways.

"Don't give me that look. You know you do." Tyler threw his keys into the dish on the table. "We both know it's not that you're lazy. You work all the time—either you're at school, or doing homework, or you're down in the shop. You don't even sleep that much."

"It's not that I can't focus," Emma said. "It's like I hyper-focus, but it's on things they don't approve of." She stuffed her hands in her jeans pockets and lifted her chin. "I'll tell you right now—I need to work with wood. I just have to. I'm not giving that up."

"Nobody's asking you to give it up," Tyler said, raising both hands.

"People think I don't have a plan, but I do. I'm going to build guitars and sell them, and save my money, and one day

;et enough together to open my own shop."

"How are you going to go about that, Emma? Selling :m, I mean."

"Well . . . it was easier when I was in business with Sonny ,ee," Emma said. "Because he had so many connections. I :hought I could work for him and ease into it. Now . . ." She shrugged. "I have some guitars already out there, mostly in Memphis. Now it's going to be hard for people to find me, though, even if they decided they wanted one. There's a limited market for the kind of work I do. I need buyers with deep pockets who know quality when they hear it."

She'd set up a blog page to promote her business while she was still in Memphis: Studio Greenwood—Custom Guitars and Expert Repair. She'd left it up since the move. Surely that wouldn't hurt. It didn't list an address or anything, just an e-mail. She'd had a few contacts through the site since she'd moved north.

"Can't you just—you know—be a kid for a while?" Tyler said.

"That's just it: I'm not a kid, and haven't been for a while," Emma snapped. "It's not my fault you weren't around to see me grow up."

Tyler flinched, and she knew she'd hit home.

"Look," she said, "I'm sorry. I didn't mean to—"

"Don't apologize to me, Emma," Tyler said. "I'm the one who should be apologizing to you." He clenched and unclenched his hands. "It would just be good for you, I think, if you made some friends. If you got out and had some fun."

Look who's talking, Emma thought. I'm a loner, just like you. That's one use for parents—once you know who they are, you can blame things on them.

"I don't have time for that," Emma said.

"Listen—I can introduce you to some people," Tyler said. "Clyde may be looking for something new. Or he could play one of your guitars at some gigs, show it off a little."

Clyde played lead guitar in Tyler's rhythm-and-blues band, Old Dogs, New Tricks. Tyler played bass. They worked steadily, every weekend, mostly local gigs, playing covers and some original music.

"Selling one guitar to Clyde isn't going to help much," Emma said. "I'll be in high school at least another year and a half. So, the way I see it, I have two years to raise enough money to start my own business."

"I can stake you," Tyler said. "I have some money put aside."

Emma resisted the urge to point out the shabby furniture, the battered refrigerator, the paint peeling off the walls. "You're going to need it for yourself," she said. "I'm guessing you don't want to work forever, and musicians don't get pensions."

"Look," Tyler said. "We don't have to settle this now. Dogs has a gig tonight, downtown. Why don't you come out with me, listen to some music, have a little fun?"

Emma groaned. "Sounds like fun, Tyler. Hanging with my daddy's band on a Friday night. Meeting the Old Dogs, trying to pitch them a guitar while they try and think of a way to say no."

Tyler stared at her for a moment, as if to say, *What's wrong with that?* Then he burst out laughing. "You're right, Emma, that sounds like no fun at all." He dug in his jacket pocket and pulled out a crumpled flyer. "Okay, I was kidding about the Dogs, but how about this? There's a place called Club

Catastrophe, down on Fourth Street. They're having a teen night tonight. Show's at seven. I could drop you off there on my way downtown."

Emma scanned the flyer.

UNDER 18 NIGHT!

FAULT TOLERANT—LIVE AND IN PERSON

ONE NIGHT ONLY! $10 COVER

"I figured it'd be a good chance for you to get out and meet some people your own age," Tyler said.

"I don't have anything in common with people my own age," Emma said. "All those cliques and who's mad at who and who's wearing whose varsity jacket . . . I don't need that."

"That's why this is a good place for you to meet people," Tyler said. "They'll be people like you—people who like music. You might relate to them better than the kids at the high school."

"Isn't it a little late for you to start managing my social life?" she said.

"Better late than never," Tyler said. "You're not doing so good on your own."

⊗ CHAPTER TEN ⊗
IF TROUBLE WAS MONEY

"**Y**ou know I don't like to go to clubs," Jonah grumbled as they turned onto West Ninth Street.

"Cheer up," Natalie Diaz said. "You'll be perfectly safe. I'll be your bodyguard."

"I've heard that before," Jonah said. "As soon as we walk through the door, you'll forget all about *that* plan. You'll all be up onstage, and I'll be left to fend for myself."

"Oh, quit whining, Kinlock," Alison said, rolling her eyes. "At least you could've shown us some skin." It seemed she'd taken her own advice. She wore a very short tank dress with a blue jean jacket, tights, and boots, feathers pinned into her purple-streaked hair, eyes smoky with kohl. Ready to rock-and-roll.

Jonah hunched his shoulders inside his leather jacket. It was October, three months since his failed rescue of Jeanette, and the weather was getting cooler. Which finally gave him an excuse to cover up.

Natalie laughed. "Maybe you could've worn a burka," she said. "You're nearly there anyway."

"Would you quit criticizing my clothes?" As soon as Jonah agreed to go to the club with them, Natalie had showed up at his door, wanting to go through his closet and put his look together. He'd flatly refused. "I'm not the one onstage," he said. "Forget it."

"You need to get out more," Natalie said. "It's not healthy to stay in your room all the time."

"I do get out," Jonah said. "I've been in—what?—four countries this month."

"I don't mean working. I mean playing."

She paused and, when Jonah didn't respond, said, "It wouldn't hurt you to get to know some girls, Jonah. Nobody's asking you to sign anything." She narrowed her eyes at him. *Or touch anybody* was the subtext.

"No."

"It's not like they're going to attack you."

That's what you think.

"You might even have fun."

"Let it go, Nat."

So Natalie Diaz let it go. She always knew just how far she could push him.

Alison, Natalie, Mose, and Rudy were in a band together—Alison on bass, Mose on guitar and vocals, Nat on drums, and Rudy on keyboards and backup vocals. They called themselves Fault Tolerant. The name was Rudy's idea. It was geek-speak for a system that continues to operate even if one element fails.

Given the arts focus of the school, bands came and went at the Anchorage like mushrooms after a rain. Fault Tolerant was different. Natalie didn't suffer fools, and she didn't put up with laziness. Neither did Rudy. And that made for a great band. They should call it Fault *In*tolerant, Jonah thought.

"I know!" Alison said. "Join the band. Then you won't be sitting alone."

Jonah snorted. "To do what? Play the tambourine?"

"We could always use more sex appeal," Alison said, smirking at him.

"Hey!" Rudy Severino called out, raking back his hair and delivering a smoldering pout. "Sex appeal right here."

"You don't need another split in those big paychecks," Jonah said.

"If you refuse to play your music in public, you should at least let us play it for you," Natalie said. "*Somebody* ought to hear it."

"*I* hear it," Jonah said. "And Kenzie. And you. That's enough." He had agreed to come after weeks of badgering from Natalie. She'd taken him on as a project ever since his meltdown in Gabriel's office. He'd been missing a lot of classes since Jeanette died, and when he came to a class, he often slept through it. Natalie suspected depression. Jonah suspected she was right, although, in his opinion, depression was a perfectly reasonable reaction to their situation.

They cut across the street, dodging traffic. They were coming up on Club Catastrophe. Music poured from the front door, and an easel out front displayed a sign: TEEN NIGHT TONIGHT FEATURING FAULT TOLERANT—LIVE AND IN PERSON.

They entered through the rear door, threading their way through a clutter of cleaning supplies, extra furniture, and paper products. They found Mose having a smoke amid the flammables. He'd driven the equipment van over, because he never would have made it on foot.

Mose was prone to self-medicating and looked the part—he was as gaunt as an end-stage addict, pierced to the max, every inch of exposed flesh covered in Gabriel's ink therapy. Like a prayer to the gods that had gone unanswered.

Jonah couldn't blame Mose for wanting to blunt the edge. A seer savant, Mose had the gift of seeing death coming before it arrived. He'd become a key asset to Safe Passage, the hospice program at the Anchorage. He and Jonah were a team. Like Dr. Death and his front man.

These days, Mose sat during their sets, and his voice had weakened considerably, but he was still the best singer in the band and he was a demon on guitar.

Maybe "Last Legs" would be a better name for this band, Jonah thought.

Mose lit up a little when he saw Jonah. He sat up a little straighter, finger-combing his hair. "Hey, Jonah! If I'd known you were coming, I'd of worn the good clothes."

"Hey, Mose," Jonah said, doing the old fist bump. "What's up?"

"I've been meaning to mention this—I've been sorting through some stuff, need to simplify, know what I mean? I wondered if you had room in that palace of yours for my vinyl collection." Mose had a stellar collection of vintage vinyl, and a sweet turntable to play it on.

"Your vinyl? No way," Jonah said. "That is *not* what you get rid of. If you're short on room, put your bed on the curb."

"I don't play them much anymore," Mose said. "Can you at least come have a look, maybe pick out some tunes?"

"Sure," Jonah said. "If you want. We'll call it a loan."

"How about tonight, right after the gig?" Mose persisted. Adopting a throaty, seductive voice, he added, "Wanna come to my place and listen to some records?"

"Tonight?" Jonah hesitated. Mose always flirted with him shamelessly, but there was a desperate undercurrent in his voice that hadn't been there before.

"Don't you think you'll be tired, after the show?" Alison said, over Jonah's shoulder. Jonah jumped. He'd forgotten she was there. "Who knows how late it'll go."

"Please," Mose said, looking Jonah in the eyes.

"Sure," Jonah said. "After the gig."

"You good, Mose?" Natalie put a hand on his shoulder and leaned down to look into his face.

"Me?" He grinned wickedly. "I'm *always* good."

Natalie chewed her lower lip. She wasn't buying it.

"I'll start setting up," Jonah said.

Music was blasting from the overhead speakers and the dance floor was crowded an hour before the official show-time. For Club Catastrophe, Teen Night was an add-on, a way to bring in customers on slow nights. They'd filled the rear of the room with billiards tables, dartboards, and vintage pinball machines to give younger patrons something to do.

As soon as Jonah appeared onstage to set up, a faint cheer went up. Fault Tolerant had a following around town. They even sometimes opened for national touring bands that Gabriel booked into the Keep.

Scanning the crowd, Jonah saw some familiar faces. Being walking distance from school, the club was a popular hangout for savants. The rest of the crowd was a mingle of Anaweir and mainliners. There was lots of Weir action in town, due to Cleveland's proximity to the seat of Weir government in Trinity.

Jonah had learned to ignore the whispers, nudges, and

pointed fingers from guildlings. Still, he couldn't help picking out a faint chant of "Labrats!" from a crowd of mainliners at two tables next to the stage.

The Anaweir were, as always, oblivious.

Jonah began hauling amplifiers onstage, taping down power cords, testing mikes, and generally making himself useful. When he'd finished the setup, he collected a soda from the bar and carried it backstage. He found a viewing spot from stage right as the club manager ran through the usual announcements about restrooms, smoking, drugs, wristbands, and warnings that Teen Nights were a privilege that could be revoked if there were any more *problems.*

"And now, without further ado, Club Catastrophe welcomes Fault Tolerant!"

Lusty shouts and foot stomping ushered Jonah's friends onto the stage. Natalie strode back to the drums, Severino took his place behind his Roland, and Alison and Mose carried their guitars out from backstage and plugged in.

All of the songs were familiar. Natalie had written most of them, some in partnership with Severino, and she and Jonah usually jammed on them before she ever brought them to the band. "Never Say Die." "Straw Man." "Caliente." "No Way Home." It was all original music. Natalie believed in controlling the whole package.

Jonah breathed in the usual crowd funk of sweat, perfume, and raging hormones. Then caught a whiff of mischief mixed in. That was his term for the nose-prickling mingle of shade magic and rotting flesh. Shades? This close to the Anchorage?

He leaned forward and peered out from the wings, scanning the crowd. Blinded as he was by the stage lights, all he could see was a murk of dark moving bodies, studded with the patches of light that denoted the gifted.

Turning up the collar of his jacket, hunching his shoulders, Jonah slipped offstage and walked down the aisle, turning his head from side to side. But he couldn't pinpoint the source, and then he lost the scent.

Ditching his sanctuary backstage, Jonah found a table in the corner closest to the door where he could keep a better watch on comings and goings. There was a price to pay, now that he was out in the open. He kept having to snarl at those who wandered over, thinking he looked lonely, sitting there by himself.

Every so often he breathed in the stench of decay or the burned-insulation scent of shade magic, but could never figure out exactly where it was coming from.

When the first set was over, the club sound track came on, and Natalie and Rudy waded into the crowd on the dance floor. Mose shuffled back outside to smoke, and Alison joined Jonah at his table.

"'Sup, Jonah?" Alison asked, tucking her hair behind her ears. She'd peeled off her jacket during the set, revealing her muscled arms. "How come you're sitting out here?"

"Do you smell anything unusual?" Jonah asked, trying not to ask a leading question.

Alison wrinkled her nose. "Dude at the next table should go easy on the cologne," she said. "And I think somebody's been smoking weed in the ladies' room. That what you mean?"

He shook his head. "I could've sworn I smelled a shade."

Alison shrugged. "I know you say you can smell them, but I can't—not from a distance, anyway. I wish I could."

Jonah grimaced. "No you don't. Trust me." He paused. "You're looking good, Shaw. Did you lose weight or what?"

She looked up, saw that he was kidding about that last part, and grinned. "I'm feeling good," she said, sipping at her drink. "I've been going to a new skin therapist. He is *amazing*."

Jonah stared at her, puzzled. Skin art was Gabriel's specialty, one of the treatments he never delegated. "Really? I didn't know Gabriel had hired anyone else."

"He hasn't. This one's an independent. Dimitri Weed. He has a clinic on Canal."

"You're going outside of the Anchorage for treatment?" Jonah said, beating down surprise.

Alison nodded. She leaned toward Jonah. "Don't tell Gabriel. Or Natalie. It's not that I don't have confidence in them. It's just, you know, an add-on."

"How'd you even find this guy?" Jonah said. "Where'd he come from? Is he a sorcerer or what?"

"He's a sorcerer," Alison said. "Some of the other savants have been seeing him. They said he works wonders, so I thought I'd give him a try."

Jonah's heart sank. Charlatans tended to prey on savants, offering them the kind of hope that Gabriel couldn't.

"Alison. You know as well as I do that skin therapy is nothing to mess around with. There are lots of quacks out there who are more than willing to take your money. They do more harm than good." He paused. "What's he charging you, anyway?"

"It's pricey," Alison said evasively. "But what if it works? How much would *you* pay for something that works?"

Everything, Jonah thought. I'd pay everything for Kenzie.

"Here. Want to see?" She slid her dress off her shoulder to display a new tattoo: a lurid, glittering snake that angled down between her shoulder blades. Jonah leaned in to take a closer look.

"What the *hell* is that?" Natalie snapped, over Jonah's shoulder, startling them both.

"Nothing." Alison jerked her dress back into place and hunched over the table.

Natalie and Rudy stood tableside, still flushed and sweating from dancing, both holding drinks. Nat had a familiar fire in her eyes. Jonah braced himself for incoming.

"I thought there was something different about you," Natalie said. "Let me see that."

"No," Alison said. "I know what you'll say."

"You went to that guy on Canal, didn't you?" Natalie slammed her drink down so hard the contents slopped onto the table. "After I told you not to."

"Leave her alone, Nat," Rudy said. "It's not your business."

"It *is* my business," Natalie retorted. "She's my friend!"

Alison scraped back her chair and stood. "If I'm your friend, you want what's best for me, right?"

"Exactly," Natalie said, eyeing her suspiciously. "That's why I—"

"Well, I've felt better since I've been seeing Dimitri than I have in two years," Alison said. "I'm sorry, but it's true. I think you're just jealous of his success."

"That's not it," Natalie said, cheeks flushed. "There just aren't that many good skin therapists out there. And you don't go to *any*one who doesn't know what meds you're taking. Besides, I can't put my finger on it, but there's something—I don't know—*wrong* about his work. I don't trust him."

"Well, I do. And so does Rudy." Alison threw a challenging glare his way.

"What does *that* mean?" Natalie asked, looking from Alison to Severino.

"Shut up, Alison," Rudy said, licking his lips nervously. "You promised you wouldn't—"

"When were you going to tell her?" Alison asked. "In the middle of a hookup? She's not stupid."

"I think you'd better tell me now." Natalie's voice had gone from fire to ice in an instant.

Jonah wanted nothing more than to escape the oppressive stew of emotions swirling around him—rage, guilt, suspicion, fear. But he was hemmed in by his three friends, with no way out.

Even worse, the shouting match in the corner was drawing attention from onlookers.

"Fine," Rudy said. "I've been seeing Dimitri, too." Slowly, deliberately, he turned and yanked up his sweater. There, at the base of his spine, curled a dragon. "I feel great, Nat," he said, over his shoulder. "I'm sleeping better, and I have more energy during the day."

Natalie stared at the tattoo, the blood draining from her face. "And I guess next you'll say you can quit anytime you like," she shouted at his back. "Oh, no, that's right, you *can't*."

"Don't be mad, Nat," Rudy said, turning back around. "Even the music is better. If you'd just keep an open mind, I—"

Natalie leaned toward him, fists clenched. "So the music is better, is it?"

"What'd I miss?" Mose had returned, limping his way through the gawkers. "We're back on in three, right?"

Fault Tolerant returned to the stage, bodies stiff, glaring at one another.

This is exactly why I don't like to go to clubs, Jonah thought. Too much drama. And since he only had four friends, this kind of drama seriously affected his quality of life.

CHAPTER ELEVEN
I'M IN THE MOOD

Club Catastrophe was in downtown Cleveland, in a neighborhood of old warehouses and commercial buildings that housed restaurants, clubs, apartments, and condominiums.

Emma tried to keep her expectations low, but she couldn't help it—her heart beat a little faster when she heard the music throbbing through the open doors.

Only Tyler seemed to be having second thoughts. "You know where you need to go to catch the Rapid home, right?" he said as Emma slid out of the car.

"I walk up Superior to Tower City and follow the signs to the trains," Emma said. "Then I take the Green Line out to Lee Road."

"You sure you have your RTA pass?"

Emma put her hands on her hips. "Are you hovering again, Tyler?"

Tyler leaned across the front seat toward her. "Maybe. Just remember—this area attracts all different kinds. And somebody's killing the gifted. So be careful."

"I'll be all right." She pointed down the crowded sidewalk. "See? There's plenty of people out on the street. And it's not like I came straight off the farm. I won't do anything stupid."

"You won't be able to reach me by phone while I'm onstage. If you need to call, leave a message, and I'll call right back during the next break. And be careful. Walk right home from the stop."

"Don't worry," Emma said even as she was thinking it was oddly fine to have somebody worrying. On impulse, she leaned through the window and kissed him on the cheek. "Bye now."

Emma paid the cover, collected her drink tickets, and extended her arm for the under-twenty-one wristband. Then, summoning her courage, she strode into the club like she belonged.

The place offered seating for maybe two hundred people, and the permanent stage in the corner said it was a serious music venue. The tin ceiling and the battered floorboards were probably original to the warehouse.

The band, Fault Tolerant, had already taken the stage, and the dance floor churned with bodies. Emma threaded her way to the front to see what she could see. The band members looked to be young—high school age—but they had some skills. Especially the drummer. She put her whole body into it. The lead guitarist played a sweet Parker DragonFly, sitting down, like one of those timeworn old blues players. He was seriously good.

More important: they all wore the glow that Tyler claimed was the mark of the gifted. In fact, there were splotches of light all over the room, like some of the dancers had individual spotlights built into their bodies. Why so many, all right here?

Emma cashed in one of her drink tickets and looked for a place to sit. Once around the room and she was still on her feet. This band drew a crowd, that was for sure. The only empty chairs were at a table in the back, a table with one occupant, who sat shrouded in shadows.

Emma moved in close, trying to get a better look before she committed herself. It was a boy—focused on his phone, the light from the screen illuminating his face, bringing his features into sharp relief as his long fingers flicked through screens.

Two things struck her right away. One: he was the kind of boy that made your heart beat faster before you ever heard his name. And two: he was the kind of boy Emma would never, ever have.

He was all muffled up, in a black leather jacket, a scarf wound around his neck, his head turtled into his shoulders. He even wore thin leather gloves on his hands.

Maybe he has one of those diseases where you're cold all the time, Emma thought.

Somehow, she found herself standing next to his table, a moth flinging itself into the flame.

"Are these seats taken?" she asked.

"Yes," he said, without looking up.

"Oh. Well, is it all right if I sit here until your friends come back?"

"No," he said, still looking at his screen.

That got on Emma's nerves. "Look, there's no other place left to sit."

He finally looked up. His skin was pale under a tumble of

black hair, his brows dark and thick, his lashes, too. Up close, she saw the lines of pain around his mouth. His eyes were a shade of indigo she'd never seen . . . eyes a person could dive into, without a second thought. Behind those eyes, beyond the reach of the light, lay the blues. A sad story that needed telling. A story she wanted to hear.

He studied her face, his eyes flicking up to her untamable hair, over her flannel shirt and jeans, her bitten-off nails. At least, that's what she guessed he was looking at.

"I'm sorry," Boy Blue said, returning to his phone. "That's not my problem."

Slamming her glass down, Emma planted her hands on the table and leaned toward him. He looked up, startled, leaning back and bringing both hands up to ward her off.

Up close, he was even more intoxicating, and she nearly lost her train of thought. Mentally slapping herself, she said, "You know what? You're damn pretty until you open up your mouth. You ought to keep it shut." Grabbing up her drink, she stalked away, feeling the burn of his gaze between her shoulder blades.

Eventually, she did locate an empty table far from the stage, back among the pool tables. She sat, tapping her foot to the music, watching the action at the tables, counting the drinks as some of the pool players grew more and more wasted. She'd spent a lifetime hugging the wall in bars. You could learn a lot that way.

Too bad they didn't give out grades for those kinds of lessons.

Now and then she looked back at the boy in the corner by the door. He still sat alone. So did she. So much for making friends her own age.

When the band took a break, one of the guitarists—a girl—walked back to Boy Blue and sat down at his table. He didn't shoo *her* away. Instead, they leaned in close, talking.

So that's how it is, Emma thought. He's with the band. She thought of going back to the bar and using her second ticket, but was afraid she'd lose her table. Some of the pool players had been eyeing it for a while. She could give up and head home, but she'd been looking forward to hearing the rest of the set. Anyway, going home was too much like giving up.

Raised voices caught her attention. Turning, she saw that Boy Blue was now surrounded by members of the band, who were all waving their hands and hissing at one another. When the lead guitarist returned, they marched back onstage, leaving Boy Blue alone again.

He looked up, found Emma staring at him, and looked away.

What just happened? Emma thought as Fault Tolerant launched into their second set.

"Hey! Labrat!"

Emma twisted around, and saw that some of the gifted who'd been playing pool had formed a half circle around her table. Two were carrying pool cues.

They didn't look much older than Emma, but none of them were wearing wristbands, and from the looks of things, they'd been taking full advantage of their legal status. They all carried beers, and they walked like people who've had a few already.

Emma blinked at them. "What'd you call me?"

"Labrat," a preppy-looking boy said, breathing beer into her face. "Or would you prefer mutant?" He had the pudgy kind of baby face that turns into jowls later on.

Emma knew better than to mix it up with a drunk. "I don't want trouble," she said. "Came to hear the band. Just move on, now." She pulled out her phone, looking for non-existent messages. Wondering what people had used for cover before cell phones.

"Time to move on," the boy persisted, thunking his beer down. "You've been squatting there all night."

"Come on, Graham," another boy said, leering at Emma. "Let her stay. Get a few drinks into her and maybe she'll show us her scaly tail."

"Eww," a tall blond girl said. "Shut up, Cam. That's disgusting. A wizard and a labrat?"

"Sometimes you wanna walk on the wild side, know what I mean?" Cam elbowed the girl. "Hey, Brooke! How about a threesome?"

Brooke pretend-slapped him.

A girl with long, sun-tipped brown hair had hung back by the pool table. Now she joined the group surrounding Emma. "Quit being jerks. If there's no place to sit, pay the tab and we'll go down the street."

"We're off the clock," Graham said. "I wanna play some more pool. Anyway, the labrat was just leaving."

"You're drunk, and you're drawing attention to yourselves, which is exactly what Rowan told us not to do," the girl said. "And we are never—ever—off the clock."

"We won't hurt her feelings, if that's what you're worried about," Cam said, nodding toward Emma. "I don't think she understands what we're saying, anyway."

"Come on, Rachel," Graham said, a note of entreaty in his voice. "Loosen up a little. Your big brother isn't here.

Uh . . . you're not going to tell on us, are you?" He put his hand on her shoulder, brow furrowed, looking a little panicked now.

"Not as long as you do what I say," Rachel retorted. Just then, her phone buzzed. "I'm going to take this call. Meantime, take care of the tab and we'll go."

The wizards watched Rachel walk away, then turned on Emma.

"See that?" Cam said. "You got us in trouble."

"Don't worry," Brooke said, sweeping back her mane of hair. "If Rowan gives us trouble, he'll have my mother to deal with."

Graham waved his cue under Emma's nose. "Come on, labrat. Fair's fair. You shouldn't sit over here if you're not playing pool." He brightened. "I know! Let's play for the tab."

The rest of them snorted with laughter.

"Do you know what that means?" Graham leaned down, hands on his knees, so he was eye level with Emma, speaking slowly. "If I win, you pay for our drinks, and give up your table. That's fair." When Emma said nothing, he added, "How about it, labrat?"

A new voice intruded into the conversation. "How about you leave her alone?"

It was Boy Blue. He stood next to Emma, so close she could breathe in the scent of leather. So close she could have reached out and touched the rivets on his jeans. She resisted the temptation to do just that.

The wizards stared at him, at first too hazy with drink to conjure a response.

"Who're you?" Graham said finally. "Her labrat boyfriend?"

"You think *he's* a labrat?" Brooke said, wrinkling her forehead in confusion. "But he's really hot."

"Eww," Graham said. "Now *you're* being disgusting."

They all laughed, but some of the confidence had leaked out of them. They resembled a herd of sheep with a wolf in their midst.

"I can take care of myself," Emma said to Boy Blue. "Don't worry."

"I'm not worried about *you*," Boy Blue said. "I'm worried about *them*."

Graham cleared his throat. "We're not talking to *you*," he said. "We're talking to *her*." He jabbed Emma with his pool cue.

Boy Blue struck like a snake, faster than Emma's eye could follow. He ripped Graham's weapon away from him, broke it like a matchstick, and dropped the pieces onto the floor.

Graham stared at him, openmouthed. "What the—that cue cost five hundred dollars!" he shouted.

"Really?" Boy Blue said. "Then you ought to be more careful about where you stick it."

Emma was thinking, Five hundred dollars? For a pool cue? That can't be right.

"You're gonna pay for that," Graham snarled. His friends muttered agreement. A crowd was gathering, spoiling for a fight. And Boy Blue seemed more than willing to give them one.

Emma didn't mean to let that happen. Not on her account. She shoved back her chair and stood, facing Graham, hands on hips. "You want to play pool?" she said. "You're on."

⊗ CHAPTER TWELVE ⊗
SHARKS

Everyone turned and stared at her. The band played on, the bass thudding through the floorboards like a pulse.

Graham looked from Boy Blue to Emma. "You've got to be kidding," he said, smirking. "All right, let's do it."

Boy Blue put his gloved hand on Emma's shoulder, sending a thrill of electricity through her. "You don't have to do this. I picked this fight. Let me finish it."

Emma glared up at him. "What—you can pick a fight, but I can't?"

For a moment, he was at a loss for words. "Well, yeah," he said. "Pretty much."

Emma turned back toward Graham. "What's the action?" she said, rubbing her fingers together. "You really want to play for the tab?"

"'Xactly," Graham said, taking in his mainliner posse with a sweep of his arm. "The tab. For all of us." His eyes flicked to Boy Blue, then back to her. "And the cost of the cue."

Emma frowned, pretending to think it over. Which she really should have been doing, considering she had $15.97 in her pocket.

Boy Blue leaned in toward her, his warm breath stirring her hair, raising gooseflesh on her neck. "Listen," he said. "Their tab'll run into big money. They've been drinking all night. And we're *not* paying for the cue."

We? Emma thought.

"What's the matter?" Graham said. "No confidence in your girlfriend here?"

Someone began a soft chant. "Tails and SCALES! Tails and SCALES!"

Emma frowned. "You know what? He's right. That *doesn't* seem fair. I don't really have a tab." She thought a moment. "How about this? If I win, you forget about the cue and buy a round for the room."

"A round for the room?" Graham scanned the crowd, as if taking a count. "I don't know. I mean, now I'll be playing with an unfamiliar cue." He pretended reluctance when she could tell he was hot for the match.

"What's the matter?" she said, shoving her hands into her back pockets, looking up at the ceiling. "You scared?"

Graham stiffened and looked back at Emma, appraising her. He must not have been impressed with what he saw, because a cocky smile broke across his face. "You're on, labrat."

"Did you all hear that?" Emma said in a carrying voice. "If I win, this fine young man buys a round for the room. If you want to lay any side bets, do it now."

All of a sudden everyone in the room was interested in the play, though nobody seemed eager to bet on Emma.

While money changed hands Emma strode to the cue rack and looked over the selection. Mostly Sterlings, handful of Furys. Pulling one down, she sighted along the length and swore under her breath. Warped. As were the next two. In the end, she chose a Sterling maple-shafted stick that wasn't quite as crooked as a dog's hind leg.

She crossed to Graham's chosen table, leaned her cue against it, and tied her hair back. "What's your game?" she said.

Graham blinked at her. "Huh?"

"You know—eight ball, nine ball, straight pool, one pocket, or snooker?"

"Um—eight ball?" he said, doubt creeping into his voice.

"Fair enough," Emma said, scooping up a triangular rack. "You got any local rules I should know about?"

"What do you mean?"

"Well, you got your Alabama eight ball, crazy eight, last pocket, misery, Missouri, one and fifteen in the sides, rotation eight ball, and like that."

Graham squinted at her, licking his lips. "I just wanna play pool. You gonna talk or play?"

"Fine," Emma said. "We'll keep it simple—classic eight ball. One game only. If you scratch on the break, you lose. Your challenge, your game, my break. Rack 'em up." She thrust the rack at Graham.

While Graham fussed with the rack, Emma walked around the table. The cloth was in bad shape, torn here and there from heavy use. She'd watched the play on that table earlier and noted that it wasn't exactly level.

By the time Graham stepped back, Emma had found her shot. She hit a soft break, but still put three balls in the pocket.

Methodically, she ran out the table while Graham watched with growing horror. When she'd cleared the table except for the money ball, she pointed her cue at the farthest pocket.

"All right," she said. "Eight ball in the upper right corner."

And she nailed it clean.

Cheers erupted all around—from people who hadn't bet on Graham. Patrons, even mainliners, slapped her on the back. Others bellied up to the bar to place their orders.

Graham swore violently. "You . . . you cheated," he said.

Emma cocked her head. "Didn't your mama ever tell you to watch yourself in a pool hall? You never know when you're going to run into a shark."

Graham extended a trembling hand toward Emma, fingers spread like he was about to hex her or something. He opened his mouth, but before he could say a word, Boy Blue had his arms twisted behind his back so he screamed in pain.

"I don't think you want to do that here," Boy Blue murmured. "Anyway, nobody likes a sore loser. I suggest you pay up and leave." Releasing Graham, he gave him a push toward the bar.

Emma stuck out her hand to Boy Blue. "I'm Emma," she said. "Thanks for the help."

After a moment's hesitation, he gripped her hand. "I'm Jonah," he said. "I guess you didn't need my help."

Emma let go of Jonah's hand, trying to think of something to say. "What was that name they kept calling us? Labrats?"

"Labrats?" He stared at her, as if confused. "I assumed you were from—" He stopped. Then shrugged. And lied . . . Emma knew he did. "I have no idea."

Emma gestured toward her hard-won table. "Would you like to sit?"

"Sit?"

"Sit. With me."

For a moment, he balanced on the balls of his feet, trapped between yes and no. Then the door to the club slammed open, and cold air swirled around them. Jonah's head came up, and he breathed in sharply, like a predator who's caught the scent of prey. "No," he said. "I can't. I have to—" He swiveled toward the door, suddenly in a hurry. "I have to go."

And, just like that, he was out the door.

Sorry, Tyler, Emma thought, watching him disappear. I guess I'm just not that good at making friends.

❧ CHAPTER THIRTEEN ❧
MONSTER TO MONSTER

Where, exactly, did you think that was going, Kinlock? Jonah thought as he exited the club. Were you hoping to work your way up from a handshake to a chaperoned slow dance?

And yet—it was such a small and simple pleasure—to talk to someone who didn't know that the thing he was best at was killing. Leaving the pool-shark girl behind was like ripping off a scab and watching himself bleed.

Focus, he thought, breathing in the night air. No, it hadn't been his imagination. A shade had just passed by, heading toward Superior.

Jonah didn't like that. He didn't like it at all. Especially since he was unarmed. You can go into a club with a gun, but just try to get in with a six-foot sword.

It was nearly nine o'clock on a Tuesday, but the bars were jumping in the Warehouse District. Across the river, in Heritage Park and around the aquarium, he could see emergency lights flashing. Maybe an accident of some kind. He hoped it wasn't something worse.

He ghosted along, following the scent, jogging left on Superior. He lost the trail momentarily, then realized the shade must have cut through the courthouse gardens and down the steps to the river. It might be on the hunt, hoping to find easy prey along the lonely route through the Flats.

He descended through the courthouse grounds, then walked west, along the river, past industrial buildings and high fences topped with barbed wire. Just as he was passing the old B&O terminal, a bell began to clamor. A bridge alarm, signaling street traffic that the bridge was opening for river traffic.

Once past the terminal, Jonah looked downriver, where several rusting lift bridges spanned the crooked river as it snaked its way to the lake.

It was the Carter Road Lift Bridge, just to his left. The barricades were down, lights flashing. As he watched, the bridge deck began to rise into the sky.

Odd. The bridge was closed for repair, and he'd understood that it would be for at least another month. Anyway, why would they be working on the bridge at this time of night?

The wind stirred his hair, and the stench of free magic came to him, stronger than ever, from the direction of the river. Turning off Canal Road, Jonah sprinted up the slight incline toward the bridge.

By the time he reached the foot of the bridge, the deck had stopped high above him. He heard faint cries for help from overhead.

Children?

The door to the access stairs was padlocked. Jonah considered crushing the lock, but disliked the notion of being caged up in the stairwell. Fortunately, the tower seemed made for climbing, a Lego maze of handholds and footrests. Halfway up, he saw the pallid face of a shade peering over the side at him, felt the shade's fear and hatred boiling down on his head.

So much for the element of surprise. Jonah climbed faster, worrying that his approach might goad the shade into a quick kill.

The higher he climbed, the stronger the scent of the shade's host. A corpse, and not particularly fresh, from the smell of it. Jonah was nearly at the top when something came hurtling over the edge, a glowing patch of white in the darkness. At first he thought it was the shade, trying to escape, but it emitted a high-pitched wail as it fell, its arms and legs windmilling. A little girl.

Jonah leaped sideways to intercept her. In a split second, he wrapped both arms around her, shifted her to the crook of one arm, and grabbed back on to the tower with the other hand. She continued to kick and wriggle and screech into his ear, nearly deafening him.

"Shhh," he said. "Hey. It's all right. I've got you."

At the sound of his voice, she stopped struggling and buried her face in his sweatshirt as if trying to burrow in. She was sniffling, but no longer screaming, at least. She glowed, like an illuminated painting in a church.

His weary synapses finally fired. She was gifted. A wizardling.

She lifted her head and looked at him. "It's not polite to stare," she said.

"You're right," he said.

"I was trying to grab the zombie's knife, and he pushed me, and I *fell*," she said, as if she thought the situation needed explaining.

"I hate when that happens," Jonah said. "Can you ride piggyback?"

"Of *course*."

"Climb on."

He turned and she clambered onto his back, wrapping her legs tightly around his middle, her arms around his neck in a choke hold.

The shade peered over the side again, a long, sharp knife in one hand, and something in his other hand that reflected an iridescent light. Jonah flinched sideways, worried it might be some new kind of weapon.

Playing it safe, he ducked under the road deck, leaping from handhold to handhold, and surfaced on the far side of the bridge. Pulling himself up onto the deck, he crouched and the girl climbed down.

She studied him with grave brown eyes. She wore a white T-shirt bearing the legend TRINITY MONTESSORI. "I'm Olivia."

"I'm Jonah."

"You're a good climber," she said, licking a finger and dabbing at a scratch on her arm.

"And you're brave." Jonah pointed to the inner wall of the bridge tower. "Stand right there while I kill the . . . the monster. Don't move."

To Jonah's relief, Olivia nodded, eyes wide, and flattened herself against the inside wall of the bridge tower.

Jonah turned to face the shade.

It stood, clothed in a rotting corpse, a cohesion of desperate need in a decaying shell.

Behind him, a dozen small children huddled at the center of the bridge deck. Holding hands, some of them whimpering. They all wore the same white T-shirts with TRINITY MONTESSORI printed on them, and they all shone with the auras of the gifted. They were nearly all wizards, with a few other mainliners sprinkled in.

Trinity. That was the headquarters of the mainline guilds.

Children? Really? Shades are going after children now? Wizard children in particular? Now, why would that be?

Using children as hosts had never been of much interest to shades. Not when they had a choice. Children were small and not very strong, and grown-ups felt the need to pen them up. Shades needed strength and size and freedom of movement. That's what they aimed for in a borrowed body.

Jonah looked around for potential weapons. Ripping a rusting cross-brace free, he hefted it in his hands, hoping it wasn't anything structurally critical. He preferred a sword, with its cutting edge, but he often used a staff when sparring in the gym. This would do.

"Hey, Jonah," the shade said, speaking mind to mind. "'Sup?"

Jonah nearly dropped his staff. "You know who I *am*?" This was another of Jonah's double-edged gifts. He was the only savant who could communicate, mind to mind, with free shades. Some hosted shades could emit screeches, howls, clicks, and the like, but that was about it.

"You mean you don't recognize me?" The shade's tone was bitter, faintly mocking.

"I'm sorry, I don't," Jonah said, taking a step closer. "I'm guessing you've changed a lot since we last met."

"I'm Brendan Wu," the shade said.

The name was familiar. Jonah paged through mental files. "I can't quite place where I—"

"I lived at Safe Harbor," Brendan said. "You'd come there to see Kenzie all the time." He paused. "I used to watch those nature videos?"

A faint image came to Jonah's mind. An older boy with stick-straight black hair and bright, intelligent eyes, who spent hours every day in the whirlpool because his skin blistered and sloughed off constantly. A boy who lived with agonizing pain most of the time.

Brendan had died four years ago. Another miss for Safe Passage.

"I remember you, Brendan," Jonah said. "We used to talk about Antarctica."

"I loved Antarctica," Brendan said wistfully. "So cold and clean." He paused. "I always wished I had a brother like you. But everyone else in my family died in Brazil."

"That's what I don't get . . . after all you've been through, how could you kill children?"

"Why are you killing *us*?" Brendan snapped back. "Wizards are to blame for . . . for all of this." He waved his hand, taking in the children, the bridge, the river below. "We're all victims of wizards. So why are you fighting against us and not them?"

A question Jonah had asked a thousand times. And yet . . .

"Brendan," he said softly. "Wouldn't you like to be at peace?" Memory strobed, like a camera flash. Thing One had used almost the same argument on Jonah. About Kenzie.

Brendan laughed bitterly. "I'm aiming a little higher than that."

"It's wrong to kill children," Jonah said with conviction. His was a strange and brutal life, with few moral anchors, but that was one of them.

"This isn't about revenge. It's about our survival. Yours, mine—all of the victims of Thorn Hill. You're killing *us*. What's so different about killing *them*?"

"You think four-year-olds are a threat to you?"

Brendan shook his head, jarring several teeth free. They clattered onto the asphalt. "Of course not. But sometimes sacrifices are necessary. And who better to pay this price than mainliners?"

During this conversation, Jonah had eased forward. Now he was close enough to make out the object the shade held in its hand. It was a bottle made of brilliant glass, with an elaborate stopper.

"What's the bottle for?" Jonah asked.

"It's for blood magic." Brendan held up the bottle and tilted it so it caught the light. "This bottle is specially made to capture it. Killing the gifted frees it. The death of a gifted child is the most powerful source."

Jonah forced back a shudder. "What do you want it for?"

"Give me these guildlings, and I'll tell you."

"I can't give them to you," Jonah said, slapping the iron bar against his palm. "They don't belong to me."

"Jonah," Brendan pleaded. "Please listen to me. Things are different now. You'll see. We're organizing, we're getting stronger. We're not going to have to skulk in alleyways anymore, trading bodies every few days."

Jonah thought of the army of shades that had attacked the

canal boat in London. "Why? What's changed?"

"Everything," Brendan said eagerly. "Blood magic is the key. We want to partner with you, with everyone at the Anchorage."

"Who's 'we'?" Jonah asked. "Are you the one who's organizing the shades?"

"No," Brendan said. "You and I would be the liaisons. Lilith wants to meet with Mr. Mandrake."

"Lilith? Who's that?" The name was vaguely familiar. Maybe someone he knew at Thorn Hill?

"Lilith Greaves. She's our new leader. She's amazing. We think that if you just understood what we were planning, you would all come on board."

All Jonah could think of was that this was some kind of trap, a trick to gain access to Gabriel and the members of Nightshade.

"Fine," he said. "Tell me what you're planning."

"No," Brendan said. "Forgive my mistrust, but you've slaughtered more of us than the rest of Nightshade combined. First, we require a show of good faith." He tilted his head at the children and extended the bottle toward Jonah. "Help me extract blood magic from these mainliners. Then I'll take you to Lilith and she'll explain how it's used."

"No," Jonah said. "Let them go. Then I'll hear whatever Lilith has to pitch."

"Suit yourself," Brendan said. He raised his hand, a signal.

"Jonah!" Olivia screamed. "Look out!"

◈ CHAPTER FOURTEEN ◈
SHADESLAYER

Jonah swung around, to see shades swarming over the sides of the bridge deck from all directions. They lined up on either side, cadavers of all shapes, sizes, and degrees of crowding in behind. They encircled him, all rotting flesh and protruding bones, resembling the cast of a high-budget horror movie.

The children crouched and covered their heads with their arms. It looked kind of like a preschool disaster drill. With zombies.

Jonah assumed a fighting stance, but Brendan held up his hand, and the shades settled in place, making no move to attack.

And then, ludicrously, Jonah's phone buzzed. He looked, and saw that he had a screenful of texts from Alison. *Where the hell are you?* Swiveling, he took photographs of the shade army and the bridge and texted them back.

"Shadeslayer!"

The voice came from high above him. He looked up, and there, on the rusting framework of the railroad bridge, stood a woman . . . rather, an apparition in the form of a woman, lighting up the entire riverbed. Her garments writhed around her like brilliant vapors, and her arms trailed streamers of light.

"Or would you rather I call you Jonah?"

"You must be Lilith," Jonah said. "But I still don't know exactly *what* you are."

Unlike the rest of the shades, Lilith did not occupy a corpse, but she didn't resemble a free shade either. Even to a slayer with an amulet, a free shade looked more like a wraith than a person. But this one was remarkably detailed, fully formed, and stable in outline, with silver-blond hair that rippled past her shoulders.

"I'm a Thorn Hill survivor. Like you. I believe the term you use is 'shade'?"

"If you're a survivor, you're not a shade," Jonah said.

"Oh, is *that* how you justify killing us? The excuse that we're already dead?" Lilith asked. "I'm as alive as you."

"If you're fine the way you are, then why are you constantly stealing other people's bodies?"

"I didn't say we were *fine*," Lilith said. "I said we were *alive*. I suppose you could say we view bodies as prosthetic devices."

"Think of Kenzie," Brendan said. "His body is damaged, but he uses adaptive equipment to interact with the world."

"Leave Kenzie out of this," Jonah said.

"Kenzie is in this, whether you like it or not," Lilith said. "As are you."

Jonah's skin prickled. He didn't like their easy familiarity with details of his life. They were cutting too close to his heart. "Brendan said you have a plan," he began, eager to change the subject.

"Indeed. That's why I asked him to fetch you."

"You brought me here on purpose?" Jonah looked around at the circle of shades, feeling foolish. The legendary Slayer, Jonah Kinlock, had walked right into a trap.

"Brendan said you were fond of children," Lilith said. "Given your history as a slayer, I didn't believe him, but here you are."

"Here I am," Jonah said. "What do you want, then? Why am I still alive?"

"I wanted to talk to you about alternatives to this road we're going down now."

"I'm listening," Jonah said.

"We would like to partner with the Anchorage. We're hoping you can use your persuasive skills to bring Gabriel Mandrake on board, too."

"If your plan involves killing mainliners, he'll never sign on for it."

"Even if he doesn't, we're hoping you will," Brendan said. "We know you and Gabriel don't always see eye to eye."

"I still don't know what your plan is," Jonah said. "Or what the blood magic is for."

"And you won't know until you commit to us," Lilith said.

"By killing children."

"Something *you* seem to be incredibly good at," Lilith snapped. "How many of us have you killed so far? My own daughter died at Thorn Hill. I've been looking for her ever since. But maybe you've already killed her." She paused. "Tell me, Shadeslayer," she said softly. "What would you do if you ran into Marcie?"

Jonah's palms were sweating, his heart thudding painfully. Lilith seemed to know exactly how to find his open wounds. "I'd want to save her from . . . from this," he said, gesturing at the assembly of decaying corpses.

"Then we are allies," Lilith said. "Why do you think I'm doing this? Why are *these* children . . ." She gestured toward the preschoolers on the bridge. "Why are *they* more important than my daughter, and your brother and sister?"

"I never said they were."

Brendan took a step toward Jonah, extending the bottle toward him. "Then do it, Jonah. Take the gloves off. Free *these* children," he said. "I'm told that being killed by you is a very pleasant experience."

"Why do you insist that I murder children?" Jonah asked. "Is this some kind of hazing ritual?"

"This way there's no turning back," Lilith said. "We're trying to help you, but we won't allow you to keep killing us. All of us have a chance at a new life—except for the ones you finish off. Either join us now, with the body you have, or . . . what's that term you use? Once you're *freed*, you'll join us anyway."

"No," Jonah said.

"Can you at least convince Gabriel to leave us be? To remain neutral in this fight? Negotiate a truce?"

"And in the meantime, you keep on killing mainliners?" Jonah nodded toward the children. "He won't go for that."

"These are mostly wizards," Lilith said. "Why shouldn't they give back to us, to make up for what they did?"

"I might agree, if you went after those that did the

killing," Jonah said. "These children weren't even born yet."

Lilith sighed. "It's a shame," she said. "You—by design—are the perfect predator: strong, quick, agile, with exceptionally acute senses and an uncanny beauty that draws people in. Someone with your gifts . . . you would be extremely valuable to the cause."

Something that Lilith said echoed in Jonah's ears. *By design*, she'd said. What did she mean by that?

"And your cause is taking revenge? That's it?"

"My cause is the survivors of Thorn Hill. The cause that Gabriel tries to claim for his own while he conspires to kill us off. Gabriel has given up, but I have not. I can't. Just because he has failed doesn't mean that I will. I'm a much better sorcerer than he will ever be." Lilith laughed. "You should see your face. Poor Jonah. Gabriel likes to keep you in the dark, doesn't he?"

That truth vibrated through Jonah like a plucked string.

"One thing I don't get," he said. "What do you have against the other guilds? Besides wizards, I mean? We were all mainliners, once."

Lilith snorted. "They ridiculed those of us who went to Thorn Hill, seeking a better life. Called us misfits and dreamers. When the massacre happened, they said we got what was coming to us. Do you know how many children were slaughtered, right after it happened? That was mainliners who did that. They justified it by calling them monsters."

"Not all guildlings are like that," Jonah said. "Many of them contribute to the—"

"Ah, yes," Lilith said. "They love helping Gabriel's kids. It makes them feel virtuous. Just don't show them any of the ugly ones. Tell me this: Do you have any guildling friends?

Ever had a mainliner over to your house?" When Jonah said nothing, she laughed. "I thought not. This life is all we have, Shadeslayer. Would you rather we simply dissipate, like a stench on the breeze? I want something better for them . . . for us." The wind stirred her clothes and hair, so she resembled a goddess in a painting.

Jonah's gaze swept over Lilith's shade army. He glanced back at the children, huddled together, whimpering on the bridge.

He turned back toward Lilith. "No," he said. "Can't do it."

"Then we will destroy you," Lilith said. "Whether you join us or not, you'll be blamed for the deaths of mainliners. See what kind of justice you'll get from them."

She gestured to Brendan. He opened a plastic bag and emptied it over the bridge deck. Jonah flung his arms up to protect his head, but there was no need. The contents floated down, all around, littering the cement like flower petals or ashes.

Jonah had no time to investigate, though, because Lilith called out to the waiting army. "Kill the guildlings. Leave the Slayer alone unless he gets in the way. Bring their blood magic to me." She blinked out.

With a roar and a rattle of bones, the shades attacked.

Jonah charged forward to meet them, his makeshift staff a bright blur in the darkness, knocking down four at a time. They fell in a jumble of bones, some of their limbs still twitching. He had to beat them up into little bits of parts before they left off trying to attack him.

He wished he had Fragarach. A sword was much more efficient when it came to dismemberment. And he needed efficiency, because more shades kept coming, foaming over the edge of the bridge, an army of dead on the move. There was no time to finish them off, only to deprive them of their physical hosts.

They aimed for the children. It took all of Jonah's strength and speed to intercept them.

"Don't run!" he shouted at them. "Don't go near the edge. That's what they want."

Just as he said this, a little boy broke away and ran, screaming, from a corpse that reached bony arms toward him. Jonah just managed to block his way and herd him back to the center. Then he turned and smashed the corpse into five smaller pieces that still jumped and vibrated on the asphalt.

It was a remarkably silent battle, save for the hiss of Jonah's staff, the whimpering of the children, and the clatter of bones. Like a deadly game of Whac-A-Mole.

"Jonah! Behind you!" Olivia. Again.

He just caught the flash of motion out of the corner of his eye in time. He flung himself forward as a razor-sharp blade hissed past his head, all but giving him a haircut. Then flipped backward as the ax blade came down again.

The shade pivoted and threw the ax straight at the children. There was no time for a pretty save. Jonah spun, swinging his staff, and batted the flying ax out of the air.

Well. Maybe it *was* a pretty save. And now he had an edged weapon.

In the time it took to realize that, three shades were nearly on top of him. He reacted, spinning, cutting them in half with one swing of his blade. The torsos and legs continued to twist and kick and try to get to him.

The ax was a blur of steel, and Jonah a blur of motion.

But sooner or later, he was going to mess up. Sooner or later, a child was going to fall over the edge and end up in the river.

"Hey! What's this?" someone shouted from the base of the bridge. "Did Halloween come early or what?"

Looking down through the framework of the bridge, Jonah saw that it was Alison, with her sword, Bloodfetcher, strapped on over the dress she'd worn to the club.

"Alison! A little help, here?" Jonah pivoted, ax in one hand, staff in the other. He slammed into three corpses at knee level. They toppled backward and disappeared over the edge.

A commotion erupted on the ground below as Alison drew Bloodfetcher and went to work. Jonah heard the crunch of bones and smelled the stench of burning flesh punctuated by occasional heartrending screams of free shades as she shivved them. Those were harder to bear than ever.

Finally, blessedly, the shades stopped coming and Jonah was able to free those already on the bridge, including Brendan. He didn't have the energy or the heart to chase the free shades down. He picked his way through heaps of bones to the edge of the road deck and looked down.

Alison was charring the last of the creatures on the ground, jetting flame at them with two-handed sweeps of her sword. Burning corpses toppled into the river, hissing as they hit the water. The surface reflected back flame in a lurid orange. And everywhere, fleeing shades, swarming like fireflies along the riverbank.

Taking a wider view, Jonah saw that the police activity on the bluff had slopped over the hill and down into the Flats. The cops would have heard the bridge alarm and then seen the platform rising on the closed bridge. *We need to get out of here.*

"Good work!" Jonah called down. "Thanks!"

Alison looked up at him, sword in hand, her hair a bright spot in the darkness. "Sorry!" she said. "I wasn't able to shiv very many of them. They were coming too fast. So now we'll have a mess of free shades to deal with."

"Can't be helped," Jonah said. "Better split. Company's coming." He pointed at the oncoming slurry of uniforms.

"What about you?"

"I'll be down in a minute. I need to clear the rest of the bridge."

Alison trotted back toward Superior as Jonah knelt on the bridge deck, looking for the bottle that Brendan had dropped. But there was something else, scattered over the ground. Plant material—shredded leaves, small purple and yellow flowers, red berries.

Nightshade.

He didn't have time to sweep up. So Jonah stuffed some of the wilted plant into his pocket, then scooped up the bottle, tucking it into the waist of his jeans.

He turned back toward the children, who huddled together, shaking and crying. All except for Olivia, who had not budged from her assigned spot. He knew he should do something, calm them down somehow. But he wasn't good with children. He always felt like he might contaminate them if he got too close.

"Is anybody hurt?" he asked.

They all started talking at once.

"Listen, I want each one of you to look at your neighbor. If your neighbor is bleeding, raise your hand."

The crying dwindled into sniffles as they checked one another out. No hands went up.

"Great," Jonah said, weak with relief.

"I want to go home," a little boy wailed.

"Soon," Jonah said. "I need to go make sure there's no monsters left on the bridge. While I'm gone, could you . . . could you all sit down and hold hands?" He pushed his hands down, and eight bottoms hit the deck with a thump. Eight pairs of eyes stared solemnly back at him.

"Let's sing a song," Olivia said, coming up beside him.

"Great," Jonah said. By now, he was ready to adopt Olivia and name her his heir. He dropped his staff, stowed his ax, and began to climb. The children's voices rose from the platform below, Olivia's louder than anyone else's.

One bright day in the middle of the night,
Two dead boys got up to fight.
Back-to-back they faced each other,
Drew their swords and shot each other.
A deaf policeman heard the noise
And ran to save the two dead boys.
And if you don't believe it's true,
Go ask the blind man, he saw it, too.

Late last night or the night before,
Twenty-four ZOMBIES knocked on the door.
I asked what they wanted, and this is what they said:
"I want to chew on your toes and bite off your HEAD!"

Not exactly soothing, Jonah thought, but . . . appropriate.

❦ Chapter Fifteen ❧
Escape from the Flats

Jonah searched the entire infrastructure of the bridge, but found no more shades lurking up there. He'd hoped that Lilith might still be in the area, maybe watching from some unseen vantage point. But there was no sign of her.

Even now, an army of free shades would be spreading throughout the city, looking for new hosts.

He looked out over the canal basin and saw that, while he'd been occupied, the police had surrounded the base of the bridge, trying not to step on scattered body parts.

Mechanics grappled with the bridge machinery, and a searchlight mounted at the top of Superior swept over the metal framework.

On the bridge deck below, the children were still chanting, playing a clapping game.

> *My boyfriend's name is Roger,*
> *He plays for the Brooklyn Dodgers.*

With a cherry on his nose and nine black toes,
And this is how my story goes.

Jonah climbed down from the tower, landing lightly on the bridge deck. The children's voices faded. They watched him, wide-eyed and silent.

"You're safe now," he said. "The . . . ah . . . the zombies are gone. Now stay put until the police officers come."

The searchlight found him, nearly blinding him, and helicopter blades whirred overhead. Jonah pulled his hood forward to shelter his face and hugged the side of the bridge tender's cabin to avoid drawing fire. He looked down to the foot of the tower, where black-clad SWAT officers were beginning to climb.

A voice blared down from one of the choppers overhead. "Drop your weapons, raise your hands, and step away from the children."

And as soon as I'm in the clear, you'll shoot me, Jonah thought. I'm not planning on dying tonight.

The bridge alarm clanged again, and with a screech of metal on metal, the bridge platform began to descend in fits and starts.

Jonah slid his body through the metal infrastructure of the lift bridge and leaped across and onto the adjacent abandoned railroad bridge. Working his way to the other side, he descended to the railbed in a series of controlled zigzag falls.

Landing on the tracks, he sprinted across the trestle and vaulted over the chain-link fence at the end. It would not do to be caught. It would not do at all.

Jonah trotted north, passing under the RTA bridge. He needed to get far enough away so that when he surfaced, the officers swarming the bridge wouldn't spot him. He couldn't keep racing through the Flats, though. That would draw unwanted attention.

Up ahead loomed the graceful arches of the Detroit-Superior Bridge. He ran up one of its buttresses, pulling himself hand over hand, and slid over the wall onto the trolley level.

He looked back at the lift bridge and saw that more and more police cars had been arriving at the bottom of the structure's towers, including a SWAT armored vehicle that resembled a tank. The police were still concentrated around the road bridge, guns drawn, awaiting the descent of the bridge deck.

He had to move fast. Once they realized he'd escaped, they would have the area cordoned off in no time. He sprinted back through the trolley subway to the east end of the bridge, leaping over barricades and gaps in the concrete floor. He surfaced just before the trolley line disappeared underground for the last time. As he climbed over the railing onto the bridge, he saw that one of the police officers stationed at the intersection of Superior and West Ninth was striding toward him.

Jonah pulled out his phone and snapped a photo of the asssortment of emergency vehicles. "What's going on?" he asked, when the officer was close enough.

"What the hell do you think you're doing here?" The policeman planted a hand on Jonah's shoulder. "Where did you come from?"

"Well, the street was blocked, so I snuck over on the lower level," Jonah said, taking three more quick photos. "Would you mind answering a few questions? I'm a freelancer, and

I just need to get a little more info before I—"

"Why are you carrying an ax?"

Damn! He'd forgotten all about the ax he'd jammed into the waistband of his jeans. Not only that; he was splattered with blood and gore.

"It's cosplay," Jonah replied, scraping up a bit of charm, touching the ax. "A costume. You've heard of the annual zombie walk, right? I do the slayer podcast. If I could just get your name and a quote from you, Officer—"

"The street was blocked for a reason," the officer roared, spinning Jonah around so he faced West Ninth. A small crowd huddled behind yellow police-line tape. "Now get back behind that line before I arrest you for disorderly conduct!"

"Of course, Officer. Right away." Jonah crossed the intersection, ducked under the police tape, and walked up West Ninth, losing himself in the crowds on the sidewalk. He ditched the ax in a Dumpster.

By now, the emergency lights and helicopters were far behind him. It was unlikely anyone had followed him on that route, but still—he didn't go directly back to school. It was just too risky. Too close to home.

He stopped at an all-night diner on Fourth Street and ordered coffee and pie, sharing the place with a bone-weary waitress and some produce brokers from the West Side Market. Lilith's words rattled around in his brain. He'd always been conflicted about his role as a slayer. So much of what she'd said echoed the voices in his own head.

He sent a brief text to Gabriel, relaying what had happened. By the time he left the diner, he had a throbbing headache. And a summons to a meeting with Gabriel and Alison the next day.

Members of Nightshade lived in the Oxbow Building, a former warehouse that had been renovated as spacious loft apartments. No shared dormitory rooms for them. It was the most secure building on campus. Gabriel occupied the penthouse.

Jonah didn't mingle much with his colleagues in Nightshade, save his few trusted friends. They had little in common save a talent for killing, and Jonah had too many secrets to keep. So he was viewed as a loner, resented as Gabriel's pet. Rumored to be especially deadly.

That, at least, was true.

When he finally walked into the duty room on the first floor of the Oxbow Building, Alison Shaw was waiting for him, still blood-grubby from the fight in the Flats.

"Thank God," she said, when he walked in. "I was beginning to worry."

"I thought it was best not to come straight back here," Jonah said. "I think half the Cleveland PD is out there."

"You could've sent me a text."

"I know. I'm sorry." He studied her. "You have blood all over you."

"Those cadavers must've been fresh," Alison said. "Lots of splash-back." She swiped at her clothes. "I know I need a shower, but I didn't want to miss you when you came in." She waited and, when he said nothing, said, "Well? What was that all about?"

Jonah really didn't want to get into it. He wished he could go up to his apartment and strip off his bloody clothes and lose himself in his music until he could lose himself in sleep.

She deserved an answer, though. She'd saved his butt.

"A shade grabbed a preschool class," he said. "From that mainliner town. Trinity. Mostly wizards."

Alison wrinkled her nose, as if nobody would possibly want a preschool class, let alone a gifted one. "A preschool class? Why?"

"Someone named Lilith has a new scheme going."

It wasn't the first time someone had tried to take charge of the shades, to organize a system for collecting and allocating bodies. But the constant hunt for new meat made it difficult to orchestrate anything.

Jonah pulled the bottle from his jeans and waved it in front of Alison. "Whatever it is, it requires blood magic. Which comes from killing the gifted."

"Blood magic?" Alison hesitated, as always, unwilling to admit she didn't know something. "What's it used for?"

"I don't know. But Gabriel will." He slid his fingers into his pocket, pulling out the bits of nightshade. "They scattered this around before the killing began." When Alison looked puzzled, he said, "It's nightshade. It looks like shades are the ones murdering mainliners, after all. And trying to blame it on us."

Alison grimaced. "You know I've got no use for mainliners, but *children*?"

"I guess so."

Alison folded her arms and lifted her chin. "What is it about you, Kinlock? Do you attract trouble or what? I wondered why you didn't stay for the second set."

Jonah rubbed blood away from a long scrape on his arm. "I smelled the shade, and I had to go check it out."

"You smelled it."

"He was wearing a corpse that was totally rank."

"I wish I had your sense of smell."

"No, you don't. Trust me, it was pretty hard to take." He slid a glance at her. Jonah had literally grown up with Alison. He understood her, though she wasn't always easy to be with.

"Anyway, I'm glad you came along when you did. I had my hands full." He rubbed his eyes with the heel of his hand. "How did the rest of the show go?"

"That's why I was trying to reach you. Mose nearly passed out during the last set," Alison said. "Natalie took him back to his place. She seems really worried."

"I'll call them," Jonah said. "See how he's doing." He paused. "Is it me, or has this been a really long day?"

Alison hesitated for a heartbeat, and then said tentatively, "I had a good time tonight." She licked her lips.

No! Jonah thought, beginning to edge toward the door. Please don't go there. Don't ruin our friendship. Don't make it awkward between us when you're one of the few friends I have.

Maybe he should imprint NO! on his black sweatshirts. *No*, I'm not seeing anyone. *No*, I wouldn't like to go someplace for coffee. *No*, I don't come here often. Just. *No*.

Alison put her gloved hand on his arm. "I just thought maybe you . . . that you might want to . . . come up to my place for a little while."

"I can't," Jonah said, knowing he had to stop her before she committed herself. So she could pretend it had never happened. What was he supposed to say now? *It's not you, it's me*? Which was the truth, after all.

He looked into her eyes, saw the spark of hope fading. "I'm sorry, Alison, I'm a mess, I really am." *In every way.* "I need to clean up and go to bed. I'm filthy, I feel awful, and I've got class in"—he checked his phone—"six hours, and you do, too." He put his gloved hand on her shoulder. "See you tomorrow."

❦ CHAPTER SIXTEEN ❧
HEIR APPARENT

When Jonah arrived in Gabriel's outer office, Alison was already there, all cleaned up from the night before. She sat in one of the guest chairs, ramrod straight, her feet planted, hands gripping the armrests as if determined to prevent herself from doing something stupid.

When Jonah walked in, she looked up at him, then quickly away. She picked at a scratch on her arm.

"Go right on in," Patrick said.

When they entered, Gabriel was sitting cross-legged on the floor in the conference area, a pick clenched between his teeth, restringing a Martin D-18. He fussed with the bridge for a few more minutes, then set the guitar aside, shaking his head. "I'll deal with that later." Pushing up to his feet, he embraced each of them in turn. "Glad you're safe," he said. He motioned Jonah and Alison to their usual seats.

"Alison," Gabriel said, studying her. "You look like you're feeling better. More robust."

She nodded. "Right," she said faintly, swallowing hard. Her gaze flicked to Jonah, then back to Gabriel. "I'm doing great. If I could just get rid of these headaches, I'd be perfect."

"Headaches? Are those new?"

Alison nodded. "It's always something."

"Ah." Gabriel tapped his long, slender fingers on a newspaper spread across the table, clearly ready to move on. "Now . . . tell me what happened in the Flats. The newspapers are full of it this morning." He held up the newspaper, and Jonah read the headline: POLICE BAFFLED AT GRISLY SCENE IN FLATS. And underneath, *Kidnapped Children Safe.*

I accomplished something, anyway, Jonah thought. But the victory tasted bitter in his mouth. "I ran into some trouble in the Flats, and Alison came to the rescue."

From the corner of his eye, Jonah caught Alison's expression of pleased surprise.

"Go on," Gabriel said, settling back in his chair, the newspaper on his lap.

"When I left Club Catastrophe last night, I caught a whiff of mischief and went to investigate. I found Brendan Wu on the Carter Road Lift Bridge."

"Brendan Wu?" Gabriel's eyes narrowed.

"Remember? He died at Safe Harbor four years ago," Jonah said. "He'd kidnapped a preschool class."

Gabriel tapped the newspaper. "From Trinity, apparently?"

Jonah nodded. "All gifted." He fished the glass bottle out of his jacket pocket and handed it across to Gabriel. "He was carrying this, to collect blood magic. He said that gifted children were the best source."

"Shades want blood magic?" Gabriel murmured, examining the bottle as if fascinated. "I wonder why."

"What's blood magic?" Alison asked. "And what's it good for?"

"It's the energy released when the gifted are killed," Gabriel said, setting the bottle on the table. "It can be captured using special ensorcelled containers like these. It's an extremely potent magical catalyst, sometimes used by sorcerers on the down-low to force together incompatible elements in order to create powerful—often deadly—magical objects and potions." Gabriel chewed on his lower lip. "I don't get it. How would shades know about that?"

"Apparently someone named Lilith is leading them now," Jonah said.

"Lilith?" Gabriel leaned forward, and the newspaper slid to the floor.

Jonah nodded. "I thought the name seemed familiar, but I couldn't place it. Brendan said she had a plan to save all of us. He wouldn't tell me specifically what it was, but it involves blood magic. Apparently, they're behind the mainliner killings."

"Oh my God," Gabriel said, rubbing his eyes with his thumb and forefinger. Jonah's mentor radiated a mingle of emotions, but one dominated them all. Fear. Gabriel knew Lilith . . . and he was afraid of her for some reason.

"This Lilith showed up, then, with an army of shades, and tried to convince me to join them in riffing the preschoolers," Jonah said. "She claimed to know you."

"I *knew* someone by the name of Lilith Greaves, who died at Thorn Hill," Gabriel said. "But it couldn't have been her. That's impossible."

"It's not impossible," Alison said, fingering her Nightshade amulet. "I mean, technically, all of the shades are dead, yet we see them all the time."

"What did she look like?" Gabriel asked. "Was she free or hosted?"

"Free," Jonah said. "She was more like a—an apparition. More detailed than your usual free shade, from what I could tell. She never let me get that close."

"So it could have been anyone," Gabriel murmured, as if trying to convince himself. He finally settled back into his seat. "Did she offer any proof of who she was?"

"She seemed to know a lot about us," Jonah said.

"I guess that's not surprising," Gabriel said. "Brendan could have filled her in . . . he or any of the other students we've lost. We've never had shades share information before."

"She wants to partner with us. Said we should be allies. At least, she wants to meet with you and negotiate a truce."

"And how, exactly, would that work?" Gabriel raised an eyebrow. "You're the only one who can communicate with shades."

"I'd act as go-between," Jonah said.

"Did she say what her plan is?"

Jonah flushed. "She wouldn't . . . not unless I committed myself by riffing some of the mainliners."

Gabriel stared at him for a long moment, as if turning that over in his mind. "No," he said. "Absolutely not. It's clearly a hoax—or a trap—and I'm not wasting time on either one." He retrieved the newspaper and folded it. "What's all this about cadavers scattered all over the Flats?"

"After we talked, Lilith ordered the shades to kill the kids. Alison and I intervened."

"How many shades would you say there were?"

"A couple hundred?" Jonah said, looking at Alison for verification.

She nodded, shifting in her seat. "There were a whole lot of them, and they didn't go down easy."

Between the two of them, they relayed the rest of the story.

"Lilith was giving the orders?" Gabriel asked. "She seemed to be in control?"

Jonah nodded. "At least, she told them to attack, and they did."

Gabriel stood, walked to the window, and stared out at the lake, hands clasped behind his back. He always did that when he needed time to think. Finally, he shook himself and turned back to them. "This person sounds extremely dangerous—someone charismatic enough to arouse the undead, and fan the flames of hatred. If you run into her again, kill her."

For once, Gabriel didn't use one of his many euphemisms for murder.

"I think we should meet with her," Jonah said bluntly. "We might learn something useful."

"Jonah!" Gabriel said. "She just tried to kill eight small children. That should tell you everything you need to know."

"I didn't say join her," Jonah said. "I said meet with her."

"No," Gabriel said.

"Look at it from her point of view," Jonah said. "We're trying to kill them. It's self-defense."

Gabriel grimaced. "That's one thing I've always loved about you, Jonah—your ability to see issues from all sides. And it seems that she's managed to engage your sympathy. But I won't meet with her. It's too risky."

"I think it's worth that risk, to find out what they're

planning," Jonah said. "You might recognize her. If she isn't the Lilith you remember, she might be somebody else from Thorn Hill."

"The answer is no," Gabriel said flatly. "I don't want to hear any more about it."

"Lilith warned me that she won't allow us to kill shades anymore. She threatened to destroy us if we keep at it. She said they will continue to kill mainliners, and we'll get the blame." He paused. "Speaking of risk, did the papers mention anything about nightshade?"

"Nightshade?" Gabriel's head came up. "What do you mean?"

Jonah tossed a handful of crushed herb onto Gabriel's desk. "They scattered this all around the killing field. It's part of the plan to eventually link it to us."

Gabriel poked at the nightshade with his forefinger. "Did anyone see either of you? Could you be identified?"

"I don't think so," Jonah said. He looked at Alison, and she shook her head.

"Good," Gabriel said. "We'll have to hope nobody makes that connection."

"Don't you think they'll find a way to make that happen?" Alison said. "I mean, we're wearing Nightshade amulets, and we have the tattoos. Assuming they know that, then . . . ?"

Gabriel sat, very still, for a long moment, then dropped his hands. "If they want a war, we'll give it to them."

He looked at Alison and jerked his head toward the door. "Alison, if there's nothing else, I'd like to speak to Jonah in private for a few minutes."

Alison stood and slumped out of the room, with many backward looks.

When she had gone, Gabriel leaned back against his desk. "I've been getting a strong vibe of frustration from you for months," he said. "It seems like you question every decision I make. Do you want to talk about it?"

No, Jonah thought of saying. But, actually, he did.

"It's a number of things. Beginning with the mission."

"Go on."

"I just don't see why it's our job to finish what the Black Rose began."

"Is that how you view what we're doing?"

"Pretty much."

"I'm sorry to hear that." Gabriel rose, crossed to the refrigerator. "Would you like something to drink? I probably have something that would—"

"No, thank you," Jonah said, unwilling to make this tiny concession.

Gabriel rummaged in the refrigerator for a few minutes, then returned to his chair empty-handed. "When I established the Anchorage, I committed myself to all of the victims of Thorn Hill—the living and the living dead. For the survivors, a home, an education, and care appropriate to their unique needs. For the others, a pathway to rest, while protecting the public. You've been critical to this effort."

"I didn't ask for this," Jonah said. Lilith's words echoed in his head. "It seems to me that the shades want to survive as much as anyone else. Who am I to put them to rest, as you call it?"

"You're not killing them, Jonah! They're already dead."

"What about Safe Passage?"

"Or nearly dead," Gabriel amended. "If you were them, what would you want?"

"That's just the thing. I *am* them."

"Fine. Would you want to spend eternity in a constant quest for somebody to slaughter so you could live in his body for a little while? And when it began to decay, try to find another victim before you were too far gone to hunt? Is that what you would want?" Gabriel's voice rose as he spoke, until he was practically shouting.

Still, Jonah was getting more fear than anger.

"What I want doesn't matter. It should be their decision. How are they a threat to us?"

"You're all right with slaughtering children?" Gabriel raised an eyebrow.

"Of course not! But why is it our job to prevent it?"

"Because we're the ones who can do it. If we don't, then who will?"

"I'd rather take a different approach—by researching what poisoned us and developing effective treatment before it's too late."

"I've been working on that for ten years," Gabriel said. "That's my area of expertise. Don't you think that if there were better treatments, I would've found them?"

Gabriel paused and, when Jonah didn't respond, said, "Is there anything I can do to make your life easier?"

"You can find someone else."

"I know Jeanette's death must have been tough on you. She was . . . a very special person."

"Yes. So special, she didn't deserve to be murdered." Tired as he was, Jonah couldn't stand to sit anymore. He shoved to his feet and crossed the office to the window. Down below, a freighter was threading its way upriver.

"All right, Jonah . . . you win," Gabriel said to Jonah's

back. "I'm going to pull you from fieldwork."

Jonah swung around to face him. "What?"

Gabriel laughed. "Oh, don't worry . . . you won't wriggle off the hook so easily. I have something else in mind for you. I wasn't going to bring this up so soon, but . . . it's time that I began thinking about a successor."

"A successor." Jonah swallowed hard, his mouth suddenly dry.

"I was hoping that you might consider taking that on."

"Me? I'm seventeen!" Jonah blurted. "How would that work?"

"You're seventeen now, yes, but you've literally grown up here. There is no one I trust more, no one who is more knowledgeable about the entire operation. We have adult staff, yes, but nobody with our history. Nobody who has invested so much of himself as you have. My thought is that you could spend the next several years as my apprentice." Gabriel smiled wryly. "I could use the help."

"How would that be different from what I'm doing now?"

"You'll spend more time here at the Anchorage. I could begin introducing you to our patrons, both Weir and Anaweir. You could get to know more about Weir politics, and make the contacts you'll need as school director. That way, when the time comes, you would be seen as my heir apparent—as school director, for the music business, and so on. Everything but Nightshade."

"I'd be out of Nightshade?" Ludicrous as it was, regret pinged through Jonah, leaving him feeling hollowed out, without purpose.

"That's what you want, right? I would ask that you continue your role with Safe Passage—for the benefit of our students. And continue training our most promising candidates in the gym. Otherwise, your role would be more . . . administrative."

"If I'm out of the field, then who's going to—"

"We'll have to work smarter somehow. Use a team approach, develop more weapons, I don't know. It's not fair to keep exploiting you just because we can."

Jonah's cheeks heated with embarrassment. "You're not exploiting me, exactly. You're doing what you feel you have to do. But—as school director—wouldn't you want someone with a gift other than . . . than killing?"

"You have many gifts, Jonah. We just need to allow you to deploy them. You have considerable charisma and persuasive ability . . . you'll be brilliant at attracting funding support."

"Even if you have to go outside of the Keep, it seems like you might want someone with a real education."

Gabriel lifted an eyebrow.

"No offense, but I've been gone more than I'm here. Even when I'm here, I'm distracted. I read a lot, but—"

"I know. We've demanded a lot of you. Now, at least, you might have the chance to focus on your education. Anyway, people won't be beating down the door to take this job. There was a time that I hoped Jeanette might." He shrugged. "The other reason I hope you'll say yes is that you're a musician, like me. I want someone who can manage it all—the club and music-promotion side as well as the foundation. It's unlikely that I'll find someone with every asset we'd like to have. But you come the closest."

"If I do this, will I have a bigger voice in policy?" Jonah asked bluntly. "In how we use resources? In deciding what the mission is?"

Their eyes met for a long, charged moment.

"Eventually, yes," Gabriel said. Which Jonah read as, *Not anytime soon.*

"Then my answer is, eventually maybe," Jonah said.

Gabriel laughed. "I guess I asked for that."

"Who'll run Nightshade, then? After you're gone?"

"Hopefully, after I'm gone, there won't be any need for Nightshade anymore," Gabriel said. "Certainly it will be a chance for someone to take the program in a different direction. Why don't we give this a try for a while? You can spend more time with the healers and educators here. I'll begin introducing you to some people. We can meet periodically and you can let me know how you're doing, and whether you want to continue on."

"All right," Jonah said. "We'll see how it goes."

"Good," Gabriel said. He thrust out his hand. "Your Nightshade amulet?"

Jonah drew back, closing his hand over the pendant, oddly reluctant to give it up. "Let's wait," he said. "We'll see how I like sitting behind a desk."

After a moment's hesitation, Gabriel dropped his hand. "It's hardly *that* boring," he said, rolling his eyes.

"Speaking of desk work, I've been wondering: Are there any files, archives, records, and like that from Thorn Hill here at school? Or are they kept somewhere else?"

That wary, guarded expression returned. "What is it you're looking for? Maybe I can help you find it."

"I'm not sure what exactly I'm looking for," Jonah said. "I'm just hoping that something will jump out at me that will help me figure out exactly what happened. You mentioned that sorcerers may have conspired with the Wizard Guild to compound the poison. I'm wondering if they might have been working at the commune."

"I'm afraid that pretty much all of that was destroyed after the massacre," Gabriel said. "As you can imagine, things were chaotic for weeks afterward. People were worried that wizards would either find or plant incriminating evidence in the records, and so a lot of material was shredded or burned. I was able to find some records from the compounding labs, and of course, I've gone over them with a fine-tooth comb, looking for anything that might be helpful to survivors. Some of the treatments we've devised have grown from those discoveries. But I think that mine's played out. You won't find anything useful here." He stood, signaling that the meeting was over. "If you have any more ideas, don't hesitate to share them with me. Sometimes fresh eyes can identify new solutions."

On his way back to Oxbow, Jonah played their conversation over in his mind. In a way, Gabriel was offering him a promotion. But it didn't feel that way. To Jonah, it sounded like good-bye. He was getting the message that he was definitely off Gabriel's A-list.

Or did Gabriel have another reason for wanting to kick him out of Nightshade?

There was one more thing that weighed on Jonah's mind. When Gabriel said that all of the records from Thorn Hill had been destroyed, Jonah read that as a lie. Which made him wonder what might be in the records that Gabriel didn't want him to see.

⪜ CHAPTER SEVENTEEN ⪐
TRINITY FAIRE

"**A**re we invited to this event or are we just crashing it?" Jonah asked as they crossed the parking lot toward Trinity Square.

"We weren't *explicitly* invited," Gabriel said. "But it's open to the public. I thought it might be helpful for you to see the seat of the Weir government and meet some mainliners in a nonofficial capacity. It's always best to get to know people when you're not asking them for something."

"What *do* we want from them?" Jonah asked.

"Right now we have no representation on the Interguild Council. I've been working to change that, but haven't been able to attract much support."

"How would it help us to have representation on the council?"

"We need to be at the table when decisions are made that affect us. Especially given the misconceptions people have about the Anchorage. Meeting you . . . interacting with you . . . that should change some minds. This is what we call outreach."

I'm the poster child again, Jonah thought, with a stab of resentment. Because I'm pretty to look at. Because my disabilities aren't obvious from the outside.

"Just remember," Gabriel said, "you're a diplomat, now. Use that Kinlock charm. Although mainliners are not at risk from us, they may not understand that. They tend to be edgy where savants are concerned."

"So I should keep that scaly tail tucked inside my jeans?" When Gabriel frowned at him, Jonah raised both hands. "Totally harmless, that's me."

They passed under a banner emblazoned with the legend TRINITY MEDIEVAL FAIRE. Jonah could hear strains of lute and recorder and the cadence of drums.

Jonah took in the crowded square—families, tourists with cameras, many clothed in period dress. "They aren't all mainliners?" Somehow, he'd expected that they would be.

Gabriel shook his head. "The town is a mix of Weir and Anaweir. Today there's lots of both. People come from all over to shop and have a good time."

Tents lined the square, mostly artists and craftpersons selling their wares, with a few armorers and purveyors of medieval clothing. Food stands sold such medieval delicacies as turkey legs, deep-fried Twinkies, and "gyros of the realm."

"Gabriel!" someone called as they passed by a booth offering handwoven clothing.

Gabriel turned aside and greeted the woman tending the booth. "Mercedes! I haven't seen you since last year's concert." They air-kissed, and then Gabriel put a hand on Jonah's shoulder. "Mercedes, this is Jonah Kinlock, one of the students I'm mentoring. Jonah, meet Mercedes Foster, sorcerer, healer, and handweaver."

Foster was all legs and arms and clouds of wiry gray hair—like a bright-eyed bird with handwoven plumage.

"Pleased to meet you," Jonah said politely, nodding to Mercedes. Thinking, This is a waste of time. Why should we come here and beg these people for acceptance?

"How did Natalie do at the clinic this summer?" Gabriel asked Mercedes.

"That girl is amazing," Mercedes said. "Especially when it comes to diagnosis. It's like she can see through a patient's skin and identify the problem. Send her back to me, please!"

Gabriel laughed. "Oh, no, that was just a loan. I need her at the Anchorage."

"Gabriel, if you have a minute, I have a question about a medicinal that I'm having trouble sourcing." The two sorcerers launched into a discussion of tinctures and extractions.

A sign had caught Jonah's eye: SWORDPLAY DEMON-STRATION—TRY YOUR HAND. Gabriel was still talking with Mercedes, so Jonah cut between two small tents to where a battered set of bleachers had been dragged alongside a fencing strip. Two fighters were going at it—a boy and a girl. Sweat ran down their faces and dripped off their bodies, spotting the piste as they thrust and parried, attacked and retreated. A small crowd of onlookers cheered them on, shouting advice, abuse, and encouragement.

The swords were not fencing blades; these were huge, heavy, and seemed to be of similar vintage to Jonah's Fragarach. But the two combatants handled them easily, and with deadly precision—as if they were an extension of their limbs. It was more of a dance than a battle. Each seemed to know where the other would be at any given moment.

Though the swords were edged, these fighters were not padded or armored; they were not wearing medieval dress at all, but had stripped down to shorts and T-shirts that showed off their muscular bodies.

"Come on, Jack!" someone shouted from the stands. "Wrap it up and give somebody else a chance."

Jonah circled the piste and sat down on the bleachers, next to a curvy girl with a mane of black curls and a wizard's glow. "Who are they?" he asked, nodding toward the fighters.

"Jack Swift and Ellen Stephenson," the girl said, without taking her eyes off the action. "You know, they're the ones who . . ." Her eyes fixed on Jonah, and her voice trailed off. "Oh—my—God. Where did YOU come from?"

"I'm from out of town," Jonah said.

"You are from *way* out of town," the wizardling breathed, her eyes alive with interest. She stuck out her hand. "I'm Leesha Middleton."

Jonah shook it with his gloved hand. "Jonah Kinlock. You were saying? About the fighters? Are they warriors, then?"

Leesha studied him, eyes narrowed. "Excuse me, but what guild are you in?"

"I'm undeclared," Jonah said. "I thought I'd try them all out first. Right now I'm thinking warrior." He nodded toward the sword fighters. "They don't seem all that serious about killing each other."

"Jack and Ellen? They're crazy in love with each other. Disgusting, if you ask me." She paused, and then continued in a low, brittle voice. "Anyway, haven't you heard? We're at peace. The Weir don't kill each other anymore."

Her grief stabbed at Jonah, fresh and hard-edged.

"I'm sorry for your loss," he blurted without thinking.

She blinked at him. "How did you—?"

"Lucky guess. Looks like they're finished."

Jack Swift and Ellen Stephenson were walking toward them, the swords safely stowed in their baldrics, arguing.

"I don't see how they could call it a draw," Ellen was saying. "I had you on the ropes, Jack."

"We were *supposed* to fight to a draw," Jack said, rolling his eyes. "Wasn't that the point? It was just an exhibition fight. It doesn't count."

"They *all* count," Ellen argued.

"I'm fine with a draw," Jack said, sliding out of his harness and setting his sword down on a blanket on the sidelines. "Why can't you be?"

"You're fine because *you* were on pace to lose," Ellen said, shedding her sword also. "Let's get something to drink before we start the open tournament."

The two warriors walked toward the concession stand.

Jonah heard more raised voices, some kind of argument, spilling down on them from higher in the stands. Leesha twisted around to look, then swore under her breath. "It never stops." Pushing to her feet, she began to climb.

Jonah turned to look. Four mainliners—a man and three women—had converged on a young wizard and appeared to be berating him about something as Leesha charged in for the rescue.

Curious, Jonah loped up the bleachers until he was within hearing distance.

"We want to know what's going on with the investigation," one of the mainliners was saying. "It's been two weeks, and we've heard nothing."

"You'll be informed of any progress, Ms. Hudson," the wizard said, raking one hand through his tumble of curls. "Ms. Middleton and Ms. Foster update me regularly." He nodded at Leesha, who'd entered the target zone.

"You should be updating *us*," Hudson said, turning her fire on Leesha. "*We're* the parents. *We're* the ones who—"

"Did you have a specific question, Ms. Hudson?" Leesha asked, her voice rich with snark.

"Who approved the field trip to Cleveland?" another parent demanded. "What were they thinking?"

"Ms. Morrison, that decision was made by the staff at the preschool," Leesha said. "For *some* reason, they thought the children would enjoy a concert at the aquarium." She paused for a beat. "I assume that you signed a permission slip?"

This is about the Flats, Jonah thought, skin prickling. That *would* be a hot topic here in Trinity.

"It should never have been allowed," Hudson fumed, turning on the young man. "You should have intervened, McCauley."

McCauley looked up, startled. "What? *I* should have intervened? I don't run the preschool. I have enough to do as is."

"The safety of our children should be your highest priority," Morrison said. "If you and Ms. Moss don't have time for that, then you need to delegate. My daughter Olivia was totally traumatized."

"From what I've heard, your daughter Olivia was totally a hero," Leesha said.

It took a few moments for Morrison to get her mouth running again. "Well, I must admit, Olivia does demonstrate natural leadership qualities; she takes after me in that regard. Certainly, in a time of crisis—"

"No doubt my son Alistair was of great comfort to the other children, too," Hudson broke in. "But I don't believe that defending against zombie attacks should be within any four-year-old's skill set."

"Zombies?" McCauley rolled his eyes. "That's the kind of talk that fans the—"

"Where is Madison Moss?" the man demanded. "Shouldn't she be here, in a time of crisis?"

"She's in school," McCauley said. "In Chicago. She'll be back in a week or two."

"If Ms. Moss wants to be in charge, she should *be* here," the man said.

"That's just it, Mr. Scavuzzo, she doesn't *want* to be in charge." McCauley turned away and pretended to focus on the field, which was difficult to do since nothing was happening.

Morrison leaned in, putting her face in front of McCauley's. "How was it that the children were so poorly supervised that they ended up on top of a bridge in the Flats?"

"That's what the investigation is for," McCauley said. "To find out what happened and who's responsible."

"It's *obvious* who's responsible," Hudson said. The other three parents nodded vigorously in support.

McCauley sighed. He seemed to already know the subtext. "Where's your proof? It doesn't make sense to spread rumors before we know what we're dealing with."

"It's suspicious that the children were found within a mile of Mandrake's school," Scavuzzo said.

Jonah stiffened.

"Not at all, since they were also within a mile of the aquarium," Leesha said.

"Really?" Scavuzzo sneered. "The preschool sponsors

field trips all the time without a problem. And yet, the first time they visit *that* neighborhood, our children are kidnapped. Who else could it be? We're not talking mainline magic here, after all. We're talking monsters."

"We may be talking monsters," Leesha said, "but it's not just a local problem."

"How do you know?" Morrison demanded.

Leesha bit her lip and turned away.

It's true, what Gabriel said, Jonah thought, resentment smoldering in his midsection. Mainliners blame us for everything.

"The fact is, they shouldn't put that kind of institution right in the middle of a city," Morrison said. "It should be in a remote area, where it doesn't present a danger to normal people."

"The Anchorage has been there for ten years," McCauley said. "There's never been a problem before. How can you—?"

"Just because we haven't heard about any problems doesn't mean there haven't been any," Hudson said. "Who knows what goes on there? I've seen photographs from Thorn Hill, and let me tell you, they were bloodcurdling."

McCauley stood up and said, "Look, this isn't really the time or place to discuss this, all right?"

"If not now, when?" Morrison sniffed.

"If you have a complaint, bring it to council," McCauley said. Turning his back on Morrison, he walked away.

"I'll tell you one thing, McCauley," Morrison shouted at his back. "I'm going to hold you personally responsible if anything happens to my daughter."

⊚ CHAPTER EIGHTEEN ⊚
INTERGUILD PLAY

After listening to that exchange, Jonah just wanted to go somewhere—anywhere—to get away from mainliners. Being a diplomat was harder than he'd thought.

He was thinking he'd go find Gabriel, but as he was descending from his vantage point in the bleachers, Jack Swift and Ellen Stephenson returned to the field and faced the stands.

"All right," Jack said. "Now it's time for the audience-participation part of the program. If you've ever wanted to try your hand at swordplay, now's your chance. No experience necessary."

Unable to resist, Jonah sat down again, in the far left seat in the bottom row, next to a young girl whose fine brown hair was scraped back into a ponytail. The girl stared at him with frank curiosity. A minute later, Leesha Middleton plopped down on his other side. "This is Grace Moss," Leesha said, pointing to the younger girl. "Madison Moss's little sister. She's here for school." Reaching across Jonah, she patted

Grace on the knee. "Quit staring, Grace," she said. "He's a little old for you."

"I'm not staring," Grace said, and shifted her gaze back to the field.

Go away, Jonah thought, glaring into space. I know what mainliners think of us.

When nobody spoke up, Ellen surveyed the crowd in the bleachers. "Come on, somebody step up and give it a go! Your pick, Jack or me."

"We'll be using blunted weapons," Jack said. "No worries."

The spectators avoided eye contact, staring down at the ground. After the show Jack and Ellen had put on, nobody wanted to take them on. A couple of audience members even slipped from their seats and slinked away, as if afraid they'd be called upon.

"How about two of you against one of us?" Jack suggested. "Or we can each pair up with someone, and then you won't be onstage by yourself." A haze of chatter rose over the crowd as people elbowed one another and tried to get their neighbors to volunteer.

"Are there two of you who would like to spar against each other?" Ellen persisted. "We could—you know—give pointers."

"Here's your chance," Leesha urged, leaning toward Jonah. "You can try out being a warrior." She paused and, when he sat in stony silence, added, "You look like you want to whack something."

He did, actually.

Before he could think, Jonah was up on his feet. "I'll give it a try," he said.

The crowd applauded madly, thrilled to be off the hook,

excited at the prospect of a new spectacle, mad with curiosity about the stranger in town.

Jack shook his hand and clapped him on the back. "Thank you, Mr.—"

"Kinlock," Jonah said, resisting the temptation to add, *Jonah Kinlock.*

"What's your pleasure, Kinlock?" Jack asked. "Me or Ellen?" He leaned in closer and said in a loud stage whisper, "I'll give you fair warning. She's ruthless. And she cheats."

The crowd hooted and catcalled.

Jonah tilted his head, pretending to be thinking. Finally, he shook his head. "I can't decide. Can I play both of you?"

Jack and Ellen looked at each other. "Um. Sure, if you're up for it," Ellen said, shrugging, "since no one else seems eager to play. Which one of us do you want to play first?"

"No. I meant both of you at once," Jonah said. "I don't think I'll have time to play you separately."

As the crowd exploded into laughter, Jonah removed his sweatshirt, revealing a tight-fitting T-shirt. This resulted in some oohing and aahing from the crowd. Leesha Middleton, for one, seemed delighted with this turn of events.

"You choose first," Ellen said generously, gesturing toward a dozen rebated weapons set out on a blanket. Jonah chose an English rapier, which was closest to the sword he was used to wielding.

"You're sure you want that one?" Ellen asked. "A heavier sword will wear you out quicker. And it may slow you down."

Jonah tried a few thrusts and parries. It might be heavier than the others, but it felt featherlight in his hand after Fragarach.

"I'm good with it," Jonah said. "Unless you want it."

He extended it toward her, hilt first.

Ellen shook her head. She and Jack chose rapiers as well.

"Can we ditch the piste?" Jonah asked, nudging the fencing strip with his toe. "And play the whole field?"

Jack and Ellen looked at each other. Jonah didn't have to read minds to know what they were thinking. Two on one, it would be to Jonah's advantage to narrow the field so that only one of them could come at him at a time. They probably thought he was a fool—or unschooled at best.

"If that's what you want," Jack said. He and Ellen rolled up the fencing strip and set it to one side.

The two warriors faced off with Jonah. "Do you want to just spar a little bit, get used to your weapon?" Ellen asked.

Jonah shook his head. "Let's do it," he said. "First blood, right?"

And the lopsided duel began.

Jonah soon realized that he'd been overconfident, taking on both warriors at once. He was accustomed to wielding his sword against shades and untried shadeslayer packs. While his ability to read intentions and his uncanny speed and agility gave him an edge, these two were better trained at swordplay. They were considerably more experienced than he was at fighting against somebody who fought back.

They probably practice together constantly, Jonah thought, leaping backward, arching his back to avoid Ellen's questing sword, then spinning to avoid a flank attack from Jack. Jack's momentum carried him past Jonah, but he nimbly evaded Jonah's quick thrust.

Jonah was all over the field, which, of course, the reason he'd asked for that change in the rules. It was too easy to get trapped on a narrow strip. This way, he could use his superior speed. At one point he literally leaped over the warriors' heads, landing on the other side.

"Do you have wings or what?" Jack grumbled.

"He's just like you," Ellen said, dabbing at a scratch on her cheek. "He won't stand still."

Despite the grumbling, Jonah could tell that the two warriors were having the time of their lives, taking a simple pleasure in the physical game. It was infectious—Jonah couldn't help joining in. Gradually, they developed a strategy to counter Jonah's strengths, scissoring in on him, trading off in order to tire him out. When Jack finally nailed him with a thrust to the left torso, Jonah was just as glad to concede rather than fight on.

Besides, he'd looked up to see Gabriel standing at one end of the bleachers. Scowling. It seemed that public sparring didn't fit in with Jonah's new role as diplomat.

The warriors, on the other hand, were practically giddy with joy. Not so much about the win, but about the play—the dance. Fighting was art to them, so different from Jonah's methodical butchery.

"Want to go three rounds?" Ellen asked, blotting sweat from her face with her sleeve. "Best two out of three?"

"You could play us one-on-one now," Jack suggested, grinning. "Or maybe find a partner." He scanned the crowd again for likely prospects.

"No, thank you," Jonah said, rolling his eyes. "I think I'll quit while I'm only one bout behind."

The crowd began to disperse, realizing that the fighting was over for the day. Soon it was just the three of them, clustered together, and Gabriel, at a distance, clearly waiting for Jonah to break away.

Ellen handed Jonah a bottle of water, which he drained at one go. She began gathering up gear, loading it into the back of an old Jeep, but Jack's sharp blue eyes were still fixed on Jonah. "You're gifted, I can tell that, but you're not exactly . . . readable," he said. "You're not a warrior, are you?"

At least Jack hadn't guessed enchanter right out of the gate.

Jonah shook his head. "Nope. Not a warrior."

When Jonah didn't elaborate, Jack tried again. "Where did you learn to fight? You have some great skills."

"I got most of my training at school. And, you know, by doing."

"Where do you go to school?" Jack asked.

"The Anchorage," Jonah said, lifting his chin, waiting for the inevitable reaction.

"The Anchorage!" Jack repeated, startlement crossing his face. He followed with the typical quick look-over. "But you . . . does that mean you—"

"I'm a Thorn Hill survivor," Jonah said. "I'm what we call a savant." He paused for a heartbeat, then added lightly, "Should I have disclosed that up front?"

Ellen had come up next to Jack and heard that last exchange. "Not to us," she said. "Jack's kind of a mongrel himself, and, let me tell you, he's not above using it to his advantage in a fight."

"Mongrel?" Jonah said. "What do you mean?" But neither one of them heard, intent on each other as they were.

"One time," Jack muttered. "Just that one time. When you were trying to kill me."

"If I were trying to kill you, Jack, you'd be dead," Ellen said sweetly.

"Hey!" Jonah shouted, louder than he intended. The two warriors swiveled to look at him. "What do you mean, mongrel?" he repeated.

"Jack's kind of a hybrid," Ellen said. "He was born a wizard, but had a warrior stone implanted. Which means he's a little bit nasty, but still has some redeeming qualities." She brushed her fingers over Jack's ripped pectorals.

"Is—is that common?" Jonah said, frustrated at his own ignorance.

"No," Jack said. "It's . . . unusual. Unique, you might say. I'm the only one."

"It's also a long story," Ellen said. "Listen, we have a sparring field set up in one of the city parks, and we work out several times a week. You could come join us. If you wanted to." She held out her phone. "Give me your cell number and I'll text you when something's happening."

Jonah hesitated, weighing Ellen's phone on his palm. A half hour ago, he'd wanted nothing more than to retreat into the safety of the Anchorage. But this might be an opportunity to learn more about the mainliners. Maybe even things Gabriel didn't want him to know.

The truth was . . . he *liked* the two warriors. He couldn't help himself.

"Please say yes," Ellen urged. "I'm tired of fighting the same-old same-old." She shot a glance at Jack. "In the interest of full disclosure, I should tell you that some of the warriors we play are dead, but if you're okay with that—"

"I'm okay with that," Jonah said, entering his cell number into Ellen's phone. "Actually, dead people are kind of my thing."

≪ CHAPTER NINETEEN ≫
KINLOCKS ON THE CASE

Late that night, Jonah went to see his brother. He often went to see Kenzie after the bars were closed and most of the stragglers had straggled off the street. When day-shift therapies were less likely to interfere.

The air was crisp and cold, and Jonah was glad he'd worn a hoodie under his leather jacket. Close to his destination, he stopped in at an all-night pizzeria he knew. He ordered a large deluxe pie with extra cheese and hoped it would stay warm until he got to Safe Harbor.

As usual, Kenzie heard him coming long before Jonah knocked.

"Hey, bro," Kenzie said. "Come on in."

When Jonah opened the door, Kenzie was sitting up in his wheelchair next to the window, his hands fluttering in his lap like panicked birds. He wore a red concert T-shirt, the only spot of color in the otherwise white-and-beige room.

Jonah set the pizza box on the broad window ledge. "I was afraid you might be in bed already."

"Nah. Just trying to outlast the white coats, as always," Kenzie said.

Jonah looked around the room. "So they're actually doing the minimal stimulation thing?"

"Yeah. They're trying to do me in—killing me with boredom. And all because I keep driving off my tutors."

"Well, if you'd stop setting things on fire," Jonah said. "They seem to find it off-putting."

"Wimps," Kenzie said.

Jonah plucked at Kenzie's brilliant T-shirt. "This your idea?"

Kenzie nodded. "Can we go out?"

"It's cold out," Jonah warned him, shedding his leather jacket.

"I don't care. I'm tired of being in a sensory-controlled environment. I really need some sensory input."

"Maybe after you eat."

Kenzie scowled. "There's no maybe. Only yes or no."

"Yes or no, then."

"Asshole," Kenzie said affectionately. "What'd you bring?"

"Deluxe from Bernini's."

"Did you bring me some lyrics?" Kenzie asked.

"What do you think? Got any tunes for me?"

"What do *you* think?" Kenzie said with breezy confidence. "I've got tunes that will rip your skin off."

Jonah dropped his backpack on Kenzie's bed and unzipped it. Pulling his MP3 player from the front pocket, he plugged in Kenzie's headphones. It took Kenzie a couple of tries to get them settled properly over his ears and find the play button. Jonah clenched his fists, resisting the temptation to help.

"Here's what I did with the last tab you sent me. If you like what you hear, I'll copy the files for you," Jonah said. It was a recording of Jonah singing, accompanying himself on the guitar.

Kenzie nodded, closing his eyes, losing himself in the music. Gradually, the frenetic movements slowed, then stopped entirely. His flexed muscles relaxed, his head dropped back, and he smiled dreamily.

That was how the music thing had started. Right after Thorn Hill, Kenzie had been severely psychotic—plagued with hallucinations, voices, seizures, and other kinds of brain misfires. The healers caring for him worried that the repeated seizures would damage his brain beyond repair.

Jonah had discovered that he could calm Kenzie's demons with music, especially when accompanied by Jonah's voice. He wished he could embrace his brother, wished they could share the comfort of touch. But he could only touch him through his voice and his presence. He didn't dare do more. Jonah had killed his sister with his terrible gift. He hoped he could somehow save his brother.

He rooted around in the small refrigerator, pulled out bottles of water, twisted free the caps, and set them on the window ledge next to the pizza. He dug two plates from the cabinet. Kenzie always ate more when Jonah joined him.

Setting his plate aside, Jonah sat down at Kenzie's workstation, bypassed the voice-recognition software, and opened the music folder. He moved two new poems into their shared folder. Once Kenzie read them, he'd scarcely need to look at them again. He had a photographic memory.

Jonah moved back to the window ledge, watching Kenzie, eyes closed, chewing thoughtfully. Kenzie opened his eyes and grinned at Jonah. "Good shit," he said, cheerfully profane. Yanking off the headphones, he reached out, grabbed another piece of pizza, and devoured half of it in one bite.

"Mose is here," Kenzie said. "Did you know?"

"He is?" Worry rippled through Jonah as he realized that he hadn't seen Mose Butterfield since the gig at Club Catastrophe. "Since when?"

"Yesterday. He's on five, back of the building. Natalie stopped in to see me after handling his admission."

"I need to go see him," Jonah said, recalling that Mose had wanted him to come over the night of the show at Club Catastrophe. One more item to add to the guilt list.

Jonah and Kenzie sat companionably, downing pizza, licking their fingers, and chugging water until the pizza was gone.

"Too bad," Jonah said, pulling a long face. "No leftovers." He stuffed the empty box into the wastebasket and cleared away the plates.

Kenzie blotted at his lips with his napkin. "I ate too much," he said.

"Maybe you should wear the headphones whenever you eat," Jonah said. "It might make it easier."

"How was the show?" Kenzie asked.

Jonah relayed what had happened at the club, and afterward, in the Flats.

"So you don't know what this Lilith has in mind?"

Jonah shook his head. "I'd like to know more about it, but Gabriel isn't interested." He paused, took a deep breath. "I have some good news. I should be around a lot more than before. I'm out of Nightshade."

"What?" Kenzie yanked the headphones away from his ears. "When did that happen?"

"A week ago."

Kenzie eyed him shrewdly. "Whose idea was it? Yours or Gabriel's?"

"Gabriel's, I guess," Jonah replied. "He wants me to spend more time with him. Learn the business."

"Which business? Music or medicine or mayhem?"

Jonah snorted. "Anyway, I should have more time to research on my own. I'd like to find out more about Lilith. She claims she was a sorcerer who died at Thorn Hill. I'd like to verify that, somehow, and also identify anyone who either left Thorn Hill right before the massacre or was there and survived it."

"Adults, you mean," Kenzie said.

"Right," Jonah said. "Sorcerers, especially. Gabriel thinks that someone at Thorn Hill collaborated with the Black Rose to poison the wells. It's a long shot, but I have to start somewhere. I want to generate a short list of suspects."

"I thought there were no adult survivors," Kenzie said.

"Yeah. That's what we've been told."

"Did you ask Gabriel?"

"He says there aren't any records from Thorn Hill here at school, but I'm not so sure. Would there be a way to check?"

"I don't have to check. There are all kinds of databases from the commune. Sorcerers are natural geeks. I used some of that info to track down Jeanette. Now, whether it will help us here, I don't know."

Kenzie frowned, thinking. He swiveled back toward his keyboard and slid his headset back into place. "Harry. Search THLIS databases," he said into the mouthpiece. He scanned the screen, then turned to Jonah. "Hmm. 'File not found.' It was just there a few weeks ago. Let me dig deeper. Nothing is ever totally deleted, know what I mean?"

"What site are you accessing?" Jonah asked. "How did you get into it?"

"The server is located somewhere here on campus. I can give you the IP address if you want, but it likely won't do you any good. Gabriel has a kick-ass data security system. I have to keep running to stay ahead of this one." Kenzie continued to murmur commands into the headset.

"Is there anything I can do?" Jonah asked.

"Get me a pop from the fridge," Kenzie said.

When Jonah returned with cans of pop, Kenzie was moving files around. "Got it. I'm going to copy all this over to a safe place so we make sure they don't disappear again."

"Can you tell when the files were removed?"

"Harry. Show info." Kenzie's eyes scanned over lines of data. "Looks like it was in the last couple weeks. I guess I could've compromised something when I was looking for Jeanette."

"Maybe," Jonah said.

Once he had the files where he wanted them, Kenzie rummaged through them.

"Harry. Scroll down. Search Thorn Hill work-share logs. Scroll down. Select October twenty-third week." He paused and, when the record came up, said, "Open spreadsheet, data entry view."

"What are the work-share logs?" Jonah whispered so Harry wouldn't overhear.

Kenzie hit mute on his second try. "Everyone at Thorn Hill was required to contribute work to the commune every week," he said. "They didn't tolerate slackers. They weren't good about keeping track of comings and goings, but they were sticklers about work records. These are the last sets before the massacre. By comparing the work schedule with the casualty lists, we should be able to identify anyone who was at Thorn Hill immediately prior to the massacre, but who doesn't show up on either the casualty or survivor lists. Now, what's this sorcerer's name?"

"Lilith Greaves."

Kenzie turned back to his screen. "Harry. Search THLIS databases. Scroll down. Select casualty lists. Select survivor lists. Open work sheet. Data sort on last name."

Through this process, Kenzie verified that a sorcerer named Lilith Greaves was at Thorn Hill immediately prior to the massacre, and showed up on the dead list after.

"Can you tell what kind of work she did for the commune?"

"She worked in the compounding labs, apparently. Making either weapons or health and beauty aids, depending on who you ask." He paused. "Here's another Greaves. A six-year-old girl who worked in the vegetable garden."

"Lilith said she lost a daughter in the massacre," Jonah said. So far, this all seemed to verify what Lilith had said.

Now Kenzie generated a list of four adults who were on the work-share lists immediately before the massacre who didn't appear on either the survivor or casualty list.

Jonah scanned the list. None of the names was familiar.

Then they worked their way through the four names, three men and a woman. Three were repeatedly honored in subsequent memorial services at the Anchorage and elsewhere. The fourth, Tyler Greenwood, a sorcerer, was not.

Three of the names continued to appear for a time in legal and probate records, child custody proceedings, obituary listings, and cemetery records. Then they dwindled away. The fourth, Tyler Greenwood, did not appear at all. He vanished, digitally speaking, after the massacre. His name didn't appear in Social Security death records, online obituaries, any of that.

"Well," Jonah said. "It *was* a major disaster. Maybe he just got overlooked somehow."

Kenzie frowned. "People don't just vanish. These days they live on, digitally, anyway. As you can see, there's always a bit of a backwash, even if they're dead." He flipped back to the work-share records. "He was a musician," Kenzie said. "Some of his work shares had to do with that. He also did general maintenance and worked in the labs and the gardens. From what I can tell, he wasn't at Thorn Hill very long." He narrowed his eyes, a predator on the hunt. "I'll just go backward in time until I find him."

Jonah's mind drifted, his brother's voice a reassuring buzz in his ears.

"Search Google for Tyler Greenwood. . . . Scroll down. . . . Search Google for music and Tyler Greenwood."

When had he last slept well? Jonah wondered. He couldn't remember. . . .

"Jonah."

Jonah startled awake. "What?"

"I'm finding a Tyler Greenwood, a musician who was in and out of a number of rock-and-roll and blues bands," Kenzie said. "He was based in Memphis. Here's a photo from, um, fifteen years ago."

Jonah leaned toward the screen. It was a promotional

photo for a rock-and-roll band. Tyler Greenwood had a bass guitar resting on his hip, the head pointed toward the floor. He looked to be twenty-something, handsome. Probably biracial.

"He continued to show up in records here in the States until about ten years ago. He must have gone back and forth to the commune, if it's the same man."

"Nothing since the massacre, then," Jonah said, his heart sinking.

"Don't give up yet," Kenzie said. "Harry. Search Tennessee vital records."

The next thing Jonah knew, Kenzie was crowing.

"What?" Jonah rubbed his eyes.

"Tyler Greenwood was married to someone named Gwyneth Hart," Kenzie said. "What do you think of that?"

"Really? How do you know?"

"It was in the vital records. Here's a newspaper article." Kenzie turned the display so Jonah could see it.

It was from the society pages of a community newspaper. *Garrett and Samantha Hart of Shaker Heights and Miami Beach held a reception to celebrate the marriage of their daughter, Gwyneth Marie, to Tyler Greenwood, of Memphis. The couple married in a private ceremony. Ms. Hart coordinates humanitarian projects. Mr. Greenwood is a professional musician.*

And there they were—the handsome young musician from the band photo and a pale-haired beauty at a fancy party.

"Search the work records for Gwyneth Hart and Gwyneth Greenwood," Jonah suggested.

Kenzie did as asked. She wasn't there.

"So Tyler Greenwood went to Thorn Hill. But Gwyneth

Hart didn't," Kenzie concluded. "Maybe Tyler Greenwood is our man. But he's disappeared."

"If he was involved in the poisoning, then he had a reason to disappear," Jonah said. He yawned and stretched.

Kenzie didn't reply. He was frowning at the display. "I have a Tyler Greenwood, listed as a son of a Sonny Lee Greenwood, recently deceased in Memphis."

That brought Jonah sharply awake. "What? Let me see that."

It was a newspaper story, dated mid-July, headlined BEALE STREET MOURNS LOCAL LUTHIER. Displayed beneath the headline was an undated photograph of four musicians jamming at what was identified as a local blues club.

According to the article, Sonny Lee Greenwood, musician and builder of custom guitars, had died from a fall in his shop. Some of his friends suspected foul play, but the police had found no proof of that. His only son, Tyler Greenwood, was listed in the death notice as having predeceased Sonny Lee. One unnamed granddaughter survived.

"I guess that settles that," Jonah said.

Kenzie shook his head. "It doesn't smell right. If Tyler Greenwood had a surviving father and a daughter, he wouldn't have just disappeared from the records when he died. There'd be an obituary, and paperwork. If there's a daughter, she'd be getting Social Security death benefits, and like that."

"How do you *know* this stuff?" Jonah asked.

Kenzie flashed him a smile. "Mind if I dig deeper on this?" he asked. "I've got time."

"Be my guest," Jonah said, trying to keep a spark of hope alive.

Kenzie found a handful of other news stories, mostly

summaries of the elder Greenwood's life and contribution to the music scene. Kenzie surfaced a bit of video from a Memphis television station, apparently taken at Greenwood's funeral. The reporter spoke with several blues musicians who had attended the wake. No family was mentioned.

Kenzie searched for the Harts, and found that they'd been killed in a private plane crash in Belize years ago.

"People around Tyler Greenwood are dropping like flies," Jonah murmured.

"Here's something," Kenzie said. "Somebody put up a tribute site for Sonny Lee Greenwood and posted a message saying that his business, Studio Greenwood, had relocated out of state. There's a link to a Web page . . . see?"

It was a simple page with a few images of gorgeous custom guitars and testimonials from customers. And a headline: NORTHEAST OHIO'S SOURCE FOR CUSTOM GUITARS AND REPAIR.

There was an e-mail address but no street address.

"Northeast Ohio?" Kenzie muttered. "What are the chances of that?"

"How could his business have relocated if he's dead?" Jonah said.

"Maybe he had a partner." Kenzie scooted back in his chair. "Here, send an e-mail."

Jonah bypassed Harry, clicked on the link, and typed, *What would it cost to reset the frets on a vintage Yamaha acoustic? I'm in the Cleveland area. Where are you located? Can you send me your street address so I can map it? Do you have standard hours?*

Though it was four in the morning, the answer came back promptly, listing the price estimate (subject to change). *I'm in Cleveland Heights. We can meet at the Innovation Center at the Library. Evenings and weekends are best. Give me at least a day's notice and bring the guitar with you.* And it listed the address of the library.

"Cleveland Heights!" Jonah swiveled to look at Kenzie. "It's moved to Cleveland Heights?" Cleveland Heights was just a few miles to the east.

He turned back to the keyboard. *I'll need a business address, too. I can't just hand off my guitar at a library.*

There was a longer wait this time, and then Studio Greenwood replied with an address, also in Cleveland Heights.

"Let me search on that address and see what's there," Kenzie said. "Harry . . . search white pages for this address." When the result came up, he looked over at Jonah. "This house is owned by someone named Tyler Boykin. Coincidence? I think not."

"You think Tyler Boykin and Tyler Greenwood are the same person?"

"Let's make sure. Harry . . . search images for Tyler Boykin," Kenzie said.

Several photos came up, most taken at one club venue or another. They were all of the man they already knew as Tyler Greenwood. Only older.

Jonah and Kenzie stared at the screen for a long moment.

"That's him," Jonah said. "That's Tyler Greenwood. Only now his name is Boykin. Wonder why he'd change his name."

"There are lots of reasons somebody might do that," Kenzie said. "Boykin could be a professional name."

"Why did the obit list him as dead?" Jonah said. "If he'd been a partner in his father's shop, I'd think people would know better."

"Or . . . he could have something to hide," Kenzie speculated. "Do you think this might be the person we want?" He lifted his eyebrows inquiringly.

Jonah felt hope flare brighter. "Maybe," he said.

"Harry. Web search on Tyler Boykin," Kenzie said.

Compared with "Tyler Greenwood," "Tyler Boykin" was easy to find. Kenzie found him on music sites, in concert listings, on a listing of session musicians. He even found a photograph of him, onstage in New York three years ago, sitting in with a blues band. When he and Jonah compared the photographs of the two men, there could be no doubt. They were the same person.

Tyler Greenwood had transformed into Tyler Boykin, right after Thorn Hill.

"What are you going to do?" Kenzie asked.

"I haven't quite decided," Jonah said. "I'll go have a talk with Boykin, I guess." He paused. "If you see Gabriel, don't mention anything about our little project."

"Going rogue, are you?" Kenzie cocked his head. "Just be careful. If Tyler Boykin is our man, he doesn't want to be found."

"I'm always careful," Jonah said. Light was leaking in through the windows, and the racket now emanating from the hallway told them that the day shift was coming on.

"I have to go," Jonah said, packing up. "I'll see if I can work up some lyrics for the new tunes."

"So we're not going out?" Kenzie said, unable to hide his disappointment.

"Not today. Soon. Right now I've got classes."

"You know, big brother, you really need to start setting things on fire," Kenzie said. "Nobody makes you go to class. People tend to leave you alone." He smiled wistfully, and Jonah felt a twinge of guilt.

CHAPTER TWENTY
BACKDOOR MAN

The Boykin house was the shabbiest one on a leafy street in an older neighborhood. The yard was overgrown in some places, down to bare dirt in others.

Hmm, Jonah Kinlock thought. Usually, sorcerers couldn't resist using a little magic to enhance the appearance of their gardens. Find the most beautiful garden in any city, it's a good bet that a sorcerer lived there.

So . . . did that mean that Tyler Boykin wasn't a sorcerer after all?

Still, instinct told Jonah that his quarry was finally within reach. Well, that and the name on the mailbox: BOYKIN. He hoped that Greenwood/Boykin would be willing to answer his questions. Hoped that, after all this time, he'd have useful information he'd spill without hard interrogation. Maybe he'd be eager to tell his story. Jonah could hope.

Jonah was good at killing. Killing was clean. Killing was

simple. Killing was sometimes necessary, but it didn't have to be painful. Still, he was growing weary of it. He didn't much like the thing he was best at.

But if Tyler Greenwood Boykin was the sorcerer who'd helped Black Rose wizards plot the massacre at Thorn Hill . . . if he were the one who created the poison that had ended or ruined so many lives, then maybe he deserved to die. But first, Jonah needed information. If Boykin had information that would help Kenzie and Alison and everyone else at the Anchorage, Jonah needed to obtain it.

Then again, Tyler Boykin might be just another innocent victim of Thorn Hill. The only adult survivor. Or someone lucky enough to have left right before the disaster, who changed his name so death didn't come calling.

Jonah flexed his shoulders, feeling Fragarach's reassuring weight. The sword might pry free some answers if all else failed. The Answerer, it was called. It was impossible to lie with Fragarach at your throat.

Jonah was so focused on the mission that he didn't realize he was in danger until it was almost too late. A whisper of sound behind him was what saved him. Instinctively, he dove sideways, feeling the cold wake of the creature's charge brush past him, hearing the clatter of claws on the sandstone pavers of the garden path.

Claws?

Jonah rolled to his feet, Fragarach already in his hand. All around the yard, spotlights kindled, flooding the garden with light. Motion detectors, no doubt. Two shades faced him across some hydrangea bushes, a man and a woman. In the dark, they could have passed for ordinary, except for the five-inch, razor-sharp claws that sprouted from their hands.

"So . . . let me guess," Jonah said. "You work for Greenwood?"

"We work for Lilith," the man said. "We followed you here from downtown."

Jonah felt a prickle of unease. Even focused as he was now, there was very little scent. The host corpses of these shades were remarkably well preserved—no visible decay or stench of decomposing flesh.

This is what we're facing from now on. Besieged at home, under attack out in the field. With no refuge from the ongoing war. Jonah could see why Gabriel always insisted on keeping their head-quarters and their mission a secret.

Jonah feinted to the left, then charged right, putting the more substantial barrier of a stone bench between him and his pursuers.

"And you're here because . . . ?"

"Lilith wants to see you."

"It's really not a good time," Jonah said. "Could we set up something for next week?"

"She wants to see you now," the man said.

"All right," Jonah said, thinking fast, buying time. "Just let me—"

A long arm snaked forward, and a claw raked across his chest, ripping through his sweatshirt, drawing blood. Only his quick leap backward saved him from being disembow-eled. Though Jonah answered quickly, the shade managed to evade his counterthrust.

"What the hell was that?" Jonah demanded. "I thought Lilith wanted to see me."

"Lilith wants you alive," the woman said. "We aren't that

fussy. She warned you, didn't she? She warned you to stop murdering us."

"We're looking forward to seeing how you'll fare as a shade," the man said. "Don't look for a warm welcome from some of us."

Thus began a nearly silent, macabre dance around the overgrown garden, Jonah's breath pluming out in the chilly air, the only sound the crackle of leaves, the rattle of claws, and Fragarach whistling through the air.

Focus, Jonah thought. These are shades. They are quick, and smart, and they don't feel pain.

That last part, at least, made his job easier.

Finally, he circled behind a small shed, leaped over the top, and landed behind the two shades. He cut one of them in half before either of them could get his body turned around.

Howling, the other shade charged forward, leaving herself open to Jonah's two-handed swipe. When she went down, the now-disembodied shades fled. Jonah considered pursuing them, but as he'd said, it wasn't a good time.

"Tell Lilith to leave me alone!" he called softly after them as they dissolved into the night.

Jonah wiped his blade on the grass, hurdled a boxwood hedge, and landed in the deeper dark next to the house. There he waited, watching to see if more shades appeared, listening to find out whether anyone inside had noticed the lights ablaze in the garden.

Though the exterior was well lit, much of the interior was dark, with no sudden activity suggesting that an alarm had been sounded. The shades were drawn, but light leaked from the living room windows and Jonah could hear music, amped up loud, the heavy thud of bass.

According to the online city directory, Boykin lived alone.

Gabriel's rule was: no witnesses. So Nightshade operations would never be tied to the Anchorage. Maybe that didn't really matter anymore, but still . . . old habits die hard.

Jonah pulled out the close-fitting black ski mask he'd brought along and yanked it down over his face. He didn't want to have to kill Tyler Boykin if he were an innocent man.

For an innocent man, Boykin had a top-of-the-line security system. It took Jonah precious time to disable it.

Jonah entered through a basement window. After a quick visual check, he slid through, feetfirst, twisting to force his shoulders through the narrow opening. He landed in near darkness, in a fighting stance, breathing in the scent of mold and old paper, fresh sawdust and shellac. Then pulled his sword in after him.

The light from the window dimly illuminated the room he was in. It was a woodshop, with a workbench at one end, a Peg-Board with tools hung in neat rows. Wood shavings littered the floor, and sawdust coated everything. Jonah fought back a sneeze.

Large table-mounted tools lined one wall. Jonah didn't know much about woodworking, but he recognized the lathe and the band saw. Lengths of fine woods hung in racks along the wall or stood in bins by the door. Was this Studio Greenwood's new digs?

Light seeped under a door to his right, and muted sound. Somebody was working late in the basement.

Jonah soft-footed it to the door and cracked it open, noticing the thick padding on the inside. His hand tightened on the hilt of his sword as he eased the door open and peered in.

It wasn't Tyler Boykin at all. It was a girl.

She sat on a tall stool, half turned away from him, head bent over her work, so he couldn't see her face. She was tuning a guitar, swearing under her breath. Her hair was the color of scorched caramel, thick and wavy, tied back with a bandanna, her skin three shades lighter. She wore stained jeans, work boots, and a plaid flannel shirt two sizes too big.

Jonah searched for a Weirstone and found one, but his read on it had the muddled, diffuse quality he associated with savants.

A savant? Here? This wasn't in the script.

Three unfinished guitars stood in stands, glued and clamped up. Posters of old blues singers lined the walls.

Her flat-top acoustic, he could see, had a sound-hole pre-amp installed. It was feeding into a mixer and then into a laptop on her workbench. What kind of guitar was it? The letters *SG* were blazoned on the fingerboard. He didn't recognize the brand.

The girl twisted the tuning keys, plucked at the strings. Out of tune. Angry, discordant notes struck Jonah's ears, nearly bringing him to his knees. His stomach churned, and he thought his head would split open. Another quick adjustment, and the notes that now cascaded from the instrument were perfectly in tune. Aligned like stars in a perfect universe.

She leaned forward, reaching for a flat pick on the workbench, and Jonah got his first good look at her face.

Her profile was less than classic: high cheekbones, her nose a bit overlarge for the rest of her face, lush lips, bottomless brown eyes. She was beautiful, and yet there was something feral about her, something enchantingly off-key.

Hardwired wild.

Recognition flamed through him. He'd seen her before . . . but where?

And then it came to him. She was Emma, the pool-shark savant from Club Catastrophe. But what was she doing in Tyler Greenwood's basement? Did she work for him? Had the sorcerer sent her to Club Catastrophe for a reason?

She began to play, bending her head over the fingerboard, eyes closed, silently moving her lips the way guitarists sometimes do. In that instant, Jonah was lost.

He had never heard music like this. It sluiced over him, carrying away every troubled thought, filling his heart with hope and joy. He forgot everything: the sorcerer upstairs, the mission, his own imperfection, and the shame and bitterness that came with it. Jonah listened, the music dripping into him like a mainline drug, until the song was over.

He rested his forehead against the doorframe. He wished he could leave her be. There was no need for this girl— whoever she was—to be involved in what was about to happen. With any luck, between the soundproofing and her own music, he could escape without her hearing a thing.

But leaving now would violate a cardinal rule of these operations: Secure the premises first. Avoid any nasty surprises.

Jonah took a breath. Let it out.

And pushed the door open, all the way.

Emma heard her father's step on the stairs. "Are you down here again, Emma?"

"I never left," she said. "I'll come up pretty soon. I need to let these set up a bit anyway." She surveyed the guitars, lined up in stands against the wall—the first she'd produced in her new shop. They weren't really guitars, yet—just tops and bottoms of maple and spruce, bookmatched and joined, then glued up and clamped. They didn't have their songs in them yet, as Sonny Lee liked to say. Used to say.

"You do beautiful work," Tyler said, now from the foot of the stairs. "And you have a great hand with the guitar. Your grandpa would be proud of you."

"He *was* proud of me," Emma said. *This is the first thing— the only thing—I've ever been good at.*

Tyler sat down on the third step, dropping his hands between his knees as if he didn't quite know what to do with them. Emma knew she still made him nervous, but she just wasn't sure what to do about it. "Didn't you say you had some algebra homework?" he said finally.

"Come *on*, now, it's Friday *night*." Forcing away the memory of other Friday nights, Emma lifted the Oscar Schmidt Galiano twelve-string from its stand, and propped a foot on Sonny Lee's stool. She brushed her fingers over the steel strings, and they harmonized—bold, bright, and brassy like a church choir.

Her fingers found the familiar chords of "Don't You Lie to Me." At least she could play the blues—the appropriate sound track for her life right now. All she had to look forward to was month after month of failure.

It just seems like there ought to be a place I fit into, where I can be myself.

She needed a world without so many standards and restrictions and expectations—one more friendly to a girl who thought differently from other people. I need a world with a frontier, Emma thought. A wilderness I can go to, when I need it.

For a while, that frontier had been Memphis. It was a world she fit into, cradled by the call and response of twelve-bar blues. But it had turned out to be a world with no future.

"Emma," Tyler said, bringing her back to now. "Algebra?"

"I'm sorry," Emma whispered. "I could give up all my Friday nights to algebra, but I don't know that it would make a difference. It's just gibberish to me. You've put a lot of time in, and I have, and it seems like I work harder than anybody else, but—"

"No," her father said. "*I'm* sorry. When you're young, you don't think about anybody but yourself. You think the usual rules don't apply to you. You do things that you regret for the rest of your life. Your mama and I . . . we . . ." And then he stopped, as he always did, never quite finishing the apology.

He's not talking about me, Emma thought. He's talking about himself. Was he sorry he'd turned his only child over to Sonny Lee for raising? Because now she and Tyler were all but strangers. Maybe if she'd had a more regular kind of childhood, she wouldn't feel like a fish out of water all the time.

Tyler stood. "All right, Emma, I'll leave you be. I need to get some practice in for tomorrow night. But don't stay up too late, even if it's Friday night. Get some sleep, and tomorrow, I want you to at least give that homework a try. I'm gonna try to do better than I have done. Just don't *ever* think I'm disappointed in you." He rested a hand on her shoulder for a moment, then slowly, wearily, clumped up the stairs.

Emma kept playing until the sound of her father's steps receded. For a long moment, she rested her cheek in the curve of the guitar, feeling the sweet, nonjudgmental kiss of lacquered wood. Thinking about Friday nights in Memphis in the steamy summertime.

She heard the music start up again upstairs, the visceral thud of Tyler's bass guitar. Knowing Tyler, he'd be at it for a while.

Emma settled the Galiano back into its stand. Slipping down from the stool, she crossed the workshop, unlatched a case, and lifted out another guitar.

This one wasn't vintage. This one she'd made the previous summer—one of two she still owned that were entirely her work. The other two she'd sold through Sonny Lee's shop under the label Studio Greenwood, since she didn't want anyone to mistake them for authentic Greenwoods. Sonny Lee's guitars commanded prices of thousands of dollars, and she was just getting started.

Sonny Lee's maker's mark was an elaborate G inlaid in ebony and mother-of-pearl on the fret board. Emma had come up with her own logo—a simple S and G, block letters, burned into the head.

She retuned into an open G, plugged into her workshop amp, and played, pouring her frustration into the music. Head bent, eyes closed, she played, chewing on the notes the way the old blues guitarists did, ripping off bits of herself and putting them into the music. Spilling it all.

When she looked up again, the door to the dirty room was open.

A boy stood in the doorway—or maybe a man—wearing a mask, a hooded sweatshirt, and jeans. From his black leather gloves to his black boots, every inch of skin was covered, save the upper part of his face. It was almost as if he were trying to hide in his clothes.

And yet . . . somehow she knew that she'd seen him before. It was more the effect he had on her than anything about his appearance. It was like he gave off a scent that made her want to run headlong into trouble.

He stood, framed in light, like a saint in a medieval painting. But anybody who breaks into your basement in black leather and a mask is no saint.

You should be afraid, said the practical voice in her head. *You should be screaming. Or running.* But Emma did neither of those things. She sat, transfixed, as he stalked, catlike, across the room toward her. Though he was broad-shouldered and muscular, he moved with a dancer's grace. Up close, she saw something poking up over his shoulder. The hilt of a massive sword.

He wasn't looking at her, though. He was looking at her guitar.

"I've never heard a guitar like that before," he said, running long fingers over the binding. There was a player's knowledge in his touch. "Is it custom work?"

Emma looked down at the guitar, resting across her knees, as if she'd never seen it before. Fingered the maker's mark on the head, the *S* and *G*. And could not speak to save her life.

A masked boy had broken into her basement with a sword. Apparently so he could talk about guitars.

She looked up at his face again. About all she could see were his eyes, but his eyes were enough.

This boy actually *looked* at her. *Looked* and *knew* and didn't judge. A fragile thread of connection shimmered between them. It was that, and his voice, more than his physical beauty, that drew her in. In fact, she couldn't *see* his physical beauty, but she knew it was there, under his clothes.

Under. His. Clothes. Warmth rushed into Emma's cheeks. "Do I know you?" she whispered.

"No," he said quickly. "You don't. And you don't want to." He studied the guitar, as if to memorize every detail.

Emma wished he would look at her in that hungry way.

"The guitar," he said softly. "Where did you get it?"

"I built it," she said, running her fingers over the mirror-like finish.

"You built it," he repeated, shaking his head. He glanced around the shop. "I guess I should have figured that out. Are there more like it?"

"I've made four," Emma said. "I've sold two of them."

"What are you *doing* here?"

"I *live* here," she said, the spell he'd spun fraying a bit. "What are *you* doing here?"

"But . . . you're a savant," he said.

"A *what?*" This boy was just about as ADD as she was. But somehow she just kept right on answering his questions.

"Who else is here?" he asked.

"My father," Emma said, apprehension raising the hair on the back of her neck.

"What's your name?"

"Emma Greenwood."

"Tyler Greenwood is your father?" He said it like that was the worst news possible.

"Well," Emma said, "he goes by Boykin now."

His shoulders slumped, picking up weight.

He doesn't want to hurt me, Emma thought. He doesn't. He doesn't. But he's going to hurt me anyway.

"What's *your* name?" Emma said.

He hesitated, a fraction of a second. Then said, "Zorro." His eyes had fixed on the guitar again.

"Are you here to steal a guitar or what?" she asked bluntly.

"Steal a . . . ? No." He shook his head. "But . . . may I give it a try?" he asked, almost shyly.

Mutely, she extended it toward him. He took it, flipped it around, and rested one foot on the cross brace of Emma's stool. Fitting his fingers onto the frets, he brushed his other hand across the strings. Sound rippled out, like water over stone, sweeping her along. She spun helplessly in its current, unable to gain footing. He played a few riffs—bits of rock-and-roll standards. Then a haunting instrumental Emma hadn't heard before.

When he'd finished, he closed his eyes, shivering, savoring each note as it died away.

"It's like sex, isn't it?" Emma said, her mouth, as always, running ahead of good sense. She clapped both hands over her mouth, too late.

For a moment, the joy faded from his eyes. Then he laughed. "Yes," he said. "It's just like sex."

Desperate to change the subject, Emma said, "What was that last piece? I've never heard it."

"My brother wrote it," the boy said, handing back the guitar.

"Well, he has a gift."

"He does." The boy nodded, his expression softening into unguarded love.

This boy would not hurt me. This boy could never hurt me.

"I never saw anybody play guitar with gloves on before." Emma set the guitar aside, on the workbench.

"I like to challenge myself."

"You going to tell me why you're here, or not?" Maybe it was a risky thing to ask, but she couldn't stand the suspense anymore.

Zorro winced. "Right," he said. Digging in his pocket, he pulled out a bundle of cording and a pair of handcuffs. "I'm so sorry," he said. "The thing is, I'm going to have to tie you up."

Well, that broke the spell for sure.

"Oh, no," Emma said, sliding off the stool, both feet hitting with a thud. "You don't." She ran for the stairs, but the boy moved impossibly fast, easily intercepting her.

He caught her about the waist, pulling her back against him, speaking low and fast, his breath warm on her neck. "I won't hurt you, Emma, I promise I won't hurt you. Just let me do this." His voice was like Southern Comfort—smooth and sweet and just as potent. As he talked, he turned her so she faced the wall, bringing her hands behind her back with the ease of long practice.

He's done this before, Emma thought, her head swimming. He's one of those serial killers. The kind that sweet-talk you into opening your door.

He kept right on talking. "I wish I didn't have to do this, but this is the best way to make sure you don't get hurt. I just need a little uninterrupted time with your father."

She wanted to float on the current of that voice, like a chip of wood in a river at flood.

I need to find a way to stop it.

Emma slammed her head back, shooting up from the balls of her feet, feeling a satisfying crunch as her skull hit his nose. His voice stopped, his iron grip relaxed, and she ripped free, hurling herself toward the stairs.

She stumbled, though, and he caught her before she got there and dragged her back, into the dirty room, one gloved hand over her mouth, pressing her tightly against his body to prevent any further head-butting. He pushed her to the floor next to the band saw, trying to pin her with one hand, but she rolled onto her back, gouged at his eyes, ripped at his mask, kneed him in the groin—used every street-fighting trick she knew to hurt him all while he seemed to be doing his best to get her tied up without hurting her.

She screamed bloody murder, too. Likely Tyler couldn't hear her with his music going, but it did dilute Zorro's voice a little.

In the end, she lay on her side on the basement floor, her

cheek in the sawdust, breathing in that familiar scent, hands bound together behind her, feet bound, too, and handcuffed to the leg of the band-saw table, enraged and still swearing.

Was this what Tyler had been so worried about? Had she somehow brought trouble straight to her father's door after all this time?

"What do you want with Tyler?" Emma demanded while Zorro was still fussing with the cords. "What are you going to do to him? You'd better not hurt him."

Zorro's hands stopped moving. "I don't want to hurt him," he said, sitting back on his heels. "I don't plan to."

"Then promise me you won't," Emma said.

"Can you breathe okay? Are you reasonably comfortable?" Zorro asked. He wasn't nearly as charming now that he had her tied up.

"Promise me," Emma repeated, tears stinging her eyes.

"Hopefully this won't take too long," Zorro said. He stood and left, closing the door softly behind him.

CHAPTER TWENTY-TWO
MELEE

Jonah mounted the stairs, already dogged by misgivings. He'd wanted this rogue operation to be clean and uncomplicated, and already it was getting messy. There was no longer a clear win to be had, here. If Greenwood knew something, Emma would pay a price. If he didn't, well, Jonah was back where he started.

But now that he was on this path, he had to follow through. He'd risked a lot already, and he needed to come away with something, or this visit would only send Greenwood on the run again.

A wall of sound hit him when he opened the basement door—music, amped up high. It struck Jonah that Greenwood might be jamming with his band. That would be just his luck.

Jonah followed the sound, through the kitchen lined with ancient appliances, the sink piled high with unwashed dishes. Through the dining room and down the center hall to the back of the house.

Jonah found his quarry in the living room, jamming with himself, filling in the bass track alongside some vintage rhythm and blues. The Rolling Stones.

Jonah watched for a moment. Greenwood was a decent bass player, all right, so that wasn't just some kind of cover story.

Jonah ghosted forward. He was halfway across the room when Greenwood looked up and saw him. The bass guitar cut off abruptly, though the other tracks played on. In one smooth movement, Greenwood set down the guitar and came up with a pistol, pointing it at Jonah.

The sorcerer studied Jonah through narrowed eyes. Then he chuckled softly. "You're sure not who I expected," he said.

"Who did you expect?"

"Not you," Greenwood said. He paused. "Do you always bring a big old sword to a shooting match?"

"I didn't know it was a shooting match," Jonah said. "You always pack a pistol when you practice?"

"This neighborhood ain't what it used to be," Greenwood said. "What are you, some kind of ninja warrior or something?"

"Something," Jonah said. He could tell by Greenwood's puzzled expression that *something* wasn't adding up. "You're wondering about my Weirstone," he said. "Sort of broken, isn't it? Muddy, some people call it. Does it remind you of someone?" He paused, took a chance. "*Emma*, maybe?"

Everything changed. Greenwood went ashy gray, radiating a mix of love and fear of loss. His eyes flicked to the floor, as if he could look through to the workshop below, then back up at Jonah. The barrel of the gun drifted a little.

He really loves her, Jonah thought.

The gun steadied, Greenwood's face hardened, and he

took a step forward. "Who the hell *are* you?"

"I'm one of those so-called Thorn Hill survivors," Jonah said, looking into Greenwood's eyes. "I have some questions for you."

"I got *nothing* to say about Thorn Hill," Greenwood said.

"Please," Jonah said, increasing the persuasive pressure. "Put the gun down. I don't want to hurt you, and I won't if I don't have to. But I will have answers."

Greenwood hit the volume button, cranking up the Stones to teeth-rattling levels. "Don't try and charm me!" he shouted. "I'm not falling for that shit." Jonah raised both hands in surrender, and Greenwood cut the volume back to a less earsplitting volume. Still loud enough to make persuasion difficult.

"Who sent you?" Greenwood demanded. "Who else knows you're here?"

"I'm not here to blow your cover or expose you," Jonah said. "I'm just trying to save some people I care about."

"So am I," Greenwood said grimly. "Now I want you to turn around, put your hands on your head, and walk ahead of me, into the conservatory." He gestured with the gun.

Unlike Wylie, he didn't even tell me to drop my weapon, Jonah thought. Reason being, he's not going to question me, he's going to kill me.

Jonah walked ahead, pausing in the doorway of the conservatory. Glassed-in room, stone floor, with inset drains to catch any spilled water. He wants to kill me in a place where cleanup is easy. Who thinks of that?

Someone who's done this before.

Jonah lunged sideways, then turned and charged at Greenwood. The sorcerer fired, and he must've been a quicker, more accurate shot than Wylie, because he got off three shots before Jonah slammed the gun away. It went spinning back into the living room. A searing pain in Jonah's side said he'd been hit—at least once.

Greenwood could have run, but he didn't. Instead, he attacked, pitching them both through the doorway, landing hard on the stone floor of the sunroom. The sorcerer was strong and wiry, and fought with a ferocity born of desperation. Given that and the distraction of the wound in his side, it took Jonah a few minutes to pin him to the floor.

"Now," Jonah gasped. "Just listen to me a minute."

Greenwood's eyes locked on Jonah's face. When cool air kissed Jonah's skin, he realized that his mask had been ripped away in the struggle.

"I need to know what you know about Thorn Hill," Jonah said. "Specifically, about the part where everybody died."

All around them, the glass walls of the conservatory exploded inward, shards pinging on the stone floor around them. Followed by the stink of conjury as wizards crowded into the room.

They both scrambled to their feet. Greenwood swore, and took off running, back toward the living room. To fetch his gun? To find Emma? To escape?

Jonah reached over his shoulder and drew his sword, feeling blood trickling down as the wound in his side ripped wider.

Wizard flame jetted in every direction, a chaotic laser light show against a Rolling Stones sound track. Greenwood screamed as the flame caught him in the doorway, and he fell, writhing, to the floor.

Jonah lunged toward Greenwood, putting himself in the line of fire. Fortunately, his layers of clothing offered some protection, but where the torrents of flame found bare skin, it was blisteringly painful. Fragarach clattered to the floor as he raised his arms to protect his face.

At least it distracted him from the wound in his side. He scarcely noticed that now.

"Don't *flame* them, you idiots!" somebody shouted. "Immobilize them!"

Now the flames died away and a chorus of voices shouted conjury . . . immobilization charms, Jonah guessed.

Jonah knew he should cut his losses and leave, but then Greenwood would end up dead, and that door would be closed. Not to mention that he'd left Emma tied up in the basement.

He sorted through his goals: Keep Greenwood alive until he could question him. Keep Emma alive. Find out why these wizards were here, what they knew, how they knew it. Stay alive himself long enough to get all that done. And escape.

Yes. Pretending to be immobilized was the way to go. Was he supposed to collapse or freeze? Since it was easier to move from a standing position, Jonah froze in his tracks just inside the conservatory and stared straight ahead.

It was a surreal scene, lit by the moonlight that cascaded through the glass, the light shivering with the movement of the trees overhead, the room full of jittery young wizards. Well, six were young, two a little older. The younger ones looked familiar, but Jonah couldn't fathom where he'd seen them before.

Finally, blessedly, somebody killed the pounding sound track.

Why were they here? Had they known Jonah would be here? Were they (a) trying to keep Greenwood from telling what he knew? Or (b) here as reinforcements, to protect him?

Based on Greenwood's reaction to their arrival, Jonah guessed (a).

The two older wizards dragged an apparently immobilized Greenwood back into the conservatory between them.

A young woman began issuing orders—a tall girl, with shoulder-length brown hair pulled back in a ponytail. "Cameron, Brooke—secure the rest of the house. If you find anybody else, bring them back here immobilized but unharmed. Look for compounding equipment, paperwork, computers, any records that might help us."

Cameron? Brooke? Jonah took a second look. Yes, it was them, the young wizards who'd been at Club Catastrophe. They moped out of the room, looking over their shoulders as if they were worried that they would miss the big reveal.

Graham was there, too. He'd scooped up Fragarach, struggling to lift the heavy sword to waist level.

And the one in charge was Rachel, the wizard who'd ordered them to back off on their harassment of Emma at the club.

This is like a replay of Worst Days of My Life, Jonah thought. And now, to top it off, Cameron and Brooke would find Emma in the basement, helpless to escape, because of Jonah.

"All right, then," Rachel said, joining the group around Greenwood. "Somerset, Hardesty, search him."

The wizards patted Greenwood down in a businesslike manner, turning up nothing but a capo and some flat picks.

"Disable the immobilization charm, but keep hold of his arms," Rachel said. "He's more dangerous than you think."

Somerset pointed at Greenwood, muttering a charm. The sorcerer just stood there, impassive, a wizard on each arm, his eyes as flat and opaque as old pennies, perspiration glistening on his forehead. His clothing was charred, and the right side of his face had blistered up.

Rachel faced off with him. "Tyler Greenwood," she said, smiling grimly. "Finally. I was beginning to wonder if you really existed."

"My name is Boykin," Greenwood said. "I guess you have to keep looking."

Rachel tilted her head toward Jonah. "Who is this . . . your bodyguard?" she asked.

Greenwood didn't even look at Jonah. "I got no idea who that is," he said. "He just showed up. We hadn't made it to introductions."

"We heard gunshots. What was that about?"

"I was shooting at *him*," Greenwood said, nodding at Jonah. "I think I winged him, too."

"Where's the gun?"

Greenwood shrugged. "I don't know where it got to."

"Hey! I recognize him," Graham said, pointing Fragarach at Jonah. "He broke my Viking cue—the one with the Predator shaft."

"What are you talking about?" Rachel snapped.

"Remember? I got into it with him at that bar in the Warehouse District," Graham said, with a hint of swagger.

Rachel scowled. "This is *exactly* why we aren't supposed to draw attention to ourselves. You never know who you're talking to."

Graham didn't get the hint. He turned, swinging the massive sword, thrusting and parrying invisible opponents, setting Jonah's teeth on edge. "I think I should get to keep the sword. You know, in payment for the cue."

"Rowan will decide what to do with the sword," Rachel said. "And when he hears about all this, you'd better hope he's in a good mood. Getting thrown out of the syndicate is the least bad thing that can happen to you."

Graham's expression clouded. "D–does Rowan really need to know about this? I mean—"

"Would you just shut up?" Rachel turned back to Greenwood while Jonah, fuzzy-headed from pain and blood loss, struggled to recall who Rowan was. Then it came to him. Rowan DeVries, the wizard he'd seen with Wylie and Longbranch in London. Head of the Black Rose.

"Look," Greenwood said, "if you want drugs, I don't have any. I don't have much money, and what I do have is in the bank. There's nothing here worth stealing. But if you drive me to the ATM, I'll get you some money."

He's trying to get them out of the house, Jonah thought. Because of Emma.

"We're not after money," Rachel said. "You know what we want—information about Thorn Hill."

"Thorn Hill?" Greenwood shook his head, drawing his eyebrows together. "What is that?"

"We've already been to Brazil," Rachel said, ignoring the question. "There's nothing there. After it was abandoned, the property burned to the ground, except for the buildings around the mines. There must have been records, notes, lab books, something."

"Brazil? I've never been there. The only records you'll

find around here are vinyl albums and old sheet music and bills I need to pay."

"Everyone's dead, except for you," Rachel said. "Why is that? How come you're the only one that survived? Or are there others we don't know about?"

Greenwood said nothing.

The young wizard reached out and brushed her fingers against Greenwood's neck. The sorcerer went rigid, arching backward. His pain surged through Jonah like an electrical shock, but Greenwood didn't make a sound.

Empathic connection—the gift, and the curse, of enchanters everywhere. The gift of perceiving the pain and emotions of others. The curse of sharing them, whether you wanted to or not.

"What was your connection to the Black Rose, back then?" Rachel demanded. "How did you know my father? He didn't keep very good records because, you see, he didn't plan on dying."

"Tell me what you want to hear, and I'll go ahead and make something up," Greenwood said. "What makes you think I'm this dude you're looking for?"

Rachel pulled out her phone, brought up a photo, and shoved it into Greenwood's face. "Give it up. You've been on our list for years. We knew that, sooner or later, you'd slip up. And you did, in Memphis. Who are you working for now, Tyler? Who is killing wizards? Tell us what we want to know, and we'll finish you off quickly."

Rachel flamed him again, her fingers leaving behind a trail of blisters and charred skin. Sweat rolled down Greenwood's face. He's not screaming, Jonah thought. Why isn't he screaming? I would be screaming.

And then he answered his own question. Because he doesn't want Emma to hear. Because he's hoping she'll stay in the basement, out of harm's way. He doesn't know she's tied up.

Rachel snorted in disgust. "Hang on to him," she said to Hardesty and Somerset.

She turned her attention to Jonah, unzipping his jacket and sweatshirt and patting him down thoroughly. It was all Jonah could do not to flinch as her hot wizard fingers prodded his blistered skin. As she ran her hands down his sides, she jerked away and peered at her bloody fingers. "You're bleeding," she said, rubbing them together.

Jonah said nothing, because he was, of course, "immobilized."

Yanking his T-shirt free from his jeans, she lifted it up and poked at the bullet wound while sweat trickled down between Jonah's shoulder blades. "Well," she said, "they're telling the truth about that, anyway. This one's been shot—looks like a clean pass-through."

She ran both hands over Jonah's chest, found the Nightshade amulet, and pulled it out from under his sweatshirt. Standing on her toes, she lifted the chain over his head, turned, and held it up so it dangled, glittering in the moonlight. She sucked in a breath, swung around, then, and took another hard look at Jonah.

Clenching the pendant in her fist, she pointed at him, murmuring a charm. Disabling the immobilization charm, Jonah guessed, so she could question him.

"Greenwood claims he doesn't know you," she said, "that you just showed up here. Why?"

"I'm from Medieval Pizza," Jonah said. "*Somebody* here

ordered a deluxe with extra cheese." He glared around the room, as if to find the culprit.

Several of the young wizards snickered.

Rachel was unimpressed. "*Did* Greenwood shoot you? How come?"

"We had a disagreement," Jonah said. "Mr. Boykin claims he didn't order any pizza."

"What's your name?"

"Jonah."

"Jonah. Why were you at the club that night? Were you tailing us?"

"I went to the club to hear the band," Jonah said. "Didn't you?"

"And now you just *happen* to be here," Rachel continued. "Are you and Greenwood working together? Did you know we would be here tonight?"

"Yeah, we're working together," Jonah said. "That's why he shot me. Frankly, if I had known you were going to be here tonight, I would have come last night." He nodded toward the wizard posse. "What *is* this? Take-a-wizardling-to-work day?"

Rachel's lips tightened. The wizardlings muttered among themselves.

Stop it, Kinlock, Jonah said to himself. You're getting cranky. You can't afford cranky, not right now.

"I'm intrigued by your pendant," Rachel said. "Where did you get it?"

"I bought it in an antique shop," Jonah said. "I think I have a receipt for it somewhere."

She snorted. "Did you know that we've been finding nightshade flowers scattered over the bodies of murdered wizards?" Extending her hand, she opened her fingers to display the amulet, then looked up into Jonah's eyes. "I'm no botanist, but this looks very much like deadly nightshade."

"Nightshade?" Jonah held her gaze. "Oh, no," he said. "Those are trumpet flowers. Some things look deadly, but they're totally harmless. And other things look harmless, and they're totally deadly." They stood, their eyes locked, for a long moment. Rachel extended her free hand, as if to touch his face.

"Hey! Rachel?" Graham tapped her on the shoulder. "You all right?"

Rachel blinked, took a step back, shook her head. "What did you . . . ?" She took another step back, apprehension stealing over her face. "Graham. Let me see the sword."

Graham handed it over reluctantly.

Rachel turned Fragarach so it reflected the light. "This looks like a museum piece, and yet . . . very functional. Did you buy this in an antique store, too?" Not waiting for an answer, she handed it back to Graham. "I'm calling Rowan," she said, all business again. "We're going to take these two someplace more secure for questioning, someplace where we won't be interrupted."

She gestured at Jonah, spoke a quick immobilization charm, and turned away, punching numbers into her phone. After a hurried conversation, she rejoined the group. "He's coming, and bringing some help," she said.

We need to be gone before the posse arrives, Jonah thought—me and Emma and Tyler. But how to manage that? And where the hell were Cameron and Brooke?

As if called by Jonah's words, Cameron and Brooke walked in from the living room, hands raised. Followed by

Emma holding Tyler's pistol like she knew how to use it.

"Emma!" Greenwood said, his face gone ashy with dismay. "Go on! Get out of here! *Run!*"

"No," Emma said. "You're all I've got, and I am not going to lose you, too." She raised her voice. "You let my father go," she said to Somerset and Hardesty. "Then . . . all of you . . . get on out of here before I start shooting people."

The wizards looked at one another, seeming more amused than frightened.

What's *wrong* with them? Jonah thought. Aren't they the least bit concerned? Hasn't it occurred to them that this might be dangerous work? Then again, maybe not. Being at the top of the magical food chain, they weren't used to worrying about other predators.

"Don't you remember her?" Cameron said to Graham, pointing at Emma. "She's the labrat that beat you at pool."

"So a labrat with a gun overpowered two wizards?" Graham smirked. "Not your best day, Cam."

"She surprised us," Brooke complained. "And then we immobilized her, but it didn't seem to work."

And I tied her up, Jonah thought. And that didn't seem to work. Well, he *had* left her tied up in a room full of tools and sawblades.

"So you're Greenwood's daughter?" A gloating smile twitched Rachel's lips. Jonah didn't need to read minds to know what she was thinking. Emma would make a great weapon to motivate Greenwood to talk.

"I'll give you to the count of three," Emma said, shifting the gun to Cameron's temple. "Then I shoot."

"Go ahead and shoot him," Rachel said, with a shrug. "I don't care." She paused. "But you *do* care about your father, don't you? Somerset and Hardesty can kill him in an instant. Even if you shoot one, the other will kill him. So put down the gun, and let's talk, and maybe you both can survive this."

Wizards have persuasive powers of their own, Jonah thought. She's stalling, counting on reinforcements. Jonah had to find a way to end this stalemate.

Greenwood was working the same problem. The sorcerer's eyes flicked around the room, assessing his options.

Nobody noticed when the ostensibly immobilized Jonah removed his gloves and dropped them on the floor. But before he could act, Greenwood made his move.

"Emma! Run!" he shouted, jerking free and plowing into Hardesty, taking him down like tenpins and landing hard on top of him. He slammed the wizard's head into the stone floor, once, twice, three times. The last time there was a crunch, and Hardesty lay still.

Somerset extended his hand toward Greenwood. As flame spurted from his fingers, Emma set her feet and fired, and the wizard went down like he'd been axed. Cameron smashed into Emma, sending her flying into a stone fountain. She landed, draped over the base like a broken doll.

Then Jonah was on him, and Cameron was dead before he hit the floor.

After that, it was a chaotic melee of wizard flame and killing charms and burning wicker, Jonah's hands closing on bare flesh. All around him, wizard voices rose in a cacophony of nasty charms that had no effect whatsoever. Jonah flinched when they flamed him, but he was used to pain, remarkably resistant to it, unless it was somebody else's. Most of the time they missed, often hitting each other. Even wounded, he was quick, while they were painfully, fatally slow.

Graham ran for the door, slowed by the weight of Fragarach, but Jonah was there first.

"Not so fast," Jonah said, extending his hand. "I'm going to need my sword back."

The wizard slashed at Jonah, a two-handed sweep, but Jonah nimbly leaped aside, gripping the wizard's bare wrist with one hand and retrieving his sword with the other. Jonah released his hold, and the wizard crumpled to the floor.

Rachel charged toward Emma, landed rolling, and came up with the gun. "If immobilization doesn't work, let's try this." She fired four shots at Jonah in quick succession. The shots went wild, shattering glass all around. Wizards were not, generally speaking, skilled with firearms: they rarely needed them.

Jonah spun, swung, and cut Rachel down with his sword.

"Rachel!" Brooke screamed.

Even when they tried to get out of his way, even when they scrambled for the door, he intercepted them easily, cut through them like a blade through silk, leaving dead bodies behind him. Finally, it was down to Brooke, who huddled, weeping in a corner, mascara running down her face.

"Don't hurt me," she quavered, when Jonah squatted in front of her.

"This won't hurt," Jonah said softly. "I promise."

Killing wizards. He was finding that it was something he was good at . . . something that brought him a certain satisfaction in a dark and terrible world.

When it was all over, Jonah stood alone in the silent conservatory. Nobody was moving.

The porch was a charred ruin. A bamboo curtain smoldered where wizard flame had set it on fire. Furniture was overturned, and pottery smashed, dirt strewn everywhere.

And everywhere, it seemed, there were dead wizards.

Conscious of passing time, Jonah searched for his gloves, pulled them back on, then looked for Greenwood. The sorcerer was lying, facedown, amid shards of shattered glass and smears of blood.

Gently, Jonah rolled him over, searched for a pulse, and swore. He was dead.

Fury mingled with guilt and disbelief. *That's another survivor of Thorn Hill gone. One more door to hope closed. Somebody who probably actually knew something.*

What had killed him? His jeans were soaked in blood from a deep gash in his right thigh. Maybe that. Or was it

Jonah's touch, a fatal encounter in the confusion? Or a wizard's killing charm?

You're like a bull in a china shop, Jonah thought. You're not used to fighting humans, who can bleed, and die, and not get up again.

Would Greenwood be dead if Jonah hadn't come there? That question gnawed at him. But time was passing. He had no idea where Rowan DeVries was coming from, but no doubt he'd be here before long.

Jonah threaded his way through the rubble and dropped to his knees next to Emma.

Just let her be all right.

And if she is, Kinlock, what exactly are you going to do with her? Her father's dead. There are eight dead wizards in her sunroom.

One thing at a time, he told the voice in his head.

The bruise on Emma's temple was ugly purple, and her eye nearly swollen shut. At first, Jonah worried she might have fractured her skull or broken her neck, but some color had returned to her cheeks. When he picked up her wrist, he could feel the reassuring thrum of her heart, even through his gloves. She was still breathing, thank God.

Blood still welled from a wound on the side of her head, where it had struck the fountain. Gently, he moved hair around until he found it. A bad gash, but not too deep, though it was bleeding a lot, the way head wounds always do.

Gently, he straightened her tangled limbs, checking for broken bones. He didn't want to move her if doing so might injure her further. Nothing seemed to be broken, although she moaned and tried to pull away, so movement was obviously painful. She had cuts all over from the broken glass, but none of them seemed life-threatening.

All the while Jonah kept up a constant litany of soothing lies, hoping it would help her, as it did Kenzie. "Easy now, Emma, you're going to be all right, I promise."

Jonah found his sword, slid it into place on his back. Found Rachel's butchered body and pulled his Nightshade amulet from her pocket. Then he knelt next to Emma again, sliding his arms under her so he could lift her.

Something about the pressure of his arms around her roused her, and she began to struggle, flailing her long limbs, crying out, "Tyler!"

"Please, Emma, don't," Jonah said, lowering her back to the floor, pinning her with his body, pouring persuasion into her, giving it all he had. Even singing softly into her ear until her body relaxed. "Please," he said. "I'm going to have to carry you, and I can't do it if you struggle."

She opened her eyes, gazing into his face, her expression muddy with confusion. "My head hurts," she whispered, tears leaking from her eyes.

"I know," he said. "Just rest. I'm going to take you somewhere you can get some help. Is that all right?"

She nodded, her eyes still fixed on his face.

He lifted her again, cradling her against him, and she snaked her arms around his neck, slipping her hand under the collar of his jacket, raising gooseflesh across his shoulders and the hairs on the back of his neck. A sense of déjà vu, of impending danger, rolled over him, but he didn't know why.

She said something he couldn't make out, and he leaned closer to hear.

"You're—you're beautiful," she murmured. "Anybody ever tell you that?"

"Just—just close your eyes," Jonah said. "It'll be easier that way."

She licked her lips, swallowed hard, then, before he knew what was happening, pulled his head down and kissed him on the lips.

Time seemed to slow into a series of sensations. Warm lips, opening under his. Her body arching up to meet him. Her hands in his hair. His body reacting with a lifetime of backed-up desire. It was as if he'd been waiting for that kiss all his life. Which, in a way, he had, with mingled anticipation and dread.

And even when he realized what had happened, what he'd done, it still wasn't easy to pry himself away from her. Her arms were like iron bands around him. Her hands pressed against the back of his neck and between his shoulder blades, generating blazing heat where skin met skin. It was all he could do to free himself without breaking her arms, and yet the struggle, the friction between them, sent blood surging through his veins. He was strong in some ways, but weak in others, and Emma was stronger than she looked.

"Oh," she whispered, suddenly breathless. That familiar drunk and dreamy look spread over her face. That exquisite bonding, soul to soul. Joy welled up in her, spilling through the link between them.

"No!" Jonah flinched back from her as if scalded, swearing under his breath. Too late. Too late. Too late.

He knelt again, easing her onto the floor, his hands gripping her shoulders to keep her at arm's length.

Her head drooped like a heavy flower on a long stem. She smiled, her eyelids fluttering shut.

Jonah recognized the look. The look of death coming on.

Desperately, he scrubbed at her lips with the hem of his sweatshirt, as if he could wipe the toxin—and his guilt—away. Instead, he left a smear of blood.

Jonah drew his knees up to his chin and wrapped his arms around them, his body shuddering with grief.

Hearing, once again, the whispers that followed him everywhere. *That's Jonah Kinlock. He killed his own sister.* And ever since, he'd told himself: Stay away from the innocent. The best you can do is deliver peace to the afflicted and justice to the guilty. You have the killing touch.

Jonah turned his attention back to Emma. She lay still, eyes closed, barely breathing, that creepy, blissful smile still on her face. Her left hand lay across her stomach, the nails cut short, like a child's, her fingers callused at the tips. She had guitar player's hands—sinewy and strong, like his own. He gripped them between his gloved hands, as if he could hold her in the world somehow.

Stubbornly, she clung to life, breaths shivering in and out of her, tears still seeping from the corners of her eyes. *As long as she's crying, she's alive.*

"I'm sorry," he whispered, praying to the merciful gods who had never heard him before. Hoping for the most potent, head-spinning drug of them all—and knowing he wouldn't get it.

Forgiveness.

Instead, he watched helplessly as the color slowly bled from Emma's face. As her breathing slowed, became fainter and fainter until he could no longer hear it. Now, when he pressed his gloved fingers against her throat, he felt no pulse.

She was dead. The realization hit him like a knife to the

gut. Though he was out of Nightshade, he was still killing Thorn Hill survivors.

"She wasn't supposed to be here," Jonah muttered to the indifferent world, his stomach roiling with sick self-loathing. His life was an endless loop of disaster and regret, a phonograph needle stuck on a sad song. A decade of killing, and he still hadn't shed the enchanter's curse: Empathy.

Jonah heard cars pulling into the driveway, doors slamming, feet crunching on gravel. A voice in his head spoke up—some primal plea for survival that wouldn't be stilled.

Reinforcements are coming. If you're still here, you'll have to riff them, too.

He decided to leave the same way he came in—through the basement. He was barely around the corner and down the basement stairs when he heard the back door opening and somebody calling, "Rachel?"

As he passed through the workshop, he took one of the SG guitars. He knew he shouldn't do it, he knew it was stealing, but he also knew that it was the only way he'd ever hear Emma's sweet music again.

CHAPTER TWENTY-FOUR
DOWN BY THE RIVER

Kenzie pulled off the headphones, draping them around his neck, and took another bite of his spring roll. "If one person survived, there must be others."

"You've already researched that," Jonah said. "Greenwood was our best prospect."

"He's the best prospect that we know of *now*," Kenzie said. "Doesn't mean he's the only one."

Jonah snorted. "Don't try to lie to me, Kenzie. You should know better than that."

Emma's bloodless face floated before Jonah's eyes. He'd told Kenzie the whole story . . . except for the part about Emma. He rarely kept secrets from Kenzie, but this one cut too close to the bone after what had happened to Marcy at Thorn Hill.

When Jonah had returned from Greenwood's, he'd thrown his clothes into the incinerator, showered in the hottest water he could stand, and treated his wounds as best he could. In the time it took to do that, he'd received four increasingly worried texts from Kenzie. Despite his weariness, Jonah knew he wouldn't be able to sleep anyway, so he'd walked over to Safe Harbor and given his brother the bad news. Seemed like he was doing a lot of that these days.

Kenzie's voice broke into his thoughts. "What about Rowan DeVries?"

"What about him?"

"He may have some leads that we don't know about."

"He doesn't know any more than we do. That's how we all ended up at Greenwood's."

"We don't know what he knows," Kenzie argued. "You didn't really have a chance to search the house. He did. He might have come away with something useful. Plus his father was in the thick of it, back in the day. Anyway . . . we each have a piece of the puzzle. Maybe it would look like something if we put them together."

"You're saying we should partner up with him?" Jonah leaned his head back and closed his eyes. "Don't you think that the fact that I riffed his younger sister might cause a little tension?"

"He doesn't know that. I'm saying that as soon as he puts anything online, I can get at it," Kenzie said. "That's what I do."

"It doesn't matter how well you do your job, if I blow it up," Jonah said.

Kenzie snorted his disgust. "Tell me again how you picked a bloodbath from all of your other options? Oh, wait—you *had* no other options." He nudged the take-out carton toward Jonah. "Aren't you going to eat any of this? Mango curry is your favorite."

"I've had enough," Jonah said.

"You haven't had *any*," Kenzie said. When Jonah didn't respond, he added, "Fine, fair warning, the curry's mine."

"Be my guest," Jonah said.

Splat!

Jonah looked up to see that Kenzie had flung the carton of curry against the sterile white wall. The bright yellow sauce ran down in long streaks toward a heap of shrimp and vegetables at the bottom.

Jonah swung around to look at his brother. "What the hell?" he said.

Kenzie eyed the mess critically. "Adds a little color, don't you think? I'm calling it *Curry Paintball on Marshmallow Fluff.*"

When Jonah made as if to get up and get a rag, Kenzie gripped his arm. "No," he said. "Every time there's a mess, you don't have to clean it up."

"Would you quit trying to make me feel better about this?" Jonah snapped.

"Would you quit holding yourself to a higher standard than you do me?" Kenzie snapped back. Shoving himself back from his keyboard, he swiveled toward Jonah, leaning forward, his hands on his knees. "Do you have to be the superhero *all the time*? Do you have to fix things *all the time*? We're supposed to be partners, and it's really condescending, if you want to know the truth."

Kenzie's pain and bitterness slammed into Jonah, leaving him nothing to say.

"Isn't it amazing, what little Kenzie Kinlock is able to accomplish, given his disabilities," Kenzie said. His hair was beginning to halo around his head, which was always a bad sign. "Why, he can look up an *address*! And then his big brother Jonah can take that information and save the world. He *cannot fail*, because then little Kenzie will be disappointed. After all, he did *his* job."

Blue flame flickered over Kenzie's hands and arms, and he gripped the arms of the wheelchair to keep them from flailing.

"Kenzie," Jonah said, "you're burning."

"Damn right I am," Kenzie said. "Has it occurred to you that you're more likely to fail because what you're doing is *harder* than what I'm doing?" He rolled his eyes. "I know I get extra credit for being disabled and all, but I actually *enjoy* being in the digital world, because there, I'm usually the most capable person in the room. Everyone else is *dis*abled, compared to me. But you—what you've done for Nightshade, what you did tonight . . . it's totally contrary to your nature. You're a walking contradiction—a deadly predator who suffers every time he makes a kill. And yet you keep going out there."

"It's not because I'm brave," Jonah said, his voice catching. "And it's not for fear of disappointing you. It's not because I want to be a hero. I'm working this plan because I don't want to live in a world without you. I don't even want to think about it."

"Then don't," Kenzie said bluntly. "Do what I do. Now is now. Now is all we have. We can write our own music, and dance to it while we can, or we can start writing our eulogies. I'd rather have a go at life, so there's something to talk about once we're gone."

The Kinlocks stared at each other for a long moment. Gradually, Kenzie's flames dwindled and died, leaving his usual faint tremor behind.

Abruptly, Jonah rose, crossed to the closet, and pulled out Kenzie's jacket. "Let's go out," he said.

"Let's do it," Kenzie said. "Are we gonna find ourselves some wimmin?"

"It's three in the morning," Jonah said. "We probably want to avoid any 'wimmen' still walking around at this hour. And the usual rules apply. You have to promise to wear the headphones and let me know if you feel the fireworks coming on so I can toss you in the river."

Jonah pulled on his leather gloves and wrestled Kenzie into his coat. "Here." He handed a knit cap to his brother. When Kenzie made a face, Jonah was unsympathetic. "It's been a while since you've been out. It's cold now." He put on his own jacket while Kenzie navigated to the door.

"Hang on a sec. I'll make sure the coast is clear." Jonah scanned the empty corridor. "We're good." He pushed Kenzie out into the hallway, shutting the door behind them. They rolled down the corridor to the back stairway.

"Okay . . . arms inside the chair." Jonah picked Kenzie up, chair and all, and carried him down the stairs.

Out on the street, they threaded their way through the dwindling crowds in the Warehouse District, headed for the river. The cold air revived Jonah somewhat, freshening his memory of events on the east side and reminding him that Lilith was hunting him. That shades seemed to be hanging out, more and more, in the area around the Anchorage.

Now that they were outside, Kenzie used the motor function on his wheelchair, laughing as he bumped over the brick pavement. Jonah took hold of the handles again as they descended the steep slope on St. Clair, rattled across the Rapid tracks, and turned onto the walkway at Settlers Landing.

They followed the walkway along the river, their breath crystallizing in the cold air. Kenzie was in a festive mood, singing rock and roll at the top of his lungs.

"Hey now, keep it down!" Jonah warned. "You sound like you've had a few too many. You don't want to draw the local constabulary."

Unfazed, Kenzie said, "I wrote a love song . . . Wanna hear?"

Without waiting for an answer, Kenzie adopted a hangdog expression and began to sing, in a twanging country voice.

> *I ain't pretty, that is true,*
> *I know you take me for a fool,*
> *A love story in a comic book cover,*
> *Ain't never going to be your lover.*

> *Ain't hard to resist,*
> *Ain't never been kissed.*

> *If I build you castles out of words,*
> *And gardens out of nouns and verbs,*
> *Would poetry your heart ensnare?*
> *Would you let me see your derriere?*

> *Think of how fun it*
> *Would be to have done it.*

> *Some people say I aim too high,*
> *You'll never let me touch your thigh,*

If your thigh's too high, how about your ankle?
If you wear leather, I'll wear manacles.

Strap me down
And I'll be fine.

Fulfill my adolescent dream,
Let's take friendship to extremes.
I promise you plenty of courting and sparking,
If you'll consent to take me parking.

I mean, literally . . . sparking.
You'll have to drive.

Kenzie tilted his head down. "What works best—'derriere' or 'underwear'?"

Jonah snorted with laughter. "Um. I don't know how to choose between them."

"What do you think, otherwise?"

"It may not have broad market appeal."

"I'm targeting the audience for Helen Keller jokes," Kenzie said. "Now listen. I've got several possible endings. Tell me which one you like best.

I'm so outta luck
Ain't never been—

"Maybe not," Jonah said. "They won't play it on the radio."
Undeterred, Kenzie sang:

It's real disturbin'
That I'm still a virgin.

"You just keep thinking, Kenzie," Jonah said, shaking his head as they passed beneath the Detroit-Superior Bridge. Jonah gazed up at its elaborate undercarriage, then stiffened, catching the scent of free magic.

Was this another ambush? Jonah suddenly realized how vulnerable they were, all alone on the riverbank. "Hey," he murmured, resting a hand on Kenzie's shoulder. "Would you mind parking under the bridge a few minutes while I check something out?"

"You're not saving the world again, are you?" Kenzie asked, his eyes glittering in the lights from the parking lot. He swung the chair around, taking shelter next to one of the bridge pillars.

When he was a member of Nightshade, Jonah's course of action would've been clear: search and destroy. Now what? Should he call Alison? Gabriel? Or simply walk away?

Peering out from under the bridge, he saw movement on the slope down to Lockwood, dozens of free shades funneling between the buildings. And beyond, a line of savants, bristling with shivs, driving the shades toward the river.

Gabriel must've issued an "all-hands" for this riff. To anyone watching, it would have looked like a battle in which only one side showed up.

As the shades crossed into the park, another group of shadehunters rose up from hiding places along the riverbank, trapping the shades between the two groups of slayers. Both sides waded in, brandishing shivs. Shades screamed as shivs connected—a heartrending, desolate sound that only Jonah could hear.

Escaping free shades swarmed up from the killing ground, fleeing straight toward the bridge. *Thunk!* Weapons sounded overhead—an unfamiliar thwacking sound. When the missiles hit home, the shades screamed and dissolved into a shower of glittering phosphorescence that dissipated in the wind from the lake. Each time it was like a bolt fired into Jonah's soul.

Jonah crouched, and leaped high, catching hold of the archway atop the pillars with the tips of his fingers. He flipped up onto the pillar, then onto the subway railing. He pulled himself up and onto the bridge.

Alison, Charlie, and Mike were lined up along the rail, firing down at the fleeing shades with weapons that seemed to be a marriage between an air rifle and a crossbow, each reloading smoothly from a quiver of hiltless shivs. There seemed to be no shortage of shivs for *this* operation. And still, from below, the screaming.

This must be the new plan—Gabriel's more efficient alternative to Jonah.

"Stop it!" Jonah shouted, shoving Mike's weapon aside. "Can't you hear them screaming?"

The shadehunter pivoted, aiming his gun at Jonah. Then slowly lowered his weapon. "No," he said. "I can't."

"With you out of Nightshade, this is the only option we have." Alison cocked her weapon and reloaded, fired and reloaded, never taking her eyes off the target. "Speaking of . . . what the hell are *you* doing here?"

Alison seemed to have gotten over her dismay at Jonah's departure from Nightshade.

"If you'll recall, I live up the hill," Jonah said. He paused, then added, "What's going on?"

"We're doing a sweep," Charlie said, turning back to his task. "Clearing the warehouse district and the Flats of free shades to improve security."

"There's got to be a better way," Jonah said, shuddering.

"Actually, we think it's working pretty well," Mike said, sliding another shiv into place.

"We were hoping that Lilith would show," Alison said. "Would you recognize her if you saw her?"

"Why?" Jonah asked warily.

"Gabriel wants her dead." She mopped at her forehead with her sleeve. "He's offering a bonus to the slayer who takes her down."

"I think that's a mistake," Jonah said. "I think he should talk to her, and find out who she is and what she knows. Then we can decide what to do."

"And Gabriel thinks that she's charmed you somehow. Which is why you're out of Nightshade."

"They're killing mainliners in droves and blaming it on us, Jonah," Mike said. "You think we should let them keep at it?"

"I never said that," Jonah said, flinching as another shiv hit home.

"We can't fight them when they're organized like this." Charlie reloaded again. "That's why Summer's dead. Even free shades are getting stronger. If we get rid of Lilith, we can go back to our usual game. Less risk for us, less risk for the general public."

"Jonah," Alison said, holding her fire for the moment. "You can still help us. You could arrange a meeting. Tell her we want to talk terms. And when you've set it up, let us know when and where. We'll be waiting, and this thing will be over."

"No," Jonah said. "I'm out of Nightshade, remember?" He went to turn away, and Alison fired a bolt over his shoulder. Dumbfounded, he turned back to face her.

"Hey," Charlie said. "Cut it out. Jonah's not the enemy."

"He's either with us or against us," Alison said, firing off another. She meant to miss: Alison was a better shot than that, but just then Jonah didn't care. He didn't remember covering the distance between them. But he plowed into her and she went down on her back and the crossbow went flying, slamming into the guardrail. He rolled away, scooped up the weapon, and broke it in half.

Alison scrambled to her feet and charged at him, and he sidestepped easily. She turned and came at him again, and he evaded her again.

"We can keep doing this for as long as you want," Jonah said. "But I'm guessing the police won't ignore what's happening here forever."

Alison struggled to catch her breath. "When Gabriel finds out you interfered with a Nightshade operation—"

"Once you've regained your senses, I think you'll agree that it's best if Gabriel doesn't hear anything about this little exchange at all," Jonah said. "I may not be in operations anymore, but I'm not going to let you shoot at me."

By now, there was little to no activity on the ground. The shades were either dead or fled into hiding, and the hunters on the ground dispersed quickly, leaving no evidence that they'd ever been there.

A strangled cry from below distracted Jonah. He looked down and saw that Kenzie's chair had emerged from under the bridge. He was trying to escape a swarm of free shades that were leaning in, poking at him, covering his face with their hands. Harassing him.

Kenzie had no Nightshade amulet. He shouldn't have

been able to see them clearly, yet, obviously, he was aware of them, batting at them with his hands. As Jonah watched, his brother's wheelchair veered off the walkway into the grass, heading for the river.

"Kenzie!" Jonah vaulted over the side of the walkway, landing hard on the pavement below. He sprinted after his brother, intercepted the wheelchair at the water's edge, and knocked Kenzie's hand off the throttle. The chair slowed to a stop and Jonah set the brake.

He turned to face the shades, and they faded back, out of reach, then turned and fled.

Kenzie was trembling, glassy-eyed, seizing. He still gripped the MP3 player in one hand. Jonah managed to pry it free. The music had stopped.

Jonah glanced back at the bridge. Alison, Charlie, and Mike were gone.

Swearing softly, he turned Kenzie so he faced the river, knowing that once the seizure started, he'd just have to ride it out. With Kenzie, you never knew just what that would involve.

Blue flame webbed and flickered over Kenzie's skin, and Jonah hoped he wouldn't short out the chair. The flame coalesced into balls of fire that arced out over the river, hissing like Roman candles as they dropped into the water. Fortunately, none seemed in danger of hitting the wooden buildings on the other side. Kenzie's arms and legs jittered and danced, his ashen face painted by his personal light show.

"Spectacular, Kenzie," Jonah murmured, resting his gloved hands on his brother's shoulders, pulling back when the pain became intolerable. "Spectacular." He just kept talking, saying anything that came into his head, knowing that his voice was one thing that could keep Kenzie grounded.

All the while Jonah scanned their surroundings, alert for attack.

When it was over, Kenzie sat, exhausted, pale and sweating. Jonah slipped the headphones over his brother's damp hair, replaced the MP3 player in his hand, and hit shuffle.

It was nearly five A.M. when the Kinlock brothers made the long climb up St. Clair, heading home. Jonah had just settled Kenzie back in his room when his phone went off. A text from Natalie. In fact, it was the latest of several he had missed. *Mose is at Safe Passage. In the Octagon. He needs you now.*

CHAPTER TWENTY-FIVE
SAFE PASSAGE

After returning Kenzie to his room, Jonah descended to the first floor, exited out the front, then circled around and reentered through the glassed-over courtyard in back. Summer and winter, this place was an oasis in the city, filled with plants and flowers, a vegetable and herb garden, a fountain. All of the Safe Passage rooms let out onto this courtyard.

Jonah caught a whiff of Gabriel's highly potent ganja from across the courtyard. The door to Octagon stood open, and Jonah walked into a smoky haze.

The lights were dim, candles all around, each flame haloed. Mose was sprawled in one of the custom-made recliners that most clients at Safe Passage preferred to beds. He was wrapped in a fleecy blanket, his arms and legs poking out like chicken bones from a nest of feathers. Natalie sat in a chair next to the bed, her expression grim, her nose pinked up from crying, holding Mose's hand. She'd never gotten used to facing off with death . . . and losing.

Severino was sound asleep in another visitor's chair, one arm flung over his eyes.

Mose was wearing headphones, but when he saw Jonah, he slid them off and set them on the table beside the bed. Rock and roll leaked out, obviously set on maximum volume. "Jonah!" he said. "No more worries about ruining my hearing." He lifted a Corona from the cup holder on the recliner and tilted it toward Jonah. "Want one?"

Jonah shook his head. "Not tonight."

"Hey now, think it over, man," Mose said. "Bar's open. Irish wake."

"All right," Jonah said. He crossed the room and reached into the cooler next to Mose's bed, fishing out a bottle. Wiping it on his jeans, he cracked it open and took a sip. "What are we celebrating?"

Mose patted the cushion beside him. "Please. Sit down."

"I'm pretty nasty, to tell you the truth," Jonah said, brushing at his clothes. "You don't want me on your bed."

"You mess up the bed, it's not my problem."

Jonah sat on the side of the bed, rolling the bottle between his hands. "Are you in any pain?"

"No, I had me a great massage and a spell in the hot tub and few tokes on Gabriel's primo weed. Natalie's been hanging out with me . . . she's totally set on soothe. I'm feeling pretty mellow, to tell you the truth."

"So. What's going on?"

"Tomorrow—no—today's the day, man," Mose said, glancing at his phone. "Today's the day I cross over to the dark side."

"No," Jonah said, shaking his head. "No. That can't be right."

"I swear, it's true. I got back here and looked in the mirror, and *bam!* There he was—death, looking me right in the eye. Giving me that come-hither look."

"I think you messed up."

"Have I ever been wrong before?" Mose raised an eyebrow.

"You never applied your gift to yourself before," Jonah said. "And you've been sick. It stands to reason that you're off your game."

Mose snorted. "Let's go over that argument: *you've been sick, so you can't be dying.* You're going to have to do better than that, Kinlock." He propped his chin on his fist. "Persuade me. I do love to hear you talk."

Jonah looked at Natalie. He could tell by the expression on her face that Mose was right.

"What about Byron?" Jonah said, naming Mose's most recent boyfriend. "Does he know you're here?"

"Oh, Jonah," Mose said, with a heavy sigh. "That is so over."

"Yeah, but he still might want to—"

"I just want to be with my friends," Mose said. "My bandmates and you. You were ever my true love, anyway, Jonah."

"Where's Gabriel?" Jonah asked. "Does he know?"

"He was here earlier," Natalie said. "He . . . uh . . . he had to leave. He wasn't dealing with it very well."

What about us? Jonah thought. Anyone wondering how we're dealing with it?

As if he'd overheard Jonah's thoughts, Mose said, "I'm sorry to have to put you through this. It's easy for me. All I have to do is die."

"I thought Alison would be here," Natalie said. "I've texted her, but no answer."

"She's working," Jonah said. "She'll be here. Is there anyone else we should call?" Jonah desperately wanted to share responsibility with someone else.

"The priest has already come and gone. So it's official." Mose took a swig of his beer. "So. *Now* will you take the vinyl?"

Jonah cleared his throat. "I'll take it all," he said. "The turntable, too, if you want."

"And the Parker DragonFly. You know you want it. You've always lusted after it . . . just like I've always lusted after you. Kind of a love triangle, in a way."

Jonah's cheeks heated. "You should give that to Alison," he said. "She needs something to remember you by."

"Alison won't respect the guitar. You will." Mose shifted his gaze to Natalie. "Doesn't he have to honor last requests?"

"I believe he does," Natalie said, her voice low and tight, her eyes swimming with tears.

"Great," Mose said. "Request number two: Jonah takes my place in the band."

"What? . . . No!" Jonah said, dread displacing his grief for the moment.

"I want the band to be good," Mose said. "Better than it ever was. It's got to be you, Jonah."

"No," Jonah said. "I'm not the guitarist you are, and I never will be."

"Guitarists are a dime a dozen. It's a great singer that's hard to come by. I kind of like the notion that it'll take two people to replace me. Bonus: you're a songwriter. You can satisfy Natalie's unquenchable thirst for new material."

"I'll give her songs," Jonah said. "I don't play in public."

Mose opened one eye. "If I can't get what I want on my deathbed, then when can I get it?"

Jonah looked up at Natalie, who was glowering at him, making throat-cutting gestures.

"All right, you win," he said. "I'm in. I'll join the band."

"Great," Mose said, yawning. "Hold him to it, Natalie. You know I'm doing it for his own good."

Rudy had awakened during the conversation. He came and stood behind Natalie, rubbing her shoulders and neck, his face a landscape of grief.

Mose's eyes drifted shut. Jonah thought perhaps he'd gone back to sleep, but then Mose murmured, "You know what they say about a watched pot? Well, it ain't true. Not in my case."

The door slammed open, and everyone jumped, except Mose, who scarcely flinched. Alison barged in, still dressed for battle. "Mose! I didn't have my phone on. What the hell are you doing here?"

Jonah moved aside, giving her space, but Alison circled around to Mose's other side and rested her hip on the edge of the chair. She gripped his hand, as if she could hold him in the world. "You are *not* dying, Mose, so get that out of your head right now. We have three gigs on the calendar, coming up, and we can't afford to break in somebody new."

"'S'all right," Mose whispered. "Jonah's going to step in. You always wanted Jonah in the band."

Alison darted a look at Jonah, then focused back on Mose. "I'll be glad to have Jonah in the band, but that doesn't let you off the hook."

"Jonah," Mose said, a note of urgency in his voice now. "I think we're getting close."

Slowly, reluctantly, Jonah stripped off his gloves and laid them on the bedside table.

"Don't you dare!" Alison snapped, and leaned over Mose, her tears dropping on his bedclothes. "You can't die, Mose, because then . . . because then . . ." Suddenly she was sobbing too hard to speak further.

"Anyone who can't be cool about this needs to leave," Mose said. "This is going to be hard enough for Jonah as it is."

Alison turned away, burying her face in her hands, shoulders shaking.

"Jonah," Mose said, from his nest of blankets.

"I'm here."

Mose lifted up the bedclothes. "Would you mind . . . very much . . . holding me?"

And so Jonah did.

∾ CHAPTER TWENTY-SIX ∾
SURVIVOR

Voices were calling to her, as if from a great distance. Hands poked and prodded her—none too gently. Burning hands. Relentless hands. Needles. Liquid flame, running into her veins.

Clamoring voices. Harsh, squabbling voices. Strangers.

She's not responding. Some kind of poison. Or a toxin. Resistant to treatment.

She's going to die, and if she does we've got nothing. We need to bring in a healer.

No. Absolutely not. Nobody can know she's alive.

Well, if you don't get someone, she won't be for long. Gabriel Mandrake is the most gifted and knowledgeable herbalist and healer in the country. He's right here in town.

Emma opened her eyes then, and looked into their shocked faces. Strident voices washed over her, but none of the voices she wanted to hear. She closed her eyes again.

After a while, someone new came—someone whose

hands soothed her, who gave her bright liquids, one teaspoon at a time . . . liquids that tingled on her tongue, then disappeared, without her ever swallowing. Someone who sponged off her body and cooled her flushed cheeks. Who called her back from the precipice onto solid ground.

And, then . . . muttering. Unhappy muttering. Outshouted by a new voice of authority.

No you cannot question her. Not even for a few minutes. I don't care what you think she knows. Do you want me to save her life or not?

When Emma opened her eyes again, she was lying in a small, spare room with a tile floor and rough, plaster-and-timbered walls. A fire burned merrily on the hearth under a mantel layered with pumpkins, gourds, and dried flowers. Candles glowed in glass jars, emitting a fragrance of cinnamon and pine. Sunlight spilled through French doors into the room from a small garden, studded with dry seed heads and brilliant autumn grasses. Just outside, birds squabbled around a feeder.

Emma's vision blurred, then doubled, then seemed to go back to normal.

The doors stood slightly open, admitting cold, clean air. It felt good against her heated skin. She rested back against the pillows, her head all at once too heavy to lift.

She shifted under a fluffy comforter in a single bed—the only furniture save two chairs, one on either side of the bed, and a small bedside table with a lamp. Lined up on the table were bottles and jars of remedies and sickroom supplies.

Have I been sick? I don't remember being sick. But her mind practically creaked from disuse.

She focused in on the bottles, hoping that they would give her a clue, but they were unlabeled. The room was painted in soothing, neutral tones, save for the jewel colors of the medicines, whatever they were.

A girl was sitting in a chair beside the bed, sound asleep.

Emma studied her with interest. She was solidly built, tawny-skinned, her black hair tied back with a bandanna. She wore jeans, high-top sneakers, and a faded Cleveland Agora T-shirt that exposed muscled arms. A plaid flannel shirt hung on the back of her chair. Emma guessed she was close to her own age. A stranger.

Or was she? There was something familiar about her. . . .

Emma had no idea where she was and no recollection of how she had come to be there.

She also had a raging headache. Reaching up, she probed the back of her head with her fingers. Her hair had been clipped short over a small, tender area. A ridge of skin told her she'd had a gash in her forehead that had been repaired.

Did I fall? I don't remember falling.

She resisted the temptation to close her eyes, leave these questions behind, and return to the vivid intensity of her dreams. A boy, rimed in light. A kiss that arrowed into her very core. Dreams or memories? She didn't know.

"H-hello?" Emma's voice sounded loud in her ears, rough and blunt from disuse. Until she spoke, she didn't actually know if anything would come out.

The girl's eyes sprang open, and she straightened guiltily. "Oh! You're awake! I thought you might be close to waking, so I didn't want to leave you alone. I was just resting my eyes."

"Wh-who are you?"

"I'm Natalie Diaz. A healer." She looked at Emma hopefully.

"I'm Emma Greenwood," Emma said.

Natalie grinned, as if Emma had passed some kind of test by remembering her own name.

"I'm sorry . . . but do I know you?"

Natalie shook her head. "No reason you should know me. I'm the one that's been looking after you. I can't tell you how glad I am to see you open your eyes."

"Why? Am I sick?"

"Sick or injured or something." Natalie sat down on the edge of Emma's bed. "Do you remember what happened to you?"

Emma touched her forehead again. "Did I hit my head?" she guessed.

"Seems like it. Or someone hit it for you." Natalie paused again, waiting for Emma to fill in.

But Emma had nothing to say. It was like her head was full of molasses with only the occasional thought forcing its way through. "I—I'm sorry," she said finally. "I'm not usually like this."

"Give yourself a break," Natalie said. "You've been really sick. Sometimes it takes your brain a while to wake up." She touched Emma's forehead with her fingertips. Her face seemed kind, but there was a wariness in her eyes, as if she were standing on shifting ground. "Are you able to sit up?"

"I—I think so." Flattening her palms against the bed, Emma pushed until she was upright.

"Good job. Any dizziness? Vision changes? Pain anywhere?"

Emma nodded. "I'm dizzy. Some double vision. And I—I'm kind of sick to my stomach."

Natalie took her pulse and tested her reflexes.

"Do you remember what month it is?"

"Well. Last I remember, it was mid-October. Right?"

Natalie grinned in relief and approval.

"How long . . ." Emma hesitated, then gave up and spit out the standard question: "How long have I been out?"

"It's been a week," Natalie said. "I've been here the past five days. You turned a corner of sorts yesterday."

"Does Sonny Lee know?" Emma asked. Pain trickled up from a reservoir deep inside. "No. I forgot. He's dead."

"Who is Sonny Lee? Was he with you when you got hurt?" Natalie asked softly.

Emma shook her head. "He was my grandfather. He died back in the summer. He—he fell." She rubbed her forehead. Were the Greenwoods prone to falling? "I've been staying with Tyler."

"Tyler?"

"My father."

Natalie reached out and cradled Emma's hands between her own, looking into her eyes. "Look, you don't have any reason to trust me, but I'm here to help you, not to hurt you . . . do you understand?"

No! I don't understand anything, Emma wanted to say. But she nodded anyway.

Natalie leaned toward her so she could whisper in Emma's ear. "When the wizards come back, we won't be able to talk. So if there's something you want to tell me that you don't want them to hear, say it now."

The wizards? Emma took a deep breath in and out, trying

to calm her hammering heart. The wizards would be here soon. Tyler had mentioned wizards. That they were dangerous. That her mother had worked for them, was afraid of them.

Should she admit any of this to Natalie Diaz? Could she trust her?

"You're a—a healer?"

Natalie nodded. "A sorcerer savant."

Savant! Where had she heard that word before?

"Not a wizard?"

"Not a wizard. Now . . . did they do this to you?" Natalie said, her voice low and fierce. "The wizards. Did they hurt you? That's what I want to know. They refused to tell me exactly what happened. It's like blindfolding me and then asking me to do surgery."

Emma tried to focus—to concentrate. But it was as if somebody had swiped a huge eraser through her mind, obliterating a landscape of memories. "I don't know," she said. "I don't remember." She looked around, trying to regain her bearings. "Where am I, anyway? In—in a clinic? A hospital?"

"You're in a private home," Natalie said. "In Bratenahl Village. Up on the lake. It belongs to Rowan DeVries. Do you know him?"

DeVries. She did know the name. But from where? "I'm sorry," Emma said. "The name sounds familiar, but I don't know why." She hesitated. "But if I've been that sick, then shouldn't I be seeing a doctor? In a hospital?" It sounded blunt, harsher than she intended. "I—I mean, you seem like you know what you're doing, but—"

"A doctor wouldn't do you any good," Natalie said. "I know a lot about poisons, so when the wizards asked Mr.

Mandrake if he'd come take a look, he sent me instead."

Poisons? Toxins? Emma flattened herself in the bed, as if she could disappear into the bedclothes. Maybe she was still dreaming. "Wait a minute! You think somebody poisoned me?"

"Well . . ." Natalie cleared her throat. "We don't know. They said that your father was a sorcerer. Tell me: did he keep poisons, herbals, and the like on hand? They say they didn't find anything like that at your house, but . . ." Her voice trailed off as she took in Emma's expression.

"Of course they didn't!" Emma's voice trembled. "And they won't!"

Natalie seemed taken aback by Emma's reaction. "I'm not calling your father careless, but sometimes sorcerers build up a resistance and they don't realize just how dangerous—"

"I'm sorry. I don't know what you're talking about," Emma said, rubbing her aching head. Her rule was not to say anything to the authorities. Natalie didn't look like the authorities, but it was best to play it safe. "My father didn't poison me. He's a musician. He's in a band. My mother is dead. Until a few months ago, I lived with my grandfather in Memphis. I don't know who you think I am, but you've got me mixed up with somebody else."

Unbidden, Sonny Lee's words came back to her. *You need to get out of Memphis, before they come after you.*

"Have you been having symptoms?"

"Symptoms?"

"Even savants who don't have symptoms at first often develop them later on, as they age. Savants who've never been in treatment come to us in their teens, when they begin to have problems. That was what happened with me. I lived with my aunt until I was twelve, then I went to the Anchorage."

Natalie paused and, when Emma said nothing, asked, "Were you under treatment?"

"Treatment?" Emma figured it was safe to just repeat the last word Natalie said.

"Are you on meds that might have interacted with something else you took? Maybe street drugs of some kind?"

Emma's ironwood spine stiffened. "I'm *not* using any street drugs, and I'm *not* having any symptoms, and everything was basically just fine until my grandfather died. Since then, things have gone downhill real fast."

Natalie glanced at the door, then leaned in again, speaking low and fast, "Don't worry. The wizards don't know you're a savant, because they can't read stones. They can't even tell for sure that you're gifted."

Emma stared at her. "What? What's that you keep calling me?"

"A savant. See, that's why I'm here. I have experience treating savants."

"I'm just lost," Emma said wearily. "Tyler told me about the—the magical guilds, but he never mentioned—what you call it—savants."

Natalie frowned, as if puzzled. "You were at Thorn Hill, right?"

How does she know that? "I guess I was, yes," Emma admitted. "For a while. I guess I left before the . . . before the massacre."

"You did? But . . . you have a savant stone."

"I can't help that," Emma said wearily. Wishing there was at least one question she could answer.

"Do you mind?" Gripping Emma's wrist, Natalie pulled Emma's right sleeve up to expose her wrist and forearm.

Then sat back, looking confused. "Huh. You don't have the tattoo," she said.

"The tattoo?"

"All of us have these." Natalie extended her arm, displaying an inked design of flowers.

Something tugged at Emma's memory, something from childhood. "I think I remember seeing those when I was a kid," she said. "Everyone had one but me." She'd been envious of the others with the flower tattoos.

"Everyone at Thorn Hill had them," Natalie said. "But you don't."

"You were at Thorn Hill, too?"

Natalie nodded. "I know this is a really bad time, to be finding all this out. But—I'm warning you—the wizards are in a hurry to talk to you. I don't think I can keep them away much longer." She used the word *wizard* like a curse.

Apprehension settled over Emma's heart, pressing all of the air out of her lungs. "My father's dead, isn't he?"

Natalie hesitated. "I don't know for sure, but if he was with you, he may be. The wizards said that you were the only survivor."

"Survivor of what?"

"Damned if I know," Natalie growled. "I was hoping *you* might tell me, because *they* aren't talking."

"But . . . what do they care? What's their interest?"

"Apparently, wizards were among the dead, and you're the only witness." Natalie leaned in close, spoke in a low voice. "Is there any other family? Anyone else I can call? Somebody who might help you?"

"No," Emma whispered, a great well of misery churning in her middle. "I have nobody."

Just then she heard footsteps, rapidly approaching. They both stared at the door.

Natalie leaned close, speaking into Emma's ear. "Listen to me," she said. "I'll try to buy you some time. Don't be afraid to tell them you don't remember anything, if that's the case. If they think you don't know anything, they might let you go."

Emma clutched at Natalie's arm. "Are you saying I'm a prisoner?"

Natalie hesitated. "From what I've seen and heard, I believe you may be."

❧ CHAPTER TWENTY-SEVEN ❧
CAN'T WE ALL JUST GET ALONG?

The Weir sanctuary of Trinity glittered in the slanting autumn sunlight like a postcard of a New England town. But the flaming russets and golds of the trees on the square did nothing to improve Jonah's mood. He and Gabriel had been arguing all the way from downtown.

"If you could hear them, you would stop it," Jonah said.

"Well, then, it's a blessing that we can't," Gabriel said bluntly. "Why do you think I pulled you out of operations? Because I didn't want to put you through this."

"But you'll put *them* through it."

"I understand that we have a kinship with everyone who was at Thorn Hill. I recognize that none of this is their fault. But what do you expect me to do? They've declared war on us."

"We made the first move," Jonah said.

"So we should allow them to keep murdering the gifted and leaving the bodies on our doorstep?"

"We could talk to them."

"There's no point. It would only make this more difficult. I don't want any communication with Lilith, do you understand? None whatsoever." Gabriel circled the square once and pulled into the angle parking that lined the main street. "The good news is that the downtown area is finally cleared of shades again. You should be happy about that." He pushed his door open and got out, seeming eager to leave this topic behind.

What Gabriel said made sense, as it always did. But something was wrong. The emotional messages Jonah was getting were definitely mixed.

"Don't you think they'll be back?" he said, making no move to get out of the car.

"I'm hoping *Lilith* will return," Gabriel said. "I believe she's the driving force behind this. If we can just eliminate her—"

"Never mind," Jonah said. He was close to being petulant, but he didn't care.

Gabriel sighed. "Losing Mose was hard on all of us, Jonah. You especially. Every time we lose a student, I feel like we've failed."

This was the place where Jonah was supposed to say, *It's not your fault, Gabriel, everyone knows you're doing the best that you can.*

Instead, he said, "Tell me again why we have to be here? Are they actually voting on this motion today?"

Gabriel shook his head. "Mercedes has put it on the agenda for discussion. One thing I've learned in my years in the business is that personal connection is always more effective. Engagement prevents all manner of rumors from getting started. If you can just be your usual charming self, Jonah, I know it will go a long way toward allaying any fears." After a long pause, he said, "We'd better go. I don't want to walk in late."

Jonah slid out of the car.

"Promise me you won't get into any more fights with mainliners," Gabriel said as they crossed the square.

"That wasn't a fight."

"What do you call it, then?"

"Sparring."

"Still. When mainliners see that you are good with a sword, it makes them think. It makes them wonder how you developed that skill. They may remember there was a boy at the bridge."

"Saving their children's lives."

"They may not see it that way."

"So my job is to be pretty, and charming, but not too capable?"

"Your job is to be judicious about which capabilities you share with others," Gabriel said, leading the way up a flight of stone steps to the door of a church.

The sanctuary was already half filled, so Gabriel and Jonah filed up the side aisle toward the front and turned into the side chapel. Jonah spotted Jack Swift and Ellen Stephenson at the back of the chapel, sprawled across the last pew, their swords propped up beside them. Working security, no doubt. Jonah and Gabriel found their way to seats three rows from the front.

Looking forward, Jonah saw that Leesha Middleton and Mercedes Foster were seated in the front row.

About a dozen people were ranged around a conference

table that had been set up on the dais. McCauley was the only one Jonah recognized.

Mercedes Foster paused to speak with them on her way to the front of the church. "Hello, Gabriel, Jonah."

The crowd in the sanctuary was restive, seething. Some of the spectators seemed to be in an ugly mood. "This looks like a lynch mob," Jonah murmured. "Is it always like this?"

"Feelings are running high about the Montessori kidnapping," Mercedes said. "I hope you wore your bulletproof vests." She rolled her eyes. "Look on the bright side . . . it will make for a lively discussion."

"Do you think we should defer introducing the representation proposal?" Gabriel asked.

Mercedes shook her head. "I hope we'll get support, if not here, then in the town at large. Your Natalie was like a goodwill ambassador for the Anchorage when she was here. Everybody was impressed with her." The sorcerer looked around. "I thought you were going to bring her today."

"I was," Gabriel said. "But then I had a request for a healer to see a seriously ill patient. I hoped she'd be back in time to come with us today, but I understand it's been a tough case."

That's just what Natalie needed, after Mose, Jonah thought. Another tough case. Some savants lived with their extended families outside of Gabriel's complex, but many of them still came to the Anchorage for health care.

As Mercedes walked on up the aisle, Gabriel studied the crowd. "I've never seen so many mainliners at one of these meetings," he murmured.

Jonah recognized some faces from his previous visit to Trinity. The angry parents who had confronted McCauley were all there, and then some. Scanning the crowd, Jonah saw Ms. Morrison, Ms. Hudson, and Mr. Scavuzzo in the audience.

"Gabriel," Jonah said. "There's something you should know about what happened at the sparring match. Some parents seemed to think—"

Somebody tapped him on the shoulder. He turned to see Ellen leaning over the back of the pew. "Jonah! Did you get my texts? We were hoping you'd come work out."

"Oh. Right. I did get your texts, I should have answered back. I've been buried in—in schoolwork," Jonah said.

"Jonah is serving an apprenticeship with me," Gabriel said. "Learning the music business. Between that and school and his own music, he doesn't have time to do much else."

"Speaking of music, Mr. Mandrake, we're looking for a local band to play at a private party," Ellen said. "An indie band, that plays original music. Not too pricey. I thought you might have a recommendation."

"If you e-mail Patrick in my office, he'll be able to send you a list, by genre," Gabriel said.

Just then, McCauley banged his gavel. "We have a full agenda, so let's get this thing started," he said. He looked around. "I see lots of new faces here. For those of you who don't know me, I'm Seph McCauley, secretary of the council." He nodded toward a young woman on his right, who glowed brighter than anyone else in the room.

"I'm Madison Moss, council chair," she said. Madison Moss was a tall, rangy girl whose wavy hair was pulled back in a clip. She wore a long, divided skirt, cowboy boots, and a handwoven scarf wrapped three times around her neck.

"That's the Dragon Heir," Gabriel murmured. "The source of power for all mainliners."

Jonah had difficulty matching her up with the way he'd heard her described by wizards. She didn't look much like a despot, to tell the truth. Just now the notorious Dragon Heir seemed to be doodling on a sketch pad hidden under the table.

"She's not that much older than me," Jonah said.

"She's had to grow up fast," Gabriel said. "She's not entirely comfortable in this role."

"I'd like to welcome back Leander Hastings and Linda Downey," Moss said. "As y'all know, they've been cataloging the weaponry, manuscripts, and other heirloom items at Dragon's Ghyll in the UK. They'll be presenting a report on their progress."

Hastings raised one hand in acknowledgment. *He* looks more like the despot, Jonah thought. Hastings had a hard, ruthless face under a tumble of dark curls. Linda Downey stood, briefly, so she could be seen. She was small, with exquisite features and spiky black hair. Like a flare of light in the darkness, she drew every eye in the room.

"They're McCauley's parents," Gabriel said. "They were active in the underguild rebellion for years. Hastings is a wizard, Downey an enchanter."

"Really?" Jonah had never seen an enchanter in the flesh—if you didn't count looking in the mirror. He leaned forward, angling for a better view. Then, just as quickly, he shifted his gaze away. He knew what it was like to be stared at.

Madison Moss introduced the others around the table, which included representatives from each of the mainline guilds.

"We expect Rowan DeVries to be here as well, from the

Wizard Guild," McCauley said, gesturing at an empty chair. "He must have been delayed."

"Now," Moss said, scanning some notes in front of her. "Before we get into the agenda, are there announcements?"

Gabriel stood up. "We have a quick announcement," he said.

"Of course," Moss said, squinting to see who had spoken. "Mr.—"

"I'm Gabriel Mandrake," he said. "And this is my associate, Jonah Kinlock." Gabriel motioned to Jonah, who reluctantly pushed to his feet. "We want to remind you all to buy your tickets for the annual Thorn Hill benefit concert, which will be held on March fifteenth, at the Keep."

A murmur ran through the sanctuary, mingled excitement and disapproval.

"As usual, we have a fantastic lineup . . . some great local bands, as well as rare appearances by Lisbet and Fallen Angels."

"We're going, Jack," Ellen whispered, behind Jonah. "I love Lisbet."

"Tickets go on sale next week," Gabriel continued. "And they're expected to go fast. In the meantime, I hope you'll check out our silent auction online. You'll find lots of rare and one-of-a-kind artifacts and donations by musicians from all over the world. And if any of you have donations for the auction or the cause, Jonah here . . ." Jonah raised his hand. "Jonah will be happy to take your pledges."

A buzz of excited commentary followed. Fragments reached Jonah's ears. *I wouldn't set foot in that place. . . . Lisbet! Can you believe it—Lisbet!*

"Let's move on to new business," Moss said, over the muted din. "Mercedes?"

The sorcerer Mercedes Foster stood. "We have a request from the survivors of the Thorn Hill disaster to be given representation on council. I support this request, and I would like to introduce this issue for discussion in preparation for a motion."

"All right," Moss said. "Is there discussion?"

Scavuzzo raised his hand. "There are representatives from every guild on the council already. Why single them out for special treatment?"

"I can speak to that," Gabriel said. He stood. "We believe that the issues confronting the savant survivors of Thorn Hill are different enough from those of the mainline guilds that they could benefit from having a voice on council."

A seer stood up. "Will we have a representative for every kind of disability, then? How about nearsighted people?"

Linda Downey raised her hand. "It seems to me that the distinction is that here we're speaking of magical differences, not physical or racial distinctions. If the savants are magically different from the other guilds, then that might warrant their being given representation on council."

Morrison stood, claiming the floor. "It seems to me that residents of Thorn Hill are either in the magical guilds or out. If they are in the guilds, then they are represented. If they are out of the guilds, then they don't belong on this council. Jack Swift, for example, is a mongrel of sorts, yet he is considered a member of the Warrior Guild."

Jack snorted softly, behind Jonah.

Hudson chimed in. "Perhaps we should investigate the kinds of magical mutations present at Thorn Hill so that we can make a better decision."

Jonah slid a look at Gabriel, knowing he wouldn't like

that idea. As Lilith had said, he liked to keep his secrets.

"We need to move on," Moss said. "Is there a motion?"

"I move that we accept written comments over the next two months," Mercedes said. "Madison can appoint a sub-committee to summarize them and present them to council in . . . um . . . February."

And so, effectively, the idea was tabled. Gabriel looked disappointed, but Jonah figured it was better than having it voted down.

Moss seemed relieved to be moving on. "Now, to old business: Alicia Middleton and Mercedes Foster will update us on the Trinity Montessori incident."

Mercedes and Leesha stood up, so that Jonah and Gabriel were looking at their backs.

Leesha took the lead. "I spoke with a reliable source in the Trinity Police Department. According to him, the Cleveland police are pretty much stymied. They did spot a suspect on the lift bridge with the children, but somehow he got away."

A rumble of displeasure arose from the spectators.

"Why are the police investigating what is clearly a magical matter?" Scavuzzo shouted.

"The police don't know it's a magical matter, Mr. Scavuzzo," Mercedes said. "If you don't believe in magic, you don't go looking for a magical explanation. That puts them at a tremendous disadvantage. As you can imagine, they are under considerable public pressure to solve the crime."

Hudson sniffed. "Since we all agree that the police investigation is a waste of time, what have *you* uncovered in *your* investigation?"

"There were approximately two hundred corpses scattered on the bridge deck and on both banks of the river,"

Mercedes said. "I've examined the cadavers. They seem to be a mixture of fresh bodies and . . . ah . . . 'seasoned' corpses. Some of them apparently came from Mapleside Cemetery west of Cleveland. How they were transported to the Flats, we don't know." She hesitated. "The children mentioned zombies."

A murmur rolled through the crowd.

"The tabloids have been having a field day," Leesha said. "Several companies have sprung up, offering what they call Zombie Walks in the Flats."

"The corpses . . . could you detect anything magical about them?" Leander Hastings asked.

The sorcerer shook her head. "If there was any magic there to start with, it was gone by the time I arrived. They had all been chopped into little bits."

"How would that have happened?" Moss asked, looking mystified.

"We thought at first they'd just . . . you know . . . fallen apart, being old and all," Leesha answered. "But some of the bones were sliced right through or battered into pieces. The children we've interviewed mentioned a boy with . . . with a big stick, but disagreed about whether he was allied *with* the zombies or fighting *against* them."

Jonah looked down at the floor, feeling conspicuous.

"As you can imagine, the children have been difficult and inconsistent witnesses," Mercedes said. "One other thing: shredded nightshade was found scattered over the bridge surface."

"Nightshade?" McCauley said. "Then it's tied to the other attacks on the gifted."

Mercedes nodded. "We're thinking it was either the same

people, or someone trying to cast suspicion on them."

"You should send a team to the Anchorage if you want to find the culprits," Hudson shouted. She avoided looking at Gabriel and Jonah. Some in the crowd murmured in agreement.

Mercedes swung around to stare Hudson down. "Hilary, there's not one scrap of evidence linking the Anchorage to the bridge incident."

"We need to *find* evidence," Scavuzzo said, openly glaring at Gabriel. "We should hold an informal lineup. Bring in our children, and see if they recognize any of the labrats."

"We can't put the children through that," Hudson countered. "It's insane. What we should do is collect DNA from the inmates at the Anchorage. See if we can make a match with what we find at the crime scene."

"You've been watching too many episodes of *CSI*," a man shouted from the audience. "The students at the Anchorage are not criminals. They're differently gifted."

By now, a half-dozen spectators were on their feet, shouting, demanding the floor.

Jonah looked over at Gabriel, who sat calmly, apparently scrolling through messages on his phone.

"Hey! All of you . . . shut up!" The voice echoed through the nave.

The shouting died instantly.

Ellen glared around the room, fists on hips. Jack stood beside her.

"Ellen and I are here to remind you that this is a meeting, not a brawl," Jack said.

Ellen nodded. "So the next person that talks out of turn is going to get pitched right out of the window."

"So now you're using *thugs* to stifle dissent?" Morrison shouted.

Ellen vaulted over the pew in front of her and strode toward Morrison. For a moment, Jonah thought he was going to see wizards fly, but Morrison sat down quickly and Ellen returned to her seat.

Shooting a grateful look at the warriors, Moss said, "We need to give Mercedes and Leesha time to do their jobs. I know emotions are running high, and I assure you we'll follow the evidence wherever it leads. If anyone has information that might help us, contact Leesha or Mercedes. They'll keep in close touch with the police and the preschool administration and let us know of any . . . um . . . developments." She paused. "Let's move on. Is there an update on the cataloging of the Hoard?" She looked at Linda Downey and Leander Hastings.

Linda stood, but before she could speak, someone else did, in a carrying voice that rang through the church from the rear.

"Perhaps you should distribute the weapons to those of us in the guilds who need them for their own protection." It was a woman's voice, cold and cutting.

Jonah turned to look.

Three wizards stalked down the aisle—an angular woman with cropped, reddish-brown hair, a whippetlike man with an early-morning five o'clock shadow, and a young man with sun-streaked chestnut hair.

Rowan DeVries.

Jonah sat bolt upright, his heart accelerating. Then, just as quickly, he slumped down, concealing himself behind those in the rows ahead.

"What is it, Jonah?" Gabriel asked, putting a hand on his arm.

"That's Rowan DeVries. Remember? He's the wizard that was there when Jeanette was murdered." *And, oh, by the way, I killed his sister.* "I don't know the other two."

"That's Nancy Hackleford and Granville Burroughs," Gabriel said. "They're known to be longtime associates of the Black Rose. They're not on council."

Moss and McCauley exchanged glances, then waited until the trio had made their way to the table and stood behind the only empty seat. "Burroughs? Hackleford?" Moss said. "It's been a while. And Rowan? Glad you could be here."

"Sorry I'm late," DeVries said. "I was delayed by a death in the family." His amber eyes rested on Moss. "But maybe you already knew that."

Moss shook her head, eyes widening in surprise. "No! How would I—"

"My sister Rachel was murdered, along with seven other wizards," DeVries said.

"Including my daughter, Brooke," Hackleford said. "She was just seventeen."

Everyone started talking at once, their voices rising higher and higher, but they didn't drown out the voice in

Jonah's head. *You know what it's like to lose a sister. He will never, ever stop hunting you.*

Finally, Moss slammed the gavel down. "Hang on! Let's hear what he has to say!"

The din diminished.

"Unless you'd rather we took a brief recess so that we can talk in private," Moss added.

"No," DeVries said. "We want everyone on the council to hear this."

"All right." Moss sat back, giving the wizards the floor. "Tell us what happened."

"I'm still waiting for an answer to my question," Hackleford said. "Will you distribute weapons from the Hoard to those in the guilds who need them for their own protection?"

"As you know, the council voted that proposition down," Moss said.

"A council packed with representatives from the underguilds who have been conspiring against wizards for years," Hackleford said bitterly.

"A reasonable response to a thousand years of oppression," Hastings countered.

"With the guilds at peace," Moss said, "it seems likely that handing out weapons might be more of a hindrance than a help."

"So you think we are *at peace*?" Burroughs laughed bitterly. "Spoken like somebody living far from the war zone. Most of the *sefas* in the Hoard were made to be used by wizards, so it's no inconvenience to the underguilds that they are locked up." His gaze flicked from face to face, stopping on Hastings's. "How many, Hastings? How many of us are going to have to die before you take this seriously?"

"They don't care about children," Morrison shouted from the audience. "Why should they care about wizards?"

Ellen stood again, and glared around the sanctuary. A warning.

Hastings scowled, drawing dark brows together. "We do take it seriously," he said. "But why should we believe that more weapons would be helpful when we don't know who did the killing and how they managed to overpower eight wizards?"

"So if it's wizards, you don't care?" Hackleford snapped.

"I didn't say that," Hastings replied. "What I meant was, if it's wizard on wizard, or wizard on Anawizard Weir, that game has been played for a thousand years."

"Not like this," DeVries said. The young wizard's eyes darkened to bronze. "Not to this degree. Not at this pace."

"You're wrong," Downey said. "You just never noticed until wizards began dying."

DeVries turned toward her. "It's been only a few weeks since Longbranch and Wylie died in London . . . right after I visited them. And yet nothing was done."

"They were murdered?" Mercedes said. "I hadn't heard that."

"The medical examiner could not determine a cause of death," DeVries said. "Nor could the healers we called in. There wasn't a mark on either of them. This time eight wizards died, and there wasn't a mark on five of them." He paused. "Well, some of them appeared to have been scorched by wizard flame, none of them seriously. We think it may have been friendly fire."

"Friendly fire?" McCauley repeated. "What about the others?"

"One was shot to death. The others were hacked to pieces. Including my sister Rachel." DeVries turned his head and looked straight at Jonah. After a flare of momentary panic, Jonah realized that he was actually looking at Jack and Ellen, behind him. At the swords propped against the pews.

McCauley followed DeVries's gaze and scowled. "I'm sorry for your loss," he said to DeVries. "Where were they when they were killed?"

"We can't tell you that," DeVries said flatly. "Let's just say they were engaged in investigative work of their own."

McCauley and Moss exchanged incredulous looks.

"What do you mean, investigative work?" Moss asked.

"Wizards have been dying for months now," DeVries said. "And nothing has been done about it. Do you blame us for looking for the killers on our own?"

"These eight that died . . . they were all wizards?" Hastings asked. "Nobody else?"

DeVries hesitated for a heartbeat, then said, "Just wizards."

One sorcerer, and one savant, Jonah added silently. Like always, they didn't count.

"All right, then," McCauley said, like somebody who's decided to just get it over with. "Based on your own investigation, do you have a theory about the identity of the assassins?"

The three wizards looked at one another. DeVries nodded to Burroughs, who spoke. "We believe that this council is a sham intended to distract us while this—this *witch* murders us one by one." He glared at Moss.

"You think *I* did it?" Moss blurted, looking stunned.

"Who else?" Hackleford snapped. "Who else has the power to suck the magic right out of a person? Who else is immune to wizardry? Who else has powers we don't even understand? Who else is under the control of the most murderous wizard who ever lived?" He looked pointedly at Hastings.

"Oh, come *on*," Ellen said, breaking her own rule about interrupting. "Don't exaggerate. Think of all the competition he's had over the past thousand years."

"You think I hacked two wizards to death, too?" Moss had gone pale, so her freckles stood out against her creamy skin. "With what? My fingernails?"

"We think you had help," DeVries said, nodding toward Jack and Ellen. "We think you brought a team of assassins with you."

"I don't 'suck the magic' out of a person," Moss said. "I just . . . disconnect. And why would I go around murdering people? I just want to be left alone."

"Where were you last Friday night?" DeVries demanded.

"Me? I was in Chicago," Moss said, flushing.

"Prove it."

"That's enough!" McCauley said. "Maddie isn't on trial here. If you think she's guilty of something, where's your evidence? Where's *your* proof? When Moss sucks the juice out of a person, it doesn't kill them."

"I don't suck juice out of *anybody*," Moss shouted. "That's disgusting."

"Maybe we haven't seen the full range of her capabilities," Hackleford said.

"Listen," Downey said. "Mercedes here is something of an expert on poisons and toxins." She pointed at the sorcerer. "Maybe if she could examine the bodies, she could—"

"That won't be possible," DeVries said.

After a stunned silence, McCauley said, "If we don't know where they were or how they died, then how are we supposed to—"

"After three months of inaction, I don't expect you to conduct anything more than a sham investigation," Hackleford said. "Involving Ms. Foster would be like inviting one of the co-conspirators to sit in on the inquest. We'll be handling this ourselves."

"And . . . there were no survivors?" McCauley asked. "No witnesses?"

"No," DeVries said. "There never are."

He's hiding something, Jonah thought, sitting up straighter. There's something he's not telling us. Could someone have survived? If so, why hadn't that person identified Jonah himself?

"We want access to the magical technology in the Hoard," Hackleford said, "in the hopes that it might help us protect ourselves while we collect the proof we need. After all, those weapons were the property of the Wizard Guild before they were confiscated."

Hastings twisted the ring on his forefinger. "Surely you don't expect us to hand you an arsenal and send you out to seek vigilante justice for the killers. That's the kind of thing we're trying to avoid with the new constitution, the establishment of the council, and so on."

"If you want to control everything, then where's your magical police force?" Burroughs demanded. "Where's your criminal court? What system have you developed to replace the Rules of Engagement?"

"We're working on that," McCauley said. "It takes time to—"

"Well, time is running out," DeVries said. "If you're not going to protect us, then we will protect ourselves." He looked at Madison Moss. "If you're really not the guilty party, you should start magically castrating people until somebody talks. Only this time, start with somebody other than wizards."

He took a step back from the table. "My father was murdered years ago. And now my sister is dead. Don't tell me to be patient. Give me weapons that I can use against these assassins, and get out of my way. That's all I want. In the meantime, I'll keep what information I have to myself."

He turned on his heel and walked out of the sanctuary, followed by Burroughs and Hackleford.

ᔥ CHAPTER TWENTY-NINE ᔥ
IN A WORLD OF TROUBLE

The door to Emma's sickroom flew open, and two wizards walked in. A man and a woman. They looked to be in their midthirties, with lean, hard faces.

Natalie stood and turned to face them, arms folded across her chest, like a wall between Emma and the newcomers.

They froze momentarily, as if startled to see Emma sitting up. "She's awake!" the man said. "Why didn't you call us?"

He crossed the room to Emma's bedside, followed by the woman. The two wizards stood over her, looking down at her like they were hungry and she was dinner.

Emma blotted at her face with her forearm, sniffling, and Natalie handed her a tissue.

The man glared at Natalie. "Why is she crying? What did you say to her?"

"She's an emotional wreck," Natalie said, squeezing Emma's shoulder. "Can you blame her?"

"Don't encourage her," the woman said. "We don't have time for hysterics." She was dressed in a sweater, skirt, and fancy leather boots, elaborate earrings and a heavy gold necklace. Her red-brown hair had that carefully tossed look that stank of money.

"I gave her something to help her sleep," Natalie lied. "You should let her rest now, and come back tomorrow."

"She just woke up, and you gave her something to put her back to sleep? Who do you think you are?"

Natalie lifted her chin. "I'm a healer. That's what I do."

"If you say so," the woman said. "Mandrake claims that you're a gifted healer despite your disability, but I find that difficult to believe." She paused for a heartbeat. "How fortunate that he's been able to find useful work for you people."

Dismissing Natalie, she turned to Emma. "I'm Ms. Hackleford, and this is Mr. Burroughs. We're going to ask you some questions."

"Just so you know," Natalie said. "Emma's experiencing some memory loss."

"Do you expect us to believe that?" Burroughs asked, scowling. He was whip-thin, with close-cropped dark hair. He might have been handsome but for his cruel lips and empty eyes.

Natalie shrugged. "Temporary amnesia is a common reaction to emotional trauma."

Hackleford made a small, unhappy moue. "So you've already interrogated her, have you?"

"Of course not," Natalie said. "It's too risky. After all my hard work, I don't want to see her relapse."

"That's a risk we'll have to take," Hackleford said. "It's

already been a week, and the trail is getting colder by the minute. There are eight people dead, my daughter included, and we need answers."

It took Emma a moment to wick up the words. "Eight people dead?" she blurted. "What eight people?"

"Well, nine, counting your father." Hackleford obviously didn't.

"Then he *is* dead," Emma whispered. "Tyler's dead." All of the hope drained out of her. She struggled to breathe, to take in air, but it was as if her airway was closing.

Her father had never been any kind of anchor . . . she hadn't even known he existed until a few months ago. But still. She felt like she'd been cut loose and cast adrift, with no idea where she would eventually land. She finally understood the truth . . . that there would be no good news coming. Ever.

A door opened in Emma's mind, and she saw blood. Blood spattered everywhere. A crowd around Tyler. Somebody slamming into her. Her father's gun, spinning away from her. Glass raining down from overhead. She began to shake, her teeth chattering uncontrollably.

"You see what I mean?" Natalie said. "This is not the time to—"

"This is wizard business," Burroughs said. "If you want to make yourself useful, then identify the toxin. Isn't that what you're supposed to be good at? Now get out."

Natalie stood, fists clenched, and for a moment, Emma thought she might refuse to comply with the wizard's demand. But she took a deep breath, released it, and left the room, closing the door behind her with a soft click.

Hackleford gazed at Emma, lips pursed, as if studying her

for vulnerabilities. "So you see, Emma," she said, in a low, foxy voice. "We're all on the same side. We want to find out who murdered your father and my daughter and the others. We're hoping you can help us. You do want to help us, don't you?"

"We know who did it," Burroughs said. "Or at least who gave the orders. All you have to do is say the names. We'll take it from there."

"S-say what?" Emma looked from one to the other. "You already know who murdered my father?"

Burroughs sat down on the side of the bed. Emma shuddered. She didn't want him there, not at all. Meanwhile, Hackleford went and bolted the door. Emma's heart began to thud so loud that she was sure the two wizards could hear it.

"Do you recognize this person? Was he one of the killers?" Burroughs extended a tablet toward her, displaying an image of a young man with dark curls and green eyes. Totally unfamiliar.

"No," Emma said. "I don't recognize him."

The wizard's lips tightened in annoyance. "Are you sure?"

"Well . . ." Emma licked her lips. "I can't be sure—"

"So he *might* have been there?" Burroughs said, leaning forward, putting one hand on her pillow, next to her ear.

"I—I think I remember somebody with a mask."

"A mask?" Burroughs and Hackleford looked at each other. "Could it have been him?" Burroughs thrust the screen under her nose again.

"To be honest, it could've been anyone."

"How about her?" Burroughs asked, extending the

tablet again. This time the screen displayed a photograph of a young woman with long, wavy brown hair and a sprinkling of freckles across her nose.

Emma pressed her hand against her forehead. Her headache had returned with a vengeance. It hurt to shake her head, but she did it anyway. "No."

"Look at this one," Burroughs persisted. This time, it was a photo of two people, a young man and a young woman, both holding elaborate swords and looking like they knew how to use them.

"Look, I don't see the point," she said. "They may or may not have been there, I just don't remember."

"How about names?" Hackleford asked. "Do you remember any names being mentioned?" She paused and, when Emma said nothing, continued: "Seph McCauley? Madison Moss? Jack Swift? Do any of those names sound familiar?"

"M-maybe if you came back . . . tomorrow. I'd remember more."

"We need to know now," Hackleford said, "before anyone else is murdered. You don't want anyone else to be murdered, do you?"

"All we need is a yes, Emma," Burroughs said, "and we'll leave you alone." He leaned in, his copper-penny eyes fixed on hers, and brushed his fingers lightly along her jawline, leaving a nettlelike sting.

"Stop that!" She slapped his hand away. "I'm not going to lie and say yes when it's just not true. I—I'm not answering any more questions without a lawyer."

"A lawyer?" Burroughs laughed. "Who do you think we are . . . the police? Do you think we're going to read you your Miranda rights, you little—"

"Careful," Hackleford warned. "You know what DeVries—"

"DeVries needs to take off the gloves, or he won't be running this operation for long," Burroughs said. Grabbing a fistful of Emma's hair, he yanked her head back and leaned in so they were nose to nose, his cigarette breath washing over her.

"That hurts," Emma whimpered, tears in her eyes. "Please, don't. It hurts."

"This is just the beginning. Let me be clear . . . you are in a world of trouble. The only way out is to give us what we want."

Drawing back her arm, Emma slammed the heel of her hand against the bridge of the wizard's nose with a satisfying crunch. Howling in rage, Burroughs wrapped his fingers around her throat and jammed her back against the headboard, each finger like a tiny torch against her skin. Emma clawed at his forearm, struggling for air. Her head was pounding. No . . . someone was pounding at the door.

She could hear Hackleford in the background. "Burroughs! Are you out of your mind? Stop it!"

But he didn't stop. Finally, stiffening her fingers, Emma jabbed the wizard in the eyes.

Burroughs released his hold and pitched himself backward. He landed on the floor and rolled to his feet, eyes streaming tears, murder on his face.

The door slammed open, the bolt pinging as it hit the floor.

A man stood in the doorway, glowing.

"DeVries!" Hackleford cried. Both wizards stepped back in unison, as if the move had been choreographed. "We didn't think you were—"

"You didn't think I'd be back so soon?"

"No . . . I didn't, but it's good you're here," Hackleford said, quickly covering her initial reaction. "The girl's awake. We were just about to call you."

The newcomer's eyes flicked from Burroughs, who was dabbing at his eyes, to Hackleford, and finally to Emma, trembling in the bed. Swearing, he crossed the room and stood at the bedside, looking down at her. He looked to be only a few years older than her, with fair skin, streaked brown hair, and tawny eyes, like a jungle cat's.

"What's going on?" DeVries asked, focusing on Emma. "What's wrong?"

Emma shifted her gaze to Burroughs, and saw the promise of pain in those copper-penny eyes.

"Nothing," she said, resisting the temptation to explore her blistered neck with her fingers.

"Something happened," DeVries persisted.

"They told me my father was murdered," Emma said. Which was true, as far as it went. Wrapping her arms around herself, she tilted her head down to conceal her neck. "I just . . . I just want to be left alone. Could you please leave me alone?"

"I'm afraid we can't. Not quite yet." When he spoke again, it was to the wizards in the room. "Would someone else care to tell me what happened here?"

"It's like she said," Hackleford said. "When she woke, she asked about her father, and we told her he was dead."

Burroughs returned to Emma's bedside like a vulture drawn back to a fresh carcass. "I think you'll agree, DeVries, that time is of the essence if we're to win broader support from the Wizard Council before any more wizards are murdered.

As you know, I have considerable experience in interrogation. I have no doubt that, given a little time, I can obtain the answers we want."

"I am less interested in obtaining the answers we want than I am in getting at the truth," DeVries said. "I told you—both of you—that I intended to handle this interrogation myself. What was it that you didn't understand?"

"I'd hoped you'd reconsider," Burroughs said. "We can't afford to squander our only chance to make our case against the cabal in Trinity. We need to get more wizards off the fence and onto our side."

"And I don't think we want to wear our witness out talking politics," DeVries said. "We'll discuss this after I've had the chance to talk to her. Now go."

They went.

DeVries pulled up a chair and straddled it, facing Emma. He might have been a college student, in his jeans, sneakers, and a collared shirt. "I'm Rowan DeVries," he said.

"Emma Greenwood."

"You're the daughter of Tyler Greenwood and Gwyneth Hart?"

Gwyneth? Gwen. Right. "Yes."

For a long moment, he stared down at his hands, saying nothing. Then he said, "Is it true what they said? Now that they're gone, do you want to change your story?"

"Is it true that I'm a prisoner?"

His head came up quickly, his expression startled.

"Mr. DeVries. I may not know much, but I'm not stupid," Emma said.

"Call me Rowan," he said. Then added, as an afterthought, "Please."

"Rowan," Emma repeated, putting an edge on it. "If I've been so sick, then why am I not in a hospital? If I'm accused of something, then why am I not talking to the police?"

"You're not accused of anything," Rowan said.

"Then suppose you tell me what this is all about?" On the streets of Memphis, she'd learned to take the offensive when she got into a tight spot. A good bluff could sometimes save a person a world of trouble.

"We need to know what happened," Rowan went on. "How you were hurt. And we need to know now. Just tell me what you remember, whether you think it's important or not."

"I'm not talking to anyone without a lawyer," Emma said.

"A lawyer would not be helpful," Rowan said stiffly.

"Not to you, maybe."

"Look, I'll walk you through it," he said. "And you fill in what you know. We found you on the floor of the conservatory. Was that where you first saw the intruders?"

Emma folded her arms and said nothing.

Rowan's tawny eyes hardened into amber, set into a face gone pale as marble. "Don't try my patience, Emma," he said softly. "My sister Rachel is dead. She's all the family I had. I practically raised her after my father was murdered. I'd prefer not to hurt you, but I *will get some* answers."

"I can't tell you what I don't know," Emma said. "Do you want me to make something up?"

"All I want is the truth," he said. "No games. Don't try to tell me that you don't remember anything." He released a long breath and raked both hands through his hair.

"The last I remember was being in my workshop in the basement."

"Workshop?"

"I'm a luthier. I build guitars." She paused and, when he didn't ask questions about this, continued: "After that, nothing. Or almost nothing. It's just a few scenes. Like pictures, in my head. Somebody in a mask. And—and gunshots. And blood." Tears leaked from her eyes and ran down her face.

He handed her a tissue. "This masked person. Can you tell me anything else? What was he wearing? How big was he? Did he look familiar? Was he gifted?"

Emma shook her head. "It seemed like he was all bundled up, so all I could see was his eyes. He had sad eyes."

"Sad eyes?" Rowan sounded a little exasperated.

"You asked what I remembered, right? I remember that."

"Did he try to charm you?"

"Charm me?" Emma was lost. "You mean, seduce me? Or . . ."

He flushed. "Charms. You know. Spells. Conjury." He raised his hand and mimicked casting a spell.

"Oh. No."

"How old was he?"

"All I saw were his eyes."

"If you had to guess."

"From his voice, I'd say he was younger rather than older. Teens or twenties."

"Are any of these people familiar?" Rowan had his own array of photographs stored in his phone, the same people the other wizards had shown her.

"I don't recognize any of them." She handed the phone back.

"How about this one?"

It was a photograph of a girl with chestnut hair in a

tennis outfit. The resemblance between her and Rowan was striking. It pinged something in Emma's memory.

"I don't know. Maybe. Is that your sister?"

"Yes," he said, putting the phone away. "What can you tell me about Tyler?"

"I don't really know him that well."

"He's your father, right?" Rowan said, raising an eyebrow.

"I just came to live with him a few months ago."

"Where were you before that?"

"I lived with my grandfather in Memphis. After he died, I came here."

And then Emma could have sworn that Rowan did the flicker-eye thing. The lying thing. He looked down at his hands. Then back up at Emma. "So. Since you've been living with Tyler, have you seen people coming and going? Meetings at the house? Did he seem to be involved in any kind of . . . conspiracy?"

"No. Nobody ever came over. He didn't seem to have any friends. He was pretty much a homebody, except when he went out for gigs."

"Gigs?"

"He plays—played—bass guitar in a band."

"Did you ever see him work with chemicals, plants, poisons, magical devices?"

"No, never."

"He was a sorcerer." It was a half question.

"That's what I'm told. But I never saw any sign of it."

"How about you? Are you a sorcerer as well?"

Emma shook her head. "I don't know what I am. Maybe nothing. Tyler said I was gifted, but that was the first I heard about it."

Rowan seemed to have run out of questions temporarily. Closing his eyes, he rubbed his forehead, looking about as weary and heartsick as Emma felt.

"What happens now?" she asked, though she wasn't sure she wanted to hear the answer.

"We'll keep trying, Emma, until you remember more."

"And if I don't?"

"We'll cross that bridge when we come to it. But I want the truth, Emma. Nothing more and nothing less."

"Fair enough," she said. "Will you tell *me* the truth, then?"

His eyes narrowed. "It depends on the question."

"If you can't tell me the truth, tell me nothing at all," she said. "I can't stand a liar. How did they die? My father and the others?"

He shifted his gaze away. "Do you really want the details? I mean—we don't have to—"

"I'm not like other people," Emma said. "I've been told that all my life. And I want to know how my father died."

"Very well, if you insist," Rowan said. "Greenwood—your father—had a deep cutting wound to the thigh. He had some . . . he was burned, and he'd been cut by broken glass, but what killed him must have been blood loss."

"And the others?"

"Two of the dead, including my sister, were badly cut up, too. Stabbed and slashed. One was shot. The others didn't have a mark on them. We've seen that before. So we've been thinking there were several attackers, using different weapons."

"Did you call the police?" By now, Emma was fairly certain he hadn't. "Did you even do an autopsy?"

Rowan rolled his eyes, as if Emma were a hopeless case. "*That* would be a colossal waste of time."

"Really? Maybe you could use the help. You don't seem to be doing such a great job on your own." Emma's anger was bubbling to the surface again, despite her efforts to contain it. "Tell me this," she said. "What were your sister and those others doing at *my* house? I assume they weren't looking to book a gig."

Rowan chewed on his lower lip a moment, as if debating how much to say. "We've been looking for people with a connection to Thorn Hill. We think there's a connection between what happened there and a series of murders going on now. Including the killing of my sister and your father."

CHAPTER THIRTY
ASK ME NO QUESTIONS

"Thorn Hill?" Emma asked, playing dumb.

"It was a Weir terrorist camp in Brazil. All of the under-guilds were involved, to a degree, but it was mostly sorcerers. They flocked there to work in secret on weapons they could use against the Wizard Guild."

"That's not what I heard," Emma blurted, recalling what Tyler had said. "And not what I remember."

Rowan's eyes widened in surprise. "You were there?"

Brasilia. Memory poured over her. The scent of jasmine and four o'clocks in the gathering dusk. Emma and her mother, riding in a Jeep on a rutted country road, hitting bumps at full speed and flying through the air. Emma shrieking with laughter. *Go faster, Mommy.*

Of course, as a five-year-old, she had no way of telling what else went on there.

With that, Emma's beaten-down memory struggled back to life, surfacing a scrap of conversation she'd had with Tyler. About her mother.

She was working for Mr. DeVries at the time.

Mr. DeVries? Who's that?

Somebody you never want to meet. A wizard.

That was why the name DeVries was familiar. Rowan's father was the wizard her mother had worked for. The one she was frightened of. The one she fled to Brazil to get away from.

"Emma?"

Emma looked up to find Rowan DeVries staring at her. "What is it?" he said, leaning toward her, his hands on his knees. "What do you remember?"

"I was there. When I was little."

"And?"

Two impulses warred within her. Her first impulse was to withhold as much information as possible. But she realized that this might be an opportunity to learn more about her mother.

"Tyler told me that my mother used to work for your father," Emma said finally.

"Did she?" He didn't seem surprised.

"And she ran away to Thorn Hill to get away from him."

"That's certainly possible," Rowan said, nodding. "So?"

"Is it true that she used to make poisons?" Emma knew that she was taking a risk, poking and prodding, digging up the truth about her mother. *If your mother is dead, and if nobody will tell you a thing about her, you can make up whatever kind of mother you want.* But she wasn't interested in made-up mothers. Emma was a person who liked to take the truth by the throat and shake it. If there was one thing she couldn't stand, it was a liar.

Rowan rubbed the back of his neck. "Does it matter

now? Some things you're better off not knowing. Maybe you should just leave that be."

"You mean, like you let Tyler be?"

Rowan sighed. "I don't know specifics about your mother, but it seems likely that she made poisons. The sorcerers who worked for my father were primarily involved in making them." His voice was flat, matter-of-fact. "If so, she must have been good at it. He only hired the best."

"What—what would he want with poison?" Emma forced the words over a dry tongue.

"My father, Andrew DeVries, founded a syndicate known as the Black Rose. Its members solved all kinds of sticky problems for their clients, but they specialized in contract killing of the gifted. Wizards, mostly. To be blunt, I come from a family of assassins."

Emma's heart squeezed painfully as the realization hit home. *My mother was a murderer. An accessory to murder, at least.*

"The syndicate was successful from the very start. After all, why butt heads with an opponent when you can take him out of play entirely? Why negotiate with rebellious under-guilds when you can eliminate their ringleaders and frighten the rest into submission? A little judicious killing can reduce the need for bloodshed later on.

"My father didn't take sides . . . he was apolitical. He sold his services to anyone willing to pay the price. Of course, some in the wizard houses were disdainful of him . . . at first, anyway." A trace of a smile quirked Rowan's lips. "They considered poison a weapon of the underguilds, an inappropriate tactic for wizards. They preferred to settle disputes via the anachronistic elegance of the Game."

"The Game?"

"You've not heard of it? They used warrior gladiators as proxies to settle disputes. They would fight one-on-one, winner take all, under a set of rules that go back to the sixteenth century." He rolled his eyes. "Rather silly, really. It leaves way too much up to chance. My father was nothing if not efficient. People soon learned to get out of his way."

Horrified words crowded together in Emma's mind, competing to escape. "B-but . . . what would he . . . I don't understand why she would—"

"There's a lot I don't know, all right?" Rowan snapped. "I was twelve when my father was murdered. Rachel was eight. We were not involved in Father's business; we were attending private schools under aliases for our own protection. I was fourteen before I found out my real name."

"Who killed your father?" Emma asked.

Rowan straightened his sleeves. "Who indeed? So many suspects to choose from."

"Why are you interested in Thorn Hill?" Emma asked.

"The sorcerers who went to Thorn Hill had expertise in a number of areas that are of interest to us now. Much of that knowledge was lost in the accident. We're hoping to salvage something."

"The accident?" *My father called it a massacre*, she wanted to say. "What happened?"

Rowan shrugged. "Apparently some of the poisons they were working on contaminated the water supply. Nearly everyone died. A few children survived—and many of them were horribly disfigured." He frowned, appraising Emma. "You must have left before then," he said.

"I guess I must have," Emma said. "How many people died?"

"Several thousand, from what I understand." He grimaced. "So much expertise was lost. What a shame."

"Yeah. A shame about the expertise," Emma murmured. "Why does that matter now? Have you decided to go into the family business?"

"Recent events have forced my hand," Rowan said.

"What do you mean?"

"Somebody is murdering wizards. We believe we know who's doing it, but right now we're helpless to stop it. Thorn Hill was also a center for research into Weirstones. Specifically, research on ways to modify them."

"Why would anyone want to do that?"

Rowan shrugged. "I don't know . . . maybe they wanted to create a mutant army to kill wizards?"

"That's ridiculous," Emma said. "My parents would never be involved in something like that."

"You mean your mother, the assassin's accomplice, or your father that you just met?" Rowan laughed. "We're alike, you and I . . . we both spring from tainted stock."

"Why do *you* want to modify Weirstones?"

"All of our Weirstones are dependent on the Dragonheart, the source of magical energy. A small group has seized power over the Weirguilds by taking control of the Dragonheart. We're looking for a way to free ourselves from dependence on the Dragonheart while retaining our gifts. Until we're able to do this, we're helpless to fight back.

"We'd been looking for your father for a long time. Some records seemed to connect him to the Black Rose—perhaps through your mother, I don't know. He was connected to Thorn Hill as well . . . he spent some time there. So we thought perhaps he might be the link we were looking for.

"Rachel believed that she'd finally located him. She and the others went to question your father and verify who he was." Pain flickered across his face. "I should never have allowed her to go, but she was excited, hoping this would be her first big breakthrough. And I thought, of course, he's a sorcerer—what chance would he have against eight wizards?" He grimaced. "But somebody else showed up, maybe somebody who knew they were coming. My sister called for help, but I got there too late."

He lost more than I did that night, Emma thought. For me, Tyler was a link to the past and a hope for the future. But anyone could tell that Rowan really loved his sister.

"She didn't describe the killer to you?"

Rowan shook his head. "It seems she didn't plan on being dead when I got there."

"You sent eight people to question one man?"

"Most of them were young. New recruits. Like me, Rachel assumed the job was routine, and brought them along so they could gain some experience. But it's also possible that they were anticipating trouble. Anyone who can murder that many wizards is exceedingly dangerous."

"But you weren't there?"

"If I had been there, Rachel would have survived. Or I would be dead," Rowan said bluntly.

"And so . . . your sister and the others drew assassins to my house, and my father ended up dead?" Emma made no effort to keep the bitterness out of her voice.

"Either that or your father lured my sister and the others into a trap," Rowan snapped back.

"And ended up dead himself. That's a real good plan, to host a murder with his own daughter as witness."

"If he was involved, I'm sure he didn't mean for it to turn out the way it did," Rowan said. "This is the first time the murderers have left any witnesses. I don't think they meant to."

So, Emma realized, she herself was supposed to be dead, along with the others. If any of what Rowan was saying was even true.

"How did I get here?"

"At first, we thought you were dead, too," Rowan said. "You didn't seem to be breathing. And yet, you were still warm, and you had a faint pulse. We brought you back here, hoping you'd recover. When you didn't show any signs of improvement, we called in that labrat healer."

"You never considered taking me to a hospital?"

"No."

You said you wanted the truth, Emma thought. "Where are we, anyway?" she asked, looking around.

"This is my house," Rowan said. "In Bratenahl."

"What's Bratenahl?"

"It's a neighborhood. A village, I guess. Up on the lake."

"Pretty fancy house you've got."

"It was my father's."

"Who are Hackleford and Burroughs?" Emma asked.

Rowan's face armored up—even more than it already was. "They're longtime colleagues of my father's. After my father died, the organization splintered. Hackleford and Burroughs are very much interested in using the current crisis to rebuild the organization and their own power." He took a deep breath and released it slowly. "Whether or not your father was involved in the murders, we should be allies. The same killers murdered your father and my sister."

"Great," Emma said. "We're allies. Then let's go back to my original question. Am I a prisoner?"

"Don't you see?" Rowan said, as if exasperated. "It's for your own protection. We're dealing with ruthless killers. What do you suppose they'll do when they find out you're still alive?"

"And if I decide to take my chances?" Emma said, thinking of Burroughs. "Can I leave anytime I want?"

"Would you stop *pushing* me?" His voice shook. "My sister is dead. Now I'm in the middle of a power struggle with people who want to seize control of the organization my father built. If you knew anything about wizards, you'd know it's cutthroat. And you'd better hope I win. Believe it or not, right now I'm the best friend you have."

Emma dredged up courage from some unknown source. "Well, guess what? My father is dead. Or so I'm told. I didn't see any killing and I haven't seen any bodies. All I have to go on is the word of a bunch of strangers who are holding me prisoner. If what you're saying is true, then prove it. You say all these people are dead. Show me the bodies."

"I can't do that."

"Why not?"

"It's been a week," Rowan said. "We already disposed of them."

This didn't sound like the bodies of the victims were buried. It sounded more like they'd been put out with the trash.

"What do you mean, you *disposed* of them? How?"

"We burned them," Rowan said. "Cremated them, if you like, with wizard flame, which leaves nothing behind."

"My father, too?" He nodded. "You had no *right*!" Emma's voice trembled.

Rowan's lips tightened. "We couldn't very well keep them around, and we didn't want any kind of inquest."

"It sounds like that's just what you did want," Emma said, her voice low and furious. "An inquest. Then you'd know more than you do now, which is nothing."

"We'll talk again," Rowan said, standing up. "In the meantime, try to get some rest. And don't worry. Our security here is very good. We're surrounded by a fifteen-foot-high wall. So nobody will be getting in or out without our knowing it."

Sonny Lee always said, Don't ask questions that you don't want to hear the answer to. But Emma could never resist going after the truth, no matter how hurtful. Maybe it was because she'd been lied to so much.

"So where am I at the end of all this?" she demanded. "After you've squeezed every last bit of truth out of me. Are you going to turn me loose then?"

"I've got to go," he said, crossing the room to the door.

"Are you going to answer my question?"

Rowan turned in the doorway. "No, I'm not. You said that if I can't tell the truth, to say nothing at all."

And then he was gone.

❧ CHAPTER THIRTY-ONE ❧
ANAWEIR

To the west, the sun descended toward the lake, gilding the edges of the clouds and sending long fingers of crimson and orange and gold over the surface toward them. The woods along the shoreline blazed with color. The clouds looked different now than they had just a few weeks ago. They were no longer fluffy puffs, but broad, flat slices layered together.

Winter was coming to Cleveland. It would take some getting used to for a Memphis girl, assuming that she lived long enough to see it.

It was Emma who had suggested the walk, hoping it would take them away from prying eyes and ears. Natalie had backed her up, saying a little exercise would speed her recovery.

The DeVries home was probably four times the size of Tyler's house in Cleveland Heights. It was built of stone, set on a large piece of property. The back side of the house was pocked with terraces, balconies, and patios showcasing the view of the lake. A stone path wound its way from the back door to a small pavilion at the edge of a cliff. The landward side of the property was circled by a tall stone wall topped with a strand of electrified wire. Security guards were housed in a separate building, and patrolled the property continually.

"Now, what was it you wanted to talk about?" Natalie asked, leaning toward Emma.

Emma glanced back at the two guards who followed behind them. For their protection, Rowan said. The aura that framed them marked them as gifted.

Natalie looked back at them, too.

"Let's walk out a little further," Emma said.

As they picked their way down the stone path, Emma cast about for something safe to talk about.

"Which guild do you belong to?" she asked the healer, pulling up her hood to keep her hair from snaking around her face.

"I was born into the Sorcerers' Guild. And now I'm a sorcerer savant."

There was that word again—*savant*. The thing Natalie claimed Emma was. "You mean you can choose a different guild?" Emma asked, surprised.

"It was hardly a choice." By now, they'd reached the pavilion at the edge of the cliff. Here, the rush of the wind and the crash of the waves on the rocks below drowned out their conversation, making it, they hoped, difficult to overhear.

Natalie scooped up a rock and hurled it out over the water. It landed with a distant splash. "Whatever the Wizard Guild put into the water supply changed us forever. We have powers no one else has. For instance, I can see injuries and disorders through a person's skin. My friend Charlie has a gift for foreign languages. But it comes at a price. Many of us have serious health problems."

Emma frowned. "You know what: this is the third different story I've heard about what happened at Thorn Hill. Tyler said it was an accident—likely contamination from the mines. Rowan claimed that terrorists compounding poisons contaminated the water supply."

"Is that what he said?" Natalie snorted. "I guess it would be hard to admit that you poisoned thousands of people, including children too young to be terrorists."

"But, why would they *do* that?" Emma asked, stuffing her hands into her pockets.

Natalie shrugged. "I guess they felt threatened by the notion of the other guilds getting out from under their control. They assumed Thorn Hill must be the center of a conspiracy against wizards." She kicked at some leaves lying in her way. "It's *always* about them, you know. They're the center of the magical universe."

No wonder she hates wizards, Emma thought, remembering what Rowan had said about the other guilds conspiring against them. "But you lived through it?"

Natalie nodded. "All of the adults died, but some of the children survived. I guess we had more ability to repair the damage." She shoved her hands into her pockets. "We survived, but we were changed. I guess you could call us magical mutants."

"Like—like . . ." Emma blushed, embarrassed. "Like in the comics?"

But Natalie laughed. "Sort of. They nailed the discrimination thing. We prefer the term 'savants.' You know, someone with a unique and narrowly focused talent or gift."

Moving away from the pavilion, they picked their way along the edge of the cliff. Far below, Lake Erie thrashed against the rocks, foam scabbing the shoreline. The waves rapidly lost color as the light fled.

"See, that's what I don't get," Natalie said. "You said you left *before* the disaster. And yet, you have a savant stone."

"How can you tell?"

"I can read your stone. Trust me, I've treated hundreds of savants at the Anchorage. I know what they look like."

By now they'd reached another small terrace bounded by a low wall that ran along the edge of the cliff. Beyond were jagged rocks intermittently drenched in waves. Natalie boosted herself onto the wall and turned, so her feet dangled over the lake below. Emma sat down on the wall next to her, keeping her feet on the landward side.

"Was anyone ever charged with the crime?" she asked. "The poisoning, I mean."

Natalie snorted. "The Wizard Council ran things at that time. No way they were going to investigate themselves. Anyway, all the adult witnesses were dead, so it was hard to figure out who to blame."

"But—but the police—"

"Because the poison killed by damaging Weirstones, it's not toxic to the Anaweir. So involving the police wouldn't really help, and it would raise questions that nobody wanted to answer. We were foreign guests in Brazil, remember.

"There wasn't a lot of pressure to solve the crime, anyway, not from the mainline guilds. Most guildlings viewed the people at Thorn Hill either as radicals or starry-eyed fools. The consensus was that we got what we deserved, and that we should be put out of our misery."

"But . . . you weren't."

"Some of us were, actually," Natalie said, her voice catching. After a moment, she continued. "Then Gabriel Mandrake came along."

"Gabriel Mandrake? Who's that?"

"He's the founder of the Anchorage, the school I attend. And the major donor to the foundation that supports us. He's a sorcerer who didn't view us as throwaways. In fact—" Natalie seemed to catch herself again. "Sorry. I don't mean to go on and on. The bottom line is, technically, we're no longer mainliners—members of the original guilds. I guess you could say that our abilities are highly variable and focused. No two of us are alike. For instance, I'm a healer. Most sorcerers are skilled at making magical tools and compounding powerful potions, and remedies. I have a special gift for diagnosis and healing through touch.

"There's a cost, though. Savants seem to decline, over time. We call it fading. Quite a few of us have died in the past ten years, and some of the survivors are in really bad health. That's why I asked you if you were having symptoms. A lot of us depend on drugs to keep us alive."

"But I'm not magical," Emma protested. "To tell the truth, I'm a mess. I'm not gifted in any way. It seems like I have more *dis*abilities than abilities. I'm always in trouble at school. I just can't seem to concentrate."

"Hmm," Natalie said, nodding as if this confirmed something. "Isn't there anything—even *one* thing—you're especially good at? Maybe something you never really considered to be magical?"

"Well. I'm a luthier. I'm good at building guitars. Like my grandfather."

A grin broke across Natalie's face. "Really? You build guitars? Do you play?"

Emma shrugged, kicking her feet against the wall. "I play a little."

"I play drums," Natalie said, as if happy to have established that natural connection between musicians. "I'm in a band. Maybe you've heard of it. Fault Tolerant?"

Emma gaped at her. "That's why you look familiar! I saw you! I saw you play at Club Catastrophe. You were the drummer."

They slapped hands. "That is so cool," Natalie said. "Like this is fate or something. See, music is really big at school, because of Gabriel's interest in it, and because it seems to work well as a therapy for some of the students who can't be reached any other way." She paused. "These guitars you build—I'd love to see one."

"I've sold a couple," Emma said. "There are two more back at my house."

"Are they . . . *magical* in any way?"

"Magical?" Emma snorted. "How can a guitar be magical?" A memory surfaced, of afternoons in the back of Sonny Lee's shop. Blues players, young and old, shaking their heads, smitten with what her grandfather could do with maple and mahogany. Sonny Lee's guitars could make a bad player sound good, and a good player make magic.

But Emma had the feeling that Natalie was talking about something more than this.

She looked up to find Natalie studying her, her lower lip caught behind her teeth. "You know, I don't know what your plans are, but the Anchorage would be a good fit for you. And Gabriel has pledged to accept all survivors."

"Why does he do it?" Emma said. "Is he some kind of saint?"

Natalie laughed. "Oh, no. He's a music promoter, so you know he's no saint. He helped found Thorn Hill . . . he still owns the land in Brazil, so I guess he feels a commitment to us. Much of the money that supports the foundation comes from gemstone mines on the property."

Emma looked for the guards who had been tailing them. Seeing that they'd stopped moving, they had taken up a position at the far end of the terrace. She could see the glow of their cigarettes through the gathering darkness.

She fingered the ring of blisters around her neck, left by Burroughs's fingers. It was now or never.

She leaned in close to Natalie. "Speaking of plans, I need your help. I need to get out of here."

Natalie nodded, still staring out at the lake. "Go on."

"They mean to keep me here until they've wrung all the information out of me that they can get, then they're going to kill me."

"Why am I not surprised?" Natalie said, a bitter edge to her voice.

"When you leave here, could you notify the police?"

For what seemed like forever, Natalie didn't answer. Then she said, "I doubt that would do any good. Anyway, what makes you think they'll let me leave?"

Emma stared at her. "What? Of course they will! They have to."

"No. They don't," Natalie said. "Why would they? You're a very important property. They see you as the break they've been looking for. Oh, Gabriel will kick up a fuss, but they'll stand their ground. They have to. They'll say I left here to return to the Anchorage, and something must have happened to me on the way. End of story."

"So you help them out and in return they murder you?"

"That's wizards," Natalie said.

"Well, then, we both have to escape," Emma said.

"Easier said than done." Natalie stared out at the now-black waters of the lake, the only side of the property that wasn't fenced in. "Can you swim?"

Emma shook her head. "Not a lick. Not many chances to learn in downtown Memphis. You?"

Natalie shook her head. "Me neither. Listen, I'll tell them I need something from the Anchorage. A medicine or a treatment. Maybe they'll let me go. Or at least send a message."

"But . . . what good would that do?" Emma asked. "If the police can't help, then—"

"I think I know somebody who can."

When they walked back to the house, Rowan was waiting for them on the terrace. Emma had the feeling he'd been watching them for some time.

"You're looking well," he said to Emma, standing aside so they could enter through the French doors. "Are you nearly back to normal?"

"Yes. Pretty much," Emma said, without thinking.

"I'm glad to hear it." He put his hand on her arm, and she flinched away. His eyes narrowed. "Perhaps, tonight, we can talk more about what you remember about the night of the murders."

Was there a threat implicit in these words? Emma wasn't sure.

As soon as they passed into the hall, Emma stopped short.

Natalie's small suitcase and backpack were sitting by the door, with all the rest of her belongings. Natalie saw it at the same time. They both swiveled to stare at Rowan.

"Since you're doing so well, I don't see any reason to take up any more of Natalie's time," Rowan said. "We'll keep working on the memory loss on our own." He gripped Natalie's arm. "Let's load up the car, and I'll drive you back to the Anchorage."

Natalie's eyes widened. She looked from Rowan to Emma, then tried to pull away, shaking her head. "I—I . . . maybe I should stay a little longer," she said. "As long as Emma's still taking medication, I don't—"

"I know you must be getting behind in your classes," Rowan said. "It's great that you were able to spend so much time here, but I think we can manage on our own now. If Emma takes a turn for the worse, I'll call."

Natalie licked her lips. "Look, you don't need to drive me back. I'll just call one of my friends from school. I know he'll be glad to—"

"No need for anyone to drive here and back. I'm heading downtown anyway." Rowan paused, as if waiting for further protest. Natalie said nothing, but stood, face pale, fists clenched, looking desperate to escape.

Natalie's words came back to Emma. *They'll say I left here to return to the Anchorage, and something must have happened to me on the way.*

And something would happen.

Emma faced Rowan. "What do you plan to do to her?"

Rowan scowled. "What makes you think I'm planning to do something to her?"

"Are you or aren't you?"

"Can you just give it a rest?" Rowan said, his body rigid with anger.

"If you're asking me to trust you, the answer is no," Emma said, folding her arms. "If you don't mean her any harm, then let her get home any way she wants."

"Look, I need to make sure she doesn't tell anyone about you," he said. "That's all."

"So you're going to kill her."

"No. I'm not." Turning, he struck like a snake, gripping both of Natalie's hands. He spoke a charm, and she froze in place, staring blankly into the distance.

"Natalie!" Emma cried. Putting her fingers under the healer's chin, she lifted her head. Natalie stared glassy-eyed at Emma. "What did you do?"

"I just immobilized her, all right?" Rowan said. "And now I'm going to wipe her memory. And then I'm going to take her back to the Anchorage." He paused. "The only way this works is if she doesn't remember anything. Otherwise, I can't let her go. Do you understand, Emma?"

Emma nodded her understanding. She was not to give Natalie any take-away message. There would be no plea for rescue. Otherwise, he'd kill her.

Resting his hand on Natalie's head, Rowan murmured words that sounded like Latin. *"Ana memorare."*

A shudder ran through Natalie. And then another.

Rowan spoke another charm and stepped back. Shooting a warning look at Emma, he said, "Natalie? What's the matter? Are you okay?"

She flinched, as if startled. She blinked at him, then rubbed both her hands over her face. "What happened? Where am I?"

"I'm Rowan DeVries, remember? You're here to treat my cousin."

"Your cousin?" Natalie said thickly, looking around, as if for clues.

"Here." Rowan rested his hot hand on Emma's shoulder. "She's doing much better, as you can see. We were just about to take you back to the Anchorage, when you had some sort of spell."

It was a spell, all right, Emma thought.

Something must have shown in her expression, because Rowan's fingers dug into her shoulder in warning.

Natalie's expression cleared. "Oh. Right. And, so . . ." Her eyes lit on the suitcase. "And so I was just about to leave?"

"Right. I'm going to take you back to the Anchorage now."

Natalie took a step, and faltered. "Wow, this isn't like me."

"I'm sure you'll be more comfortable at home," Rowan said, letting go of Emma and moving swiftly to take Natalie's arm. "We've taken too much of your time already. I can help you to the car if you'd like."

Natalie looked at Emma. "You're sure you'll be all right?"

Emma nodded. "I'm fine," she whispered.

"You call me if you need any more medicine. Or anything at all."

Then Natalie turned away, toward the door. "If you can . . . just get my bags," she said to Rowan, "I'll walk out on my own."

Rowan picked up her bags and followed her out. He paused in the doorway and turned back toward Emma.

"Don't worry. You'll be perfectly safe while I'm gone. I've instructed security not to let anyone in or out."

When they were gone, Emma sank down onto the bench in the foyer and put her head in her hands. Once again, she was on her own.

✑ CHAPTER THIRTY-TWO ✑
DO-OVER

"Jonah! Wake up!" Jake's voice broke into Jonah's seething thoughts.

Jonah looked down, balancing himself on the edge of the platform. Four stories below, his gymnastics coach was a tiny speck against the polished wood floor.

That's what they called him, anyway—a gymnastics coach. He was more like a martial-arts instructor.

"You need to be over there." Jake pointed to the far end of the gym, to the platform under the rafters. "Get there without touching down. The timer starts NOW!"

Jonah pulled the grappling hook from his pocket, clipped it to his line, and sent it flying across the room to find a home over one of the crossbeams at the peak of the roof. After yanking back a bit to anchor it, he launched himself from the edge of the platform. At first he was falling, nearly to the gym floor, and then arcing up, up, up. At the peak of the arc, he released himself from the line and grabbed on to the metal framework that supported the lighting system. Swinging back, he launched himself again, this time ropeless. But when he arrived at where the platform should have been, it was gone.

Jake was up to his old tricks again. Testing Jonah's ability to improvise on the fly.

Just before Jonah slammed into the wall, he twisted so that he hit feetfirst, meanwhile scanning the gym for the new target. Throwing out another line, he anchored near center to give himself a little time and pushed off again.

There. Just above the floor, near the door.

Midswoop, he launched another line, at an angle so he could change direction. Folding his body so he didn't hit the floor, he dropped lightly onto the platform, turned, and assumed his ready stance.

Jake examined the screen on his phone. "Time's not bad. But you've got to keep your eyes on the prize, remember."

One of Jake's cardinal rules.

"Eyes on the prize," Jonah repeated dutifully.

"Before you shower, spend an hour with the weights," Jake advised. "Work on the abdominals. Are you keeping up with your running?"

"Well," Jonah said, "I have this calculus test—"

"Calculus!" Jake shook his head. "When you going to use that? Prioritize, man! What I teach you will keep you alive."

So Jake hadn't gotten the memo. The one that said that Jonah was out of Nightshade. "Weights. Running. Got it," Jonah said, eager to end the conversation. Because he'd spotted Natalie standing in the doorway to the gym, rigid with tension, giving him a look that said, *We need to talk.* Natalie had been working off-site for nearly a week, and all of his phone calls and texts had gone unanswered.

She probably wants to schedule a practice for the band, Jonah thought. Something he wasn't sure he'd ever be ready for.

He crossed the polished gym floor to where she stood. "Glad you're back. Gabriel said that you were completing an off-campus assignment. Were you back in Trinity again?"

She shook her head. "Something's come up. I need your help."

"Sure," Jonah said, surprised. Natalie never needed help with anything. "You know all you have to do is ask."

She looked around, then leaned in close. "Let's go someplace we can't be overheard."

"Suits me," Jonah said, glancing over to where Jake was giving him the evil eye. "Let's walk down to the river."

Leaving the gym, they crossed to St. Clair. They descended into the Flats and turned left on River Road, toward Settlers Landing. The park would be nearly deserted on a weekday, this early in the morning. And it was, nearly—just a few joggers who lived downtown.

They sat on the wall around the Ohio fountain, looking downriver, their view framed by the rusted and brilliantly painted steel of multiple bridges. The only traffic on the river was the crew team from St. Ignatius, rowing valiantly against the current. It was still early, the rising sun splintered by the buildings of downtown.

"So," Jonah said. "What's up? Where have you been? I was getting worried."

"Jonah," Natalie said abruptly. "I need help with a rescue."

Jonah stared at her, mystified. There was almost nothing

Natalie could have said that would have surprised him more. Generally she preferred to remain at arms' length from field operations.

"Go on," he said.

"Gabriel sent me to help some wizards with a patient who was dying from a mysterious ailment."

"Gabriel sent you to help wizards?" Jonah rolled his eyes. "That's taking 'Kumbaya' a little too far. Did you at least poison a few while you were there?"

"Their patient wasn't a wizard," Natalie said, ignoring that last comment. "She's a savant."

"Someone from the Anchorage?" Jonah asked, mentally sorting through all the shadehunters he knew were out in the field.

Natalie shook her head. "Someone who's new to all this." She leaned closer. "They're holding her captive because she is the only witness to a murder. They think she may be the break they've been looking for . . . that she holds the key to all the recent wizard murders."

"You're sure she's a savant?" Jonah asked.

"She was at Thorn Hill, and has a savant stone." Natalie frowned. "But I don't really know what her gift is. And she doesn't have the tattoo."

Something kindled in the back of Jonah's mind. It might have been hope. "Does she? Know something about the wizard murders, I mean?"

"Hard to say. It seems she was on the scene when a number of wizards were killed, along with her father." Natalie's eyes narrowed as she focused in on Jonah's face. "Hello? Are you feeling all right? You look like you've seen a ghost."

Jonah's heart thudded painfully in his chest, and he could

scarcely catch his breath. Sweat pebbled his skin, chilling him as the wind off the river hit him.

"I . . . Gabriel's changed my dose again," Jonah lied. "It always takes a while to get used to it."

"Huh." Natalie didn't believe him, of course. "Here. Put your head between your knees." She put her hand between his shoulder blades and pushed.

"No . . . just—just . . . back to this girl. What's her name?"

"Emma Greenwood. Why?"

Jonah gripped the top of the wall on either side so hard the stone crumbled under his fingers. A torrent of emotions raced through his mind. Emma Greenwood was alive? How was that possible? And if it *was* possible, how had she fallen into the hands of wizards?

Reinforcements. Reinforcements had been arriving as Jonah was leaving the house. Yet Jonah had stolen her guitar and left Emma there for them to find.

"Jonah, what the hell is the matter?" Natalie put her hands on his shoulders and looked him straight in the eyes. "You know you can tell me anything."

Not this, he thought. He'd killed a girl and now she'd come back to life?

"Sorry," he said. "I'm all right. It's not unusual for me to feel crappy. In fact, I feel crappy most of the time. I just try and ignore it. That's what I do." *Stop it, Kinlock! You're babbling.* "About this girl. Did you figure out what was wrong with her? Is she—how is she doing now?"

"She's doing much better," Natalie said. "And no, I don't know what was wrong with her. Some kind of poison or toxin or spell. Nothing I've seen before. She did hit her head, but that doesn't seem serious."

"Who are the wizards? Did you get any names?"

"DeVries. Rowan DeVries, a Burroughs and a Hackleford. DeVries's sister was killed, apparently."

DeVries. He'd killed Rachel DeVries that terrible night in Cleveland Heights. And Rowan DeVries had come to the Interguild Council, vowing revenge. And said nothing about a witness. Clearly, they meant to keep that information to themselves.

Jonah struggled to keep his voice polite, concerned, under control. "So they invited you in to treat this girl and then they let you go? That's so . . . unwizard-like."

"DeVries wiped my mind, not realizing that I'm immune to conjured magic. I sure wasn't going to tell him. So I played along."

"The girl. Emma. What did she say about the killings?" Jonah asked, his mouth as dry as dust. "What does she remember? Would she recognize . . . anybody who was there?"

"She remembers very little of what happened. Maybe she'll remember more as she recovers. To be honest, there's a chance that nobody was murdered at all. Emma asked to see the bodies, but DeVries claimed they'd been destroyed."

Oh, somebody was murdered, all right, Jonah thought. Nine somebodies, and it could have been ten. "If she can't help them, do you think they'll let her go?"

"That's what I was hoping for," Natalie said. "I thought they might wipe her memory and send her off. But Emma seems convinced that they intend to wring everything out of her and then kill her." Natalie put her hand on Jonah's arm. "In the meantime, they're torturing her, Jonah. She didn't say anything, but there were blisters all around her neckline."

"*Tortured!* They're *torturing* her?" Jonah surged to his feet.

"Exactly." Natalie tilted her head, noting his reaction. "Does that surprise you?" She scraped back the hair that the wind had pulled loose from her ponytail.

Maybe Emma *would* remember him, and his secret would be out. But that didn't matter. Nothing mattered except seizing this chance to undo some of what he'd done.

"Where is she? Is she still at the house in Cleveland Heights?"

Natalie shook her head. "Cleveland Heights? Who said anything about the Heights? She's in Bratenahl. Up by the lake. It's just a house—a mansion—on the lakefront, but the property is walled in, and they have an alarm system and full-time security."

"No problem," Jonah said, already building his wall of secrets. "I'll get in. In the meantime, please don't say anything about this to Gabriel or anyone else. And if I bring her back here, absolutely nobody can know that history about her."

"But Gabriel will want to debrief me on what happened when I—"

"Just tell him your patient was recovering and so you came back to school." When Natalie still looked unconvinced, Jonah resorted to begging. "Please, Nat. If you care about me. If you care about—about Emma, you won't say a word to anyone."

"All right, Jonah, I trust you."

Don't trust me, Jonah thought. I'm asking you for my sake, not hers.

"Just be careful," Natalie said, trying to smile. "We have a gig to practice for, you know."

Maybe I'll be killed in the attempt, Jonah thought, showing his teeth in a smile. Then I'll be off the hook.

❧ CHAPTER THIRTY-THREE ❧
NORTH COAST BLUES

If help ain't coming, you got to help yourself. That's what Sonny Lee always said. And so the night Natalie left, Emma began planning her escape.

She considered her options. Emma was a city girl . . . not the best coordinated or athletic person. The outer walls were high, alarmed, and guarded, so the notion of her scaling them was ridiculous. All of the trees had been cut back so that they didn't overhang the wall, so shimmying down one of them wasn't a path out.

There was an attendant at the driveway gate, so even if she managed to get hold of some car keys, it was unlikely she could bluff her way out. She could try to hide in the back of somebody's car, but she suspected that that ploy worked only in the movies.

Even getting out of the house would be a challenge. At night, they locked her in her room, and during the day, there were people everywhere.

Down was easier than up. So, like it or not, over the cliff and down to the lake seemed the most likely way out. If she managed not to fall into the water, she might actually make it.

She knew she'd need a rope of some kind. So while Rowan was driving Natalie back downtown, Emma sneaked down the basement stairs.

It was cool and damp-smelling, dark and apparently little used. She found an unlocked wine cellar and several locked doors (the torture chambers?) and, happily, a coil of sturdy nylon rope in a metal cabinet. She wasn't sure how long it was, but the cliff wasn't all that high, maybe thirty feet? Huddling in a corner, she tied knots into the rope at intervals. And that pretty much summed up the climbing plan. She'd tie one end to a tree and slide over the edge, using her feet to keep from smashing against the cliff.

In a box marked DONATIONS she found a heavy sweatshirt, a knit cap, and a pair of jeans that more or less fit her, though they seemed in danger of sliding off her hipless frame. These must have belonged to Rachel DeVries, she thought, which was creepy, to tell the truth.

She carried the rope and the clothes back to her room and hid everything between the mattress and the box spring. The next day, she rooted around in the hall closet and found a pair of leather gloves in a jacket pocket. She'd need those if she didn't want to shred the skin on her hands.

She was just closing the closet door when someone behind her said, "Going somewhere?"

Emma jumped and spun around, heart thudding. It was Burroughs. And beyond him, she saw Hackleford and DeVries. Rowan had been off-site all afternoon, strategizing with his wizard colleagues. They must have just gotten back, because they were still wearing their jackets.

Burroughs was still right there, seemingly waiting for an answer.

"Oh! I . . . uh . . . it's getting chilly, and I thought I might sit out in the garden. I was afraid my hands might get cold." She held up the gloves.

"It's supposed to storm tonight," Burroughs said, moving in so he stood uncomfortably close. "Might be best to stay inside." He reached out and tucked her hair behind her ears. There was an implied ownership in the gesture that made her shudder. But Emma also noticed a wired intensity in him that hadn't been there before, a certain *eagerness*.

Emma weighed the gloves in her hand, debating whether she could get away with keeping them. "Well, maybe I'll just hang on to them in case I—"

Suddenly Rowan was there. He gripped her wrist with one hand and ripped the gloves away with the other, stuffing them into his pocket. "I don't think you realize just how precarious your situation is. Come with me."

He half dragged her away from the others, down the hallway toward her room. Wrenching open the door, he thrust her inside and slammed the door behind them. Then stood, glaring down at her.

"What is the matter with you?" Emma demanded, rubbing her bruised wrist. "What do you want from me?"

"Two more wizards have been murdered."

"Murdered? Where?"

"Chicago," Rowan said. "Sometime yesterday."

"How?"

"Similar to the others. Cut to pieces, their heartstones

drained. Nightshade scattered over the bodies."

"It's not my fault."

"No? Well, it may as well be, because you're going to pay the price."

"What do you mean?" Emma asked, her heart plummeting.

"Think the Mafia, Emma, only a thousand times worse. For what it's worth, I believe that you're doing the best you can. But this situation has fueled speculation about whether I have the right temperament for this job. Whether I'm ruthless enough to lead the syndicate. Some of my colleagues are less interested in the truth than in the political advantage to be gained if you implicate members of the Interguild Council. You are the wedge that drives support to my enemies. And that can't happen—not right now. If I lose control of the Black Rose, there's no way my successors will leave me alive."

"And, so . . . I am the sacrifice."

Rowan's lips tightened. "You are the sacrifice. Unless you can give me what I need."

"Unless I lie, and say I remember when I don't."

"That's one option," Rowan said. "Tonight, members of the Wizard Council are meeting here at the house. I'll question you in front of the council. You'll need to confirm that McCauley and Moss were there for sure, and maybe some of the others. That will bring those wizards who are wavering over to our side. You may be asked to sign a statement. Just make sure you're convincing, or no doubt Burroughs will get a chance to try his hand. Neither one of us wants that." Rowan moved to turn away, but Emma grabbed his arm, pulling him back around.

"And what happens to me after that?" she demanded. "After you have what you need?"

"I think you already know the answer to that," he said coldly. "I was born into this game. I didn't make the rules. If you cooperate, you can avoid considerable pain. The ending is the same, either way."

Panic welled up inside her. She might have a sad-ass life at the moment, but it was all she had. Maybe she didn't want to hear the truth, after all.

Emma found her voice. "Just remember this: If I live, there's the chance my memory will return, and you'll have answers. If you kill me, you'll never know who really murdered your sister. You might pass the murderer in the street and you'd never know it. Someone in your own organization may be gloating about it right now. Are you good with that? Are you willing to trade a political win based on a lie for a lifetime of wondering?"

They stood, eyes locked, for one, two, three heartbeats. Then Rowan looked away. "I suppose I'll just have to take that chance," he said, a muscle in his jaw working. "Now listen. Here's how the evening will go. I expect the council members to arrive about six o'clock. You'll hear a lot of coming and going about that time. We'll be up front until about seven, then adjourn to the study that lets out onto the terrace. I'll come to get you between seven and eight." Releasing her, he dug into his jacket pocket and pulled out the gloves he'd taken from her. "Keep these, if you want." Then he was gone.

Emma stood, frowning, weighing the gloves in her hand, going back over her conversation with Rowan. *I expect the council members to arrive about six o'clock. . . . We'll be up front until*

about seven . . . I'll come to get you between seven and eight. Why
had he been so specific about times? Why had he returned
the gloves to her after taking them away?

Unless he meant for her to use them.

First, she had to get over the garden wall. Emma hauled a
chair out of her room and set it next to the wall. Then piled
cushions on top of that. When she stood on top of the trembling stack, she could just reach the top of the wall with her
fingertips. It was good that she was tall, or she'd never have
made it. At least her arms were strong from hand-sanding
and carrying wood around. As it was, she skinned both knees
through her borrowed jeans as she scrambled for a toehold.
Not a good start.

Once on the ground on the other side, she crouched
close to the wall and scanned the grounds, looking for the
two guards patrolling the compound. She watched until she
figured out the pattern. One guard generally stayed in the
guardhouse, probably watching the video feed while the other
walked the grounds. Then they would switch off. One good
thing about their presence was that there were unlikely to be
motion detectors, at least nowhere near the perimeter walls.

She waited five minutes after the guard passed by, then
fell in behind him, following the same path, every sense alert
in case he stopped somewhere along the way.

Burroughs was right. There *was* a storm coming in. The
tops of the trees thrashed overhead, sending flurries of leaves
spiraling to the ground. The day had been sultry and summer-
like, but now the northeast wind stung her skin, bringing the
scent of rain, the touch of cold places in the north. She was
glad of her sweatshirt, and jeans, and sturdy shoes. Looking

on the bright side, the sound of the incoming storm covered any noise she made. And nobody would expect her to be outside in such weather.

Emma looked back at the house. Her phone was back at Tyler's, and she didn't have a watch, so she'd have to guess the time from the rough schedule Rowan had given her. Lights were ablaze in front of the house, cars coming and going. Which meant it was just after six, so she had an hour before anyone would notice her absence and sound an alarm.

She left the path along the wall at the edge of the cliff, knowing she'd be silhouetted against the lake as she walked along the shoreline. She'd have about fifteen minutes before the second guard passed by.

The stone wall that ran along the edge of the cliff was only waist-high so it wouldn't block the view of the water from the house. Just inside the wall, a large tree shaded the terrace.

The first large drops of rain splatted down.

Swearing, Emma uncoiled her rope. She wished she knew more about knots, but who knew that such knowledge would be important one day? Hurriedly, she doubled the rope, threaded the loop around the tree, then ran the ends through the loop. She pulled on the gloves, then boosted herself over the wall.

It all but ended there. Had she not had a death's hold on the ropes, the wind howling along the cliff's edge would have blown her away.

Emma looked down, at a jumble of jagged rocks at the bottom. The cliff seemed higher now that she was getting ready to climb down it. At least it was getting dark, making it harder to see the bottom. She swallowed down the terror rising in her throat. You can do this, she told herself. And then: Don't think about it. Just do it.

She turned, facing away from the raging lake, gripped the ropes in either hand, crouched, and stepped backward.

She could tell right away that this mission would have been a total no-go without the gloves. Desperately, she clung to the increasingly slippery ropes as rain needled her face and rivulets of mingled water and sweat ran down her neck.

Cautiously, she slid one hand down the rope until it came up against a knot. She followed with the other hand, kicking off the rock and bracing her feet a bit lower.

Repeat.

Despite all her precautions, the wind caught her and slammed her against stone before she could get her feet in proper position. Swearing some more, she turned and planted her feet against the rocky wall.

In that way, she crept down the face of the cliff, agonizingly slowly. By now she was soaked through, battered and bruised, blisters already forming on the palms of her hands through the gloves. She wished there were a way to stop and rest, but there was no place to wedge herself in order to relieve the stress on her hands.

Best to get it over with as quickly as possible. At least it was not an electrical storm. That would've been terri—

The entire shoreline lit up as lightning streaked across the sky, illuminating layers of threatening gray clouds. Thunder crashed, the sound reverberating off stone.

Emma glared up at the heavens, squinting against the torrents of rain. "Hey!" she shouted. She would have shaken her fist if she'd had a hand free. "Whatever I did, I'm sorry, all right? Can you cut me a break?"

She was answered by another strobe of lightning. As she turned her head away, she thought she saw something moving on the cliff face, farther down. The shoreline went dark again as the crash of thunder seemed likely to shake her loose from her mooring.

Was somebody already climbing down after her? If so, why was he over there? And how did he get below her? Granted, she was slow, but . . . she looked up the twin ropes to where they disappeared over the cliff's edge and saw no activity, no lights . . . nothing.

She kept her eyes fixed down the shoreline to the east. When the lightning flared again, she saw nothing unusual.

You really are seeing things, she thought, and continued her painful descent.

Now the spray from the crashing waves was drenching her, adding to her general misery. Amazingly, that meant she must be nearing the bottom. Kicking out with her foot, she managed to find purchase on an outcrop of broken stone. She found a place for her other foot, then stood there, trying to catch her breath, her shoulders screaming in pain, all of her muscles quivering. Waves swirled around her feet, then receded.

She looked to her left. Heaps of broken rock formed a sort of path along the shore. If she could just keep her footing, she might be able to work her way down past the perimeter wall and find a way to climb back up to street level.

She inched her way to the left, keeping hold of the rope, hoping it would slide sideways enough to get her past the wall. Then her questing foot met nothing but air and she looked down to see boiling water far below. There was a major gap in what had seemed to be a continuous if dangerous path.

Emma slid the rope a little farther, but then it caught on an outcropping high above her. She eyed the gap, judging the distance. Could she somehow swing across it?

"Emma!" someone shouted. Sheltering her face with her arm, she looked up and saw figures milling at the top of the cliff. Her escape attempt had been discovered. Had it really been an hour?

"Emma! Don't move! Stay there and hold tight to the rope! We'll come down and get you."

It was Rowan DeVries. Even with all the wind and rain and crashing waves, she recognized his voice, his silhouette.

Not going back, Emma thought. There's trouble up top, and trouble down below. But I've already been up top.

Again, she turned and faced downshore. She set her feet, bent her knees, and pushed off, swinging in a long, low arc across the breach. Her feet had actually touched the other side when a huge wave slammed into her, hurling her sideways against the cliff. She took the impact in her shoulder, and immediately her arm went numb.

She screamed, blood welling up salty in her mouth where she'd bitten her tongue, tears of pain and frustration welling up in her eyes. She bumped against the cliff twice more before she ended up dangling against a sheer rock face. The cliff jutted out to either side, so that she was enclosed by stone on three sides. She could think of no way to get past it. It was hard enough holding on to the ropes with her injured arm.

She was trapped. Sooner or later, a wave would hit her hard enough so that she'd lose hold on the ropes and drop into the foaming lake below.

"Are you hurt?"

Emma started, nearly losing hold of the ropes. The voice came from just over her right shoulder. In fact, the speaker sounded like he was nearly on top of her. Carefully, she turned to find a boy perched on a rock outcropping like a . . . like whatever thing it is that perches on rocks. He wore black clothing that seemed to turn the rain, a nylon webbing harness overtop. His black hair was plastered to his head, but otherwise he looked like he belonged there, one leg thrust out, foot resting on a ledge below, the other bent beneath him. He had a coil of rope slung over his shoulder, gloves on his hands, and narrow-toed, high-tech sneakers on his feet.

Oh, and his eyes were so blue a person could drown in them. Blue, and somehow familiar, striking a chord that had sounded in her heart before.

"Are you hurt?" the boy repeated, those blue eyes sweeping her for damage. He seemed tightly wound, vibrating, like a guitar string tuned to a high pitch.

"Me? I couldn't be better," she said, thrown completely off balance by this turn of events. "Why do you ask?"

Something in him relaxed, uncoiled. "I heard you scream," he said. "I thought you might need help."

He must have climbed down from above. Was he Rowan's on-site cliff rescue specialist? Always on call?

As if in answer, he pulled something from a hidden pocket and held it up for her inspection. It was a harness made of webbing, connected to a sturdy line. He clipped one end of the line to an anchor in the rock and tossed the other one toward her with a low, overhand throw. "Strap this on, if you can do it without falling. I'd feel better if you were anchored to something."

Emma caught the harness with one hand, and pain rocketed through her shoulder. Black spots danced in front of her eyes.

"You *are* hurt," he said, flinching as if he felt it himself. "I thought so. Hang on. I'll come to you." He scrambled up the cliff, setting pins in the rock and clipping in his line until his rope was anchored high above his head. Pushing off, he slammed into her, wrapped an arm around her, his momentum carrying the two of them to the other side.

Now they were squeezed together on a tiny ledge, and Emma couldn't figure out where to put her body where it wasn't pressed up against his. He must have been aware of it, too, because he averted his eyes, as if he could pretend it wasn't happening. He buckled the harness on to her, his fingers deft and sure.

He, of course, had gloves on.

"You act like you've done this before," she said.

"Once or twice."

Up close, there was something familiar about him, something that pinged in her consciousness. It was as if he gave off a scent that went straight to that place in memory where the important things are stored.

Had she seen him at one of the meetings in the mansion above?

Which reminded her.

"Just so you know. I'm not going back up there," she warned. "Don't try to make me."

"No problem," he said. "We'll go down. Do you swim?"

"No, I do not," she said tartly, water streaming down the back of her neck. "I wasn't planning on getting wet."

He laughed, and the sound echoed around the cove, somehow lifting her spirits.

"Do I know you?" she asked, their faces inches apart.

Something flickered in his eyes—something almost like panic—then was gone. "Maybe," he said, turning his face away again. "Do you come here often?"

She couldn't help it: she found herself laughing. He was so charming, so self-deprecating, so . . . so . . .

"I'm Jonah Kinlock," he said. "I'm a friend of Natalie's. Remember . . . we met at Club Catastrophe? I was rude. You played pool . . . and kicked butt."

"You're Boy Blue!" Emma blurted.

"I'm who?"

"Never mind," Emma mumbled as the puzzle pieces fell into place. Boy Blue had come to the club with the band. Sat with the blond guitar player during the break. Natalie was with the band. "So . . . *you're* Natalie's friend?"

"She seemed to think you needed rescuing, so here I am." He tilted his head back and scanned the top of the cliff. His lips tightened in annoyance. "I'll explain later. Your friends up top are on their way down. It's best if they don't know I was here. In fact, it'll be *really* convenient if they think you drowned."

Emma looked down at the furious waves pounding against the cliffs below. Could still happen, she thought, panic rising in her again.

"Hey." She looked up, and the boy, Jonah, looked straight into her eyes. Rainwater trickled down his face and clung to his eyelashes. The sculpted terrain of his face invited exploration, its peaks and valleys framed by a tumble of hair, set with eyes the color of oceans under sunlight and racing clouds. He turned his head slightly, looking down at her, his eyes deepening to a smoky amethyst. His lips were just inches from hers. Her heart thudded painfully in her chest.

"Listen to me," Jonah said, his grip tightening on her shoulders. "We're going to jump into the water, landing as far away from the cliff as we can. That's the trickiest part. I'm going to swim us out farther, then follow the shoreline to a place we can get out. I want you to try to flatten your body in the water, relax, and just let me handle the swimming. I promise you, Emma . . . I won't let you drown."

She believed him.

He pulled her tightly against him. She could feel his hard muscles through two layers of clothes. "Now," he murmured, his breath warming her ear. "By all means, scream."

He jumped, carrying them both farther than she would've expected. Then they were plummeting toward the water, and Emma screamed, a screech that could have been heard in Canada.

They plunged into the lake, and the shock of the cold lake

almost made Emma suck in water. Then they were bulleting upward, Jonah kicking strongly, pushing them toward the surface.

Her head broke through the waves, Jonah beside her. They were a fair distance from shore, but the rough surf threatened to push them back in and smash them against the rocks.

"Lie on your back," Jonah said, one hand pushing against her bottom, the other against her chest, until she was in the right position. He slid an arm across her chest, pressed tight against her breasts, then stroked strongly away from the cliffs.

Emma did her best to relax as waves crashed over her face. Since it was still raining, sometimes it was hard to tell when she was above water. It was better once they got into deeper water. Eventually, Jonah turned and swam parallel to the shoreline. She could hear faint shouts in the distance. "Emma!" If she craned her neck, she could see lights sweeping over the water under the cliffs where they'd landed. But they were already out of range.

Every so often, Jonah would tilt her upright in the water and ask, "Are you doing all right? Okay to keep going?" As if there was a choice.

He didn't seem winded at all.

"You're—you must be in really good shape," Emma said.

Jonah brushed off the compliment. "I am unusually strong," he said. And swam on.

Emma was so relaxed that she didn't even notice when he turned back toward shore.

"Emma," he said into her ear. "Put your feet down."

She did, and found a mix of slippery rocks and sand. When she stood, the water was only waist-deep.

"Careful you don't fall. The waves are still high." He

grabbed her hand to steady her, and they waded onto a rocky beach. "I parked just up here."

They cut between two large houses and followed what looked like a private lane until it ended on a public street. A dog started barking in a nearby house. "Walk faster, if you can," Jonah said. "I don't want to have to explain why we're wandering around the village soaking wet."

Away from the lake, the houses were more modest. Jonah's car was parked on a side street, covered with soggy leaves blown down by the storm.

"Get in," he said, circling around to the driver's side. "We can't hang out here too much longer or some busybody is going to look out her window and call the police."

"Wait just a minute," Emma said, looking across the roof of the car at him. She knew better than to get into cars with strangers.

He waited, head tilted in inquiry.

"Before I get in, where are we going?"

"We're going to Natalie's. We both live in the dorms at a private school called the Anchorage, downtown. Maybe she told you about it?" He raised an eyebrow, but she didn't say yes or no. "I thought maybe you could stay with her until we figure out what to do."

"We?"

"If you want our help, I mean. It's up to you." From the way he shifted his weight and constantly scanned their surroundings, she knew he was worried about being spotted, eager to get them on their way.

Emma tried to fold her arms, but it was too painful, so she let them drop to her sides. "But . . . how did you know I was here? The wizards said they wiped Natalie's mind. They said she wouldn't remember anything about this. I thought I was on my own."

Jonah smiled a hard-edged, bitter smile. "There's your first lesson," he said. "Don't believe anything a wizard tells you."

❧ CHAPTER THIRTY-FIVE ❧
THE ANCHORAGE

In the end, Emma got into the car, because she was soaking wet and hurt and had no other place to go. She guessed a possible risk was better than certain disaster.

Jonah said little during the drive downtown, responding to questions with one-word answers. When Emma asked, "Don't you want to put something over the seat so I don't get it wet?" he said, "No." And when she asked, "Are you a savant, too?" he said, "Yes."

He's probably exhausted from dragging me through the lake, she thought. But he seemed more tense than weary, and preoccupied, as if he were already planning his next move.

Emma tried not to stare at him. It's really unfair for a boy to be that beautiful, she thought. Maybe *beautiful* wasn't the word. He exuded a kind of charismatic pheromone . . . a physical and emotional heat that clouded her mind and left her breathless.

What made it worse was that he didn't even appear to be

trying. In fact, he seemed to be doing everything he could to make himself unappealing.

It wasn't working.

Get a grip, Emma, she scolded herself. She was not the kind of girl who lost her head over a pretty boy. She was too street-smart for that. And aware of just where she sat on the scale of ugly to pretty.

Maybe this dizzy, drunken feeling was an aftereffect of the concussion.

She jammed herself into the corner next to the door, but it was no use. She couldn't escape whatever spell he was casting. The car just wasn't big enough.

So she stared out the window at the landscape along the Shoreway . . . dark slices of the lake broken by the brilliant stadium and the lakefront museums and marinas. Opened the window and let the cold air pour over her face, cooling her fevered cheeks.

When they left the Shoreway at Third Street and turned down Superior into an area of old warehouses, Emma grew wary again. "Wait a minute. Your school is around *here*?"

"You've heard of the Keep?"

Tyler had mentioned it, once or twice. "Yes. It's a music venue, right?"

"Right. It's Gabriel Mandrake's club. The Anchorage is adjacent to it . . . he runs both. The school is arts-focused, so this way savants can use the studios and facilities at the club. Some are involved in promotions and production. It's a great synergy. Everything is right here."

When Emma looked closely, she realized that the neighborhood didn't look as shabby as she'd first assumed. "Apartments Now Leasing" signs fronted many of the weathered brick buildings. Others had been converted into residential and commercial lofts, with restaurants and retail stores at street level.

Ahead, a bridge arced over the industrial flats. Far below, the river wound its way to the lake, spanned by gaunt iron bridges and lined with manufacturing and tech-company buildings. But Jonah turned off before they reached the bridge, entering an underground parking garage with a key card. He pulled into a space marked KINLOCK.

"You have your own parking space?" Emma blurted.

"I come and go a lot," Jonah said. He sat there for a moment, his lower lip caught behind his teeth, staring straight ahead. Then he sighed and turned to look at Emma. "I'm going to take you straight up to Natalie's so she can look at your shoulder. She's here in this building."

"You people don't really believe in regular doctors, do you?" Emma said.

"I'll take you to the urgent care if you want," Jonah said, finger-combing his damp hair. "But you're a minor. If you show up looking like that, they'll start asking you a lot of questions, wanting to call your parents, and demanding to know who the hell I am. You'll be entangled in the system before you know it and I'll probably end up in jail."

"I guess you're right, but—"

"The truth is, a lot of our injuries and illnesses aren't really treatable using conventional medicine," Jonah said. "We're usually misdiagnosed, and then the treatment makes matters worse." He pushed open the driver's-side door, looking back at her with the trace of a smile. "I'm not saying that a doctor couldn't fix a wrenched shoulder. But Nat usually gets better results."

Entry to the building required a key card, a code, and an iris scan. They took a freight elevator up to the third floor and walked down a corridor past a series of doors. Jonah pounded on the one at the end. When no one answered, he pulled out his cell phone and began punching in numbers.

"It's late," Emma whispered. "Maybe she . . ."

Before Jonah had finished, Emma could hear someone through the door, fumbling with a bolt.

Natalie yanked open the door. "Emma!" she said, looking delighted and relieved. Then she frowned, giving her a closer look. "How'd you get all wet?"

Emma delivered the ten-word explanation while Natalie ushered her inside. Jonah followed on his own, shutting the door behind them and throwing the bolt. He seemed at home there, and Emma wondered with a ping of jealousy if he and Natalie were going out.

Natalie's place was high-ceilinged and spacious, a one-room apartment that lived a lot larger, with exposed brick and beams everywhere. Glancing around, Emma noticed an electronic drum set in one corner, mikes and amplifiers, a rumpled double bed, and an efficiency kitchen.

"This is a dorm room?" Emma said. It was fancier than anyplace she'd ever lived in.

"This?" Natalie laughed. "This is the low-rent floor. Mr. Mandrake, the school director, lives in the penthouse. And Mr. Kinlock here has a much finer place."

She's been to his room, then, Emma thought. And then mentally slapped herself. This was so not her business.

Natalie looked Emma up and down. "You'd swim in my clothes," she said at last. "Since Jonah saw fit to throw you in the lake, maybe he has something that would work."

"I'll look," Jonah said, and was instantly gone.

As soon as he left, Natalie helped Emma out of her wet clothes and gave her a bathrobe she could have wrapped around herself twice.

Natalie sat Emma down in a chair and asked a million rapid-fire questions as she cleaned cuts and bruises. Then she examined her injured shoulder, gently manipulating it until the pain diminished.

When Jonah returned, he'd changed out of his wet clothes into a cotton sweater and jeans and toweled his hair dry. Now that he was cleaned up, Emma saw that he had a nasty scrape over his cheekbone. He set a pile of clothing on the couch and sat down next to it, watching silently. Now and then he glanced down at his gloved hands.

Why does he still have gloves on?

Finally Natalie gathered up her used washcloths and dropped them into a hamper. Emma carried Jonah's clothes into the bathroom and changed into them: a sweatshirt and heavy canvas pants with a drawstring waist she could pull tightly around her.

When she returned to the main room, Jonah and Natalie had their heads together, talking. They stopped abruptly when she appeared.

"Not bad," Natalie said, looking her up and down.

"Thanks for the clothes," Emma said to Jonah. She reached toward him. "Do you—did you know you had a scrape over your—"

Jonah flinched back, avoiding her questing hand like he might get burned.

"Jonah prefers to treat his own injuries," Natalie said, giving Jonah a narrow-eyed glare. "He doesn't like to be touched." She turned back to Emma. "You should be feeling better by tomorrow. I think the shoulder's just sprained."

"I feel better already," Emma said. Which wasn't entirely true. She felt jittery, unsettled, as if she'd careened from one unsolvable problem to another. At least when she was being held captive by wizards, she had a place to stay.

Sooner or later they're going to ask me to leave, she thought. Then what? Emma had felt at home on the streets in Memphis, but that was her turf. She'd known she could go back to Sonny Lee's. There was some comfort in knowing that somebody would be looking for her if she didn't show up.

Now the streets seemed mean and spiteful, ready to chew her into bits. But she didn't want to come to the attention of the county—the bogeyman of her childhood.

She looked up to find Jonah's eyes fixed on her, the blue eyes shading into a dusky twilight purple. "You're wondering what the plan is," he said.

Something about the way he said it made the words tumble out of her, all in a rush. "I just . . . I don't know what to do now. I don't have any family . . . not that I know of. Tyler was all I had left. I can't even go back home. Rowan said the killers who murdered my father might come after me, if they know I survived. I have some money in a bank account, but not much to live on. And if child welfare finds out I'm living on my own, they'll put me in a home." Her eyes filled with liquid misery. "When I lived in Memphis, my grandfather always worried about that. Because I was a truant, and ran the streets a lot, and he wasn't a good role model." She massaged her shoulder, wincing a little.

"I feel like I should go to the police, but what am I supposed to tell them? 'Intruders came to my house and murdered my father and eight other people. How do I know? Wizards told me. No, I can't show you the bodies. Wizards burned them all up. And, no, I don't really remember what happened myself, because I have amnesia.'"

"Likely the memory is still there," Natalie said, taking Emma's hand. "Sometimes we just hide away memories that are too painful to deal with at first. As you recover, you'll gradually remember more."

"Don't push it, though," Jonah said quickly. "Right now it's probably risky to stir all that up."

"Since when are you an expert on memory loss?" Natalie glared at him.

"I'm just saying that after all she's been through, she should focus on resting, and healing, and taking care of herself." He turned to Emma. "If you have no place else to go, you belong here . . . at the Anchorage. I can introduce you to Gabriel Mandrake, the founder. If you're admitted, you can just stay here, lay low, and finish high school. Then do whatever you want."

"You've got her whole life planned out, Kinlock?" Natalie rolled her eyes. "Did you think of asking her? Or did you just plan on talking her into it?"

"I just . . . I'm not trying to tell you what to do," Jonah said.

"But . . . I'll need paperwork," Emma said, thinking how easy it sounded when he said it, but knowing different. "I've been kicked out of enough schools to know you don't just go knock on another school's door and ask to be let in. They want to know what they're getting into."

"This school is different," Natalie said. "We're used to taking in strays. A lot of us don't succeed in regular schools.

Our minds don't work the same as other people's. And some of us come from bad situations, because most of us were orphaned at Thorn Hill. I lived with family for a while before I came here, but they couldn't deal anymore. And I guess I couldn't deal with them."

"You should know that some of us are damaged," Jonah said. "We're on medication, to control seizures and prevent magical accidents. To allow us to live in polite society. Just so you know what *you're* getting into." He sounded unapologetic, almost defiant. *Take it or leave it*, he seemed to be saying.

Magical accidents. I wonder what that means, Emma thought. "I don't want drugs," she said, shrinking back in her chair.

"That's up to you," Jonah said, "but some of us do better with help." He turned toward Natalie, focused the hot intensity of his gaze on her. "Nat, remember what I said. It'll be a lot less complicated if we don't mention Emma's connection to Rowan DeVries and the Black Rose."

Natalie frowned, looking puzzled. "But if Gabriel knew about this, it might convince him that you're right . . . that we need to focus more on the threat from wizards. If he realized that they have some kind of plot under way, that they're kidnapping savants, he—"

"He *knows* that, Natalie," Jonah growled, his voice ragged with frustration. "Wizards tortured and murdered Jeanette, and he's doing nothing about it. I think they kidnapped her because they're planning another Thorn Hill. I *begged* him to take action. I even volunteered to try and find out what they're up to. He said no. When I persisted, he kicked me out of Nightshade."

"Nightshade?" Emma looked from Natalie to Jonah. "What's that?"

For a moment, neither of them spoke. "It's a . . . a kind of service club," Jonah said finally. "The point is, all Gabriel cares about is tracking down shades. It's like an obsession with him. A grudge match. Meanwhile, wizards do as they please, and he doesn't care."

Emma's head was swimming. It wasn't just wizards, sorcerers, enchanters, and the like. Now it was shades, too.

"Jonah, I'm sure if you'd just talk to him—" Natalie began.

"I *have* talked to him. I get nowhere. For all I know, he'll hand Emma right back to them. To keep the peace."

"No," Natalie said, shaking her head. "He would never do that. And I'm not going to lie to him."

"If you'd said that a year ago, I would have agreed with you," Jonah persisted, an undercurrent of urgency in his voice. "But these days, I can't predict what he'll do next."

"Maybe I'd be safer out running the streets," Emma said. "No offense."

Jonah and Natalie both started talking at once, their protests mingling together. Emma put up her hand to hush them. "I'm joking, all right? I'll tell whatever story you want. But, just so you know, I'm not a very good liar."

No problem, Jonah's expression said. *We'll lie for you.*

"*You* should decide," Natalie said to Emma. "You're the one who has to live with this. What do you want to tell Gabriel about what happened?"

"Emma," Jonah said, and his voice seemed to arrow into her, as sweet and potent as Southern Comfort. "I'm just saying that the safest thing for all of us is if nobody knows you survived."

"Not fair, Kinlock," Natalie said. "Not fair doing the enchanter thing."

He just shrugged, as if to say, *Sue me.*

Enchanter thing? What had Tyler said about enchanters?

Enchanters? Stay away from them. They can talk you into anything.

But Jonah was a savant, right? Not an enchanter. But he'd never really said what kind of magical ability he had.

Emma felt pinned down, trapped between Natalie's scowl and Jonah's blue-eyed gaze. "Well," she said finally. "I guess the fewer people that know who I really am, the safer I'll be." And the less likely I'll end up a ward of the county, she added silently.

Natalie rolled her eyes. "Fine. We won't tell Gabriel."

And, once again, Jonah Kinlock got his way.

"So what can we say?" Emma asked. "Who am I supposed to be?"

"I was at the homeless shelter today," Natalie said. "I volunteer once a week. I could say I met you there."

Emma shrugged. "Sounds good to me."

"You can stay here tonight," Natalie said, "if you're okay with the couch."

"Good," Jonah said. "I'll let you get some sleep. We'll talk to Gabriel tomorrow." He stood and moved catlike to the door, as if he couldn't wait to get out of there. Then swiveled back toward them. "I think those wizards were at your house for the same reason they murdered Jeanette. They're working a plan that involves finding people who survived Thorn Hill. It may mean the Anchorage will become a target. That means all of us. From that standpoint, anyway, we're all on the same side."

Yeah, Emma thought. Rowan said the same thing. With so many allies, why do I feel so alone?

❦ CHAPTER THIRTY-SIX ❧
AUDITION

"**W**ill I have to take an admission test?" Emma asked as they turned down the alley next to the Keep. "I'm not good at test taking."

"No test," Natalie said. "Sometimes Gabriel holds auditions. To figure out how you fit in. What you need."

"Audition?" There it was: one more reason to panic. "I'm not ready. Guitar is all I know, and I don't want to try out with a guitar I've never played before."

"It's not really a tryout," Jonah said. "More like an interview, for placement. If you get stuck, just let us do the talking."

How is Mandrake going to find out about me, if they do the talking? Emma wondered.

Maybe that was the idea—the only way Emma was going to get in was if Mr. Mandrake knew nothing about her.

They climbed a narrow staircase to the second floor. Natalie and Jonah ran identity cards through a scanner and the outside door hissed open. Then they went through three staffed security checkpoints.

"Is there a lot of crime around here?" Emma asked.

"Gabriel's careful, for a lot of reasons," Jonah said, exchanging glances with Natalie.

An assistant of uncertain gender with blue hair, bronze skin, and multiple piercings met them in the outer office. "Jonah! Natalie! And you must be Emma."

"Hey, Patrick," Natalie said, which answered one question, anyway. "Can we go on in?"

"Mr. Mandrake is expecting you," Patrick said. "But he's had some unexpected visitors. Let's wait a few moments, shall we? Would you like green tea? Juice? Springwater?"

They shook their heads, so Patrick motioned them to seats and returned to his workstation.

Emma couldn't settle down, though, so she circled the room, looking over the photos displayed on the walls, mostly of Gabriel Mandrake with the royalty of the music business. With up-and-coming bands. At various benefit concerts.

Here were framed covers of *Rolling Stone* and *Time* magazine, featuring Mandrake, alongside display cases full of medals, gold records, and awards.

"Where was this taken?" she asked, pointing to a grainy black-and-white photo of Mandrake next to a remarkably beautiful child with shaggy black hair and long-lashed blue eyes. They stood outside a tent, against a jungle background, a guitar between them.

"That's Gabriel and Jonah," Natalie said. "It was taken at Thorn Hill, not long before the massacre."

"So they knew each other before Jonah came to school here?"

"Obviously," Jonah said drily.

Emma studied the photograph, trying to divine if the setting looked at all familiar. Which it should be, since she'd lived at Thorn Hill.

"He has his own artist-edition Stratocaster?" she asked, pointing to a later photo of Gabriel holding another guitar.

"He does," Natalie said, grinning at Emma's fascination with Mandrake's show-off wall.

"Jonah," Patrick said, in a low, urgent voice. He was staring at the screen on his workstation. "Mr. Mandrake suggests you wait in the washroom until his visitors have left."

Emma looked for Jonah, but he was already gone. *How does he move so fast?*

The door to Mandrake's office opened, and a man and a woman emerged, followed by a man Emma recognized as Gabriel Mandrake. The two strangers were dressed in street clothes, but Emma had spent enough time on the street to recognize police officers when she saw them.

Mandrake was dressed in blue jeans and a white collared shirt with the sleeves rolled up. His exposed arms were covered with tattoos, and Emma could see more designs peeking out of his shirt collar.

"I assure you that I'll talk to the students. If they noticed anything suspicious, we'll be in touch," Mandrake was saying.

"It would be better if we could talk to them directly," the woman said, as if continuing an argument that had started inside. "Perhaps they saw something that would help us . . . even if they don't realize it."

Mandrake's lips tightened in what looked like annoyance. "Then you'll have to come back with a court order," he snapped. "Our children are fragile, Detective. Can you imagine how traumatic it would be if they were questioned by the police about monsters and zombies?" He raised an eyebrow.

The male detective bristled. "We're not saying there were actual zombies on the bridge," he said. "Children have fertile imaginations, and they'd been through a harrowing experience. But somebody kidnapped a dozen preschoolers. And somebody seems to have emptied a graveyard and left a couple hundred corpses in the Flats. The media is going wild. We need to find out who and why."

"I agree," Mandrake said, "which is why it's a shame to see you wasting your time here."

"Is it true that Lisbet's coming here for a concert in the spring?" the female detective said eagerly. "I saw them in Pittsburgh two years ago."

"They are," Mandrake said, glancing at his watch. "I believe Patrick here has some courtesy tickets, if you know anyone who could use them."

When the detectives had gone, Mandrake turned his attention to Emma and Natalie. "I'm sorry about that," he said, his voice still edged with irritation. "The police don't always make appointments, and I figured it was easier to handle it now than to ask them back."

Jonah emerged from the washroom and quietly rejoined them, as if being asked to hide in a bathroom when there were visitors at the school was something that happened all the time. Clearly, nobody was going to offer an explanation to Emma.

Zombies on a bridge? Emma thought. Why not?

Mandrake was thin . . . gaunt as a crankster on his way

down, with close-cropped dark hair, an earring, and intense brown eyes in a sharp-boned face.

"And you're Emma Greenwood," he said, his eyes flicking over her once, twice, three times, as if to gather as much information as possible. "And you lived at Thorn Hill."

"Yes, sir."

"You're not in the south anymore, Emma," Mandrake said. "Call me Gabriel."

Emma nodded, hoping she could manage it.

"So where have you been living, since the disaster?" Mandrake asked.

"Memphis." She guessed she'd best keep her answers short. Less chance that she'd get herself into trouble.

Mandrake smiled. "Ah. I thought I heard that in your voice. Memphis is a great music town."

"It is," Emma said.

Mandrake waited, as if expecting something more. Then he said, "Well, welcome to the Anchorage. Natalie tells me that you were staying at the family shelter downtown."

She nodded, tongue-tied. Afraid she'd say the wrong thing again. Wishing she had the gift of pretty speech, like Jonah.

Who knew that someone who hated liars would have so much need of the gift of lying.

"Patrick," Mandrake said to his assistant. "I'm not in for anyone for the next half hour."

Mandrake led them back to his office, which contained more rock-and-roll memorabilia, along with several electric and acoustic guitars that Emma itched to take a closer look at. One whole wall of the office was made of glass, and before she could stop herself, she'd crossed to look outside.

The school was high on a bluff, looking down into the industrial heart of the city. Down below, the river snaked its way to the lake, lined by steelyards and railroad tracks, spanned by a series of iron and stone bridges. Downriver, a massive lake freighter was just threading its way back to open water, the bridges lifting open before it.

"Oh," Emma said, practically putting her nose against the glass before she remembered herself. "I wouldn't get anything done if I had a view like that."

Mandrake smiled. "Sometimes I do have to draw the drapes," he said. He gestured to a grouping of chairs by the window. "Please. Sit. And tell me what's happened to you."

Natalie and Emma had worked out a story that morning. Most of it was technically true. "My parents are dead . . . my mother died in Brazil, at the Thorn Hill commune. Since then, I've lived with my grandfather in Memphis. But he died . . . a stroke, I think."

"I'm sorry for your losses," Mandrake murmured, his eyes alert and fixed on her face, so that she felt like she was the only person in the world.

"I don't have any other family, and I didn't want to go to the child welfare. I'd heard about this place called the Anchorage, where you could go if you'd been at Thorn Hill. So I came to Cleveland."

Emma glanced at Jonah. He sat, head bowed, one leg thrust out straight, the other bent at the knee. Gloved hands on his thighs. A carefully casual posture, but tension thrummed through him as if he were a high-intensity power line. Was he worried she'd say something wrong?

"How did you get here from Memphis?" Mandrake asked.

"I have a car," Emma said. "It's not pretty, but it runs."

"How old are you?"

"Sixteen."

"And the shelter didn't send you to Children and Family Services?"

"No, sir." When Mandrake's eyes narrowed, Emma added, "I told them I was eighteen. That works if you're tall, and you claim you don't have ID."

Mandrake laughed. "You've worked that out, have you?" He sobered. "You say your mother died at Thorn Hill. What was her name?"

"Gwen . . . Gwen Hart," Emma said.

"Gwen Hart," he said, shaking his head. "I don't remember her, but it was a big place and I wasn't there often. I had a business back in the States to run." He woke the notebook on his desk, and the screen illuminated. "The thing is, you're not in our survivor database. We track everyone, even those who went to live with relatives, because many of them have come back to us eventually." His fingers flew over the keyboard, then he turned the screen so that she could see it.

File not found, it said.

"So I'm not in your records?" Emma said, her heart sinking.

"Neither you nor your mother are on the casualty lists," Gabriel said, turning the screen back.

"The casualty lists? But . . . I'm alive."

"Obviously," Mandrake said. "We always check, but as you can imagine, things were chaotic at the end. All the adults were dead, after all, and the survivors among the older children were quite ill. Some of the children were difficult to identify, and so it's certainly possible that you might have survived and yet be listed as dead. The records are what they are . . . imperfect." He paused. "Could I see your right forearm?" he asked, pulling back his own sleeve.

"She doesn't have the Nightshade tattoo," Natalie said. "I already checked."

"Hmm," Gabriel said.

"My father took me back to the States," Emma said. "He came back and got me, before the . . . uh . . . poisoning."

"He did? Why?"

"He was supposed to keep me until Christmas," Emma said. "I guess you could say my parents were separated."

"What was your father's name?"

"Tyler Boykin. Well, Tyler Greenwood."

"Hmm. Tyler Greenwood. I don't remember him."

"That makes sense, because I guess he never really stayed there very long," Emma said.

"As you can tell, Emma has a savant stone," Jonah said, as if eager to cut short the discussion and get to the point.

"Yes," Mandrake said. "It's consistent with what we see in survivors." He sat back in his chair, juggling a pen with supple fingers, his face unreadable. "Do you remember Thorn Hill, Emma?"

"Just—just fragments. There are scenes in my head. Like flashbacks. Mostly, I remember my mother. It's like I hear her voice in my head. Or some fragrance reminds me of her. I never know which ones are real and which ones I made up." Her voice trailed off. *Good one, Emma. Now they think I'm seeing things.* "We called it the Farm. I remember gardens, and houses in the woods . . . they looked like mushrooms. And playing games on the—on a field called the *okara*. I slept in a hammock."

"Well," Gabriel said, "clearly you were there."

Emma glanced over at Jonah, who was scanning messages on his phone, flicking through screens. He seemed to have a habit of doing that when he was hiding in plain sight.

"So . . . you've been living with your grandfather all this time?" Gabriel said. "What was his name?"

"Sonny Lee Greenwood."

Mandrake's eyes narrowed. "The luthier?"

"That's him," Emma said. "Why? Have you heard of him?"

"Anyone who's serious about custom guitars knows his work. I have one of his guitars in my collection."

Emma smiled sadly. "They're hard to find. Most people aren't willing to give them up once they get hold of one."

"Was Sonny Lee gifted?"

"Yes, sir, he was," Emma said. "But not in the way you mean."

"Emma is already a skilled luthier," Jonah said. "Like her grandfather. I'm thinking that might be her savant gift. You've been saying you want to do more of that work on-site, maybe start a training program for some of the savants. She does amazing work."

How does he know that? Emma thought. Then, answering her own question, she thought, Natalie.

"A luthier?" Mandrake eyed her appraisingly. "Aren't you rather young?"

"I pretty much lived in Sonny Lee's shop. He said I was the best apprentice he'd ever had."

Mandrake held her gaze for a long moment, then unfolded to his feet and crossed the room to where a Martin D-28 rested in a stand. Lifting it, he brought it back to Emma.

"Here," he said, handing it to her. "What would you do with this one?"

Mellow, mellow Martins, Emma thought, brushing her fingers across the strings. This one sounded as warm as the sun on a summer day. Except for the buzz. She sighted down the fingerboard.

"This is just my eyeball guess," Emma said. "The action's too low. I'd start with the saddle height and nut-slot depth. Without my feeler gauges, I can't tell you which and how much. If that doesn't do the trick, you might want to look at the neck relief. But get somebody that knows what he's doing."

"Like you."

"Like me. But I'm not the only one."

Mandrake smiled. "I think we can find a place at the Anchorage for Sonny Lee Greenwood's granddaughter."

"I should tell you up front, I'm not much of a student," Emma said.

Jonah gave her a look that said, *Shut up.* As in: *Why are you telling him that? You trying to get him to turn you down?*

"No worries," Mandrake said, lacing his fingers. "If you don't work out as a student, maybe you can join the faculty." He stood. "Jonah . . . ask Patrick for keys to eight hundred in Oxbow. Take Emma over there, and get her settled in."

"In Oxbow?" Jonah looked astounded. "You're putting her in Oxbow?"

"That's what I said, didn't I?" Mandrake shifted his gaze to Emma. "You'll find clothes, groceries, soap, and so on at the store in the student center. Not a great selection, but enough to get you through until you can go out shopping. Put it on the school account. Jonah will show you the woodshop, too. If you need some specialized tools and supplies, make a list of what you need, and sources, if you know them, and I'll bring it all in."

"You want *me* to give her a tour?" Another surprise for Jonah, and one he didn't look happy about. "Isn't there someone else who—"

"It's good practice for an administrator-in-training," Gabriel said. "Now, if you'll excuse me, I need to make some calls."

∝ CHAPTER THIRTY-SEVEN ∝
BORN UNDER A BAD SIGN

Jonah knew he was walking a tightrope, an abyss to either side. To make matters worse, he wasn't in command of his own destiny. Any small misstep could collapse the house of lies and omissions he'd built.

It was a predicament of his own making, and yet, looking back, he couldn't see how he could have done things differently—at least once he'd committed to searching out Tyler Greenwood. When he learned that Emma was alive, he had to go after her. When he found out she was a savant with no place to go, he had to bring her back to the Anchorage. It was the safest place. It was where she belonged.

Jonah wasn't going to send her to foster care. He was the one who'd orphaned her, after all.

Would she figure it out on her own? Jonah tended to stick in people's memories. The more time they spent together, the more likely she'd recognize him. Jonah's plan had been to get her admitted to the Anchorage, and then disappear . . . at least until he was sure her memory loss was permanent. In the past, that would have been easy, given his busy travel schedule. Now that he was out of Nightshade, though, Jonah was landlocked, and both Gabriel and Natalie seemed determined to fling Emma and him together.

"Hey!" Emma's voice broke into his thoughts. He looked back, to find her clinging to a light post, breathing hard. "Can you slow down? Or are we running a race and you just didn't tell me?"

"Sorry," Jonah said, walking back toward her. "I didn't mean to run away from you. Here, let me carry that." He reached for her shopping bags, and she yanked them back.

"Just point me in the right direction and I'll go there on my own," Emma said. "No need to take up your time, being as you're in such a hurry."

Jonah shook his head, pricked by guilt. "You'll never get into the place on your own. Anyway, we're almost there. That's the Oxbow Building up ahead." They'd already been to security, and to the student center, and he'd scarcely spoken a word the whole time.

It's not her fault you have so many secrets to keep.

It's not her fault that you've spent your whole life driving people away.

What should he be telling her, if he were giving a campus tour? He pointed. "That's the dispensary on your right. Gabriel or one of the other healers will do an initial eval, and develop a treatment plan."

"I'm fine," Emma said. "I don't need a treatment plan."

Jonah chose not to argue. "Here's the fitness center. It's brand-new, and it's amazing. Here, let me show you." He turned down the walk, but Emma stayed rooted to the sidewalk.

"I don't work out," she said. "I'll probably never use it."

"Come see it anyway? Please?"

In the end, she complied, of course, and he showed her the weight room, the dance studio, the gymnasium, the massage studios, and the open sparring gym. Tilting her head back, Emma studied the climbing wall, the obstacle course, the network of gymnastic equipment. "Is this where you learned to climb up cliffs?" she asked.

"Yes," Jonah said. "Here, and out in the field."

"Out in what field?"

"Well, you know," Jonah said lamely. "On real cliffs."

Physical therapists were working with some of the more fragile students in the warm-water pool.

"Jonah!" One of the therapists, Ramon, handed off his client and walked toward them. "I didn't know you were in town. Who's this?"

"New student," Jonah said. "Emma Greenwood, this is Ramon Perez, one of the therapists."

"Welcome, Emma," Ramon said. "I hope you like it here. Jonah . . . do you have a minute? I have a question about Kenzie's treatments."

"I'm showing Emma around right now," Jonah said. "Maybe we can—"

"Go ahead," Emma said. "I can wait." She crossed to one of the whirlpools, squatted, and dipped a hand in the water.

Jonah turned back to Ramon. "What's up?"

"I've been looping your music during Kenzie's therapy sessions, like you suggested," Ramon said. "It's really improved his exercise tolerance. I'd like to try it with some of the other clients, if that's all right with you."

Jonah hesitated. His first impulse was to say no. "The

music . . . it's just something Kenzie and I share. It seems to help him, but maybe that's because we're brothers. I have no idea what effect it would have on other patients."

"That's what we want to find out," Ramon said. "You know, kind of an experiment."

"What if it's harmful?"

"All right, confession time," Ramon said, rolling his eyes. "I've already tried it on one patient who'd been in steep decline, and I've seen some improvement."

After that, of course, Jonah couldn't say no. Not to Ramon, who'd been fighting a lonely, losing battle for years.

"All right," Jonah said. "But go slow, all right?"

"Awesome!" Ramon grinned. "I'll keep you posted."

Jonah looked for Emma, but she'd disappeared.

"Emma?" She was nowhere to be found in the hydro-therapy area, nor in the gym they'd just come from.

He finally found her in front of the door to one of the sparring gyms. The display next to the door said CLOSED SES-SION. Jonah could hear the thud of bodies colliding behind the door, shouts of triumph, and screams of pain.

"What's in here?" Emma asked, trying the door, which was locked, of course. "It sounds like people fighting."

"It's martial arts," Jonah said.

"Can I see?"

"It's a closed session," Jonah said. "Look, we'd better get you over to Oxbow. We still haven't been to the woodshop, and I've got to get to class."

Emma hesitated for a moment, her hand on the door handle. Then she turned away. They were almost to the other end of the hall, when the door to the sparring gym slammed open.

It was Alison Shaw, Bloodfetcher in hand.

"Jonah!" she cried, sprinting toward them.

Instinctively, Jonah thrust Emma behind him and stood, facing off with Alison, balanced on the balls of his feet.

Alison's face registered surprise, which quickly turned to anger. She looked from Jonah to Emma and back again. "What did you think I was going to do?" she demanded. "Attack?"

Jonah shook his head. "No. I wasn't thinking anything," he said. "You just surprised me, is all."

"I don't believe you," Alison said. "Who's this?" she asked, peering over Jonah's shoulder at Emma.

"This is Emma Greenwood," Jonah said, shifting out of the way. "She's a new student. Emma, this is Alison Shaw."

Alison studied her. "Are you a senior?"

Emma shook her head. "Sophomore."

"I thought you looked good, for a senior," Alison said. Drawing another look of confusion from Emma. Alison rested the point of her sword on the floor and leaned on the hilt. Something Jonah had never seen her do before. Something nobody who knew anything about weaponry would do.

"So where'd you come from, Emma?" Alison asked.

Emma looked at Jonah, and Alison noticed. "I see. Keeping secrets, are we?"

"No secrets," Jonah said. "Natalie brought Emma in from the shelter. She's new in town."

"Speaking of secrets, how much do you know about our Jonah?" Alison asked, directing the question to Emma. "Not much, I'll bet. Better watch yourself. Jonah may be hot, but he's dangerous. Deadly, even. Look but don't touch is my advice."

Emma looked from Alison to Jonah. "Dangerous?"

"She's kind of slow on the uptake," Alison said, smirking at Jonah. "Don't you think?"

"Come on, Emma," Jonah said, propelling her toward the door. Thinking, This is turning out to be a disaster. I never should have brought her here.

"Jonah!" Alison called after them. "Don't forget we have practice tomorrow morning."

Practice? Jonah thought. Are we on the sparring schedule tomorrow and I just didn't—oh. Natalie had scheduled Fault Tolerant's first practice for the next morning. The first practice without Mose.

On the street, Emma eyed him quizzically. "What was that all about?"

"What was what all ab—oh, the practice? She's talking about the band. Fault Tolerant. Remember . . . the one you saw at Club Catastrophe?"

"I meant the part about you being dangerous."

Jonah shrugged. "I have no idea. We're all dangerous in our own way, I guess."

Fortunately, Oxbow was deserted at this time of day. Room 800 was an efficiency on the eighth floor, several floors beneath Jonah's apartment. Small, but replete with the high-tech gadgets Gabriel loved. Jonah showed her how the key card and the iris scanner worked, and demonstrated how to activate the security system.

Emma put her food in the refrigerator and set her purchases down on the bed. She took a quick walk around while Jonah hung out by the door. He loved the way she moved, loose-limbed and relaxed, at peace with her body. At one point, she dragged a chair over and stood on top of it to examine the sound system. She stretched up to examine the ceiling-mounted speakers, exposing a strip of flesh between sweatshirt and the waistband of her pants. His pants.

You're like one of those randy nineteenth-century dudes, Jonah thought. Aroused by a glimpse of ankle.

Finally, she rejoined him. "Can I ask some questions?"

"Sure," Jonah said. Eager to end the one-on-one, he added, "Can we walk while we talk?"

"Sure," Emma said. "You got a hot date or what?"

Jonah's cheeks burned as the blood rushed to his face. "Ah . . . no. I just—you know . . . homework."

As they left the apartment, she reactivated the security system. She seemed absolutely comfortable with devices of all kinds.

"Where's your room?" she asked as they got on the elevator.

Jonah pointed at the ceiling. "Four floors up."

"I could tell you were surprised that Mr. Mandrake put me here," Emma said, in that direct way she had. "Why?"

Jonah shrugged. "Oxbow is reserved for staff and . . . and . . . staff. So prepare to be put to work. Teaching, maybe, or repairing musical instruments, or helping with the music program."

"But he's never even seen my work," Emma said as they turned down the sidewalk. "How does he know I'm any good?"

"I don't second-guess what Gabriel does," Jonah said, which was a total lie. These days, anyway.

Emma digested this for a few moments. "So you work for Mr. Mandrake, too?"

"Gabriel."

"For Gabriel?"

Jonah nodded. Anticipating the next question, he volunteered, "I'm training with him in community relations, fund-raising, management of the club, and like that."

"And you're just seventeen?"

"Gabriel is never afraid to give responsibility to a person just because he's young," Jonah said. "We grow up fast." *Or we wouldn't grow up at all.*

"I've been meaning to ask you, Jonah. What is your gift?"

He should've been ready for that question, but it still caught him by surprise somehow.

"I'm an empath. Do you know what that is?"

Emma shook her head.

"I can read people's emotions," Jonah said. "Gabriel finds that helpful sometimes." *Along with my other skills. Like killing. Oh, right. Not anymore.*

Emma stopped dead in her tracks, embarrassment rolling off her in waves. "You read *minds*?"

He shook his head. "Feelings. I can't tell what a person is thinking, plotting, or planning, but I can sometimes tell when they're lying, or when they're afraid, angry, and so on."

She didn't look reassured. "Great," she muttered, peering at him out of the corner of her eye.

"Don't worry about it," Jonah said. "I've learned to filter most of it out. It's just background noise. Otherwise, I'd go crazy." *Liar.*

"Who's Kenzie?" she asked then.

"My brother."

"Younger or older?"

"Younger." Jonah guessed he should give more than

one-word answers. "His real name is McKenzie. So Kenzie for short. He lives at Safe Harbor."

"Safe Harbor? What's that?"

"It's a skilled facility for savants with severe disabilities," Jonah said. He pointed up St. Clair. "It's a few blocks that way."

"Oh." A blush stained Emma's cheeks to a coppery red. "He's disabled because of the . . . because of what happened at Thorn Hill?"

"Because of the poison," Jonah said bluntly. "It hit some of us harder than others. Kenzie has intractable magical seizures."

"Magical seizures? What's that like?"

"Unforgettable. Life-changing, even." He turned up the walk to the arts-and-crafts building. "The woodshop is in this building."

"Will I get to meet him?" Emma persisted.

"Do you want to?"

"Why wouldn't I?"

"He'd like that." They stood on the porch of A&C. "It's in here, first floor, to the rear. Your key card should open the door. If I leave you here, now, can you find your way back to Oxbow?"

"No problem," Emma said.

Chapter Thirty-eight
I'm with the Band

Emma awakened with a jolt, momentarily disoriented, her arms crossed over her face to ward off danger. Propping up on her elbows, she looked around. Afternoon sunlight streamed through the window, flaming dust motes in the air.

Right. She was in the Oxbow Building, eighth-floor studio, view of downtown.

She pulled her shirt away from her clammy skin. Jonah's shirt. She'd bought pajamas at the store in the student center, but when it came down to it, she'd slept another night in Jonah's clothes. She pressed the faded cotton against her nose. It still carried his scent.

They ought to bottle that, she thought. And call it Boy Blue. Or, maybe, Bad Idea.

She had nothing to bring to this game. She had no skills. It was her kind of luck to fall for a boy who could read minds. Well, emotions. Did that include lust? It was humiliating . . .

like walking around naked with someone who was fully clothed.

A just God would have given that gift to Emma . . . so she could sort out the liars.

What time was it? She groped for her phone. Not there. Where was her phone?

Oh. It was back at home. Tyler's home. It seemed so far away, now. Just one more dream that fades upon waking. A stopping place on a journey to nowhere.

Her groping hand found the notebook paper with her wish list on it—the notes and measurements she'd taken at the woodshop the day before. The shop at the Anchorage was top-shelf, just like everything else on campus. Still, it had an air of neglect, as if the administration had sunk a lot of money into it at the front end, but nobody had paid much attention to it since. It didn't *smell* like any woodshop she'd ever been in. Not even any sawdust on the floor.

She'd made a slow circuit of the larger tools, trying them out with scrap lumber she found in the discard bin. The tools looked nearly new, though some of the blades needed sharpening and everything was covered with a fine layer of dust. She was used to Sonny Lee's tools and their quirks. For instance, how the pulley on the table saw would slip on the shaft and bind against the body of the saw and you had to act quick if you smelled burning rubber or you might burn up the belt. Or how you had to give the old disc sander a spin to get it going because the capacitor didn't work and it wouldn't start up on its own.

There wasn't much in the way of materials—woods, fittings, and the like. Wistfully, she recalled the racks of seasoned woods she'd left behind at Tyler's, and wondered if they were still there. I need to get back there, she thought. Somehow.

Propping herself up in bed, she scanned the rows of tiny, precise handwriting, making a few additions and clarifications. New saw blades. Lubricants. The specialized wood glue Sonny Lee always ordered from Germany. And woods: birch and ebony and book-matched maple.

Setting her list aside, she slid out of bed and padded across the floor to the bathroom. She was at a boarding school, where they had set times for things. She'd probably already missed breakfast. She didn't want to miss lunch, too.

A blinking light in one corner of the mirror caught her attention. She squinted at it, puzzled. Then poked at it with her finger without result.

Then she remembered. Jonah had said something about a digital display embedded in the mirror.

A remote was propped against the backsplash. She scooped it up and began hitting buttons until a message appeared.

We're in the practice rooms on the first floor. Take the elevator down (use your key card). Entry key is GIST27. Nat.

Emma pulled on the jeans she'd bought the day before, crispy and new. She chose a black T-shirt with SECURITY in stark white letters on the back and a line drawing of a castle keep on the front. She tugged a brush through her resistant hair, twisted it into a knot, grabbed a hunk of crumb cake from the refrigerator, and went to find the practice rooms.

Emma stepped off the elevator on the first floor. To her left, toward the front, was a common area, with a flat-screen television, comfortable furniture, and a fireplace. It was deserted.

The rear of the warehouse was a rough-finished workspace that showed its warehouse bones, partitioned off with dividers. She walked down a short hallway lined with doors.

Displays next to each door listed the room schedule for the day.

As she neared the end of the hallway, she began to feel the thud of percussion under her feet, and heard the faint, anguished cry of a blues guitar, the wail of keyboards. Next to the last door, the display said simply DIAZ.

Through the door, she heard a voice that all but brought her to her knees.

> *Just one kiss,*
> *That was never meant to be.*
> *Just one kiss*
> *One more bitter memory.*
> *A blighted love, a mortal sin,*
> *A doomed encounter skin to skin.*

She eased the door open. It was Jonah, a vintage Stratocaster slung low on his hips, knees bent, head thrown back, eyes closed as he searched out the chords with his fingers. Which should have been difficult, since he was wearing fingerless gloves in studded black leather. Who wears gloves, even fingerless ones, to play guitar?

And why was Jonah playing with the band she'd first heard at Club Catastrophe? She looked them over. Their lead guitarist was missing—the one who'd played the Parker DragonFly.

The other players were the same. Natalie hunched over a drum kit, her sticks a blur, face gleaming with sweat. The purple-haired girl from the fitness center played an Ibanez bass guitar, and the boy who played keyboards was the same, too.

Emma leaned against the doorframe, head swimming as Jonah's voice poured over her.

> *Just one kiss,*
> *Was enough to break my heart.*
> *Just one kiss,*
> *A disaster from the start.*
> *Like the kiss of frost that chars the rose,*
> *An assassin in a lover's clothes.*

Jonah prowled back and forth, exuding a feral heat, his movements mesmerizing, his T-shirt plastered to his washboard abs, jeans riding low on his hipbones.

Get ahold of yourself, girl, Emma thought. You of all people know better than to fall for a musician.

Just then, the music tangled up in itself and dwindled away amid laughter and good-natured swearing.

"What the hell was *that*, Severino?" Nat asked.

The keyboardist blotted his face with his sleeve. "I was . . . you know . . . improvising."

Natalie snorted. "I thought maybe you were starting your own band, right here and now."

Severino looked up and spotted Emma in the doorway. "Hel-lo there! Who are you?"

Jonah had been trying out some riffs, but now the guitar cut off abruptly. He stared at Emma with a stricken, guilty, almost horrified expression. The kind you get when you've been caught making out with your best friend's boyfriend.

"Emma!" Natalie said, grinning. "You're finally up. How are you feeling this morning?"

"What are *you* doing here?" Jonah demanded.

He's blushing, Emma thought. He's actually blushing.

"I invited her," Natalie said.

"Why?"

"Because she said she wanted to hear us play," Natalie said, giving Jonah a *behave* kind of look.

"Great to see you, too, Jonah," Emma said. She strode over to the keyboardist and stuck out her hand. "Hi, I'm Emma Greenwood, from Memphis."

"Rudy Severino," Rudy said, grinning at her. He was good-looking, and knew it, but sometimes confidence looks good on a person. It was more stage presence than arrogance.

"And this is Alison Shaw," Natalie said, pointing at the bass player. "Rudy, Alison, this is Emma Greenwood, a new student here at the Anchorage."

"We've already met," Alison said, around the pick in her teeth.

"Don't let me interrupt," Emma said. "Pretend I'm not here." She straddled a chair, resting her arms on the back. "Was that one of your original songs? The one you just played?"

"Yes," Jonah said, keeping his eyes fixed on his fingerboard, busily tuning a guitar that was already in tune.

"That one's brand-new," Natalie said. "Jonah and his brother collaborate on songwriting."

"Your brother Kenzie?" Emma asked. "The one you mentioned?"

"Yes," Jonah said. "There's nothing wrong with his mind."

"He's a genius," Natalie said.

Ducking out of the strap, Jonah set the Strat in its stand and grabbed up a water bottle. Tilting it, he took a drink, the long column of his throat jumping as he swallowed, and wiped his lips with the back of his hand.

Wrenching her eyes away from him, Emma focused on the Strat. How long had it been since she'd held a guitar in her hands? A week? It seemed like an eternity. It was all she could do to keep from crossing the room and snatching it up. But she knew how people could be about their guitars. Herself included.

Somehow, she had to get home and get back what was hers.

Jonah was taking his time. It was like he was intentionally stalling. Like he didn't want to play in front of Emma.

"Hey!" Natalie said. "Let's get back to it," she said. "I have to be in clinic at four."

Jonah lifted the Strat and slid back into it. "Let's move on to something else. I think we've got that one down."

They played another original, something called "Doomtime," which was less bluesy and more rock and roll, with a thrumming percussion and in-your-face lyrics. Jonah sang lead, and Severino layered in a harmony. It was the kind of song that made you want to get up and move, with a refrain that stayed in your head. Next was a song called "A Tientas." Natalie sang lead on that one, with Jonah harmonizing. The lyrics were in Spanish, but it seemed to be a song they both knew well. Next was a bluesy ballad, something called "I'll Sit In."

> *I don't play no love songs,*
> *I just can't harmonize.*
> *There'll be no sweet kisses in the dark,*
> *I'll never look into your eyes.*

But if you're here to play the blues, I'll sit in.
When it comes to songs of heartbreak, I'll fit in.
For emotional disaster
You know I am the master.
If you're here to play the blues, I'll sit in.

Severino got a phone call, and the band took a break. Emma nodded toward the Strat. "Do you mind if I give that a try?"

Jonah gazed at the guitar for a long moment, a muscle in his jaw working, then shifted his gaze to Emma. His expression was an odd mix of dread and anticipation. "Do you play?" he whispered.

"I play a little."

"Be my guest," he said.

She lifted the fine weight of the Stratocaster onto her lap. "Nineteen-fifties?"

Jonah nodded. "'Fifty-seven, yes."

"Do you know about vintage guitars?" Natalie asked, toweling off.

"Vintage is where I live." Emma launched into the opening riff of "Heart of Stone." Feeling that rush that always made picking up a guitar worthwhile. Hearing the sweet sound of the Strat beat against the practice room walls.

"So sweet," Emma breathed as the last notes faded. The action was a little high for her taste, but otherwise this guitar made it easy to sound good.

She looked up to find three people staring at her, Natalie grinning as if delighted, Alison looking stunned, Jonah wearing an odd mix of pain and longing and apprehension on his face.

"You're lucky to have this," she said, running her fingers over the saddle. "It must've been pricey."

"Gabriel has a large collection of guitars," Jonah said, his voice hoarse and strange. "He's a total geek for equipment."

Emma tried to hand the guitar back to Jonah, but Natalie put a hand on her arm and said, "Play something else."

"No, really, I—"

"Play something else," Natalie ordered. "Do you sing, too?"

"Natalie," Jonah said, shaking his head. "I don't think we—"

"Play something else. *And sing*," Natalie said, glaring at Jonah.

It was just way too tempting. Like a street junkie confronted with the offer of a fix, Emma couldn't say no. For the first time since leaving Memphis, she felt like she was in the right place, wearing the right clothes, jamming with the right people. She flexed her fingers, pitched her voice low like they did down on Beale Street, and said, "This here is a little number by Big Mama Thornton called 'Ball 'n' Chain.'"

She wrung everything she could out of that Stratocaster, pouring weeks' worth of rage and pain and grief into voice and fingering. Partway in, Natalie began a soft cadence with brushes and sticks, providing a floor for Emma's anguished flights of notes.

Emma kept sliding glances at Jonah, assessing his reaction. He looked torn, his hands twitching, mirroring her fingering, his face wistful. Yet his eyes were shadowed, shifting, all greens and cool blues, like the light in a forest when the treetops are moving.

When they'd finished, Natalie slid off her stool and crossed the practice room to where a guitar case leaned against the wall. She undid the catches, lifted out a Parker DragonFly, and plugged it into the amp.

This place is like Christmas for guitars, Emma thought.

"Here," Natalie said, thrusting the guitar at Jonah. "Try this one."

"Natalie," Jonah protested, holding the Parker on his lap like it was a child with a full diaper.

"Don't be a baby," Natalie said, settling back behind the drums. "You play the Strat all the time."

"It's not that," Jonah said. "I just—"

"Would you rather Emma played the DragonFly?"

"That's not fair," Emma protested weakly, cradling the Strat in her arms, her hair sliding over its shining surface. "These are Jonah's guitars."

"The DragonFly is only newly his," Natalie said. "It belonged to our lead guitarist, Mose Butterfield. He died recently, and left the guitar to Jonah."

"He's dead?" Emma's heart stuttered. "You mean the one I saw at Club Catastrophe last month? What—what happened?"

They all looked at one another. Anybody could tell they'd been friends forever. Emma was an outsider for sure.

"Mose had been in ill health for quite a while," Natalie said finally. "A combination of the effects of the poison and heavy use of street drugs."

"I'm sorry to hear that," Emma said. "Is that why Jonah's sitting in?"

"We've wanted Jonah in the band for a good long time," Alison said. "That's the only good that's come out of it."

"So," Natalie said, as if eager to dispel the gloom. "You're *damn* good. I'd like to hear more. You play mostly blues?"

Emma nodded. "Mostly. That's what I grew up on."

"I'm wondering what songs we know that you might know," Natalie said, furrowing her brow. "We don't play a lot of covers, but—"

"Actually . . ." Emma glanced at Jonah, who had apparently resigned himself to jamming with her, because he was correcting the tuning on the DragonFly. "Actually, I have some ideas about the song you just played. 'Doomtime,' wasn't it?"

Natalie nodded, a wicked smile curving her mouth.

"Could you run through it again? Jonah, you just do your thing and I'll see what I can do." Having the guitar in her hands had restored her confidence. *This is the only thing I've ever been good at.*

They played through "Doomtime." Emma wasn't aggressive . . . she just threaded in and out of Jonah's chords. Sonny Lee always said it was like putting embroidery on a silk dress or necklaces on a pretty woman.

By now, Severino was back. "Hey!" he said. "You never mentioned you were bringing in a ringer."

"Let's try something else," Natalie said. Emma was finding out that she was as intense about music as she was about healing.

They played through their repertoire. "A Tientas." "Logjam Blues." "I'll Sit In." "Ask Me No Questions (I'll Tell You No Lies)." "Ruined." And covers of a few rock-and-roll standards.

Jonah sang lead on most of the songs, Natalie and Rudy added scraps of vocal harmony. Emma wove through Jonah's guitar work, each time adding more to the web of melody. He was a natural collaborator, seeming almost to anticipate what she was going to do before she did it, and turning on a dime to respond to what she did. With each song, they stepped on each other's toes the first few times, but by the last run-through, it was more of a marriage of equals, each claiming his own space.

Natalie tilted her head, puzzled. "I can't tell which of you is playing lead, and which rhythm guitar," she said.

"Exactly," Emma said. "That's the whole point. I've got six strings on my guitar—or twelve—and I want to use them all."

"Where'd you learn to play like that?" Natalie asked. "Have you been in a lot of bands?"

"Nothing serious, or for very long," Emma said. "But I sit in a lot. Or I used to." She cleared her throat. "When I lived in Memphis. If you're jamming with players you don't know, you have to figure out how to meet in the middle real quick."

"Hmm." Natalie shot a look at Severino, looking like a cat with a canary or two put away for later. Severino grinned back and gave her a thumbs-up.

"Natalie," Jonah said, as if he knew exactly where this was going. "Don't you have to get to the clinic?"

"It's perfect, Jonah. You said our sound was thin. We need another layer. Not just icing on the cake. *Actual cake.*"

"You sound like a jilted lover on the rebound, Nat," Alison said, unplugging the Ibanez and settling it back into its case. "Ready to rush into a new relationship with someone you hardly know."

"Give her time to settle in before you go recruiting her," Jonah said, beginning to break down his equipment. "She may find she has better options. Besides, it's not fair to put

Emma at risk so you can play in a better band!" His blue eyes glittered green.

Sonny Lee always said that Emma had an ironwood backbone—hard as iron, resilient as wood. And now it came into play.

"Hey!" she shouted.

They all swung around to look at her.

"Am I invisible or what?" She slid down from her stool, unplugged the Stratocaster, and returned it to its stand.

"Emma," Natalie began. "I don't think we—"

Emma bulldozed right over her. "I'll be straight with you, because that's the way I am. I don't know whether any of this will work out—the school, the band, the town—any of it. But I like what I've heard and seen so far, and I'm clean out of options. I've had a good time today . . . better than I've had in a while. I'll take a chance on you, if you take a chance on me. No contracts, no obligations. I'll sit in for a few practices, if you want, or play one gig, then you can decide. Or decide right now, I don't care. Just don't argue about it in front of me. That's rude. I was raised on the streets, and even I know that."

They all looked at one another. Severino burst out laughing. "I think she fits in real good," he said.

"Now I'll get going, so you all can talk amongst yourselves." Emma paused. "If you decide you want me to sit in, though, there's one condition."

"What's that?" Natalie asked, shooting a smug look at Jonah.

"I need to go back home and get my guitars."

"**P**lease stay in the van," Jonah said, for probably the thousandth time. "Just tell me what you want, and I'll go get it."

Emma shook her head. "I won't know what I want until I take a look around. And you don't know where things are."

It was just after midnight. They were sitting in the driveway of Tyler's house, in a van that Fault Tolerant used to haul equipment. Continuing an argument that had begun across town.

"They're probably watching the house," Jonah said. "They'll be expecting you to come back here."

"They think I drowned, remember?"

"Maybe. But they'll know differently if you get up onstage. Which is why you shouldn't do it."

"Which is why it's best we do this now, before we play a public gig."

Ever since the practice session, Jonah had missed no

opportunity to tell Emma why joining the band was a bad idea. It was beginning to get on her nerves, because she wasn't sure it was the right thing to do either, but she really wanted to be in the band, and she didn't need anybody trying to talk her out of it.

"You can't bring everything," Jonah said, staring straight ahead, through the windshield of the van. He gripped the steering wheel with his gloved hands as if it might try to get away.

"I don't want to bring everything," Emma said. "But you can't expect me to leave my entire life behind . . . again."

"I just . . . don't you think it will be hard, to go back in there?" Jonah said. "I just don't want you to be hurt more than you have been already."

"I don't think that's possible," she said, her insides one great hollow of loss.

"I'll go in first, then," Jonah said, turning his impossibly blue eyes toward Emma. His voice thrummed through her like sweet rum, heating her insides and clouding her head. "You wait here while I make sure it's not—"

"No!" she shouted, far too loudly for the inside of a van.

He flinched back, startled, raising both hands in defense.

"No," she said, more quietly. "I need to sort out who's telling the truth and who isn't. I want to see where my father died, and I don't want you to clean up first. I might notice something that other people wouldn't. If DeVries's sister died alongside Tyler, then maybe he and I *are* allies."

"So you're saying I should have left you hanging off a cliff?" Jonah said, his body rigid, his face a mask of disbelief. "I should have left you to be tortured and—"

"No," Emma said, sliding open the van door and jumping

down to the driveway. "I said *allies*. I didn't say I wanted to be anybody's prisoner."

Somehow, Jonah was out of the van and standing between her and the house. "You're not like other girls," he said. He looked down at her, the night breeze stirring his hair.

"You're not the first one that's noticed," Emma said, rolling her eyes. When he tilted his head, brow furrowed in confusion, she added, "Come on, Kinlock, you're going to have to do better than that. Admit it, that's a pretty lame line."

He stared at her for another long moment, then snorted, his lips twitching into a smile. "It *is* lame, I admit it, but I got nothing else. I haven't had much practice at flirting."

"Is *that* what that was?"

And then they were both laughing helplessly, a muffled, smothery kind of laughing.

You don't need to flirt, Emma thought. You just need to *be*.

When they regained control, Jonah said, "Can I at least walk in ahead of you and take the bullet for you, if need be?" His tone was light, but his body was taut as a leopard's.

She was about to follow him up the steps to the porch, when he blocked her path, holding her back with one hand.

"Do you have a silent alarm?" he asked.

"Tyler had a security system," Emma said, pointing at the metal sign in the yard.

"I know. But there's also a motion detector here on the porch." He stood, frowning, hands in his back pockets, his gaze flicking over the front of the house. Finally, he nodded and pointed into the maple tree overhanging the porch. "There's the camera. It's set up to film whoever comes in or out. It may be attached to a silent alarm, too. And, given that there are wizards involved, there may be magical traps as well. Those may or may not work on us, depending on what kind of magic they've used."

A cold finger brushed Emma's spine. *This isn't play pretend. You've got to remember that.*

"Do you mind if I try and find another way in?" Jonah said.

"Be my guest," Emma said, thinking, Easier said than done.

And, somehow—*somehow*—he swung up into the maple tree and onto the porch roof. She heard his light footsteps overhead, a window sliding up.

Moments later, he opened the door from the inside. "I disabled the alarm system," he said. "But I broke the window latch. Sorry."

"How did you do that?" she demanded.

"I forced it."

"No! I mean, how did you get up there? And how do you know about alarms?"

"It's not so different from climbing up a cliff." When she kept on staring, he added, "We have a diverse curriculum at the Anchorage."

They offer a *burglary* track? Emma thought, following him into the house.

Emma stepped inside, onto the old landing with the cracked linoleum that Tyler had been meaning to replace. On a hook inside the door hung the battered leather jacket he'd bought at a thrift store. Lined with fleece, it was the closest thing he had to a winter coat.

Impulsively, Emma lifted the jacket down. It was heavy

aviator leather . . . so old it didn't even smell like leather anymore. Instead, she caught a faint whiff of tobacco and that hair oil he used. The scent of late nights and good times.

The enormity of loss hit her, like a punch to the gut. She wrapped her arms around her middle, folding a little.

"Emma?" Jonah had turned back toward her. "Are you all right?"

"I'm fine," she said, sliding into Tyler's jacket as if she were armoring up for the battle to come. It fit big on her slim frame, and the sleeves were a little too long, but she could live with that.

They walked through the kitchen, past the bulletin board. The calendar pinned to it was still showing September, the gigs written in on the weekends. The message light on the answering machine was blinking. Emma hit the playback button.

Here was Tyler's familiar voice. "Leave me a message, and I just might call you back." Followed by a throaty laugh. Goose bumps prickled Emma's arms.

There were a series of hang-ups and several increasingly angry messages from club owners and band mates, asking after Tyler. The last one was bitter and brief, from a woman. "Least you could do is call me, Tyler. I mean, *come on!*"

Leaving the kitchen, Emma walked toward the front of the house. She might not be able to remember what happened the night of the murder, but she had a clear memory of how the house had looked before then. What was different?

The hall table was in its usual place, Tyler's keys in the old margarine tub where he always threw them when he was at home. Something was different, though. The walls had been scrubbed down—no—repainted a subtly different color.

The hardwood floors had been sanded down and refinished. The changes might fool most people, but they wouldn't fool Emma, since the place looked better than it ever had while Tyler lived there. It was like she'd walked onstage, and found it set up for a different band.

"Somebody's cleaned this place up," she murmured. "Who would've done that?"

Emma padded down the hallway, feeling invisible. Like an actor with a walk-on part in a play. I'm a ghost in this house, she thought.

She turned aside, into the office. As she entered, the tiny hairs rose on the back of her neck, and she shuddered. Even the simplest animal—a lobster—can learn to avoid those places where it was hurt before. Hadn't she read that somewhere?

Methodically, she studied the room. Her laptop was missing, and objects on the desk had been subtly shifted. She looked in the drawers and could see that the contents had been disturbed. There might be some folders gone, too.

"It looks like they searched the place," she said, looking around for Jonah. But he wasn't there. He hadn't followed her in. After all that fuss about going in her place, now he seemed to be hanging back, so as not to intrude.

She turned to the bookcase to the left of the door and pulled out the shelf that hid the gun safe. The safe was locked. She entered the combination, but it still didn't open. Apparently, the combination had been changed. Was Tyler's gun still inside?

Someone had gone to a lot of trouble to make it look like nothing had happened. Emma felt like her life had been rubbed out, like a stray pencil mark.

Emma walked on down the hallway, through the living

room, to the conservatory. Pausing in the doorway, she scanned the room before she entered.

It looked much as she remembered, except for what was missing. The wicker set with the peeling paint was gone, as were most of the lamps. The battered bamboo roller shade had been replaced and the drapes removed. The windows were the same style as before, but even without the daylight, she could tell they were new. For one thing, the windows in Tyler's house were never clean. When she breathed deeply, she could smell a charred, burned odor.

Getting down on her knees, she ran her finger along the baseboard.

"Ow!" Yanking her bleeding finger away, she sucked on it. She'd cut it on a bit of broken glass.

"Emma?" Jonah stood in the doorway to the conservatory, shifting from one foot to the other.

Emma held up her bleeding finger. "I cut my finger on some glass. No big deal." She stood. "Rowan said that this is where my father and the others were killed."

Jonah glanced around. "You wouldn't know to look at it. Somebody must have cleaned it up." After a pause, he added, "We should collect your things and go. I don't want to be here any longer than necessary."

He's as jumpy as a cat on hot asphalt, Emma thought. It was making her jumpier than she already was.

"All right, then help me bring up some things from the basement," she said. She descended the stairs, apprehension prickling her skin. Halfway down, she paused, a shudder rippling through her. Something had happened, here on the steps.

She looked up at Jonah, two steps above her. "I'm glad

you're here," she said. "This house is full of ghosts."

He must've felt it, too, since he looked half sick to his stomach.

At the bottom of the stairs, she didn't head immediately to her workshop. She stood and turned in a slow circle, looking for clues. It looked the way it always did. Maybe nothing bad had happened down here. Here was her bicycle, the tires a little flat. There was the washer and dryer, the laundry basket under the clothes chute that extended from the third floor to the basement.

Her workshop seemed undisturbed, familiar . . . the nearly finished guitars in their stands around the room, awaiting fingerboards, frets, and so on. The scent of shellac and wood glue was fainter now.

"What should I carry up?" Jonah asked, from the doorway. It was spooky, the way he just appeared like that. Like the devil, when you called him.

Emma nodded toward the clean room. "You'll find my grandfather's guitar collection in there. I already picked the best to bring from Memphis, so I want to take them all. The ones in cases, take them on up and put them in the van. The ones on display, there should be a case for each one in the storeroom. If you have any questions, give a yell."

He nodded but didn't move. He looked around the room, as if committing it to memory. "This is your workshop?"

"It is. Was," she amended.

He gestured toward the guitars in their stands. "And you . . . you made those?"

"I did," Emma said, brushing her fingers over the fret board of the one that was finished.

Hang on. She swiveled, looking around the room once

again. Then, squeezing her eyes shut, she tried to re-create in her mind the way it had looked before.

again. Then, squeezing her eyes shut, she tried to re-create in her mind the way it had looked before.

"That's odd," she said.

"What's odd?"

"One of my guitars is missing," she said. "I had two that were finished. I was playing one of them the night . . . the night all this happened. That one's gone."

For three heartbeats, Jonah said nothing. Then he cleared his throat. "Could it be somewhere else in the basement?"

"I don't see why it would be."

They searched the rest of the basement, anyway, including the coal bin. Nothing.

"Could it have broken, if . . . if there was a struggle?" Jonah asked. "Somebody's cleaned up the place. If it was broken, they might have thrown it away."

"I could have fixed it," Emma said, fisting her hands. "I'm a luthier!"

"Well, I'll start carrying," Jonah said, turning away.

"I'll be up in my room, packing some things," she called after him.

At the top of the front stairs, she turned right, toward her father's room at the far end of the hall. Past the main bathroom, where Tyler's razor, comb, and deodorant still littered the sink.

The towel Emma had used to dry her hair still hung over the shower bar, and Tyler's was wadded up in the tub, stinking of mildew.

Life, interrupted.

Emma had rarely ever gone into Tyler's room. Since she didn't really know what it was supposed to look like, it was hard to tell if anything had been shuffled around.

She opened Tyler's closet and pushed through a forest of

plaid flannel shirts. Blue jeans and T-shirts were piled on the shelf. All the wardrobe his life had required. On impulse, she pulled two flannel shirts from their hangers and laid them out on the bed.

Back in the closet, she pulled the cheap fiberboard storage boxes out of the way so she could get at the safe, and dropped to her knees. It took her two tries to get the safe open, her hands were trembling so much. She reached in, deep, and pulled out a bulky cloth bag, setting it on the floor beside her. Reached in again, and her groping hand found a much smaller bag . . . velvet.

That was it.

Closing the safe, she carried her findings back to the bed and set them down next to the flannel shirts. Picking free the knot that closed the velvet bag, she dumped the contents—something gold and glittery—onto the threadbare bedspread.

She scooped it up in her hand. It was a pendant on a gold chain. A flower with delicate petals that peeled back from a central spike, bracketed by clumps of berries. It looked familiar.

It was the same flower the Thorn Hill survivors had inked into their skin. Nightshade.

Emma looped the chain around her neck so that the pendant rested between her breasts, pleasantly warm.

She thumbed through several of the packets of bills. They were twenties and fifties. Half the stash was fresh and crisp, like it had never been touched. The rest had the look of money that had been accumulated over years, little by little. Not a windfall or payoff, but the result of months and years of blood and sweat and providing the bass-line heartbeat for a multitude of bands.

She looked around the bedroom, at the peeling wallpaper, the water-stained ceiling. Tyler could've used this money. Why didn't he spend it?

She had no idea how much it added up to, and she didn't want to take the time to do that math.

Emma opened the binder. A note was paper-clipped to the inside cover.

The money's from me. I hoped you might use it for college, or to start a business, or buy a house. It won't make up for what I took from you, but it's what I can give you now. Don't bother with the house . . . it's mortgaged to the roof, and you'll be too easy to find if you stay. My advice is: take the money and run.

I hope you'll take the time to read over these old songs. Maybe learn a few of them. One thing you can say about the blues . . . it tells the truth, if you ever want to hear it.

P.S.: The pendant belonged to your mother. I thought you should have it.

Tyler

Emma flipped through the notebook. It was tablature for dozens of old blues songs and spirituals. Not a bass line, which she might have expected from Tyler. It was six-string guitar. Pages and pages and pages of guitar tablature and lyrics, all apparently handwritten by her father. Some were songs she knew, others she'd never heard of. This was her father's legacy to her. *The truth, if you ever want to hear it.*

I always want to hear it, she thought.

She hadn't even known Tyler could read music. That

was one thing she could do . . . and do well. Sonny Lee had sent her to music-theory classes since she was little. "You're gonna do more than play by ear," he said. "You're gonna own it."

She was coming to realize that there was a lot she didn't know about her father. Would never know now.

The first song? "Motherless Child."

Emma sat back on her heels and thought a moment, chewing on her lower lip. Taking a pillow off the bed, she pulled off the frayed pillowcase. Working quickly, she stuffed the money and the binder into the pillowcase.

Then she dragged his battered suitcase out of the back of the closet and carried it and the pillowcase down the hall to her own bedroom . . . the one she'd occupied for a few months.

Pausing in the doorway, she took a good look around.

Her bed was a heap of tumbled bedclothes, just the way she'd left it. Her cell phone was still on the floor next to her bed, plugged in to charge. A few Memphis club posters were taped to the wall, her notion of decorating. If somebody'd been in the room, she couldn't tell.

She set the suitcase on the bed and zipped it open. Crossing to her closet, she pulled out her old backpack and set it next to the suitcase. Her music and electronics went into the backpack, clothing and shoes into the suitcase. She shoveled everything in, choosing quickly, going with her gut, not giving it a lot of thought.

When she looked over her selections, it struck her once again how much her wardrobe resembled her father's. Jeans. Flannel shirts. T-shirts and sweatshirts. They were more alike than she'd realized. Then why had they spent so many years apart? If he'd ever made even the teensiest effort, she wouldn't feel so divided . . . guilty and resentful and grief-stricken and pissed off.

I didn't want your money, Daddy. I wanted you. Hot tears pricked her eyes, and she slumped down on the bed, weeping.

> *Sometimes I feel like a motherless child*
> *A long way from home. A long way from home.*

"Emma? Are you all right?" It was Jonah.

"I'm fine." Emma wiped her nose on her sleeve, waving him away. She buried her face in her pillow, wishing she could disappear. It smelled of a previous life, and she cried harder.

Of course, he didn't go. "Is there . . . can I . . . get you something?"

"No," she mumbled into her pillow.

She heard the floorboards creak as he crossed the room to her. Then sat down next to her, his blue-jeaned thigh against hers. She could feel his heat through two layers of denim. "I am so sorry, Emma," he whispered. "So very sorry."

After a moment's hesitation, he gently stroked her hair, murmuring soft reassurances, his voice like sweet caresses to the soul. Her guilt and sorrow seemed to flow out of her at every point of contact. Like a ship that had reached safe harbor, she drifted, anchored by his voice.

As if he sensed the effect he was having, he lay down beside her, turned on his side, and pulled her to him so they lay like nested spoons. Wrapping his arms around her, he pressed her body to his, still murmuring soft apologies and reassurances, his warm breath stirring the hair on the back of her neck. And the jagged pain within her dulled to an ache. Replaced by the flame of desire.

He was reacting to her, too, at least she thought he was. His muscles trembled as if barely controlled, and his breathing was quick and shallow.

She squirmed against him, trying to turn around to face him. Her shirt rode up, and they were skin to skin at the base of her spine, and she thought she just might catch fire. His arms tightened, pinning her in place, which had the effect of pulling her in even closer. He was incredibly strong.

"No," he said, his voice as thick and sweet as molasses in the cold. "No, Emma. Just let me hold you. Please. Just like this."

"But . . . I just want to . . ."

"I know," he whispered. He swallowed, hard, as if swallowing down pain. "I want to, too, but we can't. It's too dangerous."

Dangerous? Emma couldn't make sense of this. "What do you mean? You're afraid the Black Rose will come back? Or you're afraid we'll go too far?"

"I mean we can't ever do this, Emma. We can't be together . . . not now, and not at any other time. I shouldn't be doing this either, but . . . I just can't stand for you to be in pain, and it seems to help."

Hurt and confused, Emma went over his words in her mind. *It seems to help.*

Finally, she understood. *He's an empath. He sensed your pain and grief, and he's trying to relieve it.*

He's doing it out of compassion. Which was a fine thing, but not what she wanted.

She turned her head, and saw that his face was turned

sharply away, chin lifted so she couldn't see his expression. It was as if he couldn't stand to look at her. As if touching her was something he could barely endure. That tension in him wasn't desire. It was . . . well, she didn't know what it was.

Emma's ironwood spine stiffened. "Let go of me right now."

And he did. He was off the bed and halfway across the room, as if the contact between them was actually painful. He stood, fists clenched, chest heaving, his eyes closed as if to shut out the view.

"I'm sorry," he said. "I just have a . . . I just have a problem with touching anyone."

Anyone? Emma wondered. Or just me? "No harm done," she said, sliding off the bed, straightening her clothes. "I kind of lost it for a minute there, but I'm okay now. I'm just about finished. Is there much more to load downstairs?"

Jonah opened his eyes, the blues rising up in them like thunderclouds on a midsummer day. "No, everything's loaded," he said, his voice thick and uneven. "You might want to do a final check to make sure I haven't overlooked anything."

"I'm sure that won't be necessary," Emma said, zipping the suitcase shut. "I'm sure you've done a perfect job."

"I'd feel better if you checked, because we aren't going to be able to come back." Jonah grabbed the suitcase before she could. "I'll take this out to the van and wait there for you."

In the end, she was glad she had a chance to say good-bye to the shop on her own. Each time she moved to a new place, she left another piece of herself behind. Each time, it was a little easier. Maybe, eventually, she'd disappear completely.

When she walked out the back door, Jonah was standing

in the driveway, staring at his phone, his face a mask of fear and disbelief.

"What is it?" Emma demanded, her hurt forgotten. "What's happened?"

"There's been an explosion at Safe Harbor," Jonah said. "We've got to get back."

∞ Chapter Forty ∞
War Games

Jonah scarcely remembered the drive from Cleveland Heights to downtown . . . just that it seemed to take forever and cars kept getting in his way. It had begun to rain, and gaudy ribbons of light smeared the pavement and bloodied the car windows as they hurtled through the darkness, careened around corners, and muscled through intersections. Once it was only Jonah's lightning-fast reflexes and nimble maneuvering that kept them from ending their journey in a tangle of metal.

"Hey!" Emma said, putting her hand on his arm. "You won't do anybody any good if we never get there. And those other people deserve a chance to get home, too."

After that, Jonah slowed down fractionally.

"Who called you?" Emma asked.

"Gabriel."

"Did he give you any details? Did he say if anyone was hurt?"

"No."

Ahead, St. Clair was barricaded, the area beyond swarming with emergency personnel and vehicles. Jonah resisted the temptation to plow through the barricades. Instead, he talked his way through.

Jonah left the van in a parking lot on St. Clair and charged toward Safe Harbor, leaving Emma to keep up as best she could. As he approached the scene, he saw that a fire truck was pouring water over the roof. Smoke billowed out of the building, though he saw no flame. Firefighters and Safe Harbor staff were escorting residents out of the building, carrying those who couldn't walk on their own.

One entire corner of the building was gone, as if someone had taken a wrecking ball to it.

Jonah mapped the building in his mind. The area destroyed was mostly day-use areas—clinics and treatment rooms, the reception area, and the gym. Areas that emptied out at night. The fist in his heart unclenched a little.

Gabriel was in the alley, helping to triage the students as they emerged from the building.

"Jonah!" he said, with a quick nod of acknowledgment. "Kenzie's out. We're taking all the evacuees who don't need hospital treatment to the Steel Wool Building. He's over there."

"Is he . . . ?"

Gabriel hesitated. "You know that everything's harder on Kenzie than on anyone else. Help us get the rest of the students out. Then you'd better go sit with him."

"What can I do?" Emma asked over Jonah's shoulder, startling him. He didn't realize she'd caught up.

Gabriel looked her over. "Since you don't know this

building, head over to Steel Wool and see if the healers need any help."

"Which one's Steel Wool?" she asked.

"Follow the stretchers," Gabriel said. "Natalie and Ramon are over there. They'll tell you what to do."

As Emma turned away, Jonah touched her shoulder. "Here," he said. "If Kenzie doesn't have his music, give him this." He dropped his phone along with a set of earbuds into her hand. "Tell him I'll be there as soon as I can." Their eyes met briefly, and then she was gone.

"Casualties?" Jonah asked, swiveling back toward Gabriel.

"Two, that we know of," Gabriel said. "Lucile Benning was the RN on duty. And Liberty Jones is dead. She must have been caught in the explosion. We found her in the street. We're not sure how she came to be there."

"She liked to go out and smoke on the side porch at night," Jonah said. Liberty was fourteen, and always had something snarky to say. Therefore, she and Kenzie got along famously. Her death would hit him hard.

"Do we know what happened?" Jonah asked.

"No," Gabriel said, too quickly. "We'll have to wait for the results of the investigation." He turned away from Jonah and walked back into the building.

But Jonah knew Gabriel too well. Slowly turning, he scanned the brick wall of the building that faced the alley. Scrawled in white paint across the brick was the legend GOOD LABRAT = DEAD LABRAT. And SAVE THE CHILDREN—KILL A LABRAT. And PEDOPHILES. ZOMBIES. LABRATS . . . with the first two words crossed out. Also the nonspecific GET OUT OF TOWN. Some of the tagging was signed THE EXTERMINATORS.

For the next hour, Jonah boomeranged from Safe Harbor

to Steel Wool, escorting the students who could walk, carrying some, propelling wheelchairs and equipment over the
rough pavement. The plan was to house Safe Harbor residents in Steel Wool temporarily until repairs could be made.
It wasn't ideal. Steel Wool was a dormitory that had emptied
out as the student population dwindled. Unlike Safe Harbor,
it wasn't tailored to meet the needs of physically challenged
residents.

While he worked, Jonah kept his eyes and ears open.
Especially to the conversations between Gabriel and police
and fire officials.

"I understand protocol, Stan," he heard Gabriel say to the
fire officer in charge, "but trust me when I tell you that we
can best meet the needs of these children right here. They are
emotionally fragile, and an unfamiliar environment might be
enough to cause a massive decompensation. Nobody wants
that. Anyone who's medically stable should stay here."

The police detective in charge of the crime scene kicked
a bit of rubble away. "We're treating it as arson—some kind
of explosive device. Has there been any friction with the
neighbors? Any trouble prior to now?"

"No," Gabriel said, "I don't know of any town-gown
troubles. Our school is small, and for the most part, our students keep to themselves. About the only place they interact
with the locals is through our community music programs
and the volunteers who provide services. Most are too young
to go to the clubs in the district." He shook his head. "I'm
guessing it was a hate crime . . . people fear and hate what
they don't understand. Or possibly someone with a grudge
against me. And no, I don't know who that would be."

"We'll figure it out," the detective said.

No, you won't, Jonah thought. Not unless you're open to a magical explanation.

"Thanks for being here, Paul," Gabriel said. "I know you'll want to interview some more students. Let's work together to make that as quick and painless as possible."

Paul put a hand on Gabriel's shoulder. "I'm sorry this had to happen, Gabriel. These kids have enough on their plate as it is."

"Ah, Jonah, there you are," Gabriel said, noticing Jonah's approach. "Paul, I'd like you to meet Jonah Kinlock, my assistant. Jonah, this is Paul Whipple from homicide."

Jonah acknowledged the introduction with a curt nod. "I'm just curious, Detective," he said. "How will you go about investigating this incident?"

"We'll interview witnesses," Whipple said. "We'll look for people who have grudges against faculty or students. We'll compare it with similar crimes in the area, see if there's a pattern. And, of course, forensics and the arson squad will go over the property with a fine-tooth comb, collecting evidence." He paused. "Why do you ask? Is there something you think we're overlooking?"

"Jonah's younger brother lives at Safe Harbor," Gabriel put in, before Jonah could open his mouth. "Naturally, he's concerned. I think we're about done here, Jonah. Why don't you go see about Kenzie."

Jonah knew when he was being dismissed. But he wasn't leaving without putting a word in. "Is Detective Whipple aware of the possible connection to the Carter Road Lift Bridge incident?"

"Don't you think that's kind of a long shot, Jonah?" Gabriel said, with a warning look.

"We're interested in everything, even long shots," Whipple said. "What do you mean?"

"Some parents of the Trinity Montessori children have suggested that students from the Anchorage might have been connected to the kidnapping," Jonah said. "Because, you know, we're close by. Some have had ugly things to say about us . . . that we shouldn't be here." He shrugged. "I know it sounds far-fetched, but I thought you should know about it."

Whipple scribbled some notes. "I may be able to get this information from the team investigating the kidnapping, but is there a contact person at the school that you know of?"

"What do you think?" Jonah asked Gabriel, pretending not to notice his headmaster's scowl. "Mercedes Foster? She's been the liaison between the parents and the police, right?"

Gabriel nodded grudgingly. "She would be a good choice," he said. "Though it's hard to believe that people in Trinity would come all the way over here to menace our students. Or would know how to go about putting together an explosive device."

"Trinity may be a small town, but it's extremely diverse," Jonah said. "You might be surprised." He met Gabriel's eyes, a look that said, *If you want a rubber stamp, Gabriel, look somewhere else.* "Now, if we're done here, I'll go see about Kenzie."

The scene at the Steel Wool Factory was one of well-controlled chaos, with a desk set up in the reception area, staffed by three caregivers, including Natalie.

Emma stopped at the desk. "I came over to help, but I have something Jonah sent over for Kenzie." She held up the phone, the earbuds dangling.

A harried Natalie pointed over her shoulder. "Kenzie's still in intake, room four. See if you can calm him down. If you finish there, come back here and we'll tell you what to do."

I don't know how to calm people down, Emma thought. I'm more likely to get people stirred up. How likely was Jonah's brother, Kenzie, to respond to a stranger?

But she'd come to help, so she had to try.

The video screens next to each room had been reprogrammed to display numbers 1 through 4, along with the name of the patient inside. Light flared from the doorway of room 4, as if somebody had a strobe light going. She peeked around the doorframe.

The room was nearly empty, except for a thick pallet on the floor. A boy huddled on the mattress, wearing a thick robe made of what looked like terry cloth and wrapped in multiple blankets. A pile of additional blankets lay on the floor next to him. The blankets must have been flame-resistant . . . because the boy was on fire.

Emma stared, fascinated. Flames flickered over his skin, giving him an oddly blurred appearance. The fire was nearly transparent save for occasional flare-ups, but she could feel the heat from where she stood. Sparks arced away from the boy, leaving scorch marks on the mattered wooden floor.

How was it even possible that he was still alive?

An aide wearing scrubs stood ten feet away from him, as close as she dared come. She held a bottle of dark brown liquid and a medication spoon. "Kenzie," she coaxed, "you'll feel better if you can just get this down."

He didn't respond. He trembled uncontrollably, his teeth chattering as if from cold, when it seemed like he should have been overheated.

Emma edged into the room. She could see the resemblance between Jonah and his brother. Kenzie shared Jonah's beautiful blue eyes and fine features, though his hair was a deep reddish brown while Jonah's was almost black. He appeared thinner than Jonah, though it was hard to tell, muffled up as he was, and his complexion had the pallor of the chronically ill. And yet there was an ethereal beauty about him, like a watercolor compared to Jonah's rich pigments.

Before you know it, these Kinlock boys will have you writing poetry, Emma thought.

The aide noticed Emma, frozen in the doorway. "Don't come in!" she cried. "He's extremely reactive right now. He doesn't need any more stimulation." Her voice carried the impatient edge that came with fear.

"I have something for him. His brother sent it over." She held up the phone.

"Jonah sent it?" The aide's expression softened and she crossed to where Emma stood. "He's so thoughtful," she said. "I just wish—" She shook her head. "I just don't see a happy ending to this."

"I'm Emma Greenwood," Emma said, extending her hand to the woman. "What's your name?"

"Martha Witcraft," the aide said. She seemed eager to talk. "I work at the dispensary. Teaching yoga. His regular nurse got called away to Metro to consult with the staff in the emergency department." She shrugged her shoulders. "I'm out of my league. I haven't worked with Kenzie before, so I don't know a lot. According to the consult, Kenzie's seizures are strongly tied to his emotional states. The explosion was close to his suite . . . in fact, it woke him up. I think it's brought back memories of Thorn Hill. Sort of like post-traumatic stress disorder. I think they thought . . . well, you know . . . meditation is helpful for people with PTSD. That's why I'm here, but it's not working out too well. The regular healers are too busy with the other casualties."

"What's that medicine you're trying to give him?"

"I don't know what it's called," she said. "It suppresses magic. They use it to dampen down his seizures. I'm supposed to give him a tablespoon. But I've got no clue how to get it into him when I can't get near him." It was obvious she was trying to help, but she was scared to death.

Emma studied the situation. It'd be no good trying to put the earbuds on him either. They were the standard variety, and they would just melt when they came into contact with his body. Yanking the earbuds out of the phone, she turned it to maximum volume. Still not very loud.

"If it's all right with you, Martha, I'll see if I can get close enough with this so he can hear it," Emma said.

Martha nodded. Clearly, it was more than all right with Martha.

Taking a deep breath, Emma walked toward Kenzie, holding the phone out in front of her. She inched in, as close as she dared, but the tinny, thin-sounding music had no effect. "Kenzie," she said softly. "I'm Emma. Jonah sent me over. He'll be here soon."

Kenzie's eyes fixed on her, but the flaming seizure continued.

"He sent you some music, if we can find a way to get it to you," Emma said. "Listen." She held out the phone again.

Kenzie shook his head. At least he was responding to her.

Emma backed away until she reached Martha.

"Would you have a speaker dock for phone or MP3 player around here somewhere?" she asked. "Something with big speakers?"

Martha frowned. "I don't usually work in this building, so I don't know. I could try to find one." She looked eager to go somewhere far away from burning boys.

"If you can't find one . . . do you know Natalie Diaz?"

"Of course," Martha said. "But I know she's tied up with triage at the moment."

"Ask her to call Rudy Severino and tell him I need a sound system for Jonah's phone. That it's for Kenzie." She stuck out her hand. "Leave me the brown stuff. Maybe I'll figure out something."

Martha looked troubled. "I shouldn't leave you alone with him," she said, looking sideways at Kenzie.

"It's an emergency, right?" Emma said.

"I guess so." Martha handed her the bottle and spoon. "Just be careful, okay?" She disappeared.

"Martha went to get us some more amps," Emma said to Kenzie. "Now, what are we going to do while she's gone?"

For a little while, she sat and talked while Kenzie burned. When she could stand it no longer, she examined the spoon. It was constructed like a kind of syringe that shot medicine into a person's mouth. She just needed to get it close enough to Kenzie's. She looked around the room for clues. Her eyes lit on the pile of extra blankets next to Kenzie, kindling an idea.

Carefully, she drew up brown stuff to the one-tablespoon measure and set the spoon aside.

Darting forward, Emma grabbed a fistful of blankets, then retreated to her starting point. Wrapping one blanket around herself, she draped another over her head, fashioning a kind of hood. She took a third blanket and wrapped it around her neck like a muffler, pulling it over the lower half of her face up to her eyes. She'd fashioned a kind of flame-resistant toga. More like one of those burkas, she guessed. Draping the remaining blanket over her arm, she scooped up the spoon and approached Kenzie again.

He seemed to know what she was up to, because he wrapped his blankets more closely around himself, burrowing in, adding another layer between Emma and the white-hot flames. When she got close, she turned away, swathed the spoon in the spare blanket with the tip poking out, gritted her teeth, and lunged toward Kenzie. On her second try, she managed to push the spoon between his lips and pressed the plunger all the way.

By now, it felt like the skin on her face was cracking and she could smell her own hair burning, despite the hood. She leaped backward, landing on her butt a few yards away. Then scooted backward like a crab.

For a moment, she worried she'd drowned Jonah's little brother. He coughed and sputtered, tears leaking from his eyes.

"Emma?"

Emma twisted around and saw Rudy Severino in the doorway, his arms loaded with equipment and power cords. He stared, nonplussed, at Emma, down on her back in her fire blanket getup. "Natalie said you needed a sound system?"

It took a few minutes to get everything in place. During that time, Kenzie's flames dwindled and finally died. He slumped over, apparently exhausted, his blue-veined hands still writhing in his lap.

Finally, Rudy hit the go button and Jonah's voice filled the air, layered with Emma's guitar and Rudy's kick-ass keyboards, Natalie's percussion the heartbeat of it all.

Kenzie smiled, tilting his head back and practically purring, like a cat that's found its spot in the sun. Rudy sat down on one side of Kenzie and motioned Emma to the other.

"I'm Emma Greenwood," Emma said, sitting next to him. "I'm new at the Anchorage."

"McKenzie Kinlock," Kenzie said gravely. "I'm sorry I was ablaze when you arrived. Thank you for putting me out." He paused. "That just seems *wrong*, somehow."

"That's Emma you hear playing lead guitar on these

tracks," Rudy said, as if eager to bring Kenzie's attention back to the music.

"Is it?" Kenzie said, taking a second, closer look at Emma.

"She's sitting in for Mose on lead guitar . . . temporarily, at least," Rudy said. "We recorded this at our last practice. What do you think, Little Kinlock?"

"I think I'm going to catch on fire again if you call me *Little Kinlock*," Kenzie said menacingly.

"No, really . . . what do you think of the tracks? Did we do justice to your songs or what?"

"Stop fishing for compliments, Severino," Kenzie said, rolling his eyes. "You know this is staggeringly fabulous." He looked at Emma. "I love how you improvised on the melody line. You're not afraid of getting in Jonah's way, but you leave room for the voice."

"He'd better worry about getting in *Emma's* way," Rudy said. "She'll run right over him."

"So you're a triple threat," Kenzie said, grinning at Emma. "Beautiful, tough, *and* talented."

"And you're talented, tough, and full of bullshit."

Kenzie laughed hard at that.

It feels good to hear him laugh, Emma thought. She tried not to think about what Martha had said. *I just don't see a happy ending to this.*

"Do you play?" she asked him. "Are you a musician? I mean."

"Only vicariously," Kenzie said. "I write the songs, and hope they don't mess them up. I can play compositions electronically—on a synthesizer—if I have time to build them. But I can't hit my targets often enough to play on a standard instrument."

Emma frowned. "I'm sorry, I don't quite understand what you mean."

"You're seeing me at my very best, because I'm pretty much wrung out right now," Kenzie said. "Usually I'm hyperkinetic . . . way too frisky for strings or keyboards." He flailed his arms around to demonstrate just as Jonah walked in, looking weary and pissed. He shed that face immediately when he saw his brother.

"Kenzie, if I've told you once, I've told you a thousand times: humans are not made to fly."

Kenzie dropped his arms to his sides. "It's just like you to walk in when all the drama is over."

Jonah studied the three of them, huddled together on Kenzie's bed. "What's going on? Natalie said you were in a bad way."

Kenzie said, "Going on? We're kicking back, listening to some tunes. Feeling ravenous."

"You're always starving after you catch fire. I asked Martha to bring back some food," Jonah said. He squatted in front of Kenzie, looking him over. "How are you feeling? Are you up to the minute on your meds?"

"I need the whole entire bedtime regimen," Kenzie said, yawning. "Except the Weirsbane. This one shot me full of it a few minutes ago." He scowled at Emma.

"*Emma* did?" Jonah took a quick breath, as if he might ask a follow-up question, but then seemed to decide against it. "Natalie says your room will be prepped in a few minutes. Are you about ready to move?"

"Not before the food comes," Kenzie said.

Just then, Martha appeared in the doorway with a stack of box lunches. "All they had left was—" She stopped, eyes wide, listening. "Who *is* that? That band is absolutely fantastic. I don't think I've heard them before."

"That's *our* band," Rudy said happily, finally basking in the praise he'd been fishing for.

Our band, Emma thought. Maybe Jonah Kinlock was crazy and they would never be together and his younger brother tended to catch fire and she was caught in a web of secrets and lies and violence, but . . . there was this. *Our band.* She really liked the sound of that.

❧ CHAPTER FORTY-TWO ❧
GOT OURSELVES A GIG

"I'm not doing it," Jonah said flatly. "No. Absolutely not."

"But . . . I already said we would," Natalie said. "You don't have plans for Halloween, do you?"

"Do I ever have plans?" Jonah rolled his eyes. "Since I haven't been traveling, I—oh, wait, I do. I'm clipping my toenails. If there's time left, I'm doing my fingernails, too."

"It's a paying gig," Rudy said. "They're offering good money, in fact. And Gabriel says they're really excited about having us come."

"Of course they are," Jonah muttered. "Don't you see? It's Halloween. Invite the monsters in to entertain at your party."

Rudy and Natalie looked at each other. "I don't think that's why they invited us, Jonah," Natalie said. "Patrick gave them a list of bands, and I guess Ellen Stephenson heard Fault Tolerant at one of the teen nights downtown, and so when we showed up on the list, they chose us."

"There are a lot of bands in town," Jonah said. "They can pick another one."

"We don't *want* them to pick another band," Rudy said. "We need to get out in front of some audiences and build some buzz. Once we get a good set list of original music, I'd like to go into the studio and record an EP. We'll need money to do that."

"Gabriel will front us the money," Jonah said. "Studio space, equipment, everything."

"Gabriel's the one who wants us to do this gig."

They were in the first-floor practice room of Oxbow, which had become their default hangout over the weeks since Mose died. Even Jonah had to admit, the more they practiced, the better they sounded. More cohesive. More than the sum of their parts. As Natalie said, the best band she'd ever been in, meaning no disrespect to Mose.

Emma had been cool and distant to Jonah since the night of the visit to Cleveland Heights. *That's what you wanted, isn't it?*

At least she'd shown no signs that she recognized him as the one who'd broken in and tied her up the night her father was murdered. Maybe Fortune had finally decided to shine on him, for some unfathomable reason.

What he hadn't expected was the relationship that was developing between Emma and Kenzie. She'd been over to see him several times since he moved to Steel Wool. They had a lot in common, in particular a knack for music theory and composition. She'd take her guitar and serve as the voice for Kenzie's flights of fancy. When Jonah asked, Emma said she liked Kenzie because he told the truth. Which to Jonah's ears sounded like a barb at the rest of them.

She knew they were keeping secrets. Jonah knew how that felt, now that he was on the outside, no longer a part of Nightshade. He knew Alison still went out on missions . . . in fact, her frequent absences were becoming an issue when it came to scheduling practices. Jonah knew the shadehunters were still holding meetings and planning strategy and launching aggressive killing operations. He just wasn't privy to their activities anymore. Was it because he didn't need to know, or because Gabriel didn't trust him?

Emma had remained silent through the argument, head bent over her fingerboard. She was playing one of her own guitars, an electrified acoustic with a fabulous voice. But she still wasn't satisfied with the action. Now she spoke up. "Who's having the party?" she asked.

"Gabriel's contacts were Jack Swift and Ellen Stephenson," Natalie said. "But the party is at Seph McCauley's house, and I think Madison Moss is cohosting. It's a kind of open house . . . members from all the guilds are invited. Apparently it's gotten to be a Halloween tradition."

"Well," Emma said. "I could stand to make some money. I'm building guitars, but I haven't had as much time to work on them, what with practice and school and all that."

"If you need money," Jonah said, "I know that Gabriel would be glad to—"

"I'm not talking about walking-around money," Emma said. "I need to make enough money to open my own shop. I've got some saved up, but not enough. I'm already living on Gabriel's dime. I don't expect him to stake my business."

"He probably would," Jonah said. "He'd love to show you off . . . 'Savant Makes Good, Starts Own Business. Film at eleven.'"

"I said no." Emma punctuated this with a trill of notes.

"I said no, too, but nobody seems to be listening." Jonah looked around the circle of faces and saw no support at all.

To buy some time, he set his guitar in its stand, crossed to the refrigerator, and pulled out a can of pop. Taking a long pull, he considered his options. He could try using his powers of persuasion, but he knew Natalie would call him on it. She had a habit of drowning him out with a drum solo whenever she felt he wasn't playing fair.

"Alison?" Jonah looked to the one person he thought might back him up, though she'd been even harder to read and predict since Mose had died. "What do you think? Do you really want to go along with this?"

"Maybe," Alison replied, with an odd, vague smile. "Can we run amok during the show? Set fire to the stage? Kill a few people?"

No help there.

"You know as well as I do that it was vigilantes from Trinity that tried to blow up Safe Harbor," Jonah said, "whether Gabriel admits it or not."

"If that's true, I'm guessing it wasn't the people hosting the party," Natalie said. "You know I'm no fan of wizards, but not everyone over there is a bigot. Mercedes Foster is really—"

"Then let the nonbigots come to the benefit concert in the spring," Jonah said. "Let them come onto our turf."

"Gabriel thinks it's a good idea. It will be good publicity for the school, and it might change some opinions about—"

"Of course he thinks it's a good idea. And he knows I'll think it's a bad idea, which is why he brought it to you and not to me. He knew what my answer would be."

"This is business," Natalie said. "This is income, and exposure, and maybe a chance to show them all what we can do."

That's the trouble with bands, Jonah thought. You join one because you love to make music, and before you know it, it's a business.

"I don't need to show anyone anything," he said. "Have you considered the fact that we might be walking straight into an ambush?"

"Jonah," Emma said. "Rowan seemed to think that people in Trinity were involved in my father's murder. You think they were behind the attack on Safe Harbor. We can all sit around here talking to each other, but if we really want to find out something, it seems to me we might learn more by going there, meeting some people, and asking some questions. Even if the people who were involved in the attack aren't at the party."

"I can't imagine what we'd learn that would justify putting you in danger," Jonah said.

"You've been complaining about Gabriel doing this very thing—avoiding confrontation," Natalie said.

"I think you're outvoted, dude," Rudy said.

"All right," Jonah said, giving in. "We'll do the gig. But if it's a disaster, don't say I didn't warn you."

"**H**ow come nobody embraces monsters, except on Halloween?" Emma said to Natalie, who was riding shotgun in Sonny Lee's old Element. "Is it kind of like St. Patrick's Day, when everybody in need of a party turns Irish?"

Natalie laughed. "Halloween is like a mix of pagan festivals, Irish folklore, All Saints' Day, and Día de los Muertos. It seems like every culture has a stake in it—pun intended."

"I always think of Halloween as the time when the veil between the living and the dead is at its thinnest," Emma said.

Natalie's smile faded. "It's always thinner than you think."

They'd taken two vehicles to the gig so they wouldn't have to travel as a pack. That way, if somebody—i.e., Jonah—wanted to leave as soon as their set was done, he could. Jonah, Rudy, and Alison had gone on ahead in the white panel van that was Fault Tolerant's usual ride, because Natalie was still working on Emma's look.

"I'm not used to dressing up," Emma had protested. "I need to be able to move to make music."

"It'll be fun," Natalie said. "It's Halloween, after all. And it will make you harder to recognize."

"That's for sure," Emma said, looking down at herself. This outfit was a compromise, though she felt like she'd given more ground than Natalie. She wore a low-cut black dress from a thrift shop that hugged her nonexistent curves and showed off her nonexistent assets. It was slit way past her knees, so at least she could walk. Overtop, a lacy jacket fastened with a red gardenia in front—she had insisted on some coverage—and lacy black gloves that extended from elbows to wrists, but left her hands bare. Emma had insisted on that, too. She was no Jonah Kinlock, who could play guitar with gloves on. Natalie had pulled her hair up, leaving a few tendrils hanging down. Then added a close-fitting hat made of black feathers, a red gardenia over one ear. Smoky eye makeup and red lipstick completed the look. Every time Emma looked in the mirror, she was startled at the stranger looking back at her.

Ah, well, she thought. Maybe I should try being someone else for a while, since being who I am isn't working out so well.

Right now the skirt was hiked up to her thighs so she could work the Element's resistant clutch.

She looked over at Natalie. Unfair. Nat had chosen a street look, with her hair teased up and tied back with a bandanna, extreme eye makeup, Converses, baggy jeans, and a flannel shirt. She looked . . . normal.

"I've been wondering," Emma said. "Where did the name of the band come from?"

"It was Rudy's idea," Natalie said. "He's the tech guy.

According to him, a 'fault-tolerant' system is one that's designed to keep working even if one part fails. Like a car that can still drive on three wheels, or a building that keeps standing even if a support fails because of rust, or fatigue, or whatever. This band has survived the loss of several members over the years. It's important enough to keep going."

"I guess, in a way, savants are like that, right?" Emma said. "We just keep going somehow."

"Some of us do," Natalie said somberly. "Not all of us."

Trinity looked like a postcard of a college town, with its stone buildings and gingerbread houses painted in soft blues, pinks, and greens. What it didn't look like was a fortress.

"How did the Interguild Council ever come to pick this little town for its headquarters?" Emma asked. "Isn't it a bit out of the way?"

"I think it had to do with the fact that some of the major players in the underguild rebellion had roots in Trinity. Linda Downey, Jack Swift, and Leander Hastings all have ties here. Because of that, when the rebels forced a change in the Rules of Engagement, Trinity was established as a sanctuary that was free of attack magic. A lot of mainliners moved into the area because of that."

Emma's pondered this. "You know that dream where it's the day of the final exam and you haven't been to class all semester?"

Natalie laughed. "You have that dream, too?"

"Well, that's the way I feel right now. Like I got started late and I'll never catch up with all this magic business." Emma downshifted as she navigated past the square and turned north toward the lake.

"Trust me," Natalie said. "The only reason I know this much is I spent a summer in Trinity apprenticing with one of the sorcerers there. Mainliner history isn't a focus of the curriculum at the Anchorage. In a way, Gabriel's still a separatist."

"Seems like it's not working out that well for him either," Emma observed.

It was nearly dark when they reached their destination, a small Victorian house on a leafy street that edged the lake. Tiny orange lights outlined the doors and windows and sparkled in the trees. Emma turned into a gravel driveway, past a large sign that said THE PARTY IS HERE! and pulled up behind Jonah's van, which was parked in the drive as close to the side door as he could get. The others must have just arrived, because they had the rear doors open and were unloading equipment onto the drive. Alison, Jonah, and Rudy were dressed casually, like musicians ready for a gig.

I knew this was a bad idea, Emma thought, plucking at her own gloves.

Jonah was kneeling in the back of the van, his muscled chest and arms flexing as he lifted amplifiers and speakers down to Rudy, his black hair ruffled by the wind from the lake. Emma's heart clenched. Jonah was just so damned pleasurable to look at.

Natalie had poked through Jonah's clothes, looking for wardrobe options. Then they'd argued for another hour. The negotiation had ended with Jonah in a skintight, paper-thin vintage Ramones T-shirt and faded blue jeans. And his trademark gloves.

When Rudy saw Emma and Natalie approaching, he nearly dropped the speaker he was holding. "Whoa!" he said. "Guess they don't need us for sex appeal."

Alison stared at them. "Nobody said we were dressing up," she said, twisting the ends of her hair.

"Meet Lady Day," Natalie announced, stepping aside to showcase her work. "Lady sings the blues."

Jonah looked up, then did a double take. Sitting back on his heels, he stared at Emma, his face transitioning from surprise to wistful resignation. Like somebody who's hungry and knows he won't ever get fed. Emma could feel her cheeks heating, pinking up under his scrutiny.

We can't be together, he'd said. *Not now, and not at any other time.*

Granted, maybe Emma was misreading him, but the signals he was sending definitely seemed mixed.

By the time she got close, he'd cleared his face of emotion. Nearly. "So," he said, his eyes on her ruby-red lips. "You're Billie Holiday?"

"Sort of," she said, "though I guess you're more of a torch singer than I am."

He smiled, reached out, and fingered a tendril of her hair. "You look amazing," he said. "It's hard to imagine that anyone would recognize you."

"Is that supposed to be a compliment?" Emma asked. "If so, it's hitting my ear wrong."

She noticed something glittering at his neck and leaned closer. It was a pendant, hanging from a chain. A flower pendant just like hers.

His blue-green eyes met hers, his gloved hand closed over the pendant, and he tucked it out of sight.

"Come on," Alison said. "Let's get this gear inside."

"What was that?" Emma asked, still staring at Jonah's neck.

"Nothing," he said, climbing down from the van. Scooping up two guitar cases, he led the way to the door.

A very tall, broad-shouldered guy wearing a black mask met them there. He wore a linen shirt with voluminous sleeves, a tight-fitting studded leather vest over it, velvet pantaloons and tights, and leather gauntlets.

Something about the mask pinged in Emma's memory. A word came back to her. *Zorro.*

"Um. Jack?" Jonah said, raising his eyebrows.

"I hoped you wouldn't recognize me," Jack replied, scowling. "Would a hat help?" He plunked a velvet hat with a feather plume on his head. Reaching over his shoulder, he pulled a lute out of a sling on his back and cradled it in his arms. "What about now?"

"You still handle that lute like it's a sword, Jack." A girl appeared in the doorway next to him. "Don't forget yourself and try and skewer someone with it." She was nearly as tall as Jack, wearing a long velvet gown with a laced bodice and cathedral sleeves that hugged her athletic frame. Her hair was tucked up under a jeweled net. "I told you black leather and gauntlets wouldn't work for a minstrel." She studied him, rubbing her chin. "Though I must say . . . leather suits you. And you should wear tights more often. You *do* have a fine leg."

"If you'll recall, I wanted to go with the gladiator costumes," Jack said, stripping off the mask and hat and tossing them aside.

"Then everybody would recognize us for sure," the girl said.

Emma guessed that these two would be recognizable in any costumes. "Who are you supposed to be?" she asked, curiosity getting the better of her.

"He's a wandering minstrel, and I'm the highborn lady who runs off with him," the girl said. "Also, an assassin." Shaking back her sleeves, she revealed twin daggers in wrist sheaths.

"I don't think the assassin part works," Jack said. "You criticize my leather, and then you—"

"Weapons go with everything, Jack," she said, twitching her sleeves down, concealing them again. Her eyes flicked over Emma in her finery. "That's a great dress," she said. "I'm Ellen Stephenson, and the man with the fine leg is Jack Swift."

Now that she heard the names, Emma recognized the two of them from the photographs Rowan had shown her of suspects in the murders at Tyler's house. As warriors, they definitely seemed capable of causing mayhem. If they recognized Emma, they showed no signs of it.

"I'm Emma Lee. I'm a new student at the Anchorage." She had that story down, at least.

"Really? I didn't know you were accepting new students," Jack said to Jonah.

"We needed a new guitar player," Jonah said, his voice cool and businesslike. "So we made an exception."

Jack got the message. "Look, Jonah, on behalf of nearly everyone, I'd like to apologize for those idiots at the council meeting. They were not the sharpest knives in the drawer to begin with, and having their children kidnapped adds that extra layer of—I don't know—hysteria."

"Don't worry about it," Jonah said. "Savants are used to that kind of talk from mainliners. Where do you want us to set up?"

"In the conservatory," Jack said. "Here, I'll show you."

Picking up an amplifier like it was made of Styrofoam, he led them to the rear of the house, to a stone-floored room with two stories of windows overlooking the lake. "We're expecting several hundred people, and this is the only room that might begin to hold them." He pointed up at a balcony overlooking the space. "The bar and the food will be set up on the balcony. We've got heaters out on the terrace, and we're hoping they will keep it warm enough that people will dance out there."

Ellen pointed them to a spot on the opposite wall from the massive hearth. "We were thinking this might be a good place for you. You're out of the line of traffic, and away from the draft from the doors, but you won't get overheated either. But if someplace else works better, let us know."

"This works," Rudy said, dropping his load of sound equipment in the corner, along an inside wall. He and Alison set to work, plugging in and testing the sound system.

Jack nudged a power strip along the wall with the toe of his boot. "You've got plenty of power here, but let me know if you need any extension cords or anything. We were thinking you could start the first set an hour after people begin arriving, play an hour, break for an hour, and then play a second hour-long set. We'll use a playlist in between. That way, most everyone coming and going during the evening will get to hear you, and you'll have time to party, too. Or . . . ah . . . not," he added, seeing Jonah's expression.

"That sounds good," Emma said. "You're warriors, right? Do you ever get to fight these days?" Well, she thought, that was about as subtle as a brick to the head.

"We get in a lot of sparring," Jack said. "We work out regularly with a diverse group of . . . of fighters." He nodded toward Jonah. "Didn't Jonah tell you? We had a great bout with him. We've been trying to get him to come out and spar with us again."

"What?" Emma swung around to face Jonah. "You never told me you were a fighter!"

"He's an *amazing* fighter," Ellen said, with frank admiration. "It took me and Jack both to beat him."

"Are you talking about martial arts, or—or—"

"With swords," Ellen said, looking from Emma to Jonah, as if puzzled by the questions.

Jonah rubbed the back of his neck. "Fencing is one of the phys ed options at school," he said, not meeting Emma's eyes. "You can sign up if you want. I'll go collect more of our gear." Turning on his heel, he walked out of the conservatory.

Troubled, Emma watched him go. She'd known he was athletically gifted . . . she'd seen him in action that night in Bratenahl . . . how strong he was, how easily he scaled the cliff face. It was one more indication of how little she knew about him . . . how little they knew about each other.

Once they got set up, they did a sound check. Emma had chosen her amplified SG, Jonah the Stratocaster, the guitar he felt most comfortable with. The acoustics weren't optimal, what with the stone floor and glass wall. They never were, for this kind of gig.

Natalie went over the set list on her tablet. "If we're doing two hour-long sets, we'll plan on about forty-five minutes of actual music for each, and fifteen minutes for chitchat and equipment changes."

"Do we *have* forty-five minutes of actual music?" Emma asked. "Let alone two sets?"

"We'll just have to play the same set twice," Natalie said.

"We'll do the tribute to Mose at the end of the first set. If we run short on the second, we can fill in with some of our older tunes, even some covers. You and Jonah can sit out." She mounted the tablet on a music stand, setting it within reach of her throne. "People are supposed to start coming about eight. We'll come back together about eight forty-five and begin the set at about nine. Sound good? Okay, we're done for now," she said. "Oh, wait a minute." She dug into her gear bag and pulled out strips of black cloth, passing out one to each person. "Black armbands, in memory of Mose."

Emma discovered that it was pretty much impossible to tie a black armband on your own arm. Jonah helped her with it, his fingers quick and sure. She reciprocated, feeling clumsy by comparison.

"I think the bar is open," Jonah said while she fussed with his armband. "I'm going up to get something to drink. Do you want anything?"

"Anything orange or lemon-lime, if they have it," Emma said, sliding the armband over his hard bicep onto his upper arm. "You must be really good with a sword, if those two are inviting you to spar with them."

Jonah cleared his throat. "They're just being polite," he said. "I don't think they were serious."

"Really? They don't seem like the type to say something they don't mean. Do you still get in a lot of practice?"

"It's something I used to do a lot of," Jonah said. "Not so much anymore."

She watched him walk away, increasing his speed as he loped up the stairs.

The party guests were a feast for the eyes, dressed in some of the most fantastic costumes Emma had ever seen: dragons and exotic birds and vampires and werewolves and knights and warriors from every possible era. It was all she could do to resist the temptation to get her phone out and start taking pictures. At least, she began to feel a little better about her own garb. Her plumage was subdued compared to some she saw, though some wore scarcely any plumage at all.

Jack and Ellen were helping with the new arrivals, taking coats and directing guests to food and drink, alongside another young couple, so brilliantly lit they were hard on the eyes. The tall boy had dark curls, an angular face, and thick dark brows. He wore several belts with large buckles, tall boots, and a handsome velvet and brocade coat. The girl wore her blond-streaked brown hair tied back with a bandanna, large hoop earrings, a hand-knit sweater, and a multicolored skirt, with tooled and painted cowboy boots. Emma guessed they were pirates. The boy, at least, looked ruthless enough to be one.

The boy looked up suddenly and caught Emma staring. He smiled at her. The smile made him look a lot less ruthless.

A gangly girl dressed as a black cat lurked in the background, sticking close to the pirates while pretending to ignore them. Typical cat, Emma thought, amused. She looked to be in her early teens. The costume was makeshift, a black hoodie over skinny jeans with both knees blown out, cat ears pinned into her mousy hair. As Emma watched, the girl nibbled at her nails, which were bitten down to the quick.

"Here's your drink," Jonah said, just behind Emma, startling her. He handed her a tall glass.

"Kinlock!" the pirate said. "We're so glad you could come." He turned to his companion. "Maddie—you remember Jonah Kinlock, who came to the council meeting with Gabriel Mandrake?"

"Oh! Jonah! I'm so sorry," Maddie said, spots of color rouging her cheeks. "I have never been so embarrassed in my life. Those people were totally out of control. I'm surprised you're willing to set foot in this town again."

"Yeah, well," Jonah said, rubbing the side of his nose, making it pretty clear that he was less than thrilled to be in Trinity.

"I don't blame you for being angry," Maddie said. Impulsively, she reached for Jonah's gloved hands. He flinched back, and then, after a moment's hesitation, he let her take them. She stared down at their joined hands for a moment, then looked up at his face, frowning as if puzzled. Gently, he extricated his hands and turned to Emma.

"Emma, this is Madison Moss, chair of the Interguild

Council, and Seph McCauley . . . you're the secretary, I guess?"

Seph nodded, heaving a sigh. "Nobody else will take the job."

"Seph, Madison, this is Emma Lee. She's lead guitarist in the band, and a new student at the Anchorage."

"Good to meet you, Emma," Seph said, extending his hand. It delivered the sting that Emma was beginning to associate with wizards. His eyes reminded her of Jonah's, though, the way their color shifted. "I know what it's like to start fresh at a new school. I hope you like it here."

"I love your outfit," Madison put in. "It's perfect." She herded the black cat girl forward. "This is my sister, Grace Moss," she said.

"We've met," Jonah said, "at the medieval fair."

"She's transferred up here to go to school," Madison went on.

Grace scowled. "Just this year," she said. "I'm going back home this summer."

"Well," Emma said, "I'm new here, too."

But Grace had eyes only for Jonah. "I didn't know you were in the band, Jonah," she said.

"We lost our lead guitarist and vocalist," Jonah explained, putting his hand on Emma's shoulder, no doubt sensing her nerves. Which made her even more nervous. "Emma and I are doing our best to replace him." He paused. "Are your parents going to be here?"

Seph nodded. "They'll make a brief appearance. It's going to be a younger crowd, though. It's our party, not theirs." His eyes fixed on the door. "Here they are now."

"Linda Downey and Leander Hastings," Jonah murmured into Emma's ear, like an announcer at the ball. "An enchanter and a wizard. The ultimate power couple."

Linda Downey drew everyone's eyes to her, like a diamond in a coal bin. She was small but finely made, with exquisite features. Her pale blond hair was threaded through with silver—not the natural silver of middle age, but a glittery, metallic kind. She wore a formfitting, strapless black dress and impossibly high silver sandals. Her nearly transparent shawl was inscribed with dragons. She gripped the arm of a tall, lean wizard with dark brows and a raptor's features. As Emma watched, Hastings leaned down and said something to Downey, and she shook her head, laughing. It seemed to take them forever to cross the room. People kept stopping them, greeting them, exchanging kisses or handshakes, looking after them when they had moved on.

Downey displayed something of the same charisma as Jonah. People just wanted to be near her.

"What's she dressed as?" Emma whispered to Jonah.

He shrugged. "An enchanter, I guess."

People were beginning to line up to greet Seph and Madison, so Emma and Jonah excused themselves.

"Make sure you get something to eat before your set starts," Seph called after them.

They returned to the bar area and filled their plates. Rudy, Natalie, and Alison had disappeared.

"Let's go out on the terrace," Emma said impulsively. "Unless it's too cold."

Jonah seemed more than willing to walk away from the growing crowd of mainliners inside.

They threaded their way through the crush of partygoers and out onto the patio, where they found Rudy and Natalie in a full-body clinch against the terrace wall. Emma and

Jonah looked at each other and, by mutual, if silent, agreement, moved to the other end and stared out toward the lake.

The grounds sloped downward in a series of terraced gardens to the lake. Small lights had come on, lighting the walkways to a small gazebo near the water's edge. Here, there were no rugged cliffs, only a rock-strewn beach. Lighted jack-o'-lanterns hung from the trees.

To the west, the sun was setting through a scrim of cloud, gilding the water's surface with gold. To the east, a hunter's moon was rising. The breeze stirred the trees overhead, carrying the scent of burning leaves, causing the jack-o'-lanterns to pitch and twist. But Emma was learning how quickly the weather could change.

The soft laughter and murmured endearments going on behind them made conversation intensely awkward.

"So," Emma said. "Any idea where Alison went?"

Jonah shook his head. Pulling out his phone, he pretended to check messages while Emma ate quesadillas.

"Isn't that hard to do?" she asked. "Using your phone with gloves on?"

"I'm used to it," Jonah said, without looking up. "These gloves are made for this. Gabriel orders them from a special tech supplier."

"Why do you wear gloves all the time?"

Now Jonah looked up. "Why so many questions tonight?"

"I'm just beginning to realize how much I don't know about you," Emma said.

It was two heartbeats before he answered. "My hands were badly damaged at Thorn Hill. I'm self-conscious about them, so I keep them covered."

Just then, the music started up, the sound blasting through

speakers set strategically around the grounds. Ellen's playlist. The crowd moved out onto the terrace, turning it into a makeshift dance floor.

A lovely, plush girl with a head of black curls made a bee-line straight for them. "Jonah?" she said. "It's Jonah, isn't it? Remember me? Leesha Middleton? We met at the Medieval Faire."

Jonah's look of puzzlement cleared, leaving no expression behind. "Right. Good to see you again."

Leesha Middleton wore a black mask and black lipstick over very pale makeup, and a red-and-black satin gown with cobweb-lace sleeves that trailed nearly to her knees. A cutaway bodice displayed her considerable physical gifts. A black choker and leather goggles completed the look. Emma crossed her arms, wondering if anybody wore hobo costumes anymore.

"Where's your costume?" Leesha said to Jonah.

Where's the rest of yours? Emma thought.

"I'm with the band," Jonah said.

"I am, too," Emma said, figuring that if Jonah wasn't going to introduce her, she'd introduce herself. "I'm Emma Lee."

"Ah," Leesha said, her kohled eyes narrowing. "So you're not . . . actually . . . together?"

Emma and Jonah looked at each other. "No," they said simultaneously.

"Wow," Leesha said. "I can sure tell you're used to harmonizing."

"How about you?" Emma asked. "What are you supposed to be?" Thinking, Dominatrix, perhaps?

Hearing the snark in her voice, Leesha pursed her black lips. "I'm a Victorian steampunk vampire, of course. Some people don't approve of cross-dressing, but—"

"Cross-dressing?" Emma took another look. No way. No fricking way.

"You know . . . wizards cross-dressing as vampires. *Some people* think it's really kinky." Leesha grinned at Emma, and Emma found herself grinning back in spite of herself.

Until Leesha turned to Jonah again. "Want to dance?"

"No, thanks. Like I said, I'm working."

"You're not working now."

"I'm not dancing either." Jonah turned his back and looked out at the lake, which hadn't changed much in the past five minutes.

Leesha stared at his back for a moment, then said, "Fine. No problem," and turned and walked away.

Incredibly, Emma found herself feeling bad for Leesha. Apparently, she wasn't the only one to feel this way, because Natalie and Rudy had drifted over during the conversation.

Natalie hissed, "It wouldn't kill you to dance with somebody."

Jonah looked her straight in the eyes. "You're right. It wouldn't kill me."

"You might find you liked it," Natalie said.

"*You* dance with her, then," Jonah snarled. And returned to his phone.

Natalie rolled her eyes, glanced at Emma, and went silent.

Natalie and Rudy returned to the dance floor. Emma might as well have been sitting by herself, for all the attention she was getting from Jonah.

"So," Emma said, "are you going out with somebody? Or don't you like girls?"

Gaah! Shut up, Emma. Shut up shut up.

Jonah focused back on Emma. "I do like girls," he said.

"I'm just not much for dancing. Or dating."

"Well, then." Emma raised her glass. "Sucks to be you."

Jonah stared at her, brows drawn together. Then the corners of his mouth quirked up and he grinned, and Emma realized then how rare it was to see him smile. Then he was actually laughing.

"Sucks to be me," Jonah said, nodding, and they clanked glasses. "How did you know?" He sat, turning the glass between his hands, momentarily lost in thought.

"Actually, I like the music," he said, looking up at Emma. "Obviously. And I do like girls. And if I danced with anyone, it would be with you. . . ." His voice trailed off and that familiar sadness came up in his eyes.

Once more, the music throbbed through Emma's veins. She just couldn't sit still any longer. She turned and gripped Jonah's arms at the elbows. "Come on, then. Dance with me."

"No," he said, shaking his head. "You dance. I'll watch."

"Maybe you haven't noticed, but nobody's lining up to dance with me," Emma said. "And they won't, long as I'm with you."

Jonah cocked his head. "Do you want me to move?"

"I want you to dance."

"I don't know how," he said, tilting his head back, scanning the couples on the dance floor. He was grasping at straws, and they both knew it.

"No worries," Emma said, tasting victory. "Dance with me, honey, and I'll make you look good."

"All right," Jonah said. He rested a gloved hand on her bare back, and every nerve in her body went on high alert. What will happen if the man ever kisses me? Emma thought. I'll probably die of joy.

Natalie was coming toward them, carrying a plate of jack-o'-lantern cookies. "Where are you two going?" she called after them. "Don't you want cookies?"

"We're dancing," Jonah said, over his shoulder. "Apparently."

It turned out Jonah Kinlock didn't need any help from Emma . . . in looking good, or dancing either. He was lithe and graceful, amazingly quick on his feet, and had no trouble mirroring every move she made. He seemed to be able to read where she would go next and be there waiting.

Yet, somehow, he always kept that little bit of distance between them . . . tantalizingly close, but never actually making contact. As if he were conscious every single moment of where his body was positioned in space.

It was Emma who kept losing her footing. She was falling for Jonah Kinlock, falling hard, even though he'd made it clear that the two of them were going nowhere.

When the song ended, applause erupted all around them. Emma looked up to find that they were the center of a small circle of dancers who had stopped to watch them.

She faced off with Jonah, hands on hips, breathless, sweat trickling down between her shoulder blades. "Liar," she said. "You said you couldn't dance."

"I never said I couldn't," Jonah said. "I said I didn't know how. But I study martial arts. And fencing. I guess some of the skills are transferable."

Emma thought of the locked gym at the fitness center. Once again, doubt wriggled to the surface. Jonah had so many secrets. But just because he had secrets . . . it didn't mean he was evil. . . . Did it?

Next came a slow dance. Amazingly, Emma talked Jonah

into staying for it. He didn't seem to be suffering through it, though. He pulled her in close, tucking her head under his chin, one hand planted on the back of her neck. Her breasts pressed against his chest, the T-shirt a flimsy barrier between them. When she pressed her cheek against his shoulder, she could hear his heart thudding in her ear.

Once, she tried to turn her face up to his, but he tightened his hold and murmured, "No. Please, Emma. Just like this, all right?"

It was all right. She rested her hand on the small of his back, her fingers just touching the waistband of his jeans. Dancing with Jonah Kinlock was like having sex with one of those gods in mythology. At the end of it you couldn't recall exactly what happened. All you knew was that you had a damn good time.

"What are you thinking about?" Jonah said, his breath stirring her hair.

Emma's face burned. "There is no way I'm telling you, Kinlock, so don't ask again."

As they turned, Emma was glad to see Leesha Middleton dancing with a tall, angular, red-haired boy in a velvet cape. It seemed she was flexible when it came to dance partners. When the dance was over, Natalie was waiting for them, grinning. She put her hand on Jonah's arm and leaned in toward him, speaking in a low voice. "What did I tell you? You two practically burned this place down. That wasn't so hard, was it? Nothing bad happened, did it?"

"It was just a dance, Nat," Jonah said, loud enough for Emma to hear. Maybe intentionally so. "Don't make more of it than it really was. Now we'd better go get organized. It's almost showtime."

CHAPTER FORTY-FIVE
SHOWTIME

It was just a dance. Don't make more of it than it really was.

The words echoed in Jonah's head, each time cutting like a blade into flesh. Double-edged. Wounding the swordsman, too.

What was that seventies song . . . "Cruel to Be Kind"?

They were in the small parlor they band was using for a green room, just off the conservatory. Rudy, Alison, and Natalie had already gone out front. Emma was still fussing with the tuning on the Studio G, her movements quick and angry, muttering under her breath. When she forced the tuning peg, the string snapped.

Jonah rested his hand on the fingerboard. "It's fine," he said. "Really, it is. You'll see."

"Of *course* it's fine." Emma sucked her finger where the string had cut it. "Who said it wasn't?" She looked up, met his eyes, and quickly looked away. "Stay the hell out of my head!"

"I wish I could," he said softly.

"I'm the one that needs to be able to get in *your* head, so I'd have a fighting chance."

"No!" he said, drawing back. "Trust me. You don't want to go there."

"Probably not," Emma said, threading the new string through the machine head.

"It's not you, it's—"

"If you tell me, 'It's not you, it's me,' I'm going to punch you, so don't," Emma warned.

"I just don't want to hurt you more than I already have," Jonah said. "This—this happens . . . every time I—"

"Don't make more of it than it really was," Emma growled, turning his own weapon against him. "And don't say you just want to be friends, because friends don't tie friends into knots."

Jonah was all out of ideas. Everything he tried to say just made things worse.

After an awkward silence, Emma said, "Why don't you go on out? I'll be there in a minute."

Jonah stood. "Just—just try and focus on the music," he said. "That's what I do. And we know that works . . . right?" He picked up the Stratocaster, fastened the strap to the end pin, and walked through the door.

Natalie woke up the house with a rattle, bang, and crash. "I'm Natalie Diaz," she said. "We are so glad to be here tonight. We're Fault Tolerant, all the way from Cleveland, Ohio, and we call this one 'A Tientas.'"

Jonah laid down the first few chords, and then Natalie came back in on drums, a pulse-pounding cadence that stirred the blood. These were Natalie's lyrics, an in-your-face kind of love song. Natalie sang lead, while Jonah harmonized.

Emma hung back a bit at first, her face a mask of concentration, till she found her footing. Gradually, she layered notes under and over Jonah's guitar line, insinuated herself into the spaces Jonah left open for her. Sometimes he was lead dog, sometimes she was. Their guitar work laced together flawlessly. Well, pretty much.

It was straight-up rhythm and blues: two guitars, drums, a bass line, keyboards. No artificial ingredients, as Nat liked to say. Jonah's Stratocaster came alive, delivering in a way it never had before. And the Studio G? That guitar was absolute magic in Emma's hands.

Maybe that's what your gift is, Emma. Building guitars that cast spells. Spellcasters.

When the set first began, Jonah kept his eyes cast downward, avoiding looking at the audience. During the guitar transitions, he stepped away from the mike and prowled around, unable to stay in one place. Energy seemed to bubble up inside him until he released it through his voice. Sweat dripped off his chin, plastered his hair to his forehead, ran down between his shoulder blades.

Finally, he dared look out, beyond the lights. He could see a mass of moving bodies, a collage of exotic colors. People dancing, people clapping or just swaying to the music.

Guitar transition. Jonah swung away from the voice mike, facing Emma. They were both in open G, the tuning allowing them to speak their minds through their instruments. She chewed on her lower lip, keeping her eyes on her fingers, a tiny frown between her brows.

Jonah lost his place, faltered, then had to scramble to get back in line. He could feel Natalie's glare, like a red-hot poker between his shoulder blades.

More vocals coming. Jonah swiveled and walked back upstage to the microphone, turned, and faced the audience. Natalie's voice curled around Jonah's, sliding over and under, deep-throated and breathy, a rogue current in Jonah's trickle of sound. Alison's bass provided the heartbeat, spinning a web of connection between the band and the audience. Drawing them in.

When the song was over, the thousand invisible threads connecting the band members to one another, and to the audience, snapped. Jonah swayed, nearly fell. Sound backwashed over them, a mingling of applause, cheering, foot stomping.

Jonah was sweating, his clothing soaked through, droplets spotting the stone floor. He blotted his face with his sleeve, grabbed a bottle of water, and drained it.

"Thank you," Natalie was saying to the audience. "Thank you *so* very much."

Jonah looked back at Emma. "Emma," he said, "sorry I stepped on you in that last—"

"Haven't you heard? There's no *sorry* in rock and roll," Emma said, leaning down to adjust the balance on her amp.

"This next piece is called 'Logjam Blues,'" Natalie announced.

This time Jonah sang lead.

They were a little rougher on "Logjam," less practiced. Jonah totally blew one of the new transitions, but the audience didn't seem to notice as Rudy's moody keyboards took over.

As the song unraveled to a rather shaky end, Natalie said, "There's lots more rock coming, but right now I'd like to take it down a notch. We call this one 'I'll Sit In,' featuring Mr. Jonah Kinlock on lead vocals."

This was Jonah's signature piece—a Kinlock & Kinlock

composition. Blues with a bit of country thrown in. Jonah set his guitar in its stand, lifted the stand mike out of its cradle, and walked to the front of the makeshift stage. Natalie began a soft cadence with brushes and Emma and Alison chimed in on guitar.

This time, Jonah sang directly to the audience.

> *If your lover ever leaves you,*
> *And you're lost in bleak despair,*
> *When your hopes and dreams are shattered,*
> *Call me, I'll be there.*

Rudy and Natalie piled in, harmonizing on the refrain.

> *If you're here to play the blues, I'll sit in.*
> *When it comes to songs of heartbreak, I'll fit in.*
> *For emotional disaster*
> *You know I am the master.*
> *If you're here to play the blues, I'll sit in.*

And Jonah was on his own again.

> *When you're lost and out of options,*
> *When you've made that big mistake,*
> *When your friends forget your number*
> *And your heart's about to break.*

He haunted the edge of the stage, stalking back and forth, casting his net of sound out into the audience. To his surprise, the energy ran both ways—from the audience as well as to it. They fed him, and he fed them. Looking off-stage, he saw the girl, Grace, Madison's sister, lips slightly parted, head tilted back, eyes closed, one toe tapping, lost in the music.

If you need commiseration, call on me,
Any time of day or night, I'm free,
When your soul begins to bleed,
I'll be just what you need,
If you're here to play the blues, I'll sit in.

He turned, faced Emma, and sang directly to her.

Don't look to me for love songs.
I just can't harmonize.
There'll be no sweet kisses in the dark,
I hope you realize.

He paused for three heartbeats, gazing at Emma.

But if you're here to play the blues, I'll sit in.
When it comes to songs of heartbreak, I'll fit in.
A sad ending to your story?
That's when I'm in my glory.
If you're here to play the blues, I'll sit in.

The end of the song was greeted with applause and rather damp cheering. Emma blew her nose and carefully wiped mascara from under her eyes.

They worked their way through the rest of their set list. With ten minutes to go, Natalie said, "Before we wrap things up, I'd like to introduce the band." She interjected a drum roll. "To my left, on keyboards and vocals, Mr. Rudy Severino!"

Rudy grinned and waved.

"On bass guitar, Ms. Alison Shaw!"

Alison executed a brief bass guitar riff, then bowed, doffing her trademark bowler.

"On guitar, from Memphis, Miss Emma Lee!"

Emma curtsied awkwardly, looking eager to get offstage.

"And, finally, Jonah Kinlock, on lead vocals and guitar." Natalie punctuated each of the introductions with a drum roll. "And I'm Natalie Diaz, on percussion. And now . . . in honor of our late lead guitarist, the immortal Mose Butterfield, a medley of his favorite guitar solos!"

Jonah kicked it off with Hendrix's "All Along the Watchtower," then Emma on Clapton's "Crossroads," Alison following with Jimmy Page's "Stairway to Heaven," Emma with B.B. King's "The Thrill Is Gone." Finally, everybody joined in on Stevie Ray Vaughn's "Pride and Joy," with Rudy absolutely spectacular on keyboards.

They finished up with "Doomtime," a cheery anthem about the end of days that had been a standard with the band for several years.

"That's it for this set," Natalie said. "We'll be back again in an hour."

People crowded in from all sides, asking questions, snapping photos, trying to get some face time with the band members. Jonah turned, and nearly smacked young Grace Moss in the face with the head of the Strat.

"Oh!" he said. "I'm sorry, I didn't see you."

Grace rubbed her cheek with the heel of her hand, smearing an inked-on whisker. She gazed up at him, eyes shining. "I just wanted to tell you—I love your music."

"Oh!" Jonah said. "Thank you."

"Too bad we don't have that EP already," Rudy muttered, with a pointed look at Jonah. "Or T-shirts."

By the time Jonah unleashed his Strat and looked for Emma, she'd disappeared.

❧ Chapter Forty-six ❧
Death Came Knocking

It was a clear night and the temperature was dropping. Emma was glad she had Tyler's old jacket, even if it looked kind of silly with her torch-singer dress. Turning up her collar, she followed the walkway down to the screened gazebo by the lake. She'd had enough of mingling . . . now she just wanted this endless night to be over.

Sonny Lee always said, "If you're worried over something you can't do nothing about, shake it off."

What about grief, Emma thought. Does it work for that, too?

This was not the kind of scrape she'd normally get into . . . falling for an unattainable man. Was it because of Jonah's gift? Or because she was trying to somehow replace the men in her life that she'd lost? She'd never subscribed to the notion that the wrong man was better than no man at all.

If Jonah was hiding something, she wondered, could it be something good instead of something bad?

Leaves had found their way into the gazebo and had collected in the corners and against the door. Emma scuffled through them and sat down on a bench, her back to the lake, the wrought iron cold under her. She could probably just hang out here until it was time for the second set. Or forever.

The interior of the gazebo was fairly large, its furniture huddling like ghosts under canvas wraps. Spiderwebs rippled like petticoats in the wind from the lake.

When she heard the crunch of gravel on the path, she thought, Stay away, Jonah. Or Natalie. Or Alison. Whoever you are . . . just leave me be.

But her bad luck ran true. The hinges squeaked as the screen door opened and closed. A tall figure stood silhouetted in the light from outside.

"So. Lady Day. It seems you were only half drowned."

Emma's heart somersaulted into her throat. It was Rowan DeVries.

"What are you doing here?" she said.

"I was invited, like everyone else." Rowan moved forward a step. There was only one door, and the wizard was standing right in front of it. Light collected on the tips of his fingers, and he extended his hand to illuminate the corner where Emma sat. "The Interguild Council wants to keep us as close as possible while they cut our throats." He eased closer. "I caught part of your set. I must say, you're an amazing guitarist. It seems you have all kinds of secret talents."

"It's no secret," Emma said. The windows were a possibility, but he'd probably get to her before she boosted herself up and over, even if she could smash through the screen.

"If you're thinking of screaming, it's unlikely anyone will hear you," Rowan said. "They have a great sound system, and the volume's cranked up all the way."

"Why would I be screaming?" Emma said. "Unless you're about to do something creepy." *Why did you have to bring that up? Well, it wasn't as if he wouldn't think of it on his own.*

"I can't believe that I fell for that amnesia story of yours. I was still grieving over Rachel . . . that's the only explanation. I actually believed that you really didn't remember anything, and the notion of Burroughs torturing you turned my stomach. I hoped that if I spared your life, I might one day find out the truth. That's why I allowed you to escape. It was a moment of weakness on my part, but it won't happen again. Unfortunately, you still managed to fall to your death . . . or so I thought."

"Am I supposed to say I'm sorry?"

"This alliance you've formed with the labrats intrigues me," Rowan said. "Is this some kind of community-service project? Frankly, I think you can do better."

"Frankly, I think it's none of your business," Emma said. Kicking off her useless shoes, she stood. "I'm going back up to the house." She tried to slide around him, but he shifted so that he was still blocking her path.

"I have another theory . . . want to hear it?"

"No," Emma said. "Get out of my way."

But, of course, he told her anyway. "Here's what I think . . . that the conspiracy didn't end with Thorn Hill at all. That the survivors who possessed the knowledge we were looking for were right under our noses, still conspiring against us. That my sister walked into a trap and you were in on it. Things went wrong, somehow, and your father was killed and you were injured. Then we came along and assumed that you were the victim."

Emma eased back one step, then another. "Here's what *I* think . . . you should stay away from those wizard drugs." She turned, planted her hands on the window frame, and boosted herself into the opening, but Rowan wrapped his arms around her waist and dragged her back. Slamming her up against the wall, he gripped her wrists with his hot hands and pinned them above her head.

He leaned in close to Emma and said, in a low, fierce voice, "Don't you think I deserve to know who murdered my sister? I swear, I have nothing against you. All I want is information."

And the thing was, Emma did think he deserved to know.

"Now," he said, "we're going to go where nobody will ever find us, and this time I'm not going to take no for an answer." He spoke a charm and Emma felt the sizzle and burn of power pouring into her.

Emma took a step toward Rowan and slammed her elbow up, freeing her wrist with a practiced twist. She smashed her skull into his nose, with a satisfying crunch of cartilage and bone. Rowan howled in pain, pressing both hands against his nose as the blood poured down.

Emma took two steps back, her head swimming with a sense of déjà vu. Why was this feeling so familiar?

"What . . . the . . . hell?" Rowan said, practically gargling blood. "But—but you're immobilized," he said. "Or you should be."

"You are wrong about so many things," Emma said. As she bolted past him, fumbling at the door, he whipped around, and extended one bloody hand toward her. She lurched to the side, smashing headfirst into the wall, knocking herself half silly, then went down on her side, twisting her ankle. That was when she realized that nothing had happened.

Rowan examined his hand, as if to see why it wasn't working. He took a step toward her, took aim again, his face twisted in fury. He's going to kill me, she thought. He's that angry.

"Leave her alone!" The voice was familiar, a razor-wire web that ensnared her . . . seductive and deadly.

Rowan half turned, and then Jonah Kinlock slammed into him and the wizard went flying, smashing into a piece of furniture.

The scene reverberated in Emma's head, a strobing flashback. Memory flooded in, to fill the empty places.

A boy slammed into her, and she flew across the room, smashing her head into a table.

Jonah dropped to his knees beside her. "Emma," he said, gently straightening her arm with his gloved hands. "Are you all right? Is anything broken?"

She opened her eyes to see a boy leaning over her, his gloved hands searching for injuries. Eyes like oceans so deep that light can only penetrate a few layers. And a scent that was life and death, joy and pain, inextricably mingled together.

Images rippled through her mind, like bodies surfacing in a murky pool: a tall, dark figure who brought death through the door. Impossibly strong. Incredibly quick. Insidiously lethal. Inhumanly beautiful.

Eyes that shaded from sapphire to tanzanite to emerald like fine black opals.

A flame kindled in her heart, a flame of truth hot enough

to burn up everything that had existed between them. She shrank back against the wall, raising both hands to ward him off.

"Please say you're all right," Jonah said.

No. She was not all right. That was something she would never be.

Jonah read her heart in that way he had. He sat back on his heels, pain flickering over his face. He glanced over at Rowan, who lay unmoving against the wall.

"Go up to the house," Jonah said. "Wait there for me." He tugged off his gloves and tucked them under the waistband of his jeans.

Emma stared at his hands. It was the first time she'd seen them bare of leather. They were beautiful hands, supple and strong, the nails clipped short.

"What's wrong with your hands?" she asked. "You said they were disfigured. They look fine to me." She reached for his hands, and he yanked them back.

"Go inside, Emma," Jonah said, his eyes glittering in the security light over the door, his cheeks hollowed by shadow.

A shiver went through her as a line from an old song came back to her.

Death came calling, and I couldn't say no. . . .

"What are you going to do?" She didn't really have to ask. She knew. She knew what was going to happen. There was death in Jonah Kinlock, and he meant to unleash it.

"Something I should have done in the first place."

"You're going to kill him, aren't you?" Emma said. "You're going to murder him, just like you murdered my father. Just like you murdered his sister. Just like you tried to murder me."

Slowly, he shook his head, as if to turn away her words. "No," he whispered. She saw the column of his throat jump as he swallowed. "No. I—I never . . . I didn't mean to hurt you, Emma."

Did that mean that he was admitting to everything but that?

"Prove it," Emma said, tilting her head toward Rowan. "Don't kill him."

"I have to."

"No."

"But . . . he tortured you. He threatened you. He'll do it again if I give him the chance. He'll never let this go."

"He lost his sister," Emma said. "He wants answers. Can you blame him?" She paused. "Anyway, you're not doing it for me. It's all about you."

Their eyes met, and held.

"Go ahead and kill him, then," Emma said, tilting her head toward Rowan. "But I'm not going anywhere. Show me how it's done." She stood, arms folded, immovable as stone.

Rowan was stirring, groaning, trying to prop himself up. He succeeded on the second try, rubbing his head, and looked around. When his eyes focused on Jonah, they widened in fear. His feet scuffled against the floor as he pushed himself to his feet.

"You want me to let him go?" Jonah said, his voice hoarse with emotion.

"Since when does it matter what I want?" Emma said.

Jonah settled back onto his heels, the deadly energy seeming to drain out of him. "Go," he said to Rowan in a hollow, flat voice.

Rowan seemed to be trying to decide whether it was some kind of trick. He edged toward the door, never taking his eyes off Jonah. Reaching the doorway, he stopped and turned to Emma.

"I'm not leaving you here with him," he said. "There's no telling what he'll do. Come on." He took a step back toward her, reaching for her arm.

"Just go!" Emma shouted, her voice clouded with tears. "Would you all quit dragging me here and there and telling me what to do?" She took a shuddering breath, almost a sob. "Go on, get out of here before I change my mind."

Rowan hesitated for a long moment, then turned, bolted through the door, and disappeared.

Emma blotted at her eyes with the backs of her hands and swung around to confront Jonah. "So. Any other murders I should know about?" she said. "Were you the one who went to Memphis and killed the person I loved most in the world? Maybe you remember him: old man with woolly hair, kind of bent over, bright-complected. Man could build a mean guitar."

"No," Jonah said. "I didn't kill anyone in Memphis."

"Think hard," Emma said. "I bet it's not easy to keep track. Probably all runs together after a while. What are you, sort of a one-night-stand assassin?"

"Emma, please," Jonah whispered, and Emma heard a prayer for forgiveness. But she'd gone deaf to Jonah Kinlock's seductive voice.

"Why am I alive? Why?"

Jonah shook his head. "I—I didn't go to your father's house to kill anyone," he said. "That was the last thing I wanted to happen."

"Accidents happen, I guess," Emma said bitterly. "Did you think it was funny . . . you having all the secrets when I had none? Me mooning after you while you're thinking I'm a fool."

"No," Jonah said.

"What, exactly, do they teach at the Anchorage? Is murder part of the curriculum or did you do this on your own? And why am I alive?" She stepped closer, too angry to worry about the danger. "Did you mess up? Or are you losing your touch? Is that it?"

Jonah stared down at his hands. "Would that I could," he murmured.

"Right. Now I should feel sorry for you?" Emma shook her head. "I'm going now. Don't follow me unless you're prepared to murder me, too."

She turned on her heel and limped away, resisting the temptation to look back.

Jonah didn't follow.

Jonah couldn't say how long he stayed in the gazebo. He remembered slumping onto the bench, pulling his gloves back on, and sitting, head down, listening to the sound of the waves on the beach and the wind in the trees.

He wished he could simply walk into the lake and keep heading north until the gunmetal-gray waves closed over his head and the fireworks exploded in his brain and the voices stopped.

But the instinct for survival had been hardwired into him, along with his deadly touch.

What would Emma do? Would she go to the police? The bodies were long gone, the evidence destroyed, the witnesses dead. She had no love for the authorities, and she had a record . . . of minor offenses, anyway.

Would she go to Gabriel? For all she knew, Gabriel had engineered the mission that had led to her father's death. Would she actually go to Rowan after she cooled off? It was hard to imagine she could believe he was the innocent in this.

And Rowan . . . how much had he heard?

It didn't matter what Emma could prove. What mattered was what she knew to be true . . . that Jonah was a killer. That he'd maybe killed her father. He had no defense. It could be true.

Guilt boiled up inside him as he realized just how alone Emma was. Everything and everyone had been taken from her. There was no one she could trust. Jonah was pretty much in the same situation, but most of it was his own fault.

By the time he left the gazebo, he was shivering in his T-shirt. He looked up at the brightly lit house. What about the second set? What would Emma do? Would she beg off? In the end he took the coward's way out and sent a text to both Natalie and Emma. *I won't be there for the second set. I'm so sorry for everything. Jonah.*

He could take the van and drive back to school. Lock himself in his room. Cross his heart and hope to die before morning. Without really making a decision, he began to climb the hill toward the house. The trees stirred and the breeze brushed past him, bringing with it the metallic scent of blood.

He heard a twig snap behind him, felt a pinch at his neck, and was unconscious before he hit the ground.

When Jonah awoke, the smell of blood was even stronger than before. He was chilled to the bone, stiff and aching from contact with the cold ground. He was lying awkwardly across a tree root. He heard voices some distance away, people laughing, scuffing through leaves. He turned his head from side to side, spitting out leaf mold from a desert-dry mouth. He felt sluggish, muddleheaded, so terribly tired.

"What's this?" somebody said. It sounded like he was just a short distance away. "Leesha!" he shouted. "Come give me a hand. Looks like this guy might've had a little too much to drink."

Leesha snorted. "Is it anybody you know, Fitch? Otherwise, maybe we should let him sleep it off." Jonah heard footsteps rapidly approaching.

"Wait a minute," Fitch said, with a new urgency. "It looks like . . . maybe he's been stabbed. There's blood everywhere."

"It's Halloween, remember?" Leesha sounded amused. "It must be part of the display. You never know what Seph and Maddie—" Her voice cut off abruptly. "I just . . . I just stumbled over . . . somebody else," she said, sounding uncertain. "It's a girl. I—I think she's dead."

Jonah tried to move, but it was like his wrists and ankles were weighted . . . too heavy to lift. When he lifted his face out of the dirt, his head was spinning, and he nearly puked. He finally managed to lift his head enough to look past the tree toward the house. He could see two costumed figures kneeling on the ground about thirty feet away. His vision swam until all he could see were blotches of color and lurid streaks of light.

"Leesha," Fitch said, his voice low and strained. "There's another body. Over that way." He pointed.

Jonah struggled to clear his head. Had he been attacked as well? Was he in shock from blood loss, or . . . ? Truth be told, he felt sicker than he'd been since—since right after Thorn Hill. And Emma . . . what about Emma? She'd gone straight back to the house after the argument, hadn't she?

Could Rowan DeVries have returned with reinforcements?

His heart froze in his chest. Was Emma lying dead with the others?

"Do you know any of them?" Fitch was asking.

"No, but there's a lot of people here I don't know," Leesha said. "And this one . . . he's wearing a mask. Do you . . . do you think I should take it off, or—"

"Don't touch anything," Fitch snapped, pulling out his cell phone. "We don't want to compromise the crime scene. Just . . . we better go back to the house until the police get here. I don't think anybody should be out here alone." He sat back on his heels, jaw set, peering into the trees. Instinctively, Jonah froze, knowing that movement would draw attention more than anything.

You're not guilty of anything, he thought. Why are you hiding? That *does* look guilty. And yet, he didn't move.

After a long moment, Fitch and Leesha stood, turned, and sprinted toward the house.

Jonah rolled over onto his back and propped up against the tree, fighting back another wave of nausea. His hand closed over something metallic. Familiar. He looked down. A dagger with a long, razor-sharp blade, smeared with blood. At first he thought it was a shiv, but no. Just a dagger.

His muddled mind tried to make sense of it. Had he brought a blade along for some reason? No. Why would he?

It seemed to take a superhuman effort to get to his knees. On all fours, he scanned the ground around him. Here was another dagger, similarly bloodied. And bits of leaves and berries, as if someone had put a fistful of plants through a shredder. His skin prickled and burned, like he'd been scalded. There was something about plants—something he should remember.

And then it came to him. Nightshade. Deadly night-shade. Belladonna. Had he been left for dead like the other victims of Lilith and her crew? Or had he been set up to take the fall himself?

Using the tree as a prop, he managed to get to his feet. His hands were smeared with blood to the elbows. His T-shirt and jeans, too. He ran his hands over his body. No obvious wounds. He felt more sick than wounded, but he probably looked like he'd been the guest of honor at a bloodbath.

Or the host.

He swayed, nearly falling before he caught himself. His head felt like it might explode. Was it possible? Could he have totally lost it, out here in the dark? Blanked out and gone on a rampage?

If he hadn't done it, then who had? Lilith? Or Rowan DeVries, making damned sure that Jonah was caught with blood on his hands this time?

One thing reassured him: none of the victims was dressed in torch-singer black. Emma was not among the dead scattered around him.

Already, he could hear sirens in the distance. He needed to buy some time. He needed to figure this out. And if he went to jail, he'd never, ever come out.

So Jonah did the only thing he could do.

He ran.

⊶ Acknowledgments ⊷

Some book births are more difficult than others. This particular project had many skilled midwives to help it along the way. First, thanks to my agent, Christopher Schelling, who suggested we say yes to readers asking for more Heir Chronicles. Then my wise editor, Abby Ranger, helped me rein in the story, define my characters, and articulate the stakes and the through-line. And, yes, Abby, I did cut back on the throw-up.

My current editor, Lisa Yoskowitz, adopted my orphaned baby when Abby moved on to new challenges. Lisa propelled the project forward, never hesitating nor flagging in her enthusiasm. I appreciate her hard work on this under trying circumstances.

Thank you to book designer Tyler Nevins and illustrator Larry Rostant, who've partnered to produce an incredible cover. Now if the book can only keep the promise the cover makes. Kudos to the publicity team at Hyperion: Lizzy

Mason, Holly Nagel, Dina Sherman, Andrew Sansone, and Lloyd Ellman, who are working hard to assure my novel gets a warm welcome.

It is an increasingly rare blessing to be able to publish eight books with the same publisher. Many thanks to Hyperion for their outstanding support over the years.

Thank you to my writing companions and early readers, as always, though there aren't as many early readers as usual due to just-in-time writing: thanks to Marsha McGregor, whose kindness and wisdom calms the waves; to Pam Daum, who is a Renaissance woman with multiple artistic facets; to readers who are game for the long read—YAckers Jody Feldman, Debby Garfinkle, Mary Beth Miller, Martha Peaslee Levine, and Kate Tuthill.

And, as always, thanks to Eric, Keith, and Rod—I couldn't do it without you! And a warm, warm welcome to Jess!

Don't miss the riveting conclusion to

THE HEIR CHRONICLES

The *New York Times* Best-selling Series
AN HEIR CHRONICLES NOVEL

CINDA WILLIAMS CHIMA

THE SORCERER HEIR

TURN THE PAGE TO START READING

❧ CHAPTER ONE ❧
CURVE BALLS

"**W**here are you off to, Alicia?" Aunt Millisandra asked as Leesha Middleton sidled past on her way to the door.

"A party," Leesha said, purposely vague. "I'll be back late."

"Is the party here in town?" Aunt Millie asked. "Will there be drinking? Will you be careful?"

This was unusual. Aunt Millie wasn't a particularly intrusive chaperone, given that she had a very clear memory of what it was like to be young, and a very poor memory of anything that had happened in the past year.

"The party is at Seph McCauley's house," Leesha said. "I don't know about the drinking, but I'm always careful these days."

Aunt Millisandra looked over the rims of her reading glasses. The glasses weren't functional—they had no glass in them. Aunt Millie didn't love the way the glass reflected, but she liked the look otherwise. "You look ravishing, my dear. It must be a very fancy party. I haven't seen you wear that dress before. And the leather goggles—is that a new fashion?"

"It's a costume," Leesha said, brushing at her vampish dress. "For a Halloween party."

"A *costume*," Aunt Millie said, emitting a shower of sparks, signifying delight. "Is it really Halloween?" She looked around wildly. "Is it beggars' night? Should I have candy? Oh, dear." She brightened. "I did make muffins the other day. Maybe we can—"

"No, Aunt Millie," Leesha said, batting out the sparks that landed on the settee. "It's not beggars' night. No worries. I'll, ah, bring home candy." Aunt Millie had many stellar qualities, but she wasn't much of a cook. The muffins could have stood in as hockey pucks. Leesha had diverted them into the trash almost immediately. Living with a wizard who was a few cards short in her mental deck wasn't always easy.

Blessedly, Aunt Millie moved on. "What are you supposed to be?"

"I'm a—a sort of Victorian vampire," Leesha said.

"It's quite fetching, dear," Aunt Millie said. "Especially the décolletage. But . . ." She pressed her lips together in disapproval. "You have such lovely jewelry, Alicia; why is it that you always wear that snake pendant?"

Leesha touched the pendant nestled between her breasts. It was a gold snake eating its tail. A talisman against evil. "It's a reminder to be careful who I partner up with."

It was also a reminder of the cost of betrayal. She'd betrayed Jack Swift to the White Rose warriormaster Jessamine Longbranch. She'd partnered up with the wizard Warren Barber, whom she hated, and betrayed Jason Haley, whom she loved. Now Jason was dead, cut down by the wizard Claude d'Orsay in a battle between the underguilds and their wizard oppressors.

Nearly two years had passed, but there would be no do-overs.

Fortunately, Aunt Millie again meandered onto a new topic. "It makes sense to be choosy, especially if you plan on biting anyone. Or being bitten. The human mouth is one of the most—"

"Not going to happen," Leesha said, cheeks burning. "I'm just hanging out with some friends."

Aunt Millie's face settled into disappointed lines. "I had hopes," she said. "You haven't had a gentleman caller since you misplaced that young man I found for you."

"I didn't misplace him," Leesha said sharply. "I've told you. He disappeared while we were out walking in London. Maybe I'm not as charming as I thought."

"Alicia Ann Middleton, you are the most charming young lady I know. No young man would willingly leave your side."

Unless he was attacked and dismembered by the walking dead. Leesha shuddered.

No! I'm not going to think about that. That never happened. Why can't I develop amnesia like every other victim of trauma?

"His family hasn't seen him since either," Aunt Millie said. "They've been terribly persistent. Why, they've even made some rather nasty accusations about you, dear. I think they should look closer to home for culprits. London can be a dangerous place, what with all those graveyards and barrows and ley lines."

Right. Ley lines, Leesha thought. "Let's not talk about that, Aunt Millie. It doesn't make sense to dwell on things you can't do anything about."

That was her new rule, and it seemed to apply to so much of her past. *I used to be so coldhearted and ruthless. What's happened to me?*

As if she'd overheard Leesha's thoughts, Aunt Millie said, "I'm worried about you, Alicia. You haven't been yourself since you went to London."

I haven't been myself since Jason died, Leesha thought. "I'm fine," she said aloud as she wrapped a black velvet cape around her shoulders. "Don't wait up. I'll be back late."

Trinity, Ohio, was a small town (!) so Leesha walked the few blocks to Seph McCauley's house. The house actually belonged to his mother, the enchanter Linda Downey, but lately his parents, Downey and Leander Hastings, the wizard, had been spending most of their time in Europe. At one time, Leesha would have envied Seph, living on his own, doing as he pleased, but right now she welcomed the distraction of having Aunt Millisandra around. The constant risk of incineration kept her on her toes.

You need something to do, Leesha thought. Something to do besides mope. A quick fling might be just the ticket. Her heart beat faster. Maybe she *would* meet someone at this party. Someone who'd never heard of the pathetic Leesha Middleton. Who wouldn't want to rehash old news or dig up the bodies of the dead.

She needed someone *fresh*.

The McCauley-Downey-Hastings home stood in a lake-side neighborhood of Victorian summer homes, built in an era when the rich birthed cottages like a cat drops kittens. Cars already lined the narrow streets nearly all the way to Aunt Millie's. Leesha heard the party long before she saw it: usually a good sign.

Leesha's former boyfriend, the warrior Jack Swift, was directing people in the foyer. He was co-hosting the party, along with his soul mate and sparring partner, Ellen Stephenson. Jack wore a leather vest, velvet pantaloons, and tights that showed off his warrior build.

"Looking good, Jack," Leesha said, flouncing her skirts, showing her glamoured fangs. Sliding easily into her usual role. "Care to expose your jugular?"

Jack took a step back and raised his weapon for a two-handed sweep—it was a pear-shaped stringed instrument.

Leesha couldn't help laughing. "What are you supposed to be?"

Jack sighed. "I'm a minstrel," he said glumly. "Not my idea."

Leesha could guess whose it was. "*Hmm.* Well, maybe you're a warrior pretending you're a minstrel," she said. "Maybe that's how you get inside the castle walls."

Jack snorted, but the corners of his mouth twitched. Leesha knew he liked that idea.

She greeted a few Anaweir high school friends who'd either stayed in the area or come home for what promised to be a stellar Halloween party. Scanning the crowd, she saw that it was mostly people she knew, a handful of non-magical Anaweir mixed in with the younger generation of gifted Weir from all over the world. The gifted belonged to one of the five magical guilds: warriors, wizards, sorcerers, seers, and enchanters. They were like five feuding gangs linked together by their dependence on the Dragonheart, the well of power controlled by Madison Moss, a.k.a. the Dragon. She'd been ruling in absentia for the past two years while attending art school in Chicago.

You could give college a try, Leesha thought. Aunt Millie had been pushing that, as an alternative to a grand tour of Europe or a year at an ashram. But could she really hang out with a bunch of freshmen?

Q: You graduated from high school *when*? What have you been *doing* all this time?

A: Preventing power-hungry wizards from taking over the world. Also, betraying nearly everyone I care about. Losing the only boy I ever loved. You?

Leesha wandered out into the conservatory. Guests in elaborate costumes danced to a wide-ranging playlist. In the makeshift stage area, people were dragging power cords around, setting up for a band. One of them was oddly dressed for a roadie, wearing a velvet cape, vest, and cravat.

"Fitch!" Leesha said. "I didn't know you'd be here. They don't have parties in Cambridge?"

"Not like this party," Fitch said, scrambling to his feet from where he'd been fussing with some sort of a connection. They shared an awkward two-handed handshake that evolved into an awkward hug.

"Will's here, too," Fitch said. "He drove up from Columbus for this. I think he's in the kitchen. Jack put him to work, too."

Will Childers and Harmon Fitch were wary of Leesha—and who could blame them? She'd sold off their lifelong friend Jack to magical traffickers. Then there was that kidnapping incident in the UK. But they'd fought on the same side in the Battle of Trinity, and they were keenly aware of Leesha's losses in that war.

Fitch retrieved a top hat from the edge of the stage and clapped it on his head. It was probably a costume, but then again it could have been Fitch being himself.

"The red hair is a good look for you," Leesha said, playing it safe. "And I love that suit. Where did you find that?"

"Thrift shop in Boston," Fitch said. "East-coast thrift is top of the line." He looked her up and down. "You look nice," he said.

"Nice?" Leesha raised an eyebrow.

He recovered quickly. "I meant, you look devastatingly gorgeous."

"That's better," Leesha said. "Are you just here for the weekend?"

Pain flickered across his face. "No, I'm here indefinitely. I'm taking a break from school."

"Taking a break?" Leesha cocked her head. "Now? Aren't you a sophomore? Isn't it the middle of the semester?"

"It is," Fitch said, "but my mom's in the hospital again, and my sibs require their older brother's firm hand and wise counsel right now." Fitch was the oldest of six kids. His mother had an autoimmune disorder and had been in and out of the hospital for years. It made it hard for her to support the family; they always lived hand-to-mouth.

Leesha put her hand on his arm. "That really sucks." She could guess how brutally hard it must be for Fitch to step away from a full-ride scholarship to Harvard.

"It's fine," Fitch said. "I'll go back eventually. I'm back working in IT for Trinity College, and they've arranged for me to continue my research and take a few classes." He stuffed his hands into his pockets. "I thought maybe you'd have left Trinity for someplace a little more exciting by now."

"I'm helping Aunt Millie with some things. That's enough excitement for me these days." She scanned the crowd. "Did Rosie come back for the party, too?"

"No." After a beat or two, he added, "We broke up."

"Oh." Way to put your foot in it, Leesha thought. She cleared her throat. "I'm sorry to hear that."

Fitch shrugged. "She's spending next year at an alternative school in Nepal. She wanted me to apply with her, and when I said no, she said I was choosing to be part of the problem. Things just escalated from there. Or deteriorated, depending on your viewpoint."

A young girl dressed as a black cat rocketed around the corner carrying a massive roll of duct tape. "Fitch? I've got the cord taped down all along the wall. Is there any—" She broke off when she saw Leesha. "Oh! Hi, Leesha."

"Hey, Grace," Leesha said, grinning. "Great costume."

"You think so?" Grace wrapped her tail around her wrist. "It's just something I came up with from stuff I had around."

"Those are the best kinds of costumes," Leesha said. She gave her skirts a twitch. "This is actually my old prom dress."

"They let you wear *that* for prom?" Grace exclaimed, then laughed when she saw that Leesha was kidding.

Leesha couldn't help liking Madison Moss's often-grouchy little sister—maybe because her mood so often mirrored Leesha's. Madison had uprooted twelve-year-old Grace from Nowheresville, Ohio, and brought her up to Trinity to go to school. Then parked her with their cousin and gone off to art school in Chicago. No wonder Grace felt out of place and abandoned.

Kind of like me.

Jack walked past, carrying an amplifier, followed by Ellen, leading some strangers through the crowd, onto the terrace. They were all carrying musical equipment, so Leesha guessed this must be Fault Tolerant, the band Ellen had been raving about since she'd seen them at a club in downtown Cleveland.

The band members were all students at Gabriel Mandrake's "special school" for magical mutants (the PC term was *savant*). Originally members of the mainline magical guilds, they'd survived a mass poisoning at a commune in Brazil that had altered their Weirstones in unique and sometimes dangerous ways. Maybe that's what made their music so exciting. Leesha was looking forward to hearing them.

She drifted closer, watching them set up, and realized that she recognized one of the band members, a tall, broad-shouldered boy with ink-black hair and smoldering blue eyes. A smoking-hot guy, in fact, and she had an excellent memory for that breed. She'd seen him at the sword-fighting demonstration at the Medieval Faire in Trinity. He'd fought Jack and Ellen both at once. He'd lost, but he hadn't embarrassed himself—not at all. In fact, Leesha thought, I'd rather watch him lose than watch a lot of other guys win.

What was his name?

"Jonah!" the drummer called over to him. "I thought you said you sent me the set list!" She peered at a tablet computer mounted next to her kit.

"I did," he called back. "I can send it again if you want."

Jonah. That was it. Jonah Kinlock.

Leesha couldn't say exactly what made him so engaging. He hadn't spent much time on his look: his timeworn T-shirt fit like a second skin and was tucked into battered jeans, the kind that start out indigo blue and then fade to a soft cornflower as they shrink to fit. Over the T-shirt, he wore a flannel shirt with the sleeves half-rolled, black leather gloves, and worn sneakers.

Maybe it was the way he moved, the way he chewed on his lower lip while he adjusted the tuning on his guitar, the interplay of light and shadow created by the planes of his face. There was something savage and elemental and feral in him. The fact that he was a savant only added to the intrigue.

I always go for the dangerous boys, Leesha thought.

"You're staring," Fitch said, nearly in her ear. "And you're not the only one."

Leesha whipped around to face him, and saw that Grace was fixed on Jonah, too, studying him with her usual intensity.

"I've met him before," Leesha said. "At the Medieval Faire in Trinity." She paused, but Fitch said nothing, just looked from Leesha to Jonah with an unreadable expression. "Well," Leesha said briskly, "I'm going to go see if Will needs help in the kitchen." Not that she knew anything about cooking, but she was good at bossing people around.

It turned out there were too many bosses in the kitchen already. When Leesha walked in, Will was busy at the sink. He was making a salad big enough to feed a small army, while pretending to ignore the raised voices leaking from the dining room next door. It was Seph McCauley and his parents.

Leesha greeted Will, slid in beside him, and picked up a paring knife, her ears wide open.

"Seph, you know we're in favor of normalizing relations among the magical guilds," Linda Downey was saying, "but your father and I think it's risky to bring all of these elements together at this particular time."

"If not now, when?" Seph said. Though she didn't have the visual, Leesha knew he was wearing his trademark stubborn scowl, so much like his father's. "Anyway, it's a little late to be second-guessing me. I sent out the invitations a month ago."

"That was before the council meeting. You heard young DeVries," Leander Hastings said. "He blames you and Madison for his sister's death, and for all of the other Weir killings. He threatened you."

"I understand that," Seph said. "But we're in the Sanctuary, and here of all places it should be safe."

"Since when has the Sanctuary been safe?" Downey's voice was low and strained. "You know better than that."

"You can't expect me to hide from him," Seph said, "especially since I had nothing to do with his sister's death."

"You do know that his father was the deadliest assassin in the Black Rose," Hastings said. "The Sanctuary's not much protection if the boy takes after his father. DeVries Senior never limited himself to magical weapons. He used whatever seemed most suitable to the circumstances: poison, firearms, blades, strangulation, killing charms . . ."

"Maybe Senior's back as a vengeful ghost," Seph said. "Maybe he's the one behind all the murders."

"We're also getting an earful about the Montessori kidnapping," Downey said. "It seems that many of the parents of the children involved believe that Gabriel Mandrake's students had something to do with it."

They were referring to a recent incident in which a group of gifted Trinity preschoolers on a field trip had somehow ended up trapped atop a lift bridge in industrial Cleveland. The children claimed they'd been attacked by zombies. Since the bridge was close to the Anchorage, Mandrake's school that served savants, some parents blamed the attack on "Mandrake's Monsters." As co-chair of the Interguild Council committee investigating the Montessori incident, Leesha had been getting an earful herself.

"Then we find out that Mandrake's students are going to be here, too," Hastings said.

"Not all of them," Seph retorted. "Maybe five? I think we have them outnumbered." After a pause (just about now he would be rolling his eyes), Seph continued. "I'm not discounting your concerns, but I don't think we should defer to a bunch of bigots with a lynch-mob mentality."

"They are concerned parents," Downey countered. "Though I admit, some of them are bigots."

"And *they're* not invited," Seph said. "This is *our* party. Madison and I think it's time we bring the guilds together in a meaningful way. It's one thing to have an armed standoff. It's another to actually normalize relations. We also need to stop stigmatizing savants as monsters and acknowledge the fact that what happened at Thorn Hill was not their fault."

"We agree," Hastings said, "and you know it."

"If you agree, then you should be supporting what we're doing," Seph said. "The only way to change opinions is to encourage contact between us and them. Anyway, are you suggesting we uninvite our guests? How d'you think *that* would be received?"

"*I'll* uninvite DeVries," Hastings said in that voice that could knock a person flat. "You don't have to be involved."

"This always happens," Seph growled. "Neither of you are on the council anymore, but whenever you're here, people start bypassing the council and going directly to you. It makes it really hard for Madison and me to do our jobs."

"What's making it difficult is that Madison is in Chicago more than she's here," Hastings said. "All of that power brings with it obligations—obligations that she is not meeting."

This was followed by a long, charged silence. Then Seph spoke. "Maddie never asked for this responsibility. She shouldn't need to be here, wielding a club to get people to behave. We're working things out in our own way."

"Yes, but you must understand that——" Hastings began, but Seph cut in.

"My point is, you can't ride in here and take over whenever you happen to be in the country. Either run this thing or don't." The swinging door between the kitchen and the dining room banged open. Seph froze in the doorway when he saw Leesha and Will, then he strode on past them and into the hall.

Whoa, Leesha thought, meeting Will's eyes. Go, Seph.

"He's right, you know," Downey said, her voice carrying from the other room. "If we're going to live in England, we're going to have to stop second-guessing him."

"You don't think a bit of counsel would——"

"You don't offer counsel, Lee," Downey said. "You have a rather unfortunate habit of bulldozing over people. When it comes to our son, you have just run into your first brick wall. Now let's go out and say our good-byes before we completely ruin this party."

Leesha and Will looked at each other, stowed the salad in the refrigerator, and fled.

By now, the dancing had started, though the band wasn't yet on stage. Nothing ventured, Leesha thought, and looked for Jonah. She found him out on the terrace with a tall girl dressed like a thirties club singer, down to the lacy gloves, finger waves, and red gardenia. A girl Leesha didn't recognize.

Something about the intimate way they stood, leaning on the wall, heads together, talking, almost convinced Leesha not to interrupt.

But not quite. She wasn't one to step back from a challenge. Nothing ventured, she repeated. "Jonah?" she said. "It's Jonah, isn't it? Remember me? Leesha Middleton? We met at the Medieval Faire."

Jonah turned away from the wall, and his gaze flicked over her, piercing her skin like icicles. "Right. Good to see you again," he said, as if it really wasn't.

Leesha's head immediately emptied. Finally, she asked, "Where's your costume?"

"I'm with the band."

"I am, too," the girl said when Jonah didn't introduce her. "I'm Emma Lee."

"Ah," Leesha said. "So you're not . . . actually . . . together?"

Emma and Jonah looked at each other. "No," they said simultaneously.

"Wow," Leesha said, not sure she believed it. "I can sure tell you're used to harmonizing."

Brilliant, Leesha thought. Entirely smooth.

"How about you?" Emma asked. "What are you supposed to be?" The sound of the South in her voice was unmistakable. As was the snark.

Leesha pursed her lips. "I'm a Victorian steampunk vampire, of course. Some people don't approve of cross-dressing, but—"

"Cross-dressing?" Emma did a double take, a look of disbelief on her face.

"You know," Leesha went on, "wizards cross-dressing as vampires. *Some people* think it's really kinky." Leesha grinned at Emma, and Emma, somewhat reluctantly, grinned back. Her smile disappeared when Leesha turned back to Jonah. "Want to dance?"

"No, thanks," Jonah said. "Like I said, I'm working."

Leesha's brain was saying, Shut up! Cut your losses and retreat. But her mouth somehow said, "You're not working now."

"I'm not dancing either." Jonah turned his back and looked out at the lake.

Leesha stared at his back for a moment, then said, "Fine. No problem," and turned and walked away, cheeks burning.

This isn't like you, she thought, this absolutely isn't like you. You're the one who says no, not the other way around.

Well. Until Jason. Jason had said no to her, which she'd

totally deserved. And then he'd never had another chance to say yes. Tears blurred her eyes, and she stumbled forward, heading for the powder room. But instead, of course, she ran smack into Harmon Fitch. The lower half of him, at least.

He gripped her elbows to keep her upright. Odd. She was suddenly conscious of the fact that his fingers had no sting to them. No sting at all. Somehow, that was a good thing.

Fitch read her blotchy face; she knew he must have, but he said nothing about it. Instead, he said, "Hey, glad I ran into you, ha-ha. Do you want to dance?"

"What?" Leesha said, like he was speaking Japanese.

"Dance," Fitch repeated. "You know, shuffle around the dance floor, figuring out where to put your chin, music playing the whole time? I didn't get in much dancing in Cambridge."

"You want to dance with *me*?" Leesha squinted at him, trying to guess his agenda.

"Look, I know there's a big height difference, but I think we can overcome that long enough to get through one dance," Fitch said.

He saw me get the stiff-arm, Leesha thought, mortified. He's being kind. And yet, Leesha decided, she would much rather dance than leave the field humiliated.

"I'd be delighted," Leesha said.

They circled the floor in silence for a few minutes. Then Fitch said, "I missed this, you know," he said.

"Dancing with me? And here I thought this was the very first time," Leesha said. It was, and they both knew it.

"No," Fitch said. "I mean being here, where it's happening. I mean the constant adrenaline, the high stakes. Saving the world, sticking up for democracy, and all that. I guess I sort of got used to living on the edge."

"Living on the edge?" Leesha forced a smile. "That'd be me, going to Harvard. No, I think I'd rather live as far away from edges as I can get."

Fitch grimaced, his cheeks pinking with embarrassment. "That was a stupid thing to say to you, and I'm sorry."

"Don't apologize," Leesha said. "You've moved on. Everybody has. I've had two years of boredom, and I kind of like it."

"Still," Fitch persisted, "considering the way it was before, with wizards pushing everyone around, isn't it better? Even though I wasn't a major player, I felt like what we were doing mattered."

"Yes," she said. "It's better." She had to think so—otherwise Jason had died in vain. "But don't diss what you're doing. That's what's important. Going to college, living your life, becoming the educated kind of genius that can make a real difference. Those are the people who save the world. Blowing things up, setting things on fire . . . that's overrated."

His eyes narrowed, focused on her. He seemed to be debating whether to say anything more. "You've changed, since—since everything."

"I'm a late bloomer," Leesha said, recalling that she'd once compared Fitch to a cockroach. Why were *those* the memories that came back to her?

Still, as they danced, Leesha felt her pain and humiliation dwindle. Sometimes life throws you curve balls. As with evil, you never know when you'll be blindsided by kindness. Maybe it was a pity dance, but she'd take it.